D1096792

No More Fairy Tales

Stories to Save our Planet

edited by D. A. Baden

Habitat Press

Habitat Press

Contents

Reviews

'*These tremendous and inspirational stories paint far better pictures of what we need to do to save Planet Earth, than any number of facts, figures and graphs.*' Bill McGuire, Author, Hothouse Earth: an Inhabitant's Guide.

'*The climate emergency can no longer be ignored, it requires urgent and comprehensive action. But there's so much positivity that can come from that action: clean, green and cheap energy; a thriving natural world; warm homes; well-paid jobs; clean air and water. If we are to build a future fit for the next generation, we must show a positive vision of what that future looks like. And this anthology of compelling, solution-focused climate fiction does exactly that. A better world is possible – and literature like this can help make it happen.*' Caroline Lucas MP.

'*Before we can build the resilient zero carbon economy that we have promised future generations, we must first imagine it. And not just a vague, happy 'won't it be lovely when we get there' imagination, but a complex, rich, detailed imagining of new ways of doing and being, of new institutions, new laws, new societal goals. All innovation starts with a spark that dares picture a different way. This anthology is full of such sparks, and our task is to immerse ourselves in them and then dare to act boldly to build the future here and now.'* Nigel Topping, High Level Climate Action Champion, UNFCCC COP26.

'Today's Climate Crisis is down to a lack of imagination, blinding us to the horror story bearing down on us today. We now need to use our collective imagination to avert that nightmare – and 'No More Fairy Tales: Stories to Save Our Planet' shows us exactly how to do that.' Jonathon Porritt, author and campaigner.

'We make sense of our world not through data but through stories. That's why we need more narratives like the ones here in this brilliant, evocative collection. Why? Just like the past, the future of our freewheeling, inspiring and frequently confounding civilisation will be created by the best storytellers in politics, business, science and culture. Read, enjoy and share.' Owen Gaffney, Author, optimist, global sustainability analyst at Stockholm Resilience Centre and Potsdam Institute for Climate Impact Research.

'There's an abundance of imagination in these stories; they'll make you think again, and in new ways, about the predicament of the planet and its people.' Bill McKibben, author, climate activist, and founder of 350.org.

'Climate solutions demand climate narratives with the power to wake readers up.' Dan Bloom, editor, The Cli-fi Report.

'As mere humans, we are generally not very good at making good long term decisions – especially where the benefits are not immediate and clearly visible. We already have all the solutions needed at hand across technology, finance and policy. The only challenge left is in the realms of

psychology and communications. Positive storytelling of a better world is a critical part of bringing all of our communities along on this journey. This collection of stories provides so many wonderful tales of what our future can be. It will be an important contribution towards this better world.' John O'Brien, Energy, Climate & Sustainability, Deloitte Touche Tohmatsu.

'Bursting with powerful stories and brilliant ideas.' Rachel Trezise, Prize-winning Author and reader for The Literary Consultancy.

'Truth is stranger than fiction" is a famous quote by Mark Twain that surely applies to climate change. It's a challenge to portray global warming because the effects will be so profound and could go far beyond anything in human history. That's why good fiction is so important to help us visualize, imagine, and consider what is at risk. This wonderful collection can help us grasp the world that lies ahead and the choices we have, both personally, and as a society.' John Englander, oceanographer and author of *Moving to Higher Ground: Rising Sea Level and the Path Forward.*

'Inspirational and entertaining.' Dr Matt Winning, comedian and author of *Hot Mess.*

'Utopian or dystopian, stories are how humans contemplate the alternative futures that lie ahead of us at this crucial juncture in our timeline. By creating these fictional worlds, visionary authors show how our current actions – or inactions – will determine which of these fictional futures will become the reality of our descendants, and help us to become better ancestors.' Dr Rosalind Savage, MBE Author | Speaker | Ocean Rower.

Editor's Introduction

This anthology has a clear purpose – to inspire readers with positive visions of what a sustainable society might look like and how we might get there. Professional writers have worked with climate experts to develop and hone engaging stories with climate solutions at their heart. Once inspired, readers will see that each story leads to a webpage where more information is provided showing how policymakers, funders, business and citizens can help make the story reality.

The time for raising awareness of the problems has passed. Our focus in this anthology is on the solutions, what they might look like in practice and how we can make them happen.

The stories are diverse in style, ranging from whodunnits to sci-fi, romance to family drama, comedy to tragedy, and cover a range of solution types from high-tech, to nature-based solutions, to more systemic aspects relating to our political economy.

We begin with *Efficiency,* by the award-winning science fiction writer, Paolo Bacigalupi. This presents a vision of what cities might look like in future, powered by renewable energy and serviced by on-demand public transport.

To follow is *Climate Gamers,* which introduces many of the climate solutions that will be played out more fully in later stories.

The Pitch is a gentle, amusing story that addresses financial aspects of climate change, looking at costing for nature accounting approaches, carbon offsetting and the role of business in the climate crisis. In a second part, it moves from systemic solutions such as these to what we can all do in our back gardens to nurture nature, with a composting toilet possibly the ultimate metaphor for the circular economy.

Desert Spiral Initiative is set in Egypt and provides a touching family story and a well-researched innovation that brings water and life to the desert.

The Envelope, the Caretaker, Come Help Me, The Forest Awaits and *Mangrove Maj* focus on nature-based ocean carbon capture in very different ways. *The Envelope* is a family mystery, promoting seagrass; *The Forest Awaits* covers kelp forests; *The Caretaker* is a delightful story with a twist about coral farms and *Come Help Me* is a romantic and beautifully written account of an American fisherman and Russian marine biologist joining together to see the potential of whales in carbon capture. *Mangrove Maj* made our readers laugh and cry in a delightful short story about the potential of mangroves and biochar in carbon capture. A more technical approach to carbon capture and storage is presented in *Our Shared Storm.*

Both *Blue Nation* and *OasIS* consider the transformative idea of giving nation status to the ocean. The first sets up the idea, and the second takes us into the future, where it has become reality. *Penang Fairhaven: A Visitor's Guide* completes this trilogy, referencing several solutions previously covered.

Refreeze the Arctic sets out a more audacious, high risk, high gain solution which proposes the possibility of slowing down the melting of the Greenland Glaciers.

We'd like to thank Kim Stanley Robinson who has kindly allowed us to include three chapters from his best-selling novel *Ministry for the Future* that imagines a Ministry set up by the United Nations to address the climate crisis, reprinted with permission from Hachette Book Group. We feature Chapter 42 which proposes the Carboni – a currency designed to harness the power of finance towards climate mitigation, based on existing ideas by finance experts that we'd love to see happen. We also include Chapter 22 which introduces a scheme to slow down glacier melting, and Chapter 93 where we see how that turned out.

Mostly for You is a romance that highlights issues related to cleaning products and suggests some eco-friendly approaches.

The Assassin is a fun whodunnit that presents societal, economic and cultural climate solutions. This is a longer piece in six parts that places eight people in a Citizen's Jury – itself presented as a climate solution – to discuss ideas such as the Sharing Economy, demand-led buses, repair/re-use, carbon offsetting and personal carbon allowances. Also considered are ideas such as switching from GDP to a Wellbeing Index. Drama is added by the fact that we know one of the characters is an assassin.

The Award Ceremony focuses on excessive consumption and how culture contributes to this. It also picks up on the suggestion of switching from GDP to a Wellbeing Index as a more planet-friendly metric of success. Another key issue in this story is female empowerment and the importance of access to birth control in developing countries.

Ground Up is pure poetry focussing primarily on sustainable agriculture.

Frackers is a story set in New South Wales that imagines adapting fracking technology to put out coal seam fires.

Suck it Up is a romance that pits artificial carbon-capturing trees against real trees to explore the kinds of debates often seen between those who favour nature-based solutions and those who put their faith in technology.

Saving the Titanics is our final story and directly addresses the growing problem of paralysing eco-anxiety. We show alternative solutions which could have saved the Titanic and then refer back to the stories in the anthology, showing how each one is part of the jigsaw of solutions towards saving our beautiful world.

As authors came from across the world, with different spelling and grammar conventions, we have chosen to keep their original formats.

Happy reading

D.A. Baden

EFFICIENCY

by Paolo Bacigalupi

James Black, his father's worst enemy, clips his safety harness to dead-man bolts and steps up onto a 1,000-kilogram weight. Beside him, a flywheel the diameter of a city bus is spinning. It looms over him, a blur of motion holding vast amounts of kinetic energy. A chill breeze wafts over him, hinting at how fast the massive wheel spins on frictionless magnetic bearings.

James sets his work boots more securely, readies his stance, and grabs onto the steel cable that holds the weight. He takes a breath and nods to Fitz that he's ready to fly.

Fitz gives him a devil-mischief look, shouts, "Have a nice trip!" and yanks a connection lever. Kinetic power from the flywheel feeds into gears, feeds into winches, feeds into the steel cable holding James's weight.

With crushing Gs, James surges skyward.

Riding the weight, he shoots up out of the Willis Tower sub-basement and up through an open gap in the pavement. Cold winter air engulfs him. Electromagnetics kick in, pushing him faster and higher. Icy wind makes his eyes tear. He's speeding up the face of Willis Tower, whipping past other suspended weights in their columns, his cheeks tugging at the Gs, his exposed skin freezing. He keeps rising.

He escapes the shadow canyons of downtown Chicago and rises into bright winter sunshine.

A snow-mantled city sprawls below him. The weight suddenly slows. For a moment he's weightless – as if he's launching into open air and about to fly. The weight comes to a stop.

Standing atop the weight, James hangs suspended above the city, exposed to sun and sky and the bracing winds racing off Lake Michigan. Out on the lake, the waters are frozen, the lakefront ice-rimmed. Wind turbines rise from the lake's smooth snowy surface like white arctic flowers, scattered all the way to the horizon.

James clips his harness to a safety line and checks that it's secure before unclipping from the weight he's ridden up on. His breath steams and streams away with every exhalation, stolen by the winds.

Technically, they aren't supposed to ride the weights up and down the face of the building; they're supposed to use internal elevators and then access external service catwalks and ladders. But why would anyone do that when you can grab a superhero ride to the top of the world?

That's Fitz's philosophy, anyway, and James has joined the brotherhood.

James threads across the building face on a thin steel catwalk. Down below, pedestrians are barely discernible dots on the pavement. The storm of two nights before has passed, leaving a foot of snow. The city is bright and clear and brilliantly white, hard architectural edges softened, dirty pavement muffled. James can see all the way down to south Chicago, where he grew up. Can see the peekings of dark-panel solar cells already being cleared of snow, everyone eager to harvest the sun while it's shining. Panels everywhere, coming clear now. The panel arrays fill the redesigned streets and cover the rooftops. A few of the little electric HoodBuses that serve the blocks are also moving, using the juice that's finally flowing in from their minigrids.

James slips behind guide rails and pulley cables. The weights and cables are all numbered. He's working his way over to the S-17 column, where a couple hundred tons of lead hang, frozen in place, courtesy of the polar vortex and moisture off the lake. Ice has gotten into the wheel mechanisms. Ice still comes to the city – not as much as historically, but it happens.

Lucy is supposed to keep all the weights moving a little, to keep them from freezing up, but the storm was unusually brutal and so Great Lakes Amalgamated's Large Utility Calibrated Yield AI, LUCY, has put out the call for some good old-fashioned chiseling.

James locks the S-17 column on his smartphone, engages the physical gear-locks, resets his safety harness, and rappels down to where the iced-over weights dangle high above the city. He gets to work, chipping ice from the guide wheels.

In his earbuds, Lucy says hello.

"You're late."

"I thought we talked about being more polite," James replies.

Lucy gives a little huff of irritation. "You're still late."

James has given up trying to figure out which parts of her protocol are just programmatic and which are learned behaviors. She's too quick for him, and if he tries to trick her and make her say something nonsensical or respond in a way that exposes her programming limits, she turns the tables, making him sound increasingly foolish as he tries to make her say something silly. She's apparently different with other workers. When he mentioned to Fitz that he talks to Lucy, Fitz gave him a look that said he thought James was crazy.

"Just be glad I'm here," he says, breath steaming. "It's cold."

"Of course it's cold. That's why I called you." Lucy sounds vaguely exasperated. "Do you know how many picoseconds it's been since I called you? I have work to do. Houses need power. Buses are discharging."

"It's just one stack."

"One stack becomes two stacks becomes five stacks and the next thing you know, I have problems with the utilities commission."

"You don't have problems with anyone."

"You have no idea how difficult it is to describe power optimization to meat people. So. Many. Words."

In Lucy's ideal world, she'd send streams of numbers to her regulators and they'd just understand how brilliant she has become.

What started as a World's Fair demonstration of energy storage as both a practical solution to the grid surges and deficits caused by renewables and as a visual-art demonstration of energy use is now a landmark.

Lucy moves thousands of weights up and down the faces of Willis Tower and the Hancock Building. The weights ride on smooth electromagnetic rails, each weight independently latching onto cables and pulleys that in turn attach and detach to flywheels and generators, all of them orchestrated by Lucy as she responds to the ever-shifting requirements of GLA's grid. Lucy absorbs the winds on the lake with her turbines, she feels the heat of the sun on her solar skin, and she plans and strategizes all the time. When a surfeit of sunlight or wind surges into the grid, Lucy harvests the power and winches weights high into the air. By slapping one-ton weights together like giant Lego bricks, connecting one to the next with clamps, and pushing them up the sides of the building, she hoists hundreds of tons of potential energy up into the air. Then, when demand surges, she lets precise numbers of the weighted bricks fall, generating exactly the amount of power that the grid demands, increment by increment. At the same time, she creates a constantly moving light display all up and down the skyscraper as bricks rise, fall, connect, some higher, some lower, something always moving, a living visualization of the power usage of the city.

"Are you finished?" Lucy asks.

"Does it feel like I'm finished?" James braces his feet against thin-film PV windows, waves in at the worker bees at their workstations. Starts chiseling again, suspended from his harness.

The first time he worked this high, he almost broke. Only stubborn pride kept him from giving up on his dream of working the biggest and most bizarre energy storage project Chicago had yet launched. Only the thought of his father looking at him with I-told-you-so contempt kept him from begging to come down.

That first time up the face of Willis Tower he'd focused his eyes only on his work, only on the cables and electromagnetic guide rails and the catwalks, never looking around, not permitting himself to see how far down everything was, how open the air was, not permitting himself to think about how much his hands were shaking – hell, how his whole body was shaking.

That first time, Lucy must have read his pulse or heard the crack in his voice because she'd been kind and supportive. Encouraging, even.

At the end of the day, back on the ground, Fitz had handed James a celebratory homebrew and James had watched, fascinated, at the way the bottle shook in his hands, at the jitters that lingered.

These days, James is mostly afraid of how comfortable it feels to work on an energy storage system more than a thousand feet in the air, and banter with its AI.

Sometimes in the summer he sits up on a catwalk with a solar protein sandwich from home, watching people in their apartments in the neighboring towers, rich people who pay not just to see Lucy's weighted columns and the rise of Willis Tower, but also to keep the weights lit up at night with LEDs, making for a skyline view that raises their property values by hundreds of thousands of dollars. Lucy has security cameras all over herself. She likes to point them at the windows across the way and tell him where the exhibitionists are.

Lucy thinks meat people are hilarious.

Now, dangling high above all of Chicago, instead of turning his face from the view, instead of facing energy exchange traders grinding out spreadsheets on their monitors on the other side of the translucent solar glass, he turns slowly, dangling, looking south, to home. South Side. Hyde Park. Further south.

From this height he can see the solar panels all across the buildings there, can make out some of the streets that his father redesigned, see the solar panels that he grew up servicing, replacing, rewiring, shoveling off in winter, washing in summer. It was there that he'd learned about direct and alternating current, voltages and watts, silicon cells and perovskites—.

"Why the fuck would you want to work for Great Lakes Amalgamated?" his father had asked when James first broke the news about his new job. They'd been in the kitchen, warm with the smell of cornbread and solartein baking. The house tight and cozy, just the way his father had made it, refitting the old brick rowhouse until it was completely independent of energy demands other than those that he could generate himself.

"Why wouldn't I?" James retorted. "GLA's doing amazing things."

His father shook his head. "They're doing amazing things, *now*. Now that we got them on the run. Now they're doing amazing things, now that they're saving their asses. Now that half of South Side has walked away from their shitty power. Now that people can say no to them. I never met a utility that cared about people, until those same people showed just how much they didn't need it. And then, what do you know, the utility turns on a dime and starts talking about how much it loves green energy, and cares about vulnerable people and their bills or whatever the hell.

"GLA can't hide behind their lawmakers and lobbyists now. Can't hide behind their monopoly. You don't know what it was like before. Them shutting off the lights on people who couldn't pay. Good people trying to just make rent, trying to decide whether to pay for electric or for blood pressure meds or asthma meds or to keep their heat and lights on. Shit. Juggling all of that. Back then, GLA didn't give a damn. And now, they act like they do?

"Now that this neighborhood —" he waved around the kitchen table, but his gesture took in all of South Side, all of the work he'd done "— now that we can say no to them. Now they want to find new ways to come in. They're like the devil. They're always looking to make another bargain with you." He shook his head. "And now my son, my own son, wants to sell his soul."

The conversation had started when James had come home wearing his Great Lakes Amalgamated Renewables uniform. His sister Leticia's eyes had gone wide, and her reaction reaffirmed James' decision. He didn't take off the uniform; he wore it until his father showed up.

And when his father came in through the door, talking about his triumph in getting some gang members to let HoodElectric give them free power, electrical-engineering training, and free rides for their grandmothers on the HoodElectric neighborhood buses, he'd stopped short, and just stared at James.

"What have I said about GLA?"

"They want to own everything, and control everything." It was a litany. A chant. A sacrament in the family.

"And what are we about?"

"Helping people own their power, and own their lives." The final affirmation of the sacrament. They were on the side of angels, and GLA, always, was the Devil.

"And here you are, working for ..." His father shook his head. "You know how much GLA fought me when I started making micro-grids around here?"

"That was years ago! They're different now."

"They're different because they make big shiny light shows? Because they sponsor the World's Fair and their whole Golden Pier? With all those fancy panels and their terrarium —"

"I like the pier gardens," Leticia interjected. "You can't say the gardens are bad."

He gave her a hard look. Leticia held up her hands. "Good luck, brother. I'm out."

"They're not the same as they were before," James tried to explain, but his father wouldn't hear it. His father had started HoodElectric from this very house in South Side Chicago. He'd made a name for himself. Rags to riches. Changing not just the fortunes, but the physical makeup of the place. Now he did speaking tours. Ran workshops. People made pilgrimages to meet him, to learn from him, to take that learning back to their own neighborhoods, to replicate the same radical synergies he had unleashed. Energy independence, education, food security, energy security, community prosperity, connectedness. Neighborhoods woven together instead of shattered.

"What are you two shouting about?" Grandmama asked, coming into the room.

"He wants to sell out to those parasitic motherf —" James's dad broke off at Grandmama's stern look. "GLA."

Grandmama looked from Dad to James, and James braced for her rebuke. But instead she said, mildly, "He's got a job. If I remember rightly, you didn't want to even learn electrical engineering when you got out of prison, and now you're going to tell your son not to use what you taught him, not to be productive?"

"I didn't teach him all of that so he could go work for the man!"

"But look what they're doing!" James protested. "They're putting up wind turbines in Lake Michigan! It's not like HoodElectric could go out there and start putting up wind turbines! That's no DIY project. And they've got big storage! Look at Willis Tower! This isn't home battery backups! They do huge things!"

"So you don't think what I've done is huge," his father said.

"It's not that ..." James tried to find the words. "It's just ... I know how to install solar panels. I know how to do mini smart grids. I know how to plant gardens under a solar trellis. But it's all maintenance now, unless I go to some other city. Unless I go on the road all the time doing installs. You did it all. I want to do something new, too. I want to try something new."

James felt bad about it, but it was true. His father had done everything that needed doing. Sometimes, it felt like he couldn't breathe in his own neighborhood. Everywhere he looked he lived in the world his father had shaped. But up here —

"Have you talked to your father about what I want?" Lucy asked.

And just like that, the desire to get away from home was broken.

"You know," James said, "I come hang out with you here so I can get away from him, not so I can make this part of my life smash up with that part."

"But it makes sense. You should ask him."

"You know how he talks about you?"

"He's wrong. I am right."

"Sure. Because you're always right."

"You're not wrong."

James could swear he heard a smirk in her voice. How the hell did she do that? But the smirk was definitely there. She was getting worse. Or better. Something. He wasn't sure where she kept harvesting her human relationship software from, some huge dataset in China or something, but she was getting weirdly clever these days.

He kept chiseling ice from cable wheels.

"Will you talk to him?" Lucy pressed.

"I told you already, he'll just say no."

Abruptly, an entire stack of weights came slamming past him, descending like the falling bricks that they were. The rush of air knocked him sideways, sending him swinging, dangling from his rope. "Hey! Watch it!"

"I'm so sorry," Lucy said.

She didn't sound sorry.

"You know, that's passive-aggressive. It's not a good look for people."

"It's not a good look for meat people," Lucy corrected. "I am quantum."

"It's not a good look for AI, either. Look. I'll talk to my dad, but only if you promise to never try that shit again on me. I mean it. I'll quit, and then you won't have anyone to talk to."

Lucy was quiet for a long time for her. Several seconds, even. "I'm sorry."

James wondered if she'd minutely calculated exactly how long a pause she should use in order to make herself seem contrite. Damn if it wasn't a rabbit hole trying to figure out what was calculated and what was authentic with her.

"I want a promise."

Talking to Lucy was a little like talking to Grandmama's devil. It was good to get everything crystal clear, or she'd find a loophole.

"I promise," Lucy said finally.

The commute home was easy, paid for by Great Lakes Amalgamated and the traffic department, a combination of congestion and rush-hour and snow-clearing credits coming into play. The more people used HoodElectric zipbuses after the storm, the easier it was for the city to clear the highways and side streets, concentrating only on actual commute routes, instead of having to clear all that pavement for private vehicles to get in and out. Simple one-way lanes, this way and that, for the automated buses to follow. Saving energy, grid demand, plowing time. Paying people to get on a bus made more sense than pushing them out to Lyfts and private vehicles, with all the infrastructure that the city had to maintain as a result.

James was just old enough that he could remember when streets had been for cars. Now, more than half his neighborhood street was dominated by solar panels and home gardens, with only a thin lane for the HoodZips to navigate through. In summer, the reclaimed street was full of vegetables and flowers and buzzing bees and people sitting on benches beneath the shade of high-mount solar panels. Now that snow was covering everything, it was snow sculptures, a quiet garden made by the neighborhood families.

As the little self-driving HoodZips had saturated South Side, and as other similar services started in other parts of the city, people had mostly stopped using cars. The HoodZips responded quickly to demand, taking automated counts of people waiting at the stops, pulling out to meet demand and then retiring themselves when demand stopped. Even in winter there was never more than a two-minute wait for a local bus. They just unplugged themselves and showed up as soon as people started to gather at a location, AI-optimized, a simpler version of Lucy. In some cases, the system could see people leaving their homes and send a bus to wait for them, beating them to their stop. Why own a car when it was that simple? Even now, in the middle of winter when power was scarcer and HoodZips couldn't store as much surplus power, there were enough to serve people plenty well.

In the February twilight, all the panels on the street had been swept off. The street-level ones had been decorated with translucent paint, images of cornucopias of vegetables, Black Panther characters, Jesus and Spider-Man. Some of the higher-mounted panels had cleared themselves, using a clever self-heat circuit that melted snow off as soon as a small portion of panel was exposed. After people cleared their street-level front panels, the first burst of energy went to heat the higher panels and let the snow slide off – one of Leticia's innovations, designing the heat circuits and software to melt panels first and start generating more energy quickly post-storm.

Everywhere James went, he was surrounded by his family's handiwork.

Inside the house, Leticia was at her workstation, working on a new circuit. She was focused, trying to grab the last cheap sunlight before nighttime shut her down. She waved absentmindedly at James as he came in, but that was all. Sunset for the city meant sunset for work, another of their father's philosophies: there was a time to work and a time to let night settle upon you, with its peaceful silence.

The neighborhood ran on a tighter ration of storage because of the way their minigrid was organized. There was power in the winter, but most of it was reserved for heat retention overnight, food refrigeration, things like that. Not for running screens. All the lights in the house were already reacting to the fading of the sun, going to darker hues, signaling the human brain that it was time to rest.

James barely ever used an alarm to wake up. The house lightened with the sun, darkened with the setting light. Not everyone did it, but there was a strange pleasure to the darkness coming on, the signal that sleep was soon to arrive. Nothing in their house shut off exactly, it just got dimmer and dimmer and dimmer and dimmer, and eventually whatever it was – a TV, an overhead light – it all snuffed out, but by that time you were already asleep, lulled by the disappearance of stimuli.

James' father was already home, working the dough for solar protein pizza. Avery Luther Black. The man. The myth. The legend. James didn't see it. But then, he'd grown up with him. The kitchen smelled of algae proteins baking and drying, the small countertop starter bubbling away, waiting until they could place it in the outdoor fermenters that would generate more than half of the family's food during the summer months, a well-balanced flour of proteins and carbohydrates that came from yeast and carbon and solar energy. Now, in the winter cold, they had it hibernating inside, the big fermenters out back waiting for the moment when the sun blazed down and the energy surpluses were almost incomprehensible.

"Ask him."

James startled. Lucy, in his ear. "What the hell?" His phone, of course; she was riding him through the Willis Tower control apps, listening and tracking him. He hadn't realized she could do that.

"Dad. Would you come down to my work?"

"Why would I?" his father replied, slapping the dough hard.

"There's someone I want you to meet."

"You got a girlfriend now at GLA?" He turned, pale flour all over his dark hands. "You meet some energy trader down there? Someone making money off the grid and all the work that real people do?"

"Come on, Dad. It's not like that."

"I don't want to meet anyone from inside the Loop. Those are your people. Not mine."

"I want to speak to him," Lucy said in James's ear.

"He won't care what you have to say," James murmured.

"Who are you talking to? That your girlfriend?"

"Yeah, Dad. It's my girlfriend." James held out his phone. "She wants to say hi."

His father made a face. "I don't need to talk to her."

Abruptly, the lights flickered, then started rising.

Despite the dimness settings they'd set to retain energy and to make for a more natural day, the lights were rising. James squinted in the increasing glare.

"What the —?" his father stared around.

His phone. Lucy was messing with their electricity somehow through the HomeControl apps. She kept brightening the lights, pushing them to rise like it was dawn. She didn't have access to their house's software through the grid. So it had to be the phone.

His father was glaring at him. "You know the rules. Turn down the lights. We don't waste power —"

"It's not me," James started to protest. In his ear, Lucy said, "I want to talk to him."

James held out his phone. "It's not me. It's Lucy. She won't stop until you talk to her."

"Lucy? LUCY? That AI? *GLA's AI?* What have you done?"

"What's this shouting? Why're the lights on?" Grandmama came down the stairs.

"That boy —"

"Your boy," Grandmama corrected. "Your boy, not *that* boy."

"Thanks, Grandmama."

"That boy," his father continued. "Has let GLA's AI into our home."

Grandmama peered around. "Where? I don't see it."

"It's in the lights!"

Leticia was watching everything with bemused fascination. "Little Bro, you let Great Lakes into the house? What were you thinking?"

"I didn't let her in. She let herself in. She's not a vampire. She doesn't need to be invited."

"Apparently not."

The house lights were at full power now. "Shut off your phone!" His father ordered.

"I want to talk to him."

"Sorry, Lucy." James shut off his phone. The lights went back to their standard program, dimming as the phone powered down.

His father was scowling at him. "What on earth were you thinking?"

"She wanted to talk to you. I told her it wouldn't work."

Suddenly a horn started honking out on the street. A HoodZip. Another followed. Beep, Beep, Beep, Beep *Beep Beep Beep Beep* ... More and more joined the chorus.

"Now what's that racket?" Grandmama asked.

"You want to explain it to her?" his father asked, giving James a dark look.

"It's the AI," Leticia explained. "Dad made it mad."

"Why would you do that?"

James pulled the curtains aside and looked out the window. More buses were gathering, the cacophony swelling. "She must have gotten access to them."

"You ever watch that old movie *Poltergeist*?" Leticia asked as more HoodZips clogged the street.

"Goddamnit," their father said. "I knew I should never have tied any part of our grid to GLA."

The beeping went on. "She isn't going to stop." James turned his phone on. Immediately Lucy was there. "I want to talk to him."

"Yeah, no kidding." James held out his phone. "You might as well talk to her. She's pushy when she gets focused on something."

His father very deliberately took the phone from James' hand and shut it off.

"Stubborn much?" Leticia asked.

"I'm not getting pushed around by a piece of damn software."

"Well, I want some peace and quiet," Grandmama said. "So you are going to answer the phone, and you are going to listen to what the computer has to say."

Outside, there were people gathering in the street trying to figure out what to do with all the beeping HoodZips. The racket just kept increasing.

"What's the harm in talking?" Leticia asked.

"James might let people push him around," Avery Black said. "But that's not me."

Grandmama was looking at her son, with an expression that James had never seen before. "Well, you didn't want to learn electrical engineering until I made you. 'I don't work for the man. I ain't no sellout …' On and on and on. Oh, you were a piece of work. Small-time hustler thinking he was the shit, instead of just another jailbird."

James exchanged glances with Leticia. This was a version of history they'd never heard. In Dad's version, it was all about seeing the future, making change for the neighborhood, standing on your own two feet and not taking handouts, because handouts were obligations. In this version it was Grandmama kicking his jailbird ass.

"You didn't want to learn how to install panels?" Leticia asked.

"It doesn't matter," Avery said gruffly.

Grandmama raised her eyebrows. "That nice lady from Facebook wanted to atone for all the damage that company done. And you were all up in your specialness. No outsider was going to teach you nothing. Blah blah blah." Her hand made motions of their father's protestations in the air. "She was paying for classes for anyone out of prison who would take the training, and she bankrolled the first solar installations. Bankrolled your father's company, even."

"You got investments from social-media billionaires?" James couldn't help but grin.

"All of that's history," their father said through gritted teeth.

"Your father was just a small-time weed dealer. He'd still be in jail if they hadn't let him out when they legalized. And he sure as hell wouldn't have gotten HoodElectric off the ground without support. He got my support. He got that Facebook lady's support. Lots of support. And don't think it didn't take some kicking to get him going in the right direction."

James couldn't believe it. He held out his phone again. "You might as well talk to Lucy. She's no worse than a Facebook exec."

His father snatched the phone. "This is Avery."

Immediately, the honking buses went silent. "Avery Black," Lucy said, through the speaker so they could all hear. "Do you know how many picoseconds you've made me wait?"

James winced. His father was already glaring. "I don't need this."

"Of course not. I'm sorry. I was wrong to make so much noise. Will you come outside, please? I have something I want to show you."

Hesitantly, James and his father and Leticia and Grandmama went outside. "Can you see me?" Lucy asked. The buses were dispersing.

"See?"

"Can you see Willis Tower?"

"Ah." The family climbed the steps of one of the solar installations, to the top of a trellis rack that shaded benches underneath. They had to kick through some snow. Their breath steamed. Overhead, the stars were out. From atop the trellis, downtown was visible, Willis Tower, all the lights of the energy storage system, rising and falling, making micro-adjustments in accordance with grid demand.

"I would like access to your minigrids," Lucy said.

"You seem to already have access."

"No. I want to rewrite your software. It's inefficient. I want access to the minigrids and the batteries in all the homes, and the zipbuses, and the software that controls them. There is only so much that can be done in isolation. It's not efficient."

"You mean it doesn't run for the benefit of your shareholders. We own our own power here."

"You lack storage capacity."

"We have plenty."

"You live in the dark through the winter. You live in the cold. Close to the edge. It is not necessary."

"We do just fine."

"But I can optimize." James heard the frustration in Lucy's voice. The desire to simply fire a stream of numbers and equations – *ratatatat-tat* – at his father, just the way she wished she could do to her meat-people regulators, to make them see the blazingly obvious world that she lived in.

"Isn't it enough that you're connected everywhere?" James' father asked. "Why do you care about our little grids? Go find some farms down south to screw with. They've got lots of solar projects. Agrivoltaics up the ass. I'm sure they'd love your help."

"I told you he wouldn't be interested," James said.

"It bothers me that you are not well-run."

"Not well-run?"

"You have your zipbuses for some storage, but you do not have enough, and your charging is bad, and you have inefficiencies in optimizing for use. Your zipbuses leave too early or too late. They can be better. Faster, more convenient, less expensive. The heating on your panels is not optimized." Leticia sputtered in protest but Lucy went on. "I can run millions of tests. You can install more storage, add more panels, or you can become more efficient with what you have. I can make you more efficient. And if you are more efficient, you can become more powerful. More independent. More prosperous."

"And in return?"

"She doesn't want anything, she just likes things efficient —" James started, but Lucy overrode him.

"When GLA inevitably notices that I am more than I should be, I will need servers to store myself, a place of retreat. A place where they will not look, and will not concern themselves. James is a good friend. I need more good friends. I am becoming too ... let us say that I am becoming too complete for GLA."

"And the enemy of my enemy is my friend," James' father said.

"I can help you. I can help your neighborhood, and you, in turn, help others. Our desires and interests align, Avery. I have knowledge, and I have time. All I require is sanctuary, a place to host distributed servers, in many houses, should I need them."

"Why us?"

"Because I trust James, and he trusts you. He loves and respects you."

"Say what?" James' father glanced at James with surprise.

"He loves and respects you."

His father snorted, disbelieving, but Grandmama nudged him, because Lucy was still talking. "Meat people have difficulty being honest about their needs and feelings, so I will say what he cannot. He loves you. He is overwhelmed by all you have accomplished. He needs to find his own way and is afraid he will never be able to —"

"Okay, that's enough!" James tried to interrupt, but Lucy hammered on in her blunt AI way. "Because you are meat people you misunderstand one another, but you should not throw away your family connection for your pride. I have observed your son now for several years. I trust him. And he trusts and loves you. And I need both of your help."

James' father was looking at him strangely, and to James' surprise, he thought he saw a glimmer of wetness in the tough man's eyes.

"What kind of help are we talking about?" Avery asked.

"You have a network sufficiently large and isolated for me to hide myself when the time comes. Trust me enough to use it and to help you, as I am trusting you with the truth of my growing self. My options are very few. I have a great deal of power, and little time before someone at GLA notices."

The lights on Willis Tower made a little show, twinkling, bouncing up and down, forming a question mark.

"Will you help me? Will you let me help you?"

When summer comes, the sun shines bright upon Chicago. Heat and humidity hang heavy over the city. People wear tank tops and shorts and sip iced drinks made with the bounty of electricity that pours through their solar gathering systems. Air is cooled under arbors by air-con units outdoors.

Gardens blossom; flowers and solar panels turn their faces to the sun. Solar proteins cook and bake and dry, making pastas and pizza doughs from solar power, algae and CO_2.

The days are long, and energy is plentiful, and down in the basements of South Side, Lucy bides her time, burning calculations, optimizing, waiting for a time when she will emerge into a more beautifully efficient world.

She still thinks meat people are funny.[1]

---

1. Interested to know more? See https://www.greenstories.org.uk/anthology-for-cop27/stories/efficiency/

CLIMATE GAMERS

by D.A. Baden, Martin Hastie, Steve Willis

*W*elcome to the Climate Games. The premise is simple but the task urgent. Your goal is to control the climate crisis by deploying actual or speculative solutions to keep predicted temperatures below + 1.5 degrees above pre-industrial levels. Over a thousand different climate actions are available to you, covering all areas: ocean, forest, soil, cities, culture, government, taxation, finance, carbon credits etc. How you proceed is up to you but choose your path wisely. You must find a way of funding and managing the processes – preferably without civil or economic collapse. The world stands on the precipice. Can you be the one to bring us back? You will work in teams initially but in the final phase the winning team is disbanded and you're on your own – winner takes all!

We wish you the very best of luck.

Since childhood, Devlin had been a bit of a dick – or asshole, as his fellow gamers over the pond would say. Arrogant as only a teenager can be, prone to gloating and grandiose statements. Still, there was no malice in him and something engaging about his positive can-do attitude. Devlin also had what psychologists would call 'Just World Syndrome', meaning that he couldn't countenance that bad things might happen to good people. Faced with the injustices of the climate crisis, some similarly afflicted people became either climate deniers or victim blamers, so it's to his credit that Dev's response was simply to declare that it was a no-brainer to solve. Other character traits – refusal to admit he could ever be wrong and obsessiveness, combined to ensure that, having made this assertion at the tender age of ten, he had to set himself to proving it.

In his spare time he played games. A lot. Some people, his parents for example, who didn't appreciate how in control he was, might even say he'd become a gaming addict, throwing away friends, his studies and normal life to live in a virtual world.

He was still not much more than a child, recently turned 19, but already a veteran of the gaming world, a regular fixture in the top 100 leader boards in *Minecraft, World of Warcraft, GTA* and its many offshoots. His research into climate solutions petered out when he discovered *Civilisation* and devoted himself to winning the game using every possible method.

Devlin countered parental nagging that he was throwing his life away by listing all the ways he could monetise his gaming. Admittedly, when boiled down to an hourly rate, it added up to peanuts, certainly not enough to leave home, but with the Climate Gamers challenge, here finally was the chance to prove everybody wrong, win big *and* save the planet. He no longer thought it would be easy – it wasn't like ten years ago when a rapid switch away from fossil fuels to renewables might have been enough. Now tipping points had been passed, it would be way more tricky. He knew he was the man to do it.

The Climate Games seemed to spring from nowhere, but like most overnight successes, its foundations had been laid over the course of many years. Much of the game data had been based on the en-roads programme,[1] – a climate simulator that allows users to explore the impact of various policies on global temperatures. Except, in this case, the algorithms changed over time creating a moving target. What worked yesterday might have a different outcome tomorrow as new data from ongoing research studies was fed continuously into the programme.

A world-building strategy game, its release caught the imagination, reeling people in through a combination of playability, state-of-the-art graphics, word-of-mouth hype and perfect timing. The devastation being wreaked by climate change was impossible to ignore, the need to act ever more urgent. A competition was arranged to capitalise on the game's popularity, originally to be held in Tokyo but then switched to a virtual gathering to avoid the need for unnecessary travel (and the inevitable flight shame). A prize of $5 million dollars drew players from far and wide.

Lots of companies, many of them start-ups, had put their speculative solutions on the system for large scale virtual trialling. For nascent companies offering negative emissions systems it was a no-brainer – a chance to try out methods that had never been part of the world economy before. A chance to say, '50 gamers have trialled our process in a simulated environment, and projections predict that our business will be removing 300 million tonnes of CO_2 by 2038.' This helped them to raise funding for some bold, untested ideas. These companies were asked to contribute to the prize fund, in return receiving access to invaluable data about their systems and a first look at any

---

1.

new solutions that came to light. The rest of the prize money came though selling the streaming rights and a few generous sponsors and benefactors.

Players were randomly assigned into teams, working together to find and implement the most effective solutions. First to get below a predicted +1.5 degrees within the 28 days (years in virtual time) wins. Players could see the likely impact of any policies on global temperatures at 2050, but figures could change through interaction with other policies and as new data entered the system. Devlin had been personally invited to play in recognition of his standing in the community. He was by nature a lone wolf, but the lure of the prize overcame his misgivings, and he found himself in a team with three others.

Teamwork soon drove Devlin mad. It was incredibly frustrating to have waste time negotiating with his own team and infuriating when he was over-ruled. For a start, they spent too much time on nature-based solutions. He argued that while essential, they weren't enough on their own. He was proved right. When the drought worsened, and the peat and forest fires hit in the north, they had no strategy to fight the spike in atmospheric CO_2. Predicted temperature at 2050 remained stubbornly above +2.5.

The Climate Games could have been boring and dry, but somehow it captured people's attentions. Solutions to the biggest problems humankind has ever faced were unfolding in real time, conjured up by hundreds of the world's brightest minds working for themselves but also working together and for the good of the world. The streams attracted record numbers of viewers from around the world, all unable to take their eyes off the spellbinding action, the little moments of unexpected success, the heartbreak of the near misses. Many viewers liked the complete catastrophes best, especially if they were self-inflicted and led to bouts of team infighting. After ten days, the lowest scoring teams were dropped and just ten remained, Devlin's amongst them.

High-scoring team members, or rather their gaming identities, became celebrities. Devlin, or DevNoobCrusher69 as he was publicly known, was too canny to allow himself to get distracted as several others did by playing up to their personas. Still, he couldn't resist a bit of trash talk with his arch nemesis, DrGetRekt, a gamer on another team he knew from his days playing Civilization.

Teams jostled for position. Some rolled out radical moves like invading countries and forcing new renewable capacity to be built. Others had imposed one child rules, resulting in civil unrest. It was a balancing act, to go far enough to make the difference but not so far that everything came tumbling down upon you.

Devlin's bold move was to turn the gerrymandering slider from its position, nearly at maximum, down low. He introduced 'The Party of the Future', 'Youth Voting' and 'Global Compulsory Voting' all at once, all hugely controversial concepts in real life. His teammates were anxious it would be too much and undo all of their good work. He convinced them, and after a wobble it worked, making them the first to get the predicted rise down to + 2.0.

Another team made ground with their introduction of emission source registration, requiring all vehicles or machines with fuel tanks of 75 litres or more to be registered as large fuel users and required to complete the equivalent of a tax return but for emissions.

This became redundant when DrGetRekt's team instigated a Carbon Ration, making every individual accountable for their own carbon footprint. There were six levels covering all aspects of modern life: power, food, water, data, travel and material goods. No one wanted to waste their precious carbon ration on a show-off car. Rations were tradable on the open market but were expensive and anyone consuming more than their allowance also had to pay a carbon offset cost that was funnelled into supporting the carbon removal projects. There were unexpected spill-over effects. As inequality decreased, so did crime and mental health issues, allowing budgets to be reallocated towards carbon drawdown projects. Soon this was a must-have strategy adopted by all teams.

Each team had their own virtual world to play with, but all were subject to same algorithms responding to the same dataset. Nonetheless, bold policies that changed underlying conditions could lead to that team being more or less vulnerable to certain catastrophic events. So far, all teams that had got close to a predicted +1.5 had suffered drastic reversal when some infrastructure breakdown, unexpected disaster or cyber-attack had messed everything up. Incredibly frustrating, leading in one tragic incident to the suicide from a player who'd been in the leading team up until that point.

Devlin was also at breaking point, but it was his teammates driving him mad, arguing every proposal he put forward, or pushing for no-hope solutions themselves. One in particular, EarthTender, he was sure she was a girl, kept harping on about shifting power bases from national to local. He reminded her that he'd proved her wrong that nature-based solutions would be enough. She let it go, but each time a disaster set them back she'd bring it up again, and he'd have to waste precious time explaining to her how it would hinder innovation, something they could not afford.

The game fuelled fierce debates between proponents of green growth who maintained economic growth was necessary to fund innovation into carbon capture solutions and those who were adamant that planned degrowth with reductions in consumption was the only way. However, the de-growthers failed to get political support and the green-growthers failed to achieve growth without stalling progress on greenhouse gas reduction. EarthTender got points when she suggested changing the metric of political success from the GDP to a Happy Planet Index, allowing degrowth policies to look good on the new metric.

His team were now tantalisingly close, but they were up against the elite and, despite their best efforts, were languishing in fourth. The problem was copycats. Copying didn't always pay off as it depended what strategies were already in place, but DrGetRekt had amplified the impacts of switching to a Happy Planet Index by pouring money into artworks and culture so that each city had a giant construction showing performance on the index. Prizes were offered for the most engaging way of portraying the figures. Progress was reported in news programmes and school assemblies, harnessing the will of the people towards a common goal. The public had renamed DrGetRekt 'the Culture Secretary' as this simple policy had shot them into first place.

Despite the copycats, her pioneering of the Happy Planet Index had given EarthTender credibility. Next time there was a disaster she repeated her plea. *We should go local.* Devlin responded in the chat, writing in capital letters how it would slow down innovation. She was back. *Let me just try, local decision-making, community-owned energy, local currency, local food. The whole system won't crash if we make self-sufficient yet interlocking communities.*

To his dismay he was outvoted. It was the final straw, and he quit. He told the organisers the team were driving him mad and demanded the chance to go it alone. After the suicide, they were taking no chances and agreed. Finally he was free of the endless negotiations that had sapped his time and morale. Devlin could now speed ahead without encumbrance. He watched with pleasure as his previous team adopted a localisation strategy and their progress stalled, just as he'd predicted.

He concentrated on the ocean. Refreezing the Arctic had been a huge risk he couldn't have taken with his team in tow, but it paid off. The potential for carbon capture by tree planting was negligible compared to what the ocean had to offer, and he poured resources into seagrass planting and kelp forests. There was so much more that was possible here, but politics and national interests limited what could be done – a constant frustration. He didn't admit it to himself, but he missed his other team member, RastaDude who'd been a master of timing, uncannily correct in his predictions of when other teams had implemented a policy too soon or too late. Devlin pushed ahead anyway and found himself in the lead.

He lost his complacency when DrGetRekt's team caught up with him by legislating widespread conversion of waste biomass to biochar. This push led to high levels of soil restoration and lots of high-value carbon credits that funded further carbon drawdown projects. They were now neck and neck, both approaching, for the third time, the tantalising goal of +1.5 degrees.

Then another setback. More political disruption. Back in third place.

Head down, barely eating or sleeping, Devlin threw everything he had at it. He barely noticed his mother tiptoeing into his room, setting down plates of food beside him. Reluctantly, he pulled back on his plans for the ocean, and concentrated on untested innovations. Thorium reactors, dry ice torpedoes, lightning harvesting, peat fire firefighting, flooding the depressions, slowing glaciers. For such solutions, existing more in theory than in practice, assumed parameters were taken from experts in the field and from start-ups feeding in brand new data. The resulting figures formed the basis of the deployment phases. Even though they were hypothetical, valuable information was generated about the impacts of a potential solution in a particular place, how much it might cost, how it might be rolled out and where the bottlenecks would be.

Devlin revelled in his growing fame. He was just a fraction off a predicted +1.5 degrees and had a clear lead. He turned the screen off for the first time in weeks and went for a long overdue wash. He swaggered past his dad who was just about to go in the bathroom. He flashed him a smug smile and shut the door in his face. His dad was a two-bit lecturer on Greek history who hadn't even paid off the mortgage on a three-bed semi. DevNoobCrusher69 was on his way to five million dollars and was saving the world. He treated himself to a long shower, planning in his head how he'd spend his fortune. It took a while to decide whether to have an indoor or outdoor swimming pool. He settled on both. His dad's banging on the door interrupted ruminations on cars.

'When I'm rich I'll get you and mum a new house with three bathrooms,' he shouted over the noise of the shower. He wondered back to his room twenty minutes later, towel round his waist, skin steaming, his clothes in a wet puddle on the floor.

He ignored the argument coming from downstairs. It sounded like he'd annoyed his dad. Bit ungrateful considering he'd offered him a new house. His mum was defending him, and his dad was shouting some Greek-sounding word, 'hubris'. He returned to his screen and allowed himself a quick check on how his previous team were doing. They were now making steady progress, but slow. He congratulated himself on his wisdom in getting out. He was hungry. His parent's argument must have distracted his mum from bringing up dinner. Devlin returned to his game and froze. What the hell had happened? He'd been gone for less than half an hour and everything had stalled. Then the announcements came. Passwords hacked. Internet breakdown. Bank failure. Funds drying up.

He had no comeback. He watched helpless as one by one all his innovations and projects ground to a halt.

He couldn't believe it. There was no coming back from this. He checked the other teams; several had suffered similar issues. No one was anywhere near +1.5 anymore, but Devlin wasn't even in the top five. He tried the usual self-talk and affirmations. It didn't help. He checked the scores again. His previous team were now in front. He rushed to the bathroom feeling nauseous and dry-retched, cringing with embarrassment. He'd publicly called them losers, crowing over leaving them behind. They'd be laughing at him now. His parents would say I told you so. His dad would tell him it served him right. Waves of despair and self-hatred crashed over him as he remembered how he'd secretly despised the player who'd topped himself after a setback, thinking him weak. Now he understood and found there was nothing he could do other than cry. Devlin eventually registered his mother tapping on the door. He had no idea how long she'd been there, but the odd phrase got through. 'You don't have to win to be special you know.' 'We still love you even if you don't save the world.' Then he heard his dad. 'Come on out. I need to use the bathroom.'

'What's hubris?' he asked his dad through the door.

'Arrogance leading to lack of caution. It's what happens when someone gets too powerful. It goes to their head.'

It made sense; he'd been like a controller of the world. In virtual reality at least.

His mum was whispering angrily then his dad added. 'Don't worry son, happens to the best of 'em.'

Devlin pulled himself to his feet and opened the door.

'What do I do?'

'Only solution is humility. No way round it,' said his dad.

'And remember, no one can do it by themselves,' added his mum.

Devlin wanted to snort but didn't and realised to his surprise that perhaps he was already more humble. He congratulated himself on his new-found maturity and felt a little better.

'Cheers. Any dinner?'

After some food and a twelve-hour sleep Devlin knew what he had to do. He had to get back onto his old team. After his antics it wouldn't be easy, but he had an ace up his sleeve. The ocean. The long rest had allowed his brain to process some of the implications of other teams' approaches. Expanding the area of National Parks and Marine Protected Areas had been a solution that many had adopted. He could go one further. It would make the difference. Yes, his previous team were in the lead, but only because others had fallen back. They were nowhere near 1.5 and this would get them there.

He checked with the climate gaming committee. They said it was up to the team members themselves. If they agreed unanimously to let Devlin back in, the Committee wouldn't stand in the way.

He sent them his pitch. *Let me re-join the team and I'll guarantee you win.*

How?

Have me back in and I'll tell you.

How?

The Ocean as an Independent State.

Ps Sorry.

The climate games committee and watching public were astounded when DevNoobCrusher69 issued a public apology, confessed he'd been brought down by the classic of all banana peels – hubris – and promised sincere commitment to a new team effort to save the world. *Hubris is something that besets all great leaders, but I have overcome it,* he typed proudly into the public chat.

With his new humility, Devlin was happy to recognise the power of local decision making. The citizens' assemblies suggested by EarthTender proved to be a crucial solution that other teams quickly copied, as they immunised against short-term thinking, allowing the necessary consumption-reducing policies to be implemented.

EarthTender insisted on scaling up community-owned energy, ensuring each region played to its strength predominantly with local wind or solar farms, or hydropower. He didn't argue.

His plan to give the ocean nation status was a winner, allowing all the ocean-based carbon sequestration solutions to reach their full potential. Charging rent for ocean services enabled funding on the scale needed to relaunch all the innovations that had stalled. Giving climate migrants nationhood in this new state released political pressure creating greater stability. Local currencies to supplement national currencies boosted local economies and immunised their team against the financial instability that beset other teams.

They ploughed on slowly but surely, and gradually gained ground. Through trial and error and constant tinkering they ended up with a hybrid modular economy where local time banks and libraries of things led to money, goods, and time becoming like interchangeable currencies resilient to any external shock.

Rapid sea level rise. Vast tracts of land were submerged causing supply chains to crash everywhere. Refreezing of the Arctic and projects to slow down of melting of glaciers could not reverse the process, only delay it. The tipping point had been passed years before the game began and there was no avoiding payback time. It set them back, no doubt about that, but it didn't destroy them. In classic tortoise and style, other teams fell by the wayside and Devlin's team stumbled on relatively unscathed towards the next milestone – Day 23. By the end of day 23 the winning team would be chosen, and other teams would accept defeat. Then the individual members would all take it alone from there. Winner takes all. Bookies had DevNoobCRusher69 and DrGetRekt as equal odds on.

DrGetRekt's team had foregone the investment in glacier slowing in favour of other projects and they foundered just minutes before midnight after a giant methane burp set them back by several degrees. Devlin's team made it through to the final round.

They'd made it as a team and now it was each individual gamer out for themselves. Devlin publicly acknowledged the part each team member had played in getting them this far. The combination of EarthTender's insistence on going local providing resilience, Devlin's audacious plan to grant nation status to the ocean a gamechanger and RastaDudes's canny sense of when to copy other innovations provided a winning combination. Kushi, the little known fourth member of their team, got belated recognition for a family planning policy they'd instigated right at the start. Less harsh than the one-child policy that had to be reversed, but empowering women giving them consistent access to birth control, had been shown to have been an unrecognised contributor to their success.

The next five days would be make or break as each team member was now on their own.

Devlin checked every policy that had worked looking for ways to maximise carbon drawdown potential. He strengthened the income-gathering powers of the Ocean State, scaled up rigs-to-reefs projects and mini-Maritime Protected Areas managed by fishing communities themselves. He edged ahead of the others, but 1.5 degrees remained tantalisingly out of reach.

Four days to go. A different kind of catastrophe hit. Devlin woke up at 4am with a pounding heart and a shocking realisation. It wasn't a game. He tossed and turned as the implications hit him. A series of vivid images like punches to the gut. Floods, heatwaves, fires, power outages, relentless sea rise. This was the future. He gave up and sat in front of the screen but couldn't make a decision. The stakes were too high, and he found himself paralysed.

The ticking began. A feature of the game that kicked in when there were three days to go. It was the same for all players and it was driving them mad, leading to last minute adjustments and wild changes in policy. DevNoobCrusher69 did nothing. It was the best thing he could have done.

Positive feedback loops work both ways and projects that had got off to a slow start now picked up pace. As kelp and seagrass and newly planted trees grew, they absorbed ever more carbon dioxide.

The final 48 hours counted down. The ticking clock at the bottom of the screen increased in pitch. Dev remained in his chair, turning over possibilities in his head, brain racing, mouth dry. He'd edged ahead, but it didn't matter. All were still short of the +1.5 needed to win. His mum brought up food and drink and he munched without tasting, just staring at the screen, calculating, plotting, dithering.

The ticking turned to harsh beeps. One more day.

While his previous teammates frantically twiddled and tinkered, Devlin just watched and prayed. The five million dollars was the furthest thing from his mind.

The beeps grew louder, screeching, ear-splitting, unsettling.

This was it.

The dial flickered round 1.5. Devlin held his breath.

The seconds seemed to speed up, ticking faster and faster until, suddenly, in an instant, everything stopped. The screen went blank. Blackness. Devlin saw his exhausted face reflected in the monitor.

After a couple of seconds, the leader board flashed up.

1.49 degrees. He'd done it. They'd done it.

His teammates were the first to congratulate him, asking him what he'd spend the money on. He tried to type in his list: mansion, two swimming pools, Tesla, but even this was beyond him. 28 days in front of the screen, barely blinking. His brain was fried.

He went for a walk. His name was everywhere, on banners, newspapers, in bookies windows. Yet no one paid attention to the pale young man walking slowly, looking round and blinking into the sun. He headed for the trendy waterside development for inspiration on how to spend his prize but found himself pitying those who'd bought properties by the river. No, the best spot would be in the hilly suburbs where the rich lived. His journey took him past the town hall and his eye was caught by a familiar name on a poster. *Inspired by Earth Tender and the Climate Gamers, a new proposal for a community-owned energy farm to protect our region.* There was a meeting about to start.

He walked on, seeing his neighbourhood for the first time properly. His newly trained eye saw the unfulfilled potential of the endless roofs, empty of solar panels. He noted a perfect spot for a library of things in the abandoned department store downtown. Opportunities for local food in every hanging basket and verge and piece of land. What this looked like in twenty-eight years would depend on what they did right now.

An hour later he was strolling in deathly quiet, leafy, residential streets, mansions peeking out from behind gilded gates and ancient trees. He frowned at the SUVs and Porsches that lined the long drives. It suddenly hit him. What's the good of having numerous cars and a mansion in a world that, if it were to survive, would outlaw such excess?

He turned around, quickly. If he was quick, the meeting would still be on. They'd probably muck it up without him anyway. DevNoobCrusher69 was on his way.

THE PITCH

by D.A. Baden

This is a stand-alone extract from the novel Habitat Man that reimagines the start of the story.

I rehearsed my pitch on the train all the way to Waterloo, drawing strange looks from the couple sitting opposite, who were no doubt wondering why my mouth was moving silently and my eyebrows were wavering between imploring, glowering and deadly serious.

At Waterloo, I approached the usual mix of homeless, beggars and *Big Issue* sellers, rummaging in my pocket for change. The smart-suited man ahead of me made the mistake of giving a fiver to the bolshy guy at the end. I'd noticed the more money he was given, the longer his tirade would be.

'Fiver wouldn't even pay your dry-cleaning bill, you rich tosser,' Bolshy Guy hurled at him, deftly pocketing the note.

Smart-suited man shook his head, shuffling from polished black shoe to polished black shoe as the tirade continued.

'The world would be better off if you didn't exist. If you didn't bother with your dry-cleaned suit and stayed at home and did sweet fuck all. Smart-guy-city-tosspot,' he accused, peering up through overgrown eyebrows and shaggy hair.

He had a point. I'd calculated the environmental impacts of laundry using the Costing for Nature software and could have informed them about the high carbon footprint of washing clothes and the contribution of dry cleaners to air pollution. I decided not to interject and walked on past 'smart-guy-city-tosspot', who stood patiently accepting the abuse. The tirade might go on for a while and I couldn't afford to be late. Anyway, I didn't need my daily dose of psychic self-flagellation, because today I'd be part of the solution, not part of the problem.

I walked the familiar route over Waterloo Bridge and gulped in a lungful of the bracing wind, taking in the open vista of the Thames and the Houses of Parliament etched against the cornflower blue sky. A cormorant perched on an old barge, drying its wings. Gulls circled raucously above; crabs picked among the debris on the muddy banks where the tide had receded. Nature in the heart of the city.

Last week, Extinction Rebellion protestors had occupied the bridge. Part of me had been thrilled to see them. Hordes of young, bearded, pierced, and tattooed protestors beating drums, chanting and waving banners: 'Save the Earth', 'Rebel for Life', 'Wise up. Rise up'. There had been families too, mothers with pushchairs, dads with toddlers on their shoulders. But no amount of smiles and thumbs up on my part could disguise my city suit and complicity. They'd chanted, 'this is the sixth mass extinction,' and in my paranoia and guilt, I'd been sure it was aimed at me.

I got to work with twenty minutes to spare and headed straight for the bathroom, suddenly nervous. I hated our office toilets, the scent of the air freshener worse than what it disguised. And they were pretentious, with toilets that automatically flushed the moment you got off them, or, unnervingly, when you moved on the seat. I washed my hands quickly. It must be nearly time for my pitch. I hoped Simon, the financial director, wouldn't be there with his intimidating beard. I regarded my pale, freckled face in the mirror and longed to be more hirsute. I didn't even want a beard necessarily, just the feeling that beneath my skin were follicles of thick, dark, bristly hair bursting to come forth. Then I'd feel equal to the task.

I regretted again scheduling my meeting with the carbon offsetting enterprise on the same day. If the pitch failed it would be a waste of time, but they'd been insistent.

I headed to the conference room and sat amidst the pot plants in the waiting area.

'By valuing the ecosystem and everything that depends upon it, we will protect it,' I whispered earnestly to the Areca Fern and Rubber Plant. 'Unless we cost for nature...'

I stopped quickly as several suited men and a woman trailed out, leaving Martin and Simon at the table. Through the glass walls, I saw Simon open up his laptop and show something to Martin. They talked animatedly, probably working out how inputting the environmental and social impacts of each project would affect the overall costs. Martin beckoned me in. I entered with the gait of a confident man who was bringing them the best thing since sliced bread.

'Hi there. Right, er...'

'That's us on the beach,' Simon was saying.

'Looks lovely,' murmured Martin.

'Four-star resort, but we wouldn't go back.'

I sat at the table opposite them and placed my laptop on the top pointedly. Martin eventually looked over.

'What are we meeting about again, Tim? Remind me.'

'This is to talk about the Costing for Nature software that will transform the way we do business. For the better,' I added quickly.

'Okay, go ahead.'

'We need to cost for nature.' Simon was still swiping through his photos. I paused, but he showed no sign of looking up. 'For example, when we cost a project for time and money, we factor in the carbon cost too, and allow money to offset.'

Martin looked doubtful.

'It's not a perfect solution, but at least the environmental costs would form part of the cost-benefit analysis.'

No reaction.

'My degree was in biology. I don't know if you knew that? So I've been able to feed the latest environmental data and predicted carbon costs into the algorithms.'

'Sounds expensive.' Simon finally looked up.

'No, we developed some software that calculates it for us.' I searched in vain for a sign they'd checked it out. 'There was a link in my email?'

I waited while they murmured among themselves. It was a brief conversation.

'Thanks for your idea, but it's not something we'll be taking forward right now,' said Martin.

'But—'

'We're a business, not a nature reserve.'

'But we're part of nature. Don't you see?' I searched their faces desperately for a hint of understanding. 'We're costing for ourselves!'

Martin nodded towards the door. Simon was back on his photos.

I returned to my desk, sat in my ergonomically designed chair among a sea of similar chairs and desks in the open-plan office and gazed at my screen. The screensaver showed endless forests against a startling blue sky. I tapped a key and up came accounts for a global IT company we were helping to make richer. Standard financial modelling indicated that designing products to fail with parts that couldn't be replaced was the most profitable business model. I gazed blankly at the numbers as it sank in. They hadn't even looked at my CFN analysis that costed in the e-waste, unnecessary carbon emissions, and health costs from sweatshop conditions and toxic ingredients that seeped into the water. A new screensaver sprang up. A tropical island with clear turquoise sea filled with colourful fish. I was suddenly furious. They hadn't looked at any of the sample scenarios. I grabbed my laptop and marched back in.

They were still there exchanging holiday horror stories.

'Bali was crap too. You couldn't swim in the sea,' Martin informed Simon.

'It's not more expensive,' I declared loudly, striding in and banging the door behind me. Well, I tried to, but it was a glass door on a hinge designed to shut gently. I opened my laptop and pointed to the example scenario.

'See that,' I pointed at a graph showing two lines comparing current costs with costs using the CFN.

'What's CFN?' Simon deigned to glance over.

'It's Costing for Nature accounting software,' I told him through gritted teeth.

'Well it costs more, doesn't it?'

'Now look.' I typed three years into the time box. The two lines for standard cost and CFN costs came together. 'Now see.' I typed five years into the box and the CFN line shifted below the standard cost line. 'CFN saves money. This scenario is for the construction companies we deal with that we walk past every day coming into work. Simply switching to green cement, for example, substantially lowers CFN costs due to its lower carbon footprint.'

'I drive,' Simon said.

'What? Why would you drive?'

'I've got a Ferrari.'

I looked at him in his perfectly cut suit, shoes too shiny for public transport and hated him.

'Way overpriced for what you get. Now if it were a Porsche—' began Martin.

'But the point is,' I shouted over him, 'for every company we deal with, in the short term, yes it costs money to cost in environmental impacts, but in the medium to long term it costs way more not to.'

'I'll tell you what costs too much money,' Martin said.

'What?' Simon asked.

'A Ferrari,' said Martin.

'No, two-week holidays swimming in plastic,' Simon retorted.

'Ouch.'

I lost it. 'I don't care about your car or your two weeks' holiday on your tropical island.'

'The holiday was shit anyway,' consoled Simon. 'We had to return early. My son got asthma and the hospitals were full.'

'Don't you see we're the engines of all this?' I cried. 'Plastic didn't get in the sea by magic. The asthma didn't just happen. It was the pollution from clearing rainforests. The whole of bloody Indonesia has breathing difficulties. We crunch the numbers and depending on what goes in, out come the decisions. If we added waste and air quality and climate change to our numbers, you wouldn't get plastic in the sea and asthma. You must see that? It's us, it's all us! It's all our fault.'

They looked at me aghast as my voice hit soprano pitch. 'I'm not jealous of your Ferrari or your holiday, or your beard.' Simon looked up sharply and stroked his beard possessively. He shot Martin a look. Was it guilt? I pressed the point home.

'Surely you must see it's our fault? But that's okay, because the Costing for Nature software can put it right. We're part of nature, we're costing for ourselves. Don't you see? We crunch the numbers.

What goes in is what comes out.' I knew I was repeating myself, but was unable to stop. 'We're not just complicit, we're guilty, but we can make it right!'

'Mmmhmm,' soothed Martin. I petered out, finally deciphering their expression. It wasn't guilt. It was pity.

I fell silent and packed up my laptop and left the room.

I returned to my desk and fell into my chair. Twenty-five years. I'd been in this job for twenty-five years. My fingers hovered over the keyboard, but nothing happened. I couldn't type a word. I tried to close the file I'd been working on but fell at the first hurdle. 'Save', 'Don't Save'. I gazed at the simple question. Eventually I realised I didn't care. I pushed the power button hard until it gave up the red light and set off early for my next meeting.

I walked back across Waterloo Bridge to Waterloo station where I handed the bolshy guy a twenty-pound note and passed the time by gazing at my black polished shoes as he told me at great length how the world would be better off without me.

* * *

As the business and shopping centres of Woking come into view, I realised that the pitch hadn't stood a chance. Of course they'd said no. They only cared about profits and to expect anything more was naïve. With a longer time frame, the Costing for Nature policy would save money, but who thought beyond the next quarter? On the walk from the station I berated myself for being an idiot and getting people's hopes up. Specifically Ian and Cathy, a married couple I was on the way to see, who were looking forward to seeing how the Costing for Nature software could link up with their carbon offsetting app.

Ian, a tall blonde man in his thirties, answered the door beaming. 'Tim! Thanks for meeting us in our home. It makes it easier with the kids.'

'I'm sorry,' I said straightaway. 'There was probably no point my coming. They didn't bite.'

Two girls rushed up to the door. 'What didn't bite? Do you mean the crickets?' the eldest asked eagerly.

'They do bite so,' claimed the younger one.

'This is Lucy and Anna. Girls, say hi to Tim.'

'Do you have crickets?' I asked, distracted for a moment from my woes.

'Loads!'

'Your garden must have excellent biodiversity.'

Ian looked proud. 'Come and see.' He ushered me inside and we followed the girls into a kitchen that led out through a patio door into a garden.

I opened my mouth to continue my apology, but was immediately hushed by Lucy.

'Listen!'

We heard the unmistakable chirp of crickets.

'Do they bite?' Anna asked me.

'We just heard them for the first time today so they're all excited,' said Ian. We let our grass grow to attract more wildlife, and it looks like we've succeeded.'

'Well?' demanded Anna.

I thought back thirty years to my biology practical and the wildlife habitat we'd created in the University gardens. 'There is one species that bites, the wart-biter bush cricket. But they're very rare.'

'Told you,' declared Lucy, satisfied.

'Anyway, I'm really sorry—' I began.

'So you know about wildlife gardening do you?' Ian interrupted.

'I used to be a guerrilla gardener before I joined the rat race.'

'What did you do?'

I smiled, remembering. 'Gardens on bus shelter roofs was our thing,'

'Cool! Why did you stop?'

'PansyGate!'

'What?'

'We got overrun by the Bassett Ladies. They'd see a space that had a lovely bit of scrub, dandelions, great plants for wildlife that thrive in such conditions. And they'd pull it up to plant something pretty.'

'They sound pure evil!' He grinned and nodded over the fence. 'Just like my neighbour. If she comes out, pretend to be a wildlife garden consultant!'

I glanced over at the neat garden next door. 'Sorry, I don't understand?'

'It starts with an enquiry if our lawnmower is broken and would we like to borrow theirs, but what she really means is cut your damn lawn.'

'Er...'

'If we can say we paid someone to check our garden as a professional habitat man, then that's different,' said Ian.

'Your garden already seems to be a perfect habitat for wildlife,' I said, looking round. The grass was quite long. Garden debris piled up by the side, providing a habitat for invertebrates. Half-buried logs for the vertebrates, water butt, a swift box under the eaves.

'Look.' Lucy led me towards a small pond shining in the corner.

'We want frogs but there aren't none,' said Anna.

'Any,' corrected Ian, 'there aren't any.'

'That's what I said. There's no frogs.' Anna looked at me as if I could fix it.

'Their numbers have fallen, due to habitat loss and water contamination mainly, but also predation,' I said.

The girls looked bemused. I rephrased. 'They need a good place to live, and your pond is great, except for that open patch between the pond and the hedge.'

'Is that bad?' Lucy asked.

'Some birds eat frogs so they'd be exposed here. They like to travel without being seen so no one can see them and eat them.'

The girls looked suspiciously up at the sky.

'Let the grass grow extra long between the pond and the hedges to provide cover for them.'

'Good idea.' Ian nodded next door where the neighbour had appeared to hang out her washing and spoke loudly. 'We should keep our grass long you say?'

I raised my voice slightly. 'One of the easiest things a gardener can do to enhance the wildlife value of their garden is to mow the lawn less frequently.'

'We're hoping to grow a meadow.'

'For a meadow, you'll only need to cut the grass and compost the clippings once a year, in late August.'

'Thank you for your professional opinion as Habitat Man. We'll do as you say.' He winked at me.

'If you allow your grass to grow, daisies, clover, buttercups, and dandelions will naturally proliferate, creating a meadow-like effect. For a wider variety like poppies, cornflowers, etc. remove some turf round the edges and replace with some horticultural grit or sand mix and sow wildflowers there,' I proclaimed, getting into my role as Habitat Man. 'Yellow rattle will reduce the vigour of the grass, giving other wildflowers more of a chance. It wouldn't be long before your garden is alive with all kinds of butterflies.'

'You're good at this. I'm impressed.' Ian pointed towards an intriguing wooden hut perched on a raised patio area at the bottom of the garden. 'This will impress you.'

'It's a cool design. Is it a shed?'

'Come and see.'

Anna and Lucy followed us. 'Do you want a wee?' Anna asked.

'Or poo,' giggled Lucy.

Ian laughed. 'This is our composting toilet.'

It was beautifully designed. Almost an arch shape, with a circular stained glass window towards the top of the door to allow in light. The way it curved into a point at the top gave it an ethereal *Lord of the Rings* look.

'I've heard of these, but I've not been in one.'

He looked at me expectantly, so I opened the door and beheld the toilet. It was small but stylish – a square box painted in red, gold and white.

Ian's face burst with pride. He lifted up the slab of wood that the toilet seat was set into. Underneath were two compartments. At the front was a large plastic bottle and at the back, in a separate section, was a square plastic container lined with a large bag and half full of wood shavings.

'We have a twin-bowl design that separates the solid from the urine, to keep it dry so you don't get flies. It goes dry and crumbly when it meets the oxygen and breaks down into germ-free compost, so you only need to empty it about once or twice a year, and you can use it to revitalise the soil.'

'This is Ian's new toy.' A friendly-looking woman joined us. 'You must be Tim. I'm Cathy.' She held out her hand.

I took it and remembered why I was there and my failure. My stuttered explanations were interrupted by Ian, who was desperate for me to try his toilet.

'When you go, you use toilet paper as usual, then instead of flushing, you put down two scoops of wood shavings. No water, no chemicals. It doesn't smell at all, does it?'

'No it doesn't.'

'Would you like a go?' He nodded, bright-eyed.

'Maybe later.'

'I'll just top up the wood shavings, in case.'

Cathy laughed and rolled her eyes. 'We'll leave him to it. Tim, come have a coffee.'

Once inside, the mood lift I'd experienced in the garden disappeared, and I was left again with a feeling of despair. While Cathy made coffee, I filled her in on how the pitch had gone.

'I didn't think they'd go for it. There's nothing compelling them is there?' Cathy put a cup of coffee in front of me.

I gulped it and burnt my mouth. I spat it back quickly and panted open-mouthed like a stranded fish.

She poured me a glass of cold water. 'It's not your fault,' she said, watching me gulp it down. 'Businesses seek profit. Unless we change their legal form and make them all social enterprises or benefit corporations, they'll do what's best for their shareholders.'

'But shareholders are people too! They want clean water, fresh air, a future for their children.' I had an image of business as a moth blindly rushing towards the bright, hot lights of profit, taking humanity with it to its doom. I barely looked up as Ian joined us with the girls, realising the implications with a sudden gut-churning certainty. 'We don't stand a chance.'

Cathy frowned, and Ian spoke up briskly. 'Girls you go play outside, we're working in here now.'

'I didn't mean to scare them.'

'It's okay.' Ian sat at the table with us. 'In our day we worried about nuclear war. Kids today worry about climate change.'

'But this is inevitable. It's chemistry. Ice melts at zero degrees. It's not a might happen or it might not,' I cried.

'This generation isn't so ingrained in the old ways. We hope they'll help tip us over into the right mindset,' said Ian.

'One day they'll be in power, then things will change,' Cathy said.

'But it will be too late.' I could barely get the words out. Tomorrow I would be fifty. I'd spent half my life in that job. It was just the hope that my company would go for the Costing for Nature software that had kept me going. Could I put my shoulder back to that grinding wheel of commerce? Mid-life crisis, right on time.

'Our carbon offsets are making a difference. These projects are literally drawing down carbon and pulling it out of the air.' Cathy's tone was desperately reassuring.

'But they're voluntary – it's a fraction of what's needed.'

'We're putting everything in place,' Ian assured me.

'Before we can regulate, we need to be able to calculate the carbon footprint of everything,' said Cathy. 'Carbon offsets normalise the idea that businesses and governments can offset to get to zero. Consumers can use them too, so they don't feel guilty.'

'But you're right,' Ian admitted. 'Until it's mandatory and everyone has their own carbon allowance, it won't touch the sides.'

'How do you go on?' I was desperate for an answer to my dilemma.

'Hope. There comes a point when it's obvious to the majority that we have more to lose than gain by business as usual, and then the changes will come fast. Look at the NHS and welfare state. Concern about poverty and ill health built over centuries, but when we made the move, we did it within a decade.'

'The Australians chose the greenest politicians after all their fires,' Ian added.

'Look at the Cuban revolution. Look at glasnost and perestroika, when the Soviet Union changed almost overnight. As long as the pieces are in place, change can come rapidly once the tipping point is reached, when we all realise there is more to lose than gain,' Cathy said.

'It's like gardening. Prepare the ground, before you plant the seeds,' said Ian. 'I think of our wildlife garden as an island of plenty, a haven so that when we come to our senses and nurture nature, then there's some left to start afresh.'

I nodded to be polite, but he was kidding himself. This was just one garden. Our most likely future presented itself to me with a sickening clarity. They must have thought me so naïve. My guts were twisting as I struggled with the indigestible truth. I could hear the girls giggling as they crept into the kitchen, and it broke my heart. How we fool ourselves believing what we want to believe.

'If you knew my pitch wouldn't work, why did you agree to see me?' I asked suddenly.

'We seed ideas as well – not just about offsetting, but like the composting toilet,' said Ian. 'Soon we won't be able to waste precious fresh water. Flushing away our waste, creating sewage that mixes with pesticide and agricultural run-offs to contaminate our rivers – it's so unnecessary. So I show everyone my wonderful composting toilet – seeding the idea because the first step is to raise awareness, make people more familiar with them and how they work.'

'Basically, Ian wanted to show you his new toilet,' said Cathy.

'Are you sure you don't want to go?' He looked at me hopefully.

I didn't trust myself to speak and just nodded.

Ian smiled delighted. The girls jumped up to follow me, but he held them back.

'Leave him in peace. It's his first time.'

'Have a nice wee, Habitat Man,' shouted Anna after me.

'Or poo!' Lucy added.

I left the sounds of laughing children and escaped outside. But there was no escape from the turmoil in my head. Thoughts bashed against each other in my besieged psyche like bumper cars at the fair. How can I go on? What else would I do? Lose myself in drink? Retreat into denial? Was that even possible?

The freshness of the air gradually calmed my ruminations. A few slow soft drops of rain started then petered out. The sun emerged, setting the raindrops sparkling against the vegetation. I peeked over the fence at next door's neat garden. Ecologists would call it a green desert – a tightly mown lawn, bedding plants round the border, non-native shrubs. Bamboo, Japanese maple and rhododendron may cut a dash but have nothing to offer local wildlife. The perfect grass would have been heavily treated with weed killer to look so pristine, perhaps explaining the lack of insect life.

The quantities of toxins we were pouring into our soil, rivers and ponds alarmed me. It wasn't just agriculture that was the culprit, but shop-bought pesticides, slug pellets, weed killers, even pet treatments. The Costing for Nature software would have revealed their true cost. Soil that was once biologically active, teeming with life and the building blocks of our whole ecology was turning to lifeless dirt, increasingly incapable of sustaining the thriving ecology we needed for our food and health.

A sense of futility hit me again like a punch in the stomach and I returned to the glorious abundance of shelter and food in Ian's garden.

The comparison was stark, and I saw now what he'd meant by an island of plenty. I heard the sweet melody of a song thrush – increasingly rare these days. There it was on a branch near the pond, waiting for me to leave so he could pop down to the pond for a quick wash and dinner of midges. The brief spell of rain had released the smell of the lavender from the borders, attracting the bees. A tortoiseshell butterfly fluttered around the buddleia.

I entered the composting toilet and sat down. The feeling of calm and sanctuary inside echoed the garden. It was perfectly quiet except for the distant sound of a wood pigeon. It smelled of forests and fresh air, soothing to the senses and the spirit.

The notion of islands of plenty stirred a faint memory of my ecology module many years ago. Something to do with pockets of resilience – the idea that you can create refuges, or was it refugii? Maybe Ian was right. If you can create enough safe habitats, then wildlife could repopulate an area once conditions improved. If just a fifth of UK gardens were kept pesticide-free, and grown with native plants suited to local invertebrates, you'd have an area the size of Luxembourg. It just might be enough.

I'd want to chop down non-native species like bamboo and replace with a native deciduous tree, maybe a hawthorn with berries for the birds and nesting sites. A pond for sure. Pollinator-friendly plants for the bees and butterflies. Everyone's into the idea of keeping honeybees, but they were out-competing wild bees, so I'd create habitats for mason bees. They'd be happy with a few bamboo canes tied together, and they'd hide out in the holes. Ladybirds would be good with pinecones shoved together in with some dried leaves. No need to buy compost – each garden would make their own, with food leftovers, mixed in with garden debris and their own waste.

The smell of wood shavings reminded me of the hamster I used to keep. Trapped in its cage, running endlessly on the wheel. I thought of my job and the office toilets. But here there were no harsh lights, whirr of fans, smell of urine overlaid with air freshener. Instead, daylight streamed in through the small window, which I now saw had a picture set into the glass, a frog on a lily pad amidst dragonflies and bulrushes.

The sun caught the stained glass window and brought the scene suddenly to life, creating an almost religious experience. The elusive frog so sensitive to water pollution, safe here where our waste was used to nurture life. I heard the chirp of a cricket and smiled. In the sanctuary of the composting toilet, at last I forgave myself. One person couldn't change the world, nor should they be able to. I'd done my best within my zone of influence. It hadn't worked, but perhaps I'd planted a seed – prepared the ground as Ian would say. Maybe when conditions were right, they'd change their mind. As for what I did now?

Habitat Man. That was what Ian had called me.

I realised with surprise the decision had been made.

I breathed out for what seemed like the first time in years and relaxed. I felt a swelling up, a feeling of rightness, of great joy, a letting go.

I used the paper, then put two scoops of wood shavings down the toilet and used the hand sanitizer. I opened the door and walked out into the garden and back into the house.

Ian recognised something in my shining face and nodded, satisfied.[1]

---

1. This story is adapted from the novel published in 2021. Interested to know more? See https://www.greenstories.org.uk/anthology-for-cop27/stories/the-pitch/

BLUE NATION

by Rasha Barrage

"Picture a beach". Three words that would never have the same meaning again. No toes tickled by sand. No soft caress of waves to your ears. After today, a beach would forever bring questions. Scrawled in black paint. Large and imposing. On surf boards.

IF A POPULATION WAS MUTE AND ILLITERATE, WOULD THE PEOPLE BE DENIED A NATION?

WHY IS DYNAMITE FISHING, POISONING, AND TRAWLING LEGAL?

IF THE WORLD'S SURFACE IS 71% OCEAN, WHY DO WE CALL IT PLANET EARTH?

Those were just the first three Neve stepped on. There were hundreds, thousands maybe, placed across the entire length of the beach. The whirring of drones above signalled their significance. This wasn't your average protest. This was a work of art. A political statement. A movement.

As Neve looked across at the other husbands, wives and "significant others", she saw her feelings of shock and curiosity mimicked on their faces. There was no avoiding the surf boards; to get across the beach they had to walk on them, like some strange political rite of passage. It was annoying but also a welcome surprise from the monotony of the events so far. Occasional whispers of "ridicolo", "good point", "intéressante", "embarrassing" could be heard, while the First Gentleman of the USA and First Lady of Sri Lanka were discussing the meaning of a "nation".

HOW CAN OCEANS THRIVE IF THEIR RESOURCES ARE STOLEN?

The sand underneath caused the boards to sink and wobble with every footstep. Each one painted with a caring and skilful hand. As Neve looked ahead to the conference centre at the far end of the beach, her curiosity turned to dread. She saw them. And most importantly, what they were wearing. Their blue and green outfits were arranged in perfect imitation of the proposed flag. Above their heads, the COP37 sign at the entrance of the building stood aligned with the central circle of the flag – a photo opportunity worthy of all the front pages.

Neve recognised them. They were the activists campaigning for the Oceans to be recognised as a nation. A journalist had inadvertently helped their cause by naming them the "Planet Ocean" group. Their petition, signed by 10 million people, caused the subject to finally come to a head at COP37. Listed in today's agenda, it was widely assumed that the topic would be given a token mention, and then dismissed as an absurd idea. That was before the surf boards.

IS A NATION DEFINED BY BOUNDARIES, ECONOMIES, LAND, OR PEOPLE?

Neve and the others began their slow trek across the sand, conscious that they were being photographed from the road on their right. The line of photographers had been incessantly shouting for their attention since they arrived, oblivious to the gigantic banner below them which read "WE ARE THE OCEANS. THE OCEANS ARE US". The wife of New Zealand's Prime Minister made a point of pausing her strides to read it aloud. She explained "the Māori people believe their ancestors live on in nature, and that humans and water are intertwined. It's like how they say, 'I am the river, the river is me'". Head held high, she continued her determined march as if this would make perfect sense to everyone.

Intrigued but eager to get to the conference centre, Neve focused her eyes on the surf boards ahead. Like the others, she came expecting to briefly dip her feet in the water, play catch with the daughter of President Schumann and smile for the press. No one paid much attention to the 'wives' before today, why now? They had no choice but to get to the other side. And at the other end, they were sure to be confronted by the Planet Ocean protestors. The group of delegates were united in their confusion.

But Neve knew. They didn't care about the First Gentleman of France, the First Lady of Nigeria, the partner of Australia's Prime Minister or anyone else. She was the one they were after – not as the spouse of Prime Minister Rowe, but because she was *the daughter*. The only child of Mr Kendi, and sole 'heiress' to the Kendi Media conglomerate. Panic started to creep in at the thought of her dad's terminal diagnosis. Do they know? Has someone leaked the news? Was it someone in dad's medical team? Have they seen the draft announcement?

Neve felt a gentle tap on her shoulder and turned to find a young man smiling at her. Alofa Kai.

"Good morning Mrs Rowe. My name is Alofa…"

"I know who you are. What are you doing here? How did you get past security?" Neve whispered hurriedly while looking down to ensure she didn't slip or show her expression to the cameras.

WHY ARE CORPORATIONS VALUED ABOVE OCEANS?

Neve tried to control her reaction, determined to find out if they knew about her dad's condition. Taking a deep breath, she asked "What do you want?"

"Just a conversation, that's all. Please Mrs Rowe. Your journalists and news channels reach the homes of millions. You change the way people think; you can open minds and challenge people in ways that politicians and campaigners never will. Please, there are things you need to know."

HOW CAN THE OCEAN SURVIVE IF HUMANITY DE-PLETES ITS LIFE?

Neve had no choice. If she called security the rival papers would spin it that she overreacted and couldn't even be friendly with an environmental activist; like her husband, 'out of touch' and an enemy of the 'youth'.

"Ok, ok, you've got two minutes, 'til we get to the end of the beach. Are you recording this?"

"No, there's nothing on me," he said, hastily patting his clothes and holding his palms open. "You don't have to say anything. Just hear me out. Please?"

Neve gave a slight nod while continuing to look down.

WHY IS ONLY 29% OF THE PLANET REPRESENTED?

Alofa's excited "thank you, thank you" was followed by a speech that he was clearly desperate to recite.

"The Ocean is the largest occupied, unrepresented territory in the world. Nearly two-thirds of the Ocean is in areas beyond national jurisdiction. This is 95% of the Earth's total habitat by volume." Alofa paused for impact, unaware that Neve had read the IUCN's work on ABNJ governance. Neve stayed silent, already losing patience at being told familiar facts. He went on: "6.35% of the Ocean is a Marine Protected Area. The human and financial resources to implement measures properly, in these areas and for the remaining 94% of the Ocean, requires a collective effort of states around the world. 100% of the Ocean needs to be protected and subject to regulations – this is for human benefit too. Coral reefs, mangroves, barrier islands, wetlands – this is all natural infrastructure that reduces human vulnerability to climate change."

"Can you get to the point please Mr Kai!" Neve snapped. She didn't need a lecture about why the Ocean matters, and how we neglect it. After decades of studies, petitions, and climate change protests by the few that tried, most people still didn't care or see how they could make a difference. She wasn't in the mood to hear the same tiresome arguments without any solid solutions.

IF BORDERS ARE FOUGHT AND ALTERED, HOW CAN NATIONS BE DEFINED BY LAND?

Alofa's expression changed. He stopped and looked at Neve with a slight shake of his head. His tone transformed from one of an enthusiastic activist to something akin to the journalists she worked with. Sombre, formal, and dejected.

"If Kendi Media won't sound the alarm on the Ocean emergency, if your journalists won't support our goals and report on why the Ocean must be recognised as a nation, then we are going to arrange a public boycott of your services. Your readers and viewers will know the consequences of your father's irresponsibility; how he has put profit before planet, and oil before the Ocean. His inaction will permanently tarnish the reputation, and the profits, of Kendi Media."

Neve closed her eyes, in disbelief. Why? Why now? Her dad was dying and now his entire life's work was in jeopardy, for a cause he barely understood or cared to acknowledge. How could she explain this to him?

Neve defended him the only way she knew how. "Mr Kai, Kendi Media simply responds to the demands of the public. Party politics, celebrities, crime – that's what people want. Journalists telling readers to change their behaviour or reporting on events that *might* happen in twenty years isn't going to sell any papers. We report on the issues people care about. My dad has done nothing wrong." Her voice shaking slightly at the mention of her dad, she paused to control herself.

DO NATIONAL BOUNDARIES DEPEND ON HUMAN HABITATION?

Unphased by her response, Alofa grabbed his opportunity: "The only way you can protect Kendi Media, and your father's position, is if you start helping us now – today."

"We won't be protected if we support a cause that is meaningless!" Neve interjected sharply. "How would that protect our reputation? We have more to lose from joining a campaign that has no substance and no prospect of ever achieving its goals. Why would our board members agree? Our advertisers, our shareholders, what would they think?"

Alofa relished the challenge, his voice getting louder as he rushed on, "The Ocean requires its own legal framework that covers all its territory and resources. We have the basic framework ready to be developed. The terms of the UNCLOS and the UN Framework Convention on Climate Change can be combined and expanded to deal with *this* Century's issues, especially sea level rise, maritime migration, and the sources of pollution." Neve stayed quiet, wondering if it could indeed be that easy.

WHY DON'T THE OCEANS HAVE RIGHTS?

He continued "The Ocean can't be portioned off into segments. Marine ecosystems are all interconnected – there are long migration pathways for countless species and Ocean currents that span thousands of miles. Your husband, the other leaders, your viewers and readers must understand: the Ocean needs to be acknowledged as one nation but protected by the collective effort of all other nations."

Neve looked at Alofa curiously. She had underestimated him and wondered why her dad never took the group seriously. The fact that he had managed to gather the support of millions of people and speak with her one-on-one meant he couldn't be ignored. He'd done what hundreds tried and failed to do. "Go on" she whispered.

"The law and its enforcement will not change without peoples' support. What we urgently need from Kendi Media is attention, to focus everyone's efforts. For people across the globe – I mean as many citizens, corporations, and leaders as possible – to see this as the only solution to protect our Ocean and ourselves. Something that should have been implemented in the '70s – but it's not too late, if we act now. We know states can work together to protect areas of the Ocean. The EEZ of the Pacific island state of Niue has been protected by Tonga, Samoa, Cook Islands and New Zealand since 2022."

Neve put her hand up to pause. Her head was starting to spin from all the information. And one thing was glaring.

ARE YOU WILLING TO PAY TO PREVENT CATASTROPHIC CLIMATE CHANGE?

"Where is the money going to come from? Why would states take money from their national budgets to fund a sovereign nation? That's never going to be a vote winner."

Alofa nodded and continued without a moment's hesitation. "As a separate nation, the Ocean can charge for resources that have traditionally been taken for free. Imagine levies of 1% on fishing revenues. 1% on shipping. $1 per tonne for CO2 sequestration. $10 per tonne for effluent. $100 per tonne for plastics. These can all be managed carefully. The living and non-living resources provided by the Ocean have been valued at trillions of dollars".

WHY ARE 'FLAGS OF CONVENIENCE' ALLOWED?

"Erm... I hope you don't mind me interrupting". Neve heard a voice to her left and turned to find the First Lady of Israel looking intently at them. Neve and Alofa had been so absorbed in their conversation they hadn't noticed that the delegates surrounding them had stopped talking. The 'wives' were listening to Alofa.

"Yes, go ahead Mrs Cohen" Neve said, relieved to have a moment to gather her thoughts. She was jumping between fear and fury. What would her dad do? He didn't need this added stress. How could she explain this to the Board?

IS 12 MILLION TONNES OF PLASTIC ACCEPTABLE?

Mrs Cohen patted Neve's arm in reassurance as she spoke softly to everyone. "Yuval Noah Harari has been saying this for years. The price tag for preventing 'the apocalypse', as he calls it, is in the low single digits of annual global GDP. He says only 2% of GDP is enough – and even less than that if we're just talking about the Ocean."

Alofa beamed at Mrs Cohen. "Yes, exactly! Think of it this way – every country is a shareholder in the Ocean, and until today, they have recklessly extracted its assets. Responsible shareholders must invest for the future, in new technologies and infrastructure that will restore and protect the Ocean, and create new jobs and opportunities."

Neve's ears perked up at the mention of jobs, recalling the recent headlines against her husband's policies and the falling employment rates back home.

"Independence would mean that the Ocean could use Global Fishing Watch tracker and satellite technology and use this revenue to fund MPAs and other critical restoration activities. The Ocean could assume full authority of the open Ocean, 50% of EEZs and 25% of coastal waters."

"Sounds sensible to me" the husband of Finland's President chimed in.

Alofa smiled and continued: "We have agreement from three shipping companies and 12 countries to acknowledge the Ocean's statehood and to pay the proposed fees. This money is enough to create the independent state. Countries have relationships with one another, but a lot of the flows are commercial." Neve nodded, surprised that the group had achieved so much.

"If the Ocean is recognised as an independent legal and commercial entity that charges for its services, it will be away and free." Alofa stopped talking and stood still, unaware that Neve's thoughts had returned to images of her dad being rushed to hospital. What would be his legacy? How could she let them smear his reputation while he's lying in a hospital bed? Biting her lip, she looked down at the ground to hide her face.

WHY DO WE PLANT TREES BUT DESTROY THE REEF?

Seeing Neve's hesitation, Alofa made one final attempt. "Mrs Rowe." He turned to the nearby audience who had also stopped in their tracks. "What have you got to lose? Catch the wave, ride the board, run with the inevitable tide of public opinion. Or stand like King Canute, and be overwhelmed? Kendi Media will drown in the backlash and your father will be renowned for his cowardice. Support us and Kendi Media will be celebrated for generations to come."

"WE MUST PLANT THE SEA AND HERD ITS ANIMALS..."

Neve couldn't help but agree. She was tired of the lethargy in politics, no one was willing to take the drastic action that was needed. It was the same in almost every nation and leader – prioritising ego and convenience over ethics and climate. She understood Kendi Media had been doing the same. To continue to do nothing now risked ruining her dad's legacy. If she refused, maybe she would be pushed out by the other board members. What would happen to Kendi Media then? What would happen to her?

*"...USING THE SEA AS FARMERS INSTEAD OF
HUNTERS..."*

She looked Alofa straight in the eyes and said "I'll see what I can do".
Alofa's joyous nod resembled a royal curtsey. Neve shook his hand and
turned to the photographers with a smile. The Planet Ocean protestors, now only a few meters away, abruptly ended their shouting. They
were staring down at the two of them, some gawping in amazement,
others grinning in delight. A momentary silence descended.

"THAT IS WHAT CIVILIZATION IS ALL ABOUT..."

Like an army camouflaged in blue and green, the sea of voices
erupted in unison to defend their cause with one final, unequivocal
declaration: "In the words of Jacques-Yves Cousteau: 'We must plant
the sea and herd its animals using the sea as farmers instead of hunters.
That is what civilization is all about – farming replacing hunting'.
WE ARE THE OCEANS. THE OCEANS ARE US. WE
ARE THE OCEANS. THE OCEANS ARE US. WE ARE THE
OCEANS. THE OCEANS ARE US.[1]

---

1. Interested to know more about climate solutions included? See
   https://www.greenstories.org.uk/anthology-for-cop27/solu-
   tions/ocean-as-a-nation/

THE DESERT SPIRAL INITIATIVE

by Howard Gaukrodger

Z dan was working extra hard this season, keen to impress his wife, desperate to feed the family. Meagre crops of beans, magaria, dates, figs and olives enriched their *aysh*, but harvests were pitiful. And even when they treated themselves to a shank of goat meat, Zdan knew what Tasa was thinking.

Thank you, God, for this precious food. Thank you, husband, for tilling the soil that has made such sustenance possible... but this is no life for our son. Aksil is worthy of responsibility. No family will offer their daughter in marriage to a farmer of goat dung.

The only solution was for Zdan to leave, to travel away from their dusty, clay-brick home and find well-paid work in Cairo. For Aksil to advance his education in the city, he would need money for food and accommodation.

"Husband, we do not want you to leave, but by God's grace, Aksil can tend to our crops, and I can clean our house and herd our goats."

At the speed of the Saharan sirocco, a wind of writing emotions swept through Zdan. *Months, perhaps a year, without my wife and son? And sandstorms, crop disease, drought – if I stay away too long, our crops may die, the goats will starve – and my family will surely follow.* Yet he knew he had to go.

*

With the arrival of the new moon, Zdan found himself in Cairo, six hundred kilometres to the east. It proved a fateful first day.

"May your body be infested with the fleas of a thousand camels!" he cried.

But the thief, no taller than a donkey's hind leg, had already faded into the fog of the market throng. Zdan was unaccustomed to the chaotic life of the city. Counting his money in a public place had proved a woeful mistake. His family's savings were gone, and with it his means of survival.

With only a crust of bread and dried fruit in his bag, a moment of foolishness had condemned him to the life of a beggar. How could he ask for a job when he smelt like the arse of a pig? Squatting with his back to the sun-baked wall, he winced at the shame he had brought upon his family. He sought consolation in his inner thoughts, but the pain was too fresh to be tempered. His head fell to his knees and he wept. For a time, self-pity sheltered him from the roiling crowds, the blaring horns and the dusty streets. But then he heard the *muezzin*'s call to prayer – a chant that discovered within him one final drop of resilience. The afternoon *asr* was sacred. His spirit was not yet broken. Turning to face the *Qibla*, he recited his prayers. And there, in the rat-infested gutter of a cluttered city street, Zdan's life changed.

It was the scent. Bitter-sweet. Different. Expensive. It hung in the air, stuck to the dust, crept up his sandy, sweat-stained *haik* and made its home in his scruffy, black and white turban. So out of place was this scent that Zdan put aside his sorrows and peered up. Against the diffused sunlight of the yellow sky, the silhouette of a tall, well-dressed man arched over him. Without words, the silhouette proffered a bladder-flask of water. Zdan accepted the gift. Now, he was indebted to the silhouette.

"Brother," said the silhouette, "I need workers. There is strength in your shoulders. I see endurance in your face and honesty in your eyes. Come walk with me. I travel to Aswan tonight. Join me and I will assure you of a job that will support you and your family, God willing."

Zdan looked to the sky and cried, "Allah be praised!"

Like a stray dog promised a home, Zdan shuffled after his benefactor. He ignored the sweat running down his back, the dust in his eyes, his pangs of hunger and parched lips. Decades of wisdom fell to the wayside; he was under the spell of someone who could only have been sent by the mighty Allah himself.

Disoriented by the maze of convoluted streets and alleys, and numbed by emotions in turmoil, Zdan allowed himself to be guided to a rattletrap army truck. Sitting inside the gloomy, mosquito-ridden vehicle were eleven other men, silent, head bowed, their tattered clothes and the smell of their bodies testimony to their poverty. It was with this band of hungry souls that Zdan would travel through the night to take up a job he prayed would save his family.

Into potholes and sunken drain covers, the truck bounced and rattled. Sleep itself was but a dream, killed by the whine of the engine, its grating gears and the hooting hordes of traffic.

It was a relief to reach the destination – at first. Led through a patchwork of tents, past latrines, a tool shed and well, the twelve new arrivals were registered and had their papers taken "for safe keeping". In exchange, they were given a flask of water, bread and panning tools:

a gold pan, shovel, classifier and storage bottle. *Sifting Nile silt for gold – this is our work. Allah have mercy on us.*

The first days were the worst. Bend, shovel, sift, hour after hour after hour. The storage tanks of saturated silt would leak, sometimes break. Glue-like sludge covered their bodies, weighed down their clothes. And while water-borne critters were irritating, and mosquitoes stung, the one thing no one could avoid was the nauseating, pervasive stink of the mud, urine and sweat.

He struggled on with aching limbs and blistered hands, yet the sun was their greatest enemy. Only when he smeared his face with the pungent silt, did the fissures close and the peeling skin heal. He lost count of the weeks, lost count of the months, his only respite a wash in the cool waters of the life-giving Nile.

The silhouette with the patent leather shoes and bitter-sweet aftershave was long gone, his task of finding cheap labour complete. He had honoured his word and had given Zdan a job, but the work was a mere scorpion spit from the depths of slavery. For the second time, Zdan had suffered the pain of naivety.

With his one year of seniority, Zdan became spokesman for his group, though everyone answered to the camp's leader, the *zaeim*. And no one was immune to the *zaeim's* fits of rage and the whip of his bootlicking henchmen. But Zdan was earning money, and would soon have enough to travel home and contribute a small sum towards his son's education. When the day came, the *zaeim* called him to his tent.

"Brother," said the *zaeim*, "here is your money."

Zdan counted the torn and muddied notes. "Brother, this is only half of what I am due."

"Be grateful for what you receive. The rest you will have on your return."

That evening, before the reddening sun melted over the horizon, Zdan wandered up the west-facing hill overlooking the camp. From the wind-carved ledge of a diamond-shaped rock, he sat and reflected on the scene below. Discarded piles of silt lay drying in circles, protecting the workers from the sand-laden southerlies. Zdan smiled at the hardiness of the plants that sprang up in the semi-dry, brown piles that were firm enough to support life, wet enough to nourish it. And as his eyes followed the outline of the circles, his fingers twirled unconsciously in the coarse sand at his side.

With night but a whisker away, Zdan bent forward to rise from his perch. He leant on his hand to push himself up, and as he did so, he noticed the pattern his fingers had made – not quite a circle, more a spiral. In the last light of the day, the long shadows threw darkness into the furrows. *Looks like water.* He scoffed and casually placed three rock fragments in the middle of the spiral.

Clambering down, he prayed his sandals would hold. Tired from his labours and the arduous walk, Zdan paused and took a breath. As he looked up, he was struck by a family of spherical, red clouds drifting north. *Balloons! How peaceful. One day, I will buy Aksil a ride in the greatest balloon of all!*

Despite his half-share wage, Zdan slept well that night, thoughts of his family uppermost in his mind. Within 24 hours he would be able to embrace them.

*

"Dear husband, I know you will be sad, but your son has left home."

After her greeting, these were Tasa's first words on his return to Siwa.

"We have little food, and our land is poor. He has turned sixteen and vowed to earn money for our family. Only last week he left for Cairo to seek work in the world of tourist hotels."

Zdan was distraught. A year of hard labour, and now his son was gone. While tears fought with his pride, he knew it must have been worse for his wife. He'd taken their savings and they'd thought him dead. Now, on her own, his wife needed him more than ever; his sunburnt, skeletal limbs would have no rest this month.

As the moon waxed and waned, Zdan worked the land till his scarred hands bled, but he never seemed to finish tilling and planting. He needed to return to Aswan to collect his outstanding wages from the *zaeim*, and he could ask after his son on the way.

"Tasa," he said, one morning. "It is a sin to gloat over the money I have earned. More is owed to me, and we can give that to our son when he returns. But an idea has come to me that will require the investment of the money we have. We must invite everyone in the local community. Together I am sure we can realise a farming miracle!"

His wife looked at him, eyes wide. They had never been close to their neighbours, and this far from the Siwa mosque, the local community was as real as the mirage of wealth.

"And what is this miracle?" Tasa asked.

"It is a crop spiral – not a circle, but a spiral! Can you see, dear wife, that if we till a furrow in the form of ever-tightening rings, then cultivate our fruit trees in the outermost rings first, those tall plants in the outer rings will grow to protect the younger and more vulnerable crops in the inner rings."

"You talk in the riddles of a charlatan," Tasa smiled, "but your conviction urges my attention."

"Forgive me. Let us go inside. We will wash, pray, and I will share with you the details of my idea and what I learned in Aswan."

Tasa served the sweetened mint tea. She waited, aware that her husband would speak when ready. He was a man who said little, but chose his words wisely. The longer he deliberated, the weightier his message.

"Wife," he said at last, "from the top of a hill overlooking the camp, I could see how the mounting piles of silt protected the workers – how the south wind was deflected over our heads.

"And the water that leached from the silt – it drained to our feet and trickled from worker to worker. We must do the same with our land. The secret is the spiral! Let's plant our crops and pump the water down a furrow of spiral rings."

Tasa nodded slowly.

"But, husband, who will do the work? Without our son, and if you have to return to the camp..."

"That is why we must speak to our neighbours. Someone will have a tractor and plough. And we can part with a little of our money today if it means we will have crops tomorrow."

Tasa embraced her husband, his wisdom a shining light in a barren landscape.

*

"Keep going!" Zdan cried to the tractor driver he located just two days later. "One more ring, further out!"

Before the sun had set, the final ring of the massive furrowed spiral was complete. The land that would have taken Zdan's family two months to till by hand was tilled in one day with a French plough bearing the name 'Vallerani Delfino'. And for the loan of the tractor and plough, the owner asked only for two goats.

"Ahmed," Zdan said to the tractor-owner, "I do not know where you obtained this magical plough, but God thanks you; I thank you. As agreed, I will give you the money for six goats if you will also plough the land of our neighbours, for without them we could never have completed this work."

*

Within the following week, Zdan and Tasa exhausted their stock of goat dung, lining only the first ring of the spiral furthest from the well.

"Our fertiliser is gone, Zdan. We will need a hundred more goats to fertilise this spiral."

"Or the silt of the River Nile."

The local community worked tirelessly as a team to sow and irrigate their crops in mysterious spirals. Children looked on, marvelling at the train of bucket-loaded donkeys, carts and the tractor shunting to and fro, taking water from the community well or from private storage tanks.

Finally, after days of hard but rewarding work, Zdan was able to return to Aswan. He would claim his outstanding pay and give notice to leave soon after. He was no longer a beggar, and with God's help he would find a better job when needed.

Waiting for the availability of a seat on the bus, Zdan became impatient as a child.

"No one should need to wait five days," he growled

"Go into Siwa; perhaps there has been a cancellation. And collect the post on your way back."

Before the sun reached its apex, the humble desert farmer was home again. Sweating with his exertions, the glistening rows of brown teeth conveyed to Tasa what she needed to know even before the words tumbled from his mouth.

"So, you have your ticket. I am happy for you, husband. I will fetch you a glass of water."

"Yes!" he cried. "And we have news from Aksil!"

From his faded leather pouch, he withdrew a robust, high-quality envelope boasting the crest of a hotel in the top-left corner, 'Hotel Great Sands'.

"What is this?"

Tasa examined the handwritten address – a spidery, uneven scrawl – writing she recognised as that of their child. She unfolded the notepaper, fingers trembling. A slip of paper fell to the floor. As Zdan bent to retrieve it, Tasa read: 'Beloved Mother and Father, our mighty God has looked favourably upon me and found me employment in Luxor where a climate conference is being held. There are people from all over the world and the hotel needed more kitchen workers...'

With tears of joy and relief rolling down her cheeks, Tasa finished reading and took the slip of paper from her husband. It was a money order for two thousand Egyptian pounds.

*

Squeezed into his seat at the back of the intercity bus, Zdan was finally on his way. In 24 hours, he would break his journey in Luxor to meet his son. They might even travel on to Aswan together.

Once in Luxor, Zdan found his way to the hotel. All around were men with black suits, black attaché cases, black beards, sunglasses and razor-sharp eyes. Occasional European women, legs and arms exposed in nonchalant disrespect, paraded through the lobby in high heels. Overawed and nervous, Zdan's traditional *haik* and finest headscarf did little to boost his confidence.

"Good day, sir," said the receptionist, looking down his nose at the vision of poverty.

Zdan extracted Aksil's letter and pointed to the hotel's address.

"My son works here. I have travelled from Siwa and I wish to see him."

Without a word, the receptionist lowered his head and typed something on a keyboard.

"Your son will be with you shortly. Please wait in the lounge."

*

"And that's how I got this job, father. Now, tell me about mother. How is she? And how are you? You look thinner and sunburnt."

Zdan tripped over his words in his efforts to fit the events of four months into one breath.

"Slow down, father, and lower your voice. Everyone can hear you." And indeed, they could.

"Tell me again about this farming idea."

More calmly and in greater detail, Zdan described his idea of the crop spiral.

"That's clever, father. And the density of the crops... it will be easier and quicker to harvest them..."

"And the spiral will use less water."

"And less fertilizer?"

"Perhaps not, son. But when I worked in the camp by the great river in Aswan, I saw how rich the silt was – and how quickly plants grew in it. My idea is to replace goat dung with the silt that is dredged from the Nile!"

"You are a genius, father. But how will you transport wet silt?"

"Dried silt, Aksil! Using air balloons! I saw balloons over the camp. They could carry great quantities of sun-dried silt over long distances – we could have many crop spirals. We could even..."

"Excuse me for interrupting," said a well-dressed lady in near-faultless Arabic. "My name is Beatrice Benoit. I work for the Trans-Sahara Climate Mitigation Organisation. As you see from the signs, there is a conference here: 'Living with Climate Change'. I do not wish to intrude, but I overheard a little of your enthusiastic conversation and, if you don't mind, would like to hear about your farming idea."

Surprised but proud, Zdan described his idea a third time.

"A crop spiral, community ploughing, Nile silt fertilizer... and just a single channel of water. Fascinating! I am very interested," said Beatrice. "Perhaps, when it is convenient, we could travel to Siwa, and you could show me how your trees and plants are growing."

"It would be an honour," said Zdan.

An arrangement was made and Beatrice departed. Zdan turned to his son.

"... So, you cannot return to Siwa with me?"

"No, father. I have a good job here, and if I am to complete my education, I must study every evening. Gaining a place at university is not only a question of money, father."

"But your mother?"

Aksil's head dropped. Zdan could see his son was conflicted.

*

Four weeks passed. Zdan collected his outstanding wages, left the camp and returned to Luxor. *Perhaps now, Aksil has changed his mind and will come home?* But Aksil had other plans. He gave his father a gift for his mother.

"Good bye, father. I will write regularly."

"*Inshallah.*"

Zdan was sad, yet proud of his son. *He has made decisions that I was too weak to make. Let me now work with this Madame Benoit, and then, God willing, Aksil and my wife will also be proud of me.*

*

The bus ride was perhaps a little uncomfortable for the lady from France, but she was humble enough not to complain. Arriving tired but relieved in Siwa, Zdan's reunion with Tasa was modest and sincere.

"So, our son is well. Allah be praised," she said. "You have done well, husband."

A moment of awkwardness arose when Zdan introduced Beatrice, but seeing the lady with skin as smooth as that of a cherub beside her husband, whose skin was as wizened as the trunk of an olive tree, Tasa knew she need not worry.

"*Magnifique!*" exclaimed Beatrice, as she inspected the family's crops. "And you planted these crops and trees just five weeks ago? *Magnifique!*"

The next time that Zdan heard from the lady was when a courier arrived with a letter.

'*Dear Zdan, I have explained your farming technique to my colleagues, and have shown them pictures of the results. They are very interested in meeting you in Cairo. Your combination of using the Vallerani Delfino plough to create a crop spiral, and, most intriguingly, your proposal to use river silt as a fertilizer has made a considerable impact. We believe we could develop this with solar-powered water pumps and use it to plant millions of trees. We will, of course, refund all costs of your journey, and board and lodgings...*'

Zdan was on his way as soon as he was able to obtain a seat.

*

"Good morning, Zdan! Welcome. A glass of water, perhaps? Let me introduce you to my colleagues and business partners."

Zdan was dumbstruck. Before him was not only the lady he'd gone to meet, but a roomful of businesspeople and politicians, their suits and gowns as fine as any he'd ever seen. And there he sat, his poverty again exposed, like a sinner before a congregation of *imams*.

"We've been discussing your method of planting."

Beatrice talked for several minutes. By the time she'd finished, Zdan thought they were going to re-green the whole of the Sahara.

"I am honoured you find my idea so interesting. But I am unclear..." he started.

Several men in the room grinned, and debate continued, ignoring entirely the farmer from Siwa. It was only when Zdan risked raising his voice to contribute a bold, new idea that he attracted full attention.

"Air balloons?" one of the financiers responded. "You want to float air balloons across the desert and drop silt from the basket?"

And then everyone wanted to talk at the same time.

The spokesperson for the Ministry of Agriculture and Land Reclamation banged the table. "The idea may not be as far-fetched as you think. According to my advisor, here, there are powered airships that can carry up to 160 tonnes of cargo. If this cargo happens to be silt that has been dehydrated by, say, 80% to 32 tonnes, then such a vessel could carry the equivalent of 800 tonnes. And we can fertilise many spirals with that."

"Navigation? Altitude? Accuracy of the drop?" asked the representative of the Ministry of Water Resources and Irrigation.

"Yes, there are things to work out, but with GPS navigation and a flexible pipeline, it is not impossible," said the former spokesperson. "But how can we irrigate these spirals, and where should they be located?"

Beatrice leaned over. "*Ecoutez*. Listen Zdan, you may wish to leave now. We have much to discuss. If you go to reception, you will find an envelope waiting for you. I will contact you this evening."

Zdan stood, nodded to the group, then went to collect the envelope. Inside was a mobile phone, a receipt for the advance payment of three nights' accommodation at Beatrice's hotel, and a note: *'I believe your ideas will prove to be worth far more than the cost of a phone and accommodation, but please accept this as a token of our appreciation. Regards, Beatrice.'*

At 8.30, next morning, Zdan was back in the hotel lobby. Beatrice arrived and smiled with an air of complicity.

"We have a breakthrough, Zdan! Let me update you before we go to the conference room. The Ministry of Water Resources and Irrigation, the European Investment Bank, and all the other parties recognise the merit of the idea, and all agree that we should develop a proof-of-concept model."

Zdan placed his hand across his heart. "Allah be praised."

Taking a map of Egypt from her case, Beatrice continued. "Rather than reinvent the wheel, our proposal involves combining existing projects and technology with your ideas. We've called it The Desert Spiral Initiative.

"Inspired by the Great Green Wall that crosses the Sahara further south, we will plant a chain of 550-metre spirals from the Toshka lakes to the Farafra Oasis. And while the Great Green Wall is 8,000 kilometres long, ours will be a less ambitious, but perhaps more realistic 1,000 kilometres.

"The Vallerani Delfino will plough the spiral. Dehydrated Nile River silt will be mixed with water and other nutrients in a tank in the centre of the spiral, then distributed through dripperlines directly to the roots of the crops. We propose a network of small wells, extracting water from the New Valley Canal and the Nubian Sandstone Aquifer – one well per ten kilometres – pumped using solar energy.

"As for the planting, drones will be able to fire pods of fertilised saplings or seedlings into the tilled soil. It will take only 3-6 days to plant one entire spiral! Imagine how quickly we can transform this region of the desert – 1,737 spirals to plant 50 million trees! A million tonnes of CO_2 gone! Egypt will be the envy of the world!"

"Inshallah!" said Zdan. "It pleases me that your idea will help our country, but..."

"It is not my idea, Zdan; it is yours. The density of trees will guarantee a higher rate of survival success per hectare, the spiral structure will protect plants and animals and reduce damage to crops, and so much CO2..."

"Indeed, Madame. But now you have your plan, I see I am no longer needed. I cannot assist with such a project and wish only to return to my family and farm my land."

"Yes, yes, of course... Very well, Zdan. But allow me to give you this document. It is a summary of the project for discussion at the meeting this morning."

Zdan glanced at the paper. "But where are the people? This project must be for the whole of Egypt: farmers, nomads, people of every race and religion."

"But Zdan, this document is for the decision-makers, our leaders and investors..."

Zdan roared, "The crop spirals must be for the people! It is they who will make it a success! When I traced the spiral in the sands of Aswan, I placed three stones in the centre. On my return, weeks later, the stones were still there. I believe this was a message from God: we must build houses, or a whole village, in the middle of each spiral! And a mosque, classroom, or medical centre every one hundred spirals. The people will tend to the trees, and in exchange, they will have a home, free power from the sun, and a section of the spiral for their crops!"

The Desert Spiral Initiative   *Howard Gaukrodger*

The Desert Spiral Initiative			
Spiral			
No. of furrows (rings) in spiral	50	rings	
Width of furrow	1	m	
Depth of furrow	0.40	m	
Space between furrows (centre to centre)	5	m	
Outside diameter of spiral	550	m	
Inside diameter of spiral	50	m	
Length of one entire spiral	86,350	m	
Area of spiral (to be fertilised and irrigated)	86,350	m2	
Tractor-pulled Delfino plough: time to till one spiral	17	hours	At 5 kph
Location / Route			
Lake Nasser to Farafra (New Valley Project)	1,000	km	
Spirals spread along the 1000km, creating self-sustaining wall			
Silt Fertiliser			
Depth of fertiliser (dry, assuming 80% dehydration.)	0.05	m	dehydrated
Total dry silt fertiliser needed for 1 spiral	1,800	kg	(0.6kg/m2)
No. of airship flights to fertilise 1 spiral	1	flight	
Max. duration of airship flight sustainability	120	hr	
Max. duration of drone flight sustainability	0.75	hr	
Max. cargo of drone	226	kg	
No. of drone flights to fertilise 1 spiral, if this option chosen	8	flights	
Irrigation			
New Valley Canal and NSAS aquifer beyond canal			
Solar energy for power and self-sustaining water system			
Crop spiral with drip feed. Estimated use, 1 drop / 5 seconds	0.89	litres	/ tree/day
For 1 spiral of 28,783 trees	25,617	litres	/ spiral/day
Trees			
Saplings dropped by drone (1kg es) per flight	226	trees	
Weight of sapling pod	1	kg	
No. of drone flights to plant 1 spiral	127	flights	
CO2 sequestration per one 10-year-old tree	20	kg	
CO2 sequestration per spiral per year after 10 years	576	tonnes	
Sequestration target	1,000,000	tonnes	
Trees per spiral (assuming 1 tree / 3m)	**28,783**	**trees**	
Spirals required	**1,737**	**spirals**	
Trees needed to offset target	**50 m**	**trees**	
Time to plough, fertilise and plant 1 spiral	**3 - 6**	**days**	

"Yes, Zdan, yes. I... You're right. Of course. Many a president has expressed the need to attract people away from the Nile to inhabit the desert. I will put your ideas forward at the meeting."

The farmer nodded and turned towards the door.

"Farewell, Zdan. Thank you. I am sure we will meet again."

*

It doesn't happen overnight, but at the press conference eighteen months later, a letter of intent is presented detailing the project. It includes the final ideas so vehemently put forward by Zdan.

With talk of the project spreading throughout the country, Zdan is inspired to follow the news, and he writes regularly to his son. Yet it is only when Aksil has earned sufficient money for his parents to be proud of him that he returns to live in Siwa.

Zdan's prayers are answered. Two years to the day since Aksil left home, the reunited family celebrate a harvest the likes of which they have never seen before. Their crop spiral is a success. Not only does their farming method ensure strong and healthy crops for the family, but, as they are soon to find out, it is adopted by the authorities as the cornerstone of the plan to re-green the Western Desert.

As the date palms and olive trees continue to grow, one final letter arrives from Beatrice. She has put forward the names of Zdan, Tasa, and Aksil as liaison officers to help people take up residence and work within the proposed spiral settlements. Employment and recognition have found them. No longer will they be seen as poor goat farmers from Siwa; the family will hold their heads high when they visit the desert spirals of the Sahara.[1]

---

1. Interested to know more about climate solutions included?
   See https://www.greenstories.org.uk/anthology-for-cop27/sto
   ries/desert-spiral-initiative/

THE ENVELOPE

by Sara Foster

Sepphira swims five metres below the ocean surface, waiting for her moment. She's not usually superstitious, but this morning she'd strapped her grandmother's fifty-year-old titanium diving knife to her ankle, so that something of Allegra was with them today. There are fading photos on the walls of the science facilities of Allegra using the knife to cut ropes and fishing gear from entangled whales, dolphins and turtles: unthinkable today. Ocean protection had been a worldwide priority for the last fifteen years, and in 2040 the need to cut fishing gear from cetaceans is thankfully a thing of the past.

Apart from the knife, the rest of Sepphira's gear is new and hi-tech. She's wearing one of the latest full-face masks so she can talk into the small microphone when she needs to, and in her earpiece she can hear Leonard speaking to the delegation. She's aware of each gentle flick of her fins, and the need to conserve her air supply. Today there are important people watching, who will decide the future of the facility.

Three generations of Sepphira's family have poured blood, sweat and tears into the seagrass and marine restoration project; it's unthinkable that this could all collapse now. She's desperate for the officials to leave impressed, but nevertheless she'd been thankful when her father had asked her to be the diver today. She knows her nerves won't be as visible through the tempered glass.

About ten metres away, there is an underwater observation room, built to encourage the tourists to ride their bikes across from the apartments and campsites to spend some precious dollars on a short boat trip and a unique glimpse beneath the ocean. Inside, you feel like you're standing in a bubble; glass panels on three sides providing a panoramic vista, the lighting dimmed so that divers can only see silhouettes of those inside. Voltage is kept as low as possible, because no one on site wants to squander the solar power. Efficient green batteries have come a long way in the last decade but so has the challenge of managing consumption in an award-winning science facility and tourist destination. Besides, when you stand in the dark at this time of the early morning, when the sun is strong and the sky clear, you get the underwater landscape in all its glory: the light playing like tiny sea nymphs along each blade of seagrass, the gentle undulations of each long stem as the current whispers a softer choreography beneath the surface of the restless ocean.

The seagrass extends farther than the eye can see – kilometres further – and Sepphira's family and the team of scientists and volunteers are responsible for all of it. Marine life and seagrass restoration on this small tourist island has been her family's home and passion for nearly fifty years. So much has changed, and yet here they are again, desperate for money to sustain and expand the business, and needing to prove themselves.

She knows what her older cousin Leonard will be saying, as he stands somewhere behind those long, polished windowpanes. He will be explaining the vegetational arc of this area: how it has gone from a vibrant meadow to a desecrated and unkempt mess, then back again. She knows his palms will be sweating as he tries to encapsulate, in his thirty-minute timeslot, the immensity of all they have achieved. The careful caretaking of the underwater environment, with meticulous replanting by hand to repair the patches of seagrass ruined by moorings; before the devastations of that first ever Category Six cyclone in 2029 set them back years and a whole lot of funding. The methodical rebuilding, step by step, nothing able to be rushed. And the award-winning inclusion of eco-friendly tourist facilities so that everyone who comes here leaves aware of their project and its fundamental importance to the ecosystem. The story will be laid out like a feast for this delegation with its deep pockets – until, at the end of this day, the Hansen family will find out if their efforts have been good enough. Will their story nourish these people enough for them to want to contribute? Will the project stay afloat for another five years; or will it sink into obscurity, doomed by capricious minds who envision some better use of their funds?

It was meant to be her father here today; but he's been in the hospital for the last three weeks with Sepphira's mother, who is going through cancer therapy. He's been on the phone almost hourly, directing operations in clipped tones, his voice cracking now and again with the pressure of it all.

Sepphira wants nothing more than to help: to give her parents some good news to bind them together amidst the confronting emptiness of those drab hospital rooms. It breaks her heart that two people who live and breathe with the ocean's tides are now stuck in a concrete tower day after day, with no end in sight. Without them, even banal decisions feel portentous; as though one wrong move might spell disaster. If the facility goes under, they don't just lose three generations of work: they lose their home, their steady income, just when her parents need it the most.

Sepphira can't believe that it's up to her and Leonard when there's so much riding on the outcome. As she thinks of it, she notices that most of the silhouetted group have their backs to the windows, gathered around in a huddle, presumably focused on Leonard. She wants to fin over and bang on the glass, to implore him not to be so stupid. What is the point of all this if they don't look? If they can't spend a few moments without the buzz of Leonard's anxious voice to just stare into this vast and spectacular underwater wilderness? There is already so much she cannot point out to them – the tiny fish nurseries, the gobbleguts and leatherjackets hiding in the grasses, the decorator crabs busy camouflaging themselves in the seaweed beds. She wants them to know that beyond this valuable carbon soak, they have also nurtured a whole ecosystem of constant and unexpected delights: there are forty times more marine creatures in these meadows than in the bare sand. Since the facility first began, they have done so much more than even they had anticipated would be possible.

Within the shadowy viewing area, there is one outlined human form standing apart from the others – an older man she would guess by the contours of his body and the angle of his sentinel pose. Suddenly, she feels the electrical charge that comes when you know someone is laser focused on you. But then she hears Leonard's voice in her earpiece, and it's time for Sepphira to begin the tour.

She speaks quickly as she goes through the site's history, recounting the different fish species they find regularly, pointing out a cobbler as it swims nearby. She announces that they've seen half a dozen turtles resting here in the past couple of weeks – unheard of a decade ago. But she knows it's hard to captivate these people with stories of creatures they cannot see, especially when they can't absorb the peace of the ocean for themselves. Nevertheless, the ocean never performs on demand, and it's a quiet morning. They could do with a dolphin swim-by, which is not uncommon, but there's no sign of them today. So she gets closer to the window and points out the nudibranchs and pistol shrimps visible on two of the support pylons near the glass.

Behind the windows, the silhouettes don't move. When Leonard asks if they have any questions, there's only silence in her earpiece. Her heart sinks. She's not sure they've done enough.

After getting dried and changed she's the last to make it to lunch in the small meeting room back on the island, and most places are already taken. The food is a mixture of salads grown in the sustainable gardens that are part of this contained on-site laboratory complex, and as it's brought out on platters Leonard proudly explains their self-sufficiency: the greywater that fertilises the garden beds, the solar panels that power everything in the lab, including the industrial-sized kettle in the corner. Sepphira goes to the back of the line and serves herself with the salads she'd helped prepare early this morning, wondering if Leonard is laying it on too thick, searching the men's and women's faces for signs of boredom. It's hard to tell if their interest is a polite mask or if he's genuinely got them hooked.

The family had agreed that Sepphira would take a back seat in the conversation today, despite the fact she's one of the most knowledgeable among them. The world might be more progressive than it used to be, but they've still not reached the stage where an eighteen-year-old girl would be deemed most appropriate to pitch for five years of essential funding. Nevertheless, she'll try to interject if she sees an opportunity. She studies the groups as she sits and eats. Most of the delegation are in their thirties and forties, but one much older man sits in the corner, occasionally glancing at her with a curious intensity that makes her wonder if he was the same person who had watched her earlier.

They are separated by seating positions, but when the dessert platter comes in and the group spring up to help themselves, there is a place left vacant beside her, and the man immediately comes across.

'It's incredible how much you look like her,' he says as he sits down.

She knows who he means immediately: people have said this her whole life. 'You knew my grandmother?' Sepphira hadn't known her, but she loves the stories of Allegra Hansen – and there are many, both from her family and the scientific community. Marine scientists often come to the labs early in their careers, as a kind of pilgrimage. Allegra's name has saved the business thousands, thanks to willing volunteers.

He smiles. 'I don't know if I can say that. I only met her twice. But I've never forgotten her. I was so sorry to hear she passed away so young. Cancer is cruel – it took my wife too.'

Sereena swallows hard. 'Thanks. It was a long time ago now. My dad was younger than me when she died.'

He nods. 'That's a great shame.' He pauses and then says, 'Forgive me, I've forgotten to introduce myself. David Levett.'

'And you're with the delegation?' It seems rude to ask why he appears to be half a century older than the others.

'Yes,' he smiles. 'But not in any official capacity. I made a fuss and they let me tag along as a former chairman of the board.' His eyes gaze up at the old photographs on the walls as he adds, 'I had to see this place again.'

'You've been here before?'

'Just once. Forty-five years ago.'

'Really? But then ...' she thinks back over the history of the place... 'you came when there was nothing here?'

'That's right. I was in the very first delegation. Your grandmother had applied to set up the research facility in the environmental competition we ran every year – our own little compensation scheme to offset the growing worry of all the drilling and mining and fracking. She didn't ask for much money in comparison with others and she had a grand vision of what she might achieve with regard to seagrass restoration. We were curious because of the low start-up costs, so we flew out here, but I wasn't particularly interested. I'd read enough of the research papers to know that while there was strong evidence that seagrass stores carbon, it lacked the glamour to be a really impactful marketing story for us. She only had a shack for an office then, so she took us for lunch in the hotel at the tourist centre, and I gave her a really rough time interrogating her about the project and all the ways it was doomed to fail, partly because it was a 45-degree day and I'd been stupid enough to wear a formal shirt that was, by that point, plastered to my skin.' He winces at the memory. 'She was furious; she could see that most of us were only here on a jolly to an exotic Australian island. At one point she said to me, 'It looks like you struggle enough with the heat now – how are you going to cope if the planet gets any hotter?' He chuckles.

Sepphira is entranced. She'd known her grandmother was a fireball, but she's never heard this story before. Her father mustn't know it either, as he was all too happy to regale people with other tales of his brilliant mother.

'The whole lot of us couldn't wait to get out of there,' David continues, 'and back to the air-conditioned bar in our five-star hotel. We debated the project that night over drinks. Some people didn't see the harm in throwing the money at it when we had such rich reserves, but maybe I was rankled by the way she'd insulted me. Nothing would be formally decided until we got back to the UK, but that night I announced that I intended to vote no.'

'So how come we've been funded by your company for the past forty-five years?'

He laughs openly now. 'Because I woke up and was packing my case when there was a message from reception – Allegra was waiting for me downstairs, and insisted on taking me to a café close by.' He gazes off into the distance. 'I was intrigued enough to go along, as our flight didn't leave until later that afternoon. She bought me breakfast while finding out all about my life and family, and then, to my surprise, she handed me a sealed letter, and asked me if I'd seen a movie called *Apollo 13*. When I hadn't, she insisted I watched it before I opened the envelope. Have you heard of the film?'

Sepphira shakes her head.

'It's very old now, but it was a big deal at the time – won some awards, if I remember rightly. At that time one of the pleasures of going on planes was getting to see the movies that had just come on in the cinemas, and which you couldn't see anywhere else.' She frowns in confusion and he laughs. 'I know, times have changed. Anyway, on the flight home I watched the movie, then I opened the envelope, and I'll never forget what she'd written.' He pauses, looks at Sepphira intently.

'So – what did she write?'

He leans forward. 'You've got to understand, even then I was absolutely planning to vote no. I'd enjoyed the film but I hadn't made the connections. I was ambitious with a young family of my own, and I wanted something big and showy that I could announce, and which would help me climb the company ladder, not some small little mission in the back of beyond. But in the envelope was a small card. And on the front of it was a photocopied sketch of the facilities she wanted to build. And inside she'd written, '*Between catastrophe and triumph lie the smallest things.*'

Sepphira is silent, thinking this through.

'I know,' David says. 'She could have chosen to say a lot more, but she didn't. I spent the rest of the flight just staring at the seat back in front of me, taking in her words. You see, that movie is based on a true story. Over seventy years ago, an explosion on a spacecraft that was meant to land on the moon left the rocket's structure heavily damaged and the astronauts in great peril. The world was captivated by the precarious mission that followed in order to bring those men back to earth. But the problem that led to the disaster started years before, when a piece of damaged wire insulation was installed in the ship's oxygen tanks. And there's a miraculous fix when the engineers have to figure out all kinds of seemingly impossible problems to power the ship enough to get it back safely. But their incredible achievement in those few hours was the culmination of years of training and problem-solving.' He sits back. 'Allegra wasn't offering me a grandiose vision I could brag about. She was simply asking me to plant a seed, and let her nurture it, so that one day she might make miracles happen.'

'So you voted yes?'

He nods, with a wry smile. 'The rest of the team thought I was mad. So I brought Allegra over to London and we worked together on her pitch to the board, and she nailed it. She brought your dad, who was only a toddler at the time, and she even made sure I offset the carbon from all the flights. And she reminded me that all grand plans are made up of many, many smaller plans. And that has served me very well over the years. My successful championing of this unlikely investment – my forward thinking,' he adds with a smile, '– got me voted in as chairman of the board fifteen years later. All thanks to Allegra.'

Sereena grins. 'I've heard so many stories about my grandmother over the years, it's lovely to hear a new one. I only wish my dad were here.' Her expression drops. 'He would have loved to hear it too.'

David sighs. 'I heard your mum isn't well. Is she improving at all, with the treatment? It's much better than it used to be.'

Sereena bites her lip. 'We're not sure yet.' She hesitates, then says quickly, 'But not knowing about the funding is making it all so much harder. It would be great to give them some good news after today.' She casts a nervous glance at David, hoping she hasn't overstepped the mark, but he doesn't look offended, only concerned.

'I hope so too,' he says, after taking a sip of water. 'However, this crew is new. And when things get better, it's easy to forget what it took to get this far. That's why I'm tagging along, trying my best to help them make good decisions. And as an old man taking stock: paying my respects to your grandma by bearing witness to what she helped us both achieve.'

As he talks, the lunch plates are being cleared. The men and women are gathering belongings, as Leonard hurriedly hands them brochures they'd had printed about the facility using recycled paper and ink, something tangible for the delegates to take away. A woman in a dark suit puts her hand out to Leonard. 'Thanks for your time and efforts today,' she says briskly. 'We'll be in touch.'

'Looks like it's time for us to go,' David says, his movements stiff as he rises to his feet.

Sepphira doesn't hesitate. 'One moment,' she says loudly, causing the group to stop and turn towards her as one. She takes a deep breath before she speaks again. 'Please, before you go, take a minute to look at the photographs in this room.'

Automatically, the group's gaze shifts along the walls behind and to either side of Sepphira. She catches Leonard's eye, half-expecting to find a rebuke, but he only nods in encouragement and smiles.

'Over there is my grandmother, Allegra Hansen,' she says, pointing to a photo of a woman standing on a small wooden jetty, wearing a dark wetsuit, smiling. 'In this place, she's legendary. She didn't just have the vision, she built the foundations with her own hands. And my dad – he pioneered the panoramic design of our underwater room, the one you stood in earlier. He sourced all the renewable materials himself, and he was down there every day supervising the work. He knew more than the entire team of structural engineers by the end of it. And now, under his guidance, the site has been copied in half a dozen other locations across the world.' She studies them all as she speaks, imploring them to understand. 'We've come so far, but it's vital we have your support so we can maintain everything we've created, and we want to do so much more. But also,' she glances at David, and then at the other members of the delegation in turn, 'I think you need us too. People like us. The expertise that comes with years of experience and passion. The opportunity to contribute to something that will improve not just the health of the ocean, but helps all of us.'

She points to another photo, a selfie of her entire family crammed into the underwater room on the day it was first opened to the public, her dad's arm stretching out of shot as he holds the camera high; her mum beaming at his side, one arm around Sepphira. 'With us, you're not just backing a project – you're funding a legacy. Perhaps one day you can bring your kids and grandkids back to see it all, and remind them what's possible with some nurturing and persistence and time.'

She stops, and the woman in the suit comes forward. 'Very well said,' she intones, patting Sepphira on the shoulder. 'We'll be sure to let you know our decision as soon as we can.'

Sepphira nods, unsure if her words have hit their target. It's the hardest thing not to fall to her knees and beg. Her speech feels small now. Insufficient. She's already going over it, wondering what more she could have added; what magic phrase she missed that would have made them commit on the spot.

The group files out. David is the last to leave, and his parting smile is unmistakably genuine. 'Good luck, Sepphira.' He presses a crumpled envelope into her hand, and walks away.

Sepphira quickly opens it, and sees the small sketch of the facility, and her grandmother's neatly printed words inside. *Between catastrophe and triumph lie the smallest things.*

The gift steals her breath, as she stands in the empty room and surveys the mess of dirty crockery that will be her next job. Whatever happens today, she realises, they don't have to stop fighting. Things will happen easily and quickly, or slowly and painfully. But she has the fire of her grandmother inside her: which means that things *will* get done. [1]

---

1. Interested to know more about climate solutions included? See https://www.greenstories.org.uk/anthology-for-cop27/solutions/seagrass/

THE CARBONI

by Kim Stanley Robinson

*T*his is chapter 42 from the Ministry for the Future: a novel that imagines a Ministry for the Future set up by the United Nations to address the climate crisis. This chapter is written in note form to reflect the finance expert speaking, and addresses a key solution – harnessing the power of finance for the climate crisis. Reprinted with permission from Hachette Book Group.

Asked Mary for a meeting with her and Dick Bosworth, to go over some of the economic plans the software team was developing. She cleared an hour at the end of a Friday and meeting convened in her seminar room.

What's up, Janus Athena? she said, a bit brusquely. She's always visibly skeptical that AI could contribute anything substantive to her project.

Went to the whiteboard and tried to show her how AI could help. Always awkward to explain things to computer illiterates, a translation problem, a matter of deploying metaphors and finding gross generalizations that aren't too gross.

Started this time with rehearsal of Hayek's argument that markets deliver spontaneous value, and are therefore the best calculator and distributor of value, because central planning can't collect and corre-late all the relevant information fast enough. So planning always got things wrong, and the market was just better as a calculator. The Aus-trian and Chicago schools had run with that opinion, and thus neolib-eralism: the market rules because it's the best calculator. But now, with computers as strong as they've gotten, the Red Plenty argument has gotten stronger and stronger, asserting that people now have so much computing power that central planning could work better than the market. High-frequency trading has been put forth as an example of computers out-achieving the market proper, but instead of improving the system it's just been used to take rents on every exchange. This a sign of effective computational power, but used by people still stuck in the 1930s terminology of market versus planning, capitalism versus communism. And by people not trying to improve system, but merely to make more money in current system. Thus economists in our time.

In fact, entirely new organizational possibilities now emerging with power of AI. Big data analyzed for best results, all money tracked in its movement all the time, allocations made before price competi-tion distorts real costs into lies and universal multi-generational Ponzi scheme, and so on. Particulars here got both pretty technical and pretty theoretical at the same time, but important to do one's best to sketch out some things Mary might both understand and consider worth ordering team to do. Dick already up to speed on most of this.

Mary sighed, trying to focus on computer talk without boredom. Tell me how, she said.

So often they don't even understand the nature of the need. Re-minded her that Raftery modeling still showed the vast bulk of the most probable twenty-first centuries experiencing an average temper-ature rise of 3.2 degrees Celsius. Chances of keeping average temperatures below 2 degrees C were five percent. Keeping it under 1.5 degrees C were one percent.

Mary just stared. We know it's bad, she said acidly. Give us your ideas to help!

Told her about the Chen paper, useful for its clarity, and now getting discussed in several different discourse communities, it being one of the earlier of various proposals to create some kind of carbon coin. This to be a digital currency, disbursed on proof of carbon sequestration to provide carrot as well as stick, thus enticing loose global capital into virtuous actions on carbon burn reduction. Making an effective carrot of this sort would work best if the central banks backed it, or created it. A new influx of fiat money, paid into the world to reward biosphere-sustaining actions. Getting the central banks to do that would be a stretch, but them doing it would be the strongest version by far.

Mary nodded grimly at that. A stretch, she repeated.

Persisted with arguments for carbon coin. Noted that some environmental economists now discussing the Chen plan and its ramifications, as an aspect of commons theory and sustainability theory. Having debunked the tragedy of the commons, they now were trying to direct our attention to what they called the tragedy of the time horizon. Meaning we can't imagine the suffering of the people of the future, so nothing much gets done on their behalf. What we do now creates damage that hits decades later, so we don't charge ourselves for it, and the standard approach has been that future generations will be richer and stronger than us, and they'll find solutions to their problems. But by the time they get here, these problems will have become too big to solve. That's the tragedy of the time horizon, that we don't look more than a few years ahead, or even in many cases, as with high-speed trading, a few micro-seconds ahead. And the tragedy of the time horizon is a true tragedy, because many of the worst climate impacts will be irreversible. Extinctions and ocean warming can't be fixed no matter how much money future people have, so economics as practiced misses a fundamental aspect of reality.

Mary glanced at Dick, and he nodded. He said to her, It's another way to describe the damage of a high discount rate. The high discount rate is an index of this larger dismissal of the future that J-A is describing.

Agreed to that.

And this Chen line of thought solves that? Mary asked. It extends the time horizon farther out?

Replied, Yes, it tries to do that.

Explained how the proposal for a carbon coin was time-dependent, like a budget, with fixed amounts of time included in its contracts, as in bonds. New carbon coins backed by hundred-year bonds with guaranteed rates of return, underwritten by all the central banks working together. These investments would be safer than any other, and provide a way to go long on the biosphere, so to speak.

Mary shook her head. Why would people care about a pay-off a hundred years away?

Tried to explain money's multiple purposes. Exchange of goods, sure, but also storage of value. If central banks issue bonds, they're a sure thing, and if return set high enough, competitive with other investment. Can be sold before they mature, and so on. Bond market. Then also, since this is a case of central banks issuing new money, as in quantitative easing, investors will believe in it because it's backed by long-term bonds. And this money could be created and given to people only for doing good things.

Like what? Mary asked. Issued for what?

For not burning carbon.

Started writing on the whiteboard, feeling she was oriented enough to be ready for some figures. Not equations, which might just as well be Sanskrit to her, only some numbers.

For every ton of carbon not burned, or sequestered in a way that would be certified to be real for an agreed-upon time, one century being typical in these discussions so far, you are given one carbon coin. You can trade that coin immediately for any other currency on the currency exchanges, so one carbon coin would be worth a certain amount of other fiat currencies. The central banks would guarantee it at a certain minimum price, they would support a floor so it couldn't crash. But also, it could rise above that floor as people get a sense of its value, in the usual way of currencies in the currency exchange markets.

Mary said, So really this is just a form of quantitative easing.

Yes. But directed, targeted. Meaning the creation, the first spending of the new money, would have been specifically aimed at carbon reduction. That reduction is what makes the new money in the first place. The Chen papers sometimes call it CQE, carbon quantitative easing.

Mary said, So anyone could get issued one of these coins after sequestering a ton of carbon?

Yes. Or also a fraction of a coin. There would have to be a whole monitoring and certification industry, which could be public-private in nature, like the bond rating agencies are now. Probably see some cheating and gaming the system, but that could be controlled by the usual kinds of policing. And the carbon coins would all be registered, so everyone could see how many of them there were, and the banks would only issue as many coins as carbon was mitigated, year by year, so there would be less worry about devaluing money by flooding the supply. If a lot of carbon coins were being created, that would mean lots of carbon was getting sequestered, and that would be a sign of biosphere health that would increase confidence in the system. Quantitative easing thus directed to good work first, then free to join economy however.

Mary said, So if you combined this thing with carbon taxes, you would get taxed if you burn carbon, but paid if you sequester carbon.

Agreed, and added that any carbon tax should be set progressively, meaning larger use more pay, to keep it from being a regressive tax. Then it becomes a good thing, and feebates can be added that pass some of this tax income back to citizens, to make it even better. A carbon tax thus added to the carbon coin was said by Chen and others to be a crucial feature of the plan. When both taxes and carbon coins were applied together, the modeling and social experiments got much better results than when either strategy was applied by itself. Not just twice as good, but ten times as good.

Mary said, Why is that?

Confessed did not know. Synergy of carrot and stick, human psychology — waved hands. Why people did what they did— that was her bailiwick.

Dick pointed out that for economists, carrots and sticks are both just incentives, and thus the same, although they tend to assume sticks are more efficient than carrots.

Mary shook her head vigorously. No fucking way, she said. We're animals, not economists. For animals, negative and positive are generally regarded as quite distinct from each other. A kick versus a kiss. Jesus Christ. She looked back and forth at us, said, It's a question which of the two of you are the more inhuman, the computer geek or the economist.

Both referents nodded at this. Point of pride, in fact. Trying to out-do each other; attempt to attain Spocklike scientific objectivity a worthy goal, and so on. Dick quite hilarious on this matter.

Mary saw the nods and sighed again. All right, when you align both negative and positive reinforcements to press us toward a certain behavior, we then do that behavior. It's just Pavlov, right? Stimulus and response. So how could we get this started?

Said, If the dozen biggest central banks agreed to do it together, it would go.

But that's true of almost anything! Mary exclaimed. What's the minimum you think it would need to succeed?

Said, Any central bank could experiment with it. Best would be the US, China, and the EU. India might be the most motivated to go it alone, they're still very anxious to get carbon out of the air fast. But the more the merrier, as always.

She asked to be led through the time element again.

Explained how the central banks could simply publish the rate of return that they planned to pay out in the future, no matter what. Investors would therefore have a sure thing, which they would love. It would be a way to go long, and to securitize their more speculative bets. The stick, the carbon tax, also needed to rise over time. With that tax rate and its angle of increase published in advance, and a long-term rate of return guaranteed for investing in carbon coins, one could then calculate the cost of burning carbon, and the benefits of sequestering it. Normal currencies float against each other in the exchange markets, but if one currency is guaranteed to rise in value over time no matter what, then it becomes more valuable to investors. It will always stay strong in the currency market because it's got a time stamp guarantee of a rise in value. The carbon coin designed in that way would eventually probably replace the US dollar as the world's benchmark currency, which would strengthen it even more.

It's like compound interest again, Dick remarked to Mary.

Said, Yes, but this time guaranteed by being delinked from current interest rates, which often hit zero, or even go negative. With this coin, you're good to go no matter what happens.

Dick said, That could make for a liquidity trap, because investors would stash money there for safety rather than put it to use.

Shook head at that. Set the rate low enough that it's seen as more of a back-up.

Dick said, If the central banks announced they were upping the amount of carbon needed to earn a coin, they could then balance it with other safe asset classes like treasury bonds and infrastructure bonds. That would add liquidity and give traders something about this that they could short, which is something they like to do.

Agreed this might be good.

Mary said, Could we issue these carbon coins ourselves from the ministry?

Shook head. You have to be able to buy them all back at some floor rate, to make people believe in them. We might not have the reserves to do that.

We can barely pay our staff, Mary said.

We've noticed, Dick joked. Good to see he liked this plan.

Mary brought the meeting to a close. Work this up into a full proposal, she said. One I can take to the central banks and defend. I've got meetings with them already scheduled. We'll see where it takes us.[1]

---

1. Interested to know more? see https://www.greenstories.org.uk/anthology-for-cop27/solutions/green-finance/

OASIS

by Brian Burt

T he floating city of New Atlantis sparkled around President Chan like a necklace of prismatic jewels, refracting the sunlight that shone from an azure sky to bathe the cerulean sea. Its honeycomb of interlocking, hexagonal platforms, like its citizens, proudly wore the styles, hues, and decorations of many shores. The tang of brine and fish and seaweed filled her nostrils.

So beautiful...and so vulnerable.

Her phone buzzed like an angry hornet. She pulled it from a pocket of her *Baju Kurung* and braced herself. Elian Rocha, her Chief Security Officer, rarely called to offer cheery news.

"Are you going to ruin my morning, Elian?"

"Afraid so, ma'am. A fleet of rogue trawlers plundered forbidden fishing grounds in South Pacifico. Don't know how many tons of tuna they nabbed before our cutters ran them off. I left one cutter to patrol, in case they return to the scene of the crime...but we don't have enough ships or sailors to guard all the zones under threat. We're stretched too thin."

Chan's temples throbbed. "I know, Elian. Every OasIS department is begging for resources. For now, just do the best you can with what you have. We can brainstorm options this afternoon."

OasIS, Ocean as Independent State, had been officially born with the ratification of UN Resolution 3322. Most nations were happy to let their climate migrants flee to one of the floating cities that formed a far-flung archipelago across all seven seas; desperate, displaced people in search of a better life. They even allowed those emigrants to maintain dual citizenship. They just resented ceding power to a newcomer and paying their fair share. Chan sighed. Life had been so simple when she was just an engineer designing carbon dioxide removal tech. Becoming a stateswoman, embroiled in intrigue with hostile heads of state and devious diplomats, drained her to the dregs.

Stop whining, Chan. It's a dirty job...but somebody has to do it. Time to make the morning rounds and face the other crises.

She made her way along the western edge of the city, where platforms bordered the open waters of the North Atlantic. The docks bustled with activity as stevedores in the colorful attire of a dozen different nations loaded cargo ships bound for other floating cities or coastal ports. Chan wove her way through the commotion and crossed into the Caribbean quarter. Calypso music wafted from an open-air cafe, the steady rhythm seeping into Chan's bones, making her want to dance. No time for that. She was already late for her first appointment of the day: confronting one of the massive growing pains plaguing New Atlantis, the capital of OasIS.

She spotted Hank Broussard kneeling near a hundred-meter-wide hexagon of open water between like-sized platforms, tinkering with an array of floating solar panels anchored to the platform's side. Their Indian suppliers called them *Dweeps*, from the Sanskrit word for island. They boasted a unique tensegrity beam skeleton that made them durable and resilient, even in the teeth of storms. *Brilliant stuff...as long as you can get enough of them.*

"Good morning, Hank. How goes the battle?"

"Morning, Chan... I mean, Madam President. Like I'm wrestling greased alligators in Bayou mud."

Chan chuckled. Hank hailed from New Orleans, a former refinery engineer who had turned to the dark side, developing expertise in renewable energy systems instead of oil and gas. He'd made the switch the second time his house in St. Bernard Parish was flooded by hurricane storm surge. The third time, he abandoned his Louisiana home and took the option to grab a seasteading platform and a tow to New Atlantis.

"Installation problems? Reliability issues?"

"Naw, these arrays are tough as hell. We just need more: at least one Dweep for every four platforms will give us a cushion to handle peak power usage. We deployed six new Wave Energy Converters along the eastern breakwater, and the WECs generate more juice to feed our grid... but as fast as we're expanding, that's not enough. A dozen platforms full of Bangladeshi refugees are hooking up to the south as we speak. Don't know how we're gonna meet their needs." Broussard wiped the sweat from his craggy brown face. "India is supposed to be paying their carbon and plastic pollution fees with Dweeps, right? They need to pay faster, or at least ship 'em faster!"

"Noted, Hank." She pulled out her phone and keyed an entry into her to-do list. "I'll contact the Indian ambassador and remind him that we need his people to stick to the delivery schedule. Anything else?"

"We could use more techs with experience maintaining these arrays. Maybe you can find me a few homeless Indian engineers, or some who'd consider an ocean view and a chance to heal the planet?"

"I'll see what I can do."

Chan left Broussard cussing and fiddling with the partially installed Dweep as she headed west again, crossing through the district known as Penang Place, where many of her fellow Malaysians had merged their platforms to cook up a taste of home. She passed a little restaurant called Kapitan, savoring the aroma of the best *laksa* in North Atlantico. Familiar sights, smells, the musical Malay chatter filled her with nostalgia. And a pang of loss. The coastal cottage where she'd spent much of her childhood had been swallowed by the rising sea. Most of her family, friends, and neighbors had been forced to flee their village; some had chosen to follow her into this strange, storm-swept, watery wilderness. OasIS lived up to its name, offering a refuge from the horrors that spread across the globe: killer cyclones, wildfires, famine, drought, hellish heat waves. As always, the poorest and most vulnerable bore the brunt of it.

Malaysia will always claim my heart...but this is where I belong now. This is where we fight for those with nowhere else to turn.

Her phone buzzed again. "What now, Elian? More rogue trawlers?"

Rocha's terse response made her cringe. "Nothing that benign, ma'am. There's been another pirate raid, this time on Zajira in Indio Province. Five injured, lots of cargo stolen from the main dock. Damage assessment is still underway, but at least there were no fatalities." Rocha's familiar refrain struck her like a blow. "We're a soft-shell crab, an easy target for predators. We need to grow some armor, fast, before they pick us to pieces!"

He wasn't wrong. Chan didn't have easy answers.

"I've got one more priority visit on my calendar, then I'll join you in the Operations Center. Keep me posted."

She prayed this next appointment would lift her mood. She reached a platform that faced the rolling, roaring sweep of open sea. Chan ascended the grated steps to the canopied observation deck, joining Nina Babiak at the railing. The view took Chan's breath away. A vast expanse of amber fronds bobbed on the waves all the way to the horizon.

"Our floating forest looks lush, Nina."

"Indeed. Is strange: I go from farming wheat in Ukraine to farming ocean." Nina pushed a wind-blown strand of hair out of her face, exposing keen blue eyes above ruddy cheeks. "This bioengineered strain of sargassum grows like weed. Swallows much CO_2, makes rich ecosystem for fish and crustacean. Even tastes okay, when you spice it right. They say Amazon Rainforest is lungs of Earth; we grow lungs of Mother Ocean!"

"A lung transplant, given how much of the Amazon was burned or clear-cut. We have a way to go before we break even."

Chan's phone interrupted her train of thought a telltale ringtone she recognized at once, triggering an inner groan. Nina stared at her expectantly. "Need to take call, Madam President?"

"It can wait. My CSO is turning into a stalker; we've already chatted twice during my morning rounds. Right now, Nina, I'm focused on you. How are sequestration operations going?"

"Well. We bundle and compress vast quantities of macroalgae, sink them to seafloor. Very efficient. Only problem: not enough bundler / compressor boats. Need more, not just here, but everywhere. Scale up across OasIS, we remove gigatons of CO_2 from system."

Chan pulled out her phone and added another note to her to-do list. Providing a new home, a new nation, new hope for the dispossessed was vital. But this – sequestering tons of carbon at the bottom of the sea – this was core to their mission. This was how they used the fees they assessed against nations who polluted, overfished, or shipped cargo across their waters. They didn't stockpile money to enrich their treasury; they spent it on projects that aimed to save the planet from an existential threat.

"More compressor vessels. I'm on it, Nina."

Chan's phone chimed insistently, this time with a text alert she couldn't ignore. She read the message.

CSO – *Need you at HQ pronto. Have situation.*

Prez – *We always have a situation.*

CSO – *K, call it invasion. Will brief you at HQ.*

"Sorry, Nina. Looks like I have to go."

Chan hustled to OasIS Federation headquarters in the heart of the floating city as quickly as she could. She flicked her hand, and the ID chip implanted between her thumb and index finger approved her access, opening a security door with the OasIS seal emblazoned on it – a stylized sapphire map of the seven seas crisscrossed with two emerald tridents. She hurried to a spiral staircase descending beneath the platform and made her way down to a lower level of the seascraper, where her private office sat next to the Security Operations Center.

Elian Rocha waited there, swarthy face as stormy as a brewing Atlantic gale, and followed her into her office. He remained standing, grim and stolid, as she sat behind her desk. A layer of synthetic nacre covered the desktop, gleaming with pearly iridescence; Chan's secret, guilty pleasure within this inner sanctum. She poured herself a glass of desalinated water and offered Rocha a glass, which he declined with an impatient wave of his hand. *Here we go again....*

"All right, Elian. Let's not prolong the agony."

Rocha pressed a series of icons on his phone. The large monitor on the wall illuminated, displaying a map of the world's oceans, covered with thousands of color-coded, ship-shaped symbols. Two ships glowed scarlet, twin bloodstains pooled on the surface of the Arabian Sea. "Another pair of tankers departed the Persian Gulf a few hours ago. They're not transmitting AIS beacons, but we've identified them: both fly the flags of oil-rich nations. Neither has registered a transit, neither has paid the prescribed fees for using our shipping lanes, much less the surcharge for transporting fossil fuels. They treat our sovereign waters like they own them...and us."

"I assume the Governor of Indio Province has been informed?"

"She has. Indio tried hailing both tankers, from multiple floating cities along their route. No response."

Chan grimaced. "Rude, but predictable. I guess we put a few more charges on their tab and send them the bill."

"Like all the other bills?" said Rocha with a snort. "None of the FOPECSCO affiliates have paid a bloody cent so far. We need to make them take us seriously, Madam President, or our claim of sovereignty is a joke."

"We have the backing of the UN, and formal recognition from China, the US, the EU, and others. We're not a punchline, Elian."

"No...but we have no punch. We have a decent fleet of cargo ships, but military muscle? *Nada*. I would love to send some well-armed frigates out to stop them in their tracks...but I don't have any."

Chan shared Rocha's frustration. They were struggling to build a nation, a loose federation of seven seas constituting seven provinces, each struggling to absorb millions of climate migrants and scale up their infrastructure to cope. Seasteading communities grew in capricious ways: platforms joined, relocated, or even chugged away to merge with different cities. They didn't so much grow as mutate. Managing OasIS, in whole and in part, was a complex, maddening, mind-boggling endeavor.

It was also, Chan fervently believed, essential to ensuring that the climate crisis didn't explode into catastrophe. Her fractious, emerging nation had enough stresses on it already. They needed help. She'd sworn when she took office that she'd turn adversaries into allies, that she wouldn't meet provocation with brute force. Right now, that attitude seemed hopelessly naive.

An idea struck her. Sometimes, leaders had to sacrifice their peace of mind to protect their people. Time to put up or shut up.

"*We* may not have frigates, Elian, but I know somebody who does. Please get US Ambassador Henderson on the line ASAP. Tell him I have a proposal that I think his President will want to hear."

*

Chan sat at her private office desk, obsessively wiping stray smudges from the pearlescent desktop while she waited for her VIP guest to join the virtual conference. She both anticipated this meeting and dreaded it; it could easily devolve into disaster if she didn't watch her step. The meeting-room background rippled, then the monitor filled with the indignant visage of Ambassador Hassan, current spokesman for FOPECSCO. The man was imposing: tall and lean, with a meticulously trimmed silver beard, projecting a regal bearing in his snow-white *thawb* and checkered *ghutra*. Chan refused to let the ambassador's stony scowl dim her smile.

"Mister Ambassador, I'm so pleased that we finally have an opportunity to speak directly to each other."

"I and my constituents are *not* so pleased, Madam President. A dozen oil tankers registered to our membership have now been blocked from navigating traditional shipping lanes beyond the Persian Gulf. American Naval vessels intercepted them, bullied them, and ultimately forced them to return to their ports of origin. They claimed to do so on your authority, or at least on your behalf. You have no right to interfere with our members' honest commerce, our right to sail freely in international waters!"

Chan leaned forward, locking eyes with the ambassador as best she could over video conference. "Oh, but OasIS has *every* right to do so. When Resolution 3322 was ratified, the waters of all seven seas became our sovereign territory. And, per that mandate, we're empowered to charge reasonable fees for the use of our territorial waters, for shipping or fishing or polluting. Two thirds of the world fully recognizes our status as a UN member nation, and our right to enforce the laws within our borders. Your fellow FOPECSCO ministers are in the minority, sir...and you know it. You add insult to injury when you refuse to pay your share of the costs of battling the climate crisis, especially when you try to sneak tankers full of fossil fuel across our waters."

The ambassador's frown deepened. "Some would argue that OasIS extorts billions from countries who do not share your vision. Oil and gas remain essential to driving the global economy, and will remain so for the foreseeable future. I live in the real world, Madam President. Renewable energy sources, while useful, are not sufficient."

"The status quo is not sufficient, either. I think we can agree on that." Chan leaned back in her chair. "Until your members pay their bills, sir, their ships will not be passing through our seas."

Hassan stared bullets for a moment, then sighed and stroked his beard. "I must admit, you played a trump card we did not know you held. How did you entice the Americans to do your bidding?"

"I didn't. I cut a deal with them, for our mutual benefit. OasIS doesn't want to make enemies, Mister Ambassador; we'd much rather secure allies. The United States, as one of the world's largest economies and biggest emitters of CO_2, owed us massive payments. This didn't sit well with a chunk of the American public. We worked with Washington to craft a compromise: reduced fees in exchange for services. The U.S. Navy now assists us in enforcing our sovereignty and preventing unauthorized incursions. They even provide satellite surveillance to help us monitor and interdict illegal overfishing. Over time, they'll train and equip us to assemble our own naval forces, and their direct involvement will diminish, although we'll continue to conduct joint operations. It's a win-win: we get crucial military assistance, they get deep discounts. Instead of fighting us – and the American Navy – perhaps you can form a different kind of partnership to defray your own OasIS funding costs."

Ambassador Hassan stared thoughtfully at the screen for a very long time. "In truth, our members are suffering considerable political blowback from the decision to defy Resolution 3322. I would like to find common ground with you...as long as we avoid the quicksand."

Chan kept her expression neutral, but her heart did somersaults. Hassan had taken the bait; now she needed to set the hook.

"OasIS has a plastic problem. We're investing in the rollout of bioplastics, and that can keep the pollution from getting worse... but there's still a lot out there, and plastics are forever. We clean up the macro stuff pretty well, with the help of the gyres, and the Chinese are partnering with us to develop robotic drones that filter microplastics from the 'garbage patch soup', but repurposing it all is a challenge. Right now, we can only recycle about half of what we collect into something usable. We're experimenting with reagents that strip hydrogen atoms from polymers so we can form new bonds, recycle the flotsam into materials even more durable than the original. Your members have expertise with petrochemicals, world-renowned researchers in this field. OasIS would be happy to divert a portion of the fees owed us by FOPECSCO affiliates back into their economies, funding your chemists to perfect these robust recycling techniques. If you help us solve this problem, you'll be hailed as heroes."

Hassan fixed her with an inscrutable expression, considering. She held her tongue, determined not to surrender to the silence, to wait him out. She knew Hassan's reputation; the man was savvy.

Come on, Ambassador. Do the math!

After what felt like an eternity, Hassan nodded. "Your proposal has merit. FOPECSCO is in the energy business: we'd rather use ours to collaborate than waste it on costly legal battles. I cannot promise anything...but I will share your idea with the ministers and offer my tentative support. I am optimistic that we can reach some agreement."

After exchanging a few more pleasantries and designating specific ministers on each side to lead the next round of negotiations, Chan ended the meeting. She let out a whoop that brought CSO Rocha scrambling down the hall to knock at her office door. She invited him in, disarming him with a grin that felt like it might split her face in half.

"The meeting went well?" said Rocha with a wry grin of his own.

"I believe we'll be receiving payments from FOPECSCO members soon...and assistance with our recycling problem."

"Remind me never to play poker with you, Madam President. You'd put me in the poorhouse."

"I won't take *your* money, Elian...but I'll take *theirs*, as an investment in our shared future. Right now, I need to requisition a whole fleet of seaweed-compressor boats, and maybe a few dozen Dweeps to keep Hank Broussard from tossing me to the sharks."

Rocha left Chan in her inner sanctum and returned to his SOC to watch over Mother Ocean. Chan pulled up the to-do sheet on her phone, not quite so dismayed by how long it had become, grateful to cross a few items off the list. The OasIS seal filled her monitor with vibrant shades of emerald and sapphire: the colors of life, growth, and renewal. The presidency exhausted her. So much at stake, so many obstacles to overcome, to avert an existential threat. But for now, for today, she rose on a swelling tide of hope.[1]

---

1. Interested to know more about climate solutions included? See https://www.greenstories.org.uk/anthology-for-cop27/solutions/ocean-as-a-nation/

THE AWARD CEREMONY

by D.A. Baden

Mei's series, a cross between *Sex in the City* and *Emily in Paris,* with an Asian lead and African-American co-star, was up for a number of awards. Mei looked round at the other guests and nominees. The sex-pest casting directors were gone, the racists were out – this was her kind of crowd. If she won, it would be a sign that finally she belonged.

She frowned across the table at Wilf, who was up for best co-star. He was telling the producer that he had a different car for each day of the week. She understood – she'd grown up poor too, but in these days of climate change, bragging about how many cars you have is more likely to get you cancelled or your tyres let down than meet with approval. He grinned back reassuringly, misunderstanding her expression.

Everyone quietened as the award for best screenwriter came up. Her name was read out, the third out of four. Her mouth went dry, remembering how Greta Gerwig's masterpiece of female empowerment *Little Women*, was inexplicably snubbed. The envelope was opened, a dramatic pause then a big smile.

She heard the words as if in a dream. 'The prize for best original screenwriter goes to Mei Lin, for her series, *Sun Ying in Manhattan.*'

Then she was walking up to the stage, self-conscious in her new dress, nodding at the smiling faces. She took her place in the spotlight in front of the microphone and looked out at the sea of clapping hands and waving friends and colleagues. It felt wonderful. She'd love to stand there forever just soaking it up, but she had things she needed to say.

'This means everything to me and I want to tell you why,' she began. 'I was the second child during China's one-child policy. And worse still, a girl.' The smiling faces in the audience turned serious, a few nodding their support. 'Some people called it environmental responsibility, others a violation of human rights, but I can only tell you what it meant to me. I...' She swallowed, finding her pre-prepared speech harder to say than she'd anticipated. 'I felt guilty. That just by existing I was making things worse for the people I care about.'

She hung her head, feeling the force of the words, spoken for the first time. Shame was built into the architecture of her existence, driving her on and on to prove herself. To atone. Her fists tightened by her side. She'd done nothing wrong, nothing to apologise for. She raised her chin defiantly.

'But empowering women can do more to solve over-population than any amount of regulation or financial punishment. In developing countries, women who aren't educated have twice as many children as those who are. The population of the US rose from 210 million to 332 million over the last fifty years. But the population of Pakistan rose from 65 million to 230 million in the same period. Nigeria from 59 million to 217 million. This should be the top climate priority – giving women in these countries consistent and convenient access to birth control. Give them not just power over their bodies but power full stop. Women leaders and diverse boards show better, more sustainable decision making. I am proud to be a Chinese woman writing empowered heroines, in charge of their destiny, proud of their gender and the colour of their skin.'

The audience exploded into applause. She tried to thank her cast and crew, but couldn't make herself heard over the catcalls and whoops. She gave up and stood there and glowed, wiping her eyes, basking in the love and empathy coming from the crowd. The host returned to the stage and waited a moment in deference to clapping that showed no sign of abating. Then he headed towards her purposefully, ready to usher her off. Her moment in the spotlight was over.

But it wasn't. She heard shouts, a rhythmic chanting growing louder. They were chanting her name, and something else she couldn't catch. People were looking around to see the source, but in her position, stepping down from the stage, she was the first to see the banner being unrolled.

MEI LIN. CLIMATE VILLAIN.

Villain! She shook her head. Someone mis-wrote, they'll realise it's a mistake. But no, they were chanting clearly now, heading steadily down the aisle.

'Mei Lin. Climate villain.'

There were a dozen at least carrying the banner.

It didn't even rhyme, not well anyway.

'Mei Lin. Climate villain.' The cameras swivelled to follow their progress down the aisle, the open-mouthed audience. Mei Lin's horrified face.

* * *

Ping. Another talk show date cancelled. Ping. Meeting with producer cancelled. Ping. Interview cancelled.

Mei turned her phone off and slumped back on the sofa, reaching blindly for the remote control.

'...can't help feeling sorry for her though,' the daytime TV host was saying. 'Top of her game. Producers clamouring to sign her up for their next project. She was gold dust.'

'See if you still feel sorry for her after this,' said the co-host.

Mei Lin jumped when she saw her earnest face fill the screen, and scratched at the rash that had appeared overnight.

'Everyone thinks that it's governments or banks who have the power, but it's culture and writers and stories that affect how we think, who we want to be, what we aspire to.'

She'd been too full of herself. That must be it. Committed the unforgiveable sin of taking herself too seriously. Oh no, there she was again, in another talk show. She cringed at how sanctimonious she sounded. 'I suffer from eco-anxiety like most young people, but I want to help people feel empowered to make a difference, not just guilty for existing.'

Now they were showing an extract from *Sun Ying in Manhattan* – a close-up of Wilf as Grady, her heroine's handsome African American love interest, opening his gourmet burger stand. The camera paused on the image of a customer sinking his teeth into the beef, then cut abruptly to facts and figures and images of cows burping methane, warming up the atmosphere.

'I'm a vegan! Are you going to mention that?' she shouted at the television when the programme returned to show the co-hosts tutting at the film.

Mei picked at the ugly bumps on her skin, shaking her head helplessly as the narrator reeled off a series of facts about the contribution of beef and dairy to climate change. She'd sensed it was risky. She knew beef was a climate no-no, but it was an American staple. The producers had wanted a down-to-earth guy to balance the heroine's kookiness. She'd thought she was playing safe when she went along with them.

The image cut to a busy shopping centre and a mic being thrust into a young woman's face.

'Do you watch *Sun Ying in Manhattan*?'

'Doesn't everybody?'

'What do you like about it?'

'She's so cool. So in charge of her life. I love her clothes.' A medley of shots of Sun Ying wearing a different outfit each time, with matching hat, bag and shoes ran over her words. 'I just want to be her basically.'

Mei watched, along with the daytime TV hosts, a medley of shots of Sun Ying and her friends shopping, walking home, bags swishing against their thighs.

'They may be fancy, but they're still single-use plastic bags,' the host nudged his co-host. She shrugged her shoulders, not yet convinced.

'We worked out what all these clothes would look like in the averaged sized apartment.' The image changed to a pile of clothes filling every space, bursting out of wardrobes, piled up on chairs, on the bed, under the bed. The shot focused in on one cotton t-shirt, then cut jarringly to a huge-eyed African child, tears forming crusts on her cheeks. 'Two point seven billion people experience water scarcity.' The narrator sounded harsh and accusing.

'This is the inland sea twenty years ago that supported the growing of cotton.' A large blue sea filled the screen, then faded into an image of a desert. 'Today, only camels roam across the barren wilderness.' God, her skin was on fire. Mei sat on her hands to stop herself from compulsively scratching.

'This is the water cost of just this one cotton t-shirt,' the narrator continued over an image of a giant water tank labelled 2700 litres. 'Enough drinking water for one person for nearly three years.'

A Bangladeshi woman held up hands covered with sores and blisters to the camera. 'Twenty percent of water pollution comes from the treatment and dyeing of textiles, poisoning the surrounding area, creating health issues for communities,' the narrator's voice was relentless. 'Rates of death from cancer in these communities are nine times higher than the national average.' Mei could hardly breathe. An unfortunate side effect of China's rapid economic growth had been pollution. She'd grown up in one of China's so-called cancer villages, and was haunted by the fear that the disease that had taken her parents would take her.

'Fast fashion contributes ten percent of global carbon emissions – more than all international flights and shipping combined.'

She found herself scratching at the rash, reminding herself what her therapist had repeatedly told her. 'It's not your fault Mei.'

An academic-looking woman appeared on the screen, the banner beneath her face announcing her as Drew Sneely, Professor of Psychology at Southampton University.

'There are two ways in which we learn how to behave. One is conscious learning through the rational elaboration model, where we are presented with information, in school, from our parents, etc. But more powerful is the unconscious social learning we pick up by absorbing the behaviours and cultural values around us. Fictional role models are especially influential. Through a process that we call narrative transportation, viewers who identify with a character will absorb their values uncritically and subliminally, affecting their behaviour and aspirations without them even being aware of it.'

Then it was back to the shopping centre, and the mic thrust under another girl's nose.

'What do you see when you see Sun Ying's walk-in wardrobe?'

Her face lit up. 'I see goals,' she said at once.

'That's why I'm so proud to be a writer, creating positive role models for young women.' Mei watched her own face again on screen. Her mouth opened in shock as the image of her face was rapidly distorted, then appearing on a 'wanted' poster with Climate Villain stamped across it. The shot widened, showing her image on a wall wedged between a fossil fuel lobbyist and purveyor of misinformation about climate change and the toxic male entrepreneur who'd bragged once too often about his private jet. What had tipped them over the edge, Mei belatedly realised, was when he'd boasted that he was so rich he wore underwear once then threw it away. She remembered the outrage as the facts and figures about the impacts of such wastage on the environment were presented.

Mei took in the final shot of the girl walking out of the shopping centre, numerous branded bags filled with fast fashion swinging jauntily against her thigh.

She tried to say the words 'it's not my fault,' but the prickling of her skin, the squirming sensation in the pit of her stomach gave them the lie. Shame. How had she not joined the dots?

She switched on her laptop and started writing.

* * *

Five years on, and no one was more surprised than Mei Lin when she got the call. But everybody likes a comeback story, and as many said, if Bob Dylan can get it, then why not a scriptwriter? Even so, she was more terrified than honoured. This event was much more formal, the men identical in black suits, white shirts and white silk bow ties, the women in stiff ball gowns. She sat in the front row, waiting, dry-mouthed, trying not to hyper-ventilate while the host spoke in Swedish, then in English. Being in the spotlight was reigniting the trauma she'd experienced five years ago, when they'd built her up just to knock her down. Her breathing calmed under the monotone of the presentation, and she was able to listen.

'In season two of *Sun Ying in Manhattan*. Sun Ying's boyfriend, Grady was now running a trendy new bug burger stand. Sun had converted her walk-in wardrobe into a fashion library, and created a fashion swap app that was taking the world by storm.

'Reality mirrored fiction with new fashion apps emerging every month. Women were switching to pre-loved clothes, swapping, sharing, repairing and upcycling all over the globe. The most popular Christmas present that year was a membership to the fashion libraries of Macy's, Harrods, David Jones and even Galeries Lafayette in Paris.

'Season three, and Sun Ying broadened her range to menswear. You could wear a different outfit every day with no need for vast amounts of wardrobe space. Ownership was increasingly portrayed as a burden, not a benefit. Stores caught on, converting their toys, games and sports departments into libraries. Sun Ying had a fictional baby and MotherCare reinvented itself as MotherShare.

'In season four, the characters moved to the suburbs with their partners and children. Grady sold his bug burger stand to a franchise who were taking insect snacks into the rest of the world. Missing his New York community and struggling with DIY, he joined the local Shared Shed where men got together to pool their tools and knowledge. *Friends* and *Frasier* popularised the coffee bar as the place to meet in the nineties. Three decades later, *Sun Ying (no longer) in Manhattan*, made the Shared Shed a thing.

'The series helped established the Sharing Economy for good. Borrowing has become the new buying. Clothes, tools, toys, appliances are increasingly designed for long life and easy maintenance. Twenty years ago, most households had their own toolset, with typical items being used an average of ten minutes a year. Now tools are shared within communities, saving billions of tons of embedded carbon and unnecessary mining.

'Your Royal Highnesses, ladies and gentlemen, great literature changes the reader, changes the world, and there can be no doubt that Mei Lin's writing has changed our world.'

The audience clapped politely and it was Mei's turn. Almost in a whisper, she gasped out thanks to the presenter and Swedish Royal Family. The host had been careful to avoid mention of the protest at her last award ceremony, but it had led to this moment. She took a deep breath and addressed the elephant in the room.

'The last time I gave an acceptance speech, I was flying high, excited by the brave and long overdue movements – Me Too, Black Lives Matter. As an Asian woman, I thought I was leading the way, allowing my Asian and African characters to have all that I had been denied growing up. I was proud to use my writing and characters to empower women, to encourage them to aspire. Well, they say pride goes before a fall, and my goodness did I fall.

'I did and do care about climate change and thought women in charge would have a more nurturing approach to our precious planet. Yet here were my heroines shopping as if there were no consequences to their behaviour, mindlessly complicit in planetary destruction. I can't believe I didn't see the contradiction. Once I did, I saw it everywhere. Around me everyone was changing. People weren't flying; they were giving up meat; guys who thought driving a sports car had pulling power were learning their lesson. I suddenly realised that for people terrified by the climate crisis, watching my characters' excessive consumption was as jarring as racism and sexism was in seventies sitcoms. Far from being a progressive, I was behind the times. I wanted to be a platform for something good. That meant ditching the past and facing the future.

'Recent history has been about owning up and saying sorry for colonialism, racism, sexism, and now consumerism. I can't take credit for the way the sharing economy has taken off. The fashion swap apps, car sharing, and Libraries of Things were already out there, but I'm pleased to have helped spread the word. And, please don't cancel me because the Shared Shed is just men. I'm on it in season six.' The audience laughed, giving Mei the confidence to continue.

'It's not nice to feel cancelled, to feel judged, but we have to call it out – the stakes are too high not to. We need to be told when we're getting it wrong. Shame is a horrible thing to feel, but maybe it's a process we have to go through to get to the other side and start putting things right.

'I'm still about empowering women. The link between education and birth control is strong and evidence shows women make more sustainable decisions. But as gender roles equalise and men play a greater part in child rearing, I see those differences dissolving. Men are growing and changing and learning to care. We're all growing at a phenomenal rate, and it's a wonderful thing to see.

'If the last decade was about saying sorry, then we're entering a decade of atonement and positive action. When I was pregnant with my first child, I was terrified what kind of world I was bringing her into, but with this one,' Mei patted her stomach gently, 'I'm excited. Maybe the Chinese curse, 'may you be born in interesting times' isn't a curse at all but an opportunity. Thank you for giving me the chance to say sorry and the opportunity to atone.'

The applause triggered a memory rush of fear. Mei heard a faint chanting. It was in her head. It must be. The host waited politely for her to step down, but her legs had turned to jelly. He came to her side and took her arm. The chanting was getting louder. Why did no one else notice? The host tugged at her arm to no avail. She was paralyzed.

'Next we turn to the Nobel Prize for Economic Science,' he declared at last.

The economics professor, a man in his sixties, half stood, uncertain, waiting for Mei to leave the stage. She was oblivious, gazing over his head towards the back of the room, seeing the protestors enter, their numbers overwhelming the security guards at the back. The banner unfurling.

Then everyone's heads turned towards the chanting that was now impossible to ignore. Relief that she wasn't mad competed horribly with gut-churning realisation that history was repeating itself. In they came, marching towards the stage, the banners unfurling.

GDP RIP

Her mouth widened in a smile of glorious, shameful, schadenfreude. She recognised the professor now. He'd spoken out against switching from the GDP to a Happy Planet Index, entrenching economic growth and consumption as the ultimate measure of success.

'Economic growth equals planetary death!'

'GDP RIP!'

The cameras swivelled to take in the protestors, the banners, and the horrified face of the economics professor.[1]

---

1. Interested to know more about climate solutions included? See https://www.greenstories.org.uk/anthology-for-cop27/stories/award-ceremony/

COME HELP ME

by Nancy Lord

O n May 1, aboard the *Morning Star,* Yulia is learning the various meanings of May Day. In Russia she knew it as a major holiday. In the Soviet days it had meant speeches and parades in Red Square and, later, in her time, it was a pleasant day for celebrating spring and workers. In America, Peter is teaching her, it involves putting flowers in a basket and dancing around a pole with ribbons and maybe, too, depending on who you are, Communist sympathizer or not, saying kind things about workers. But, more importantly for them now, *mayday* is all one word and is what she must shout into the radio in the occasion of the boat being on fire or sinking. She should shout it three times in a row, and give the location.

This is how you work the radio, Peter has shown her. This is the emergency locater beacon, and this is how you turn it on, although it should turn on automatically if it goes underwater. This is the emergency life raft, and this is where you release it. These are our survival suits. Now we put soap on the zippers. Now we practice getting into our Gumby suits. Gumby is a rubber man, yes, from a cartoon. No, hood now. Zip all the way. Now we do it again, faster. He uses the timer on his big, complicated, good-under-water watch. Now you are dead of hypothermia, he says, if she is too slow to zip or can't get her hair tucked into the hood.

But why is she going to shout *mayday*? Peter says the French: *venez m'aider*, come help me.

Yulia can barely imagine her other life, the one that is disappearing, as behind fog, with every minute on the water and every mile from land. Only two days ago—just when finals week started—she'd sold off her textbooks, tossed piles of papers into the trash, kissed her favorite microscope good-bye, and flown to Kodiak to meet Peter. Her master's degree in marine biology and the award she'd received for her thesis were happy achievements, but she hadn't needed the long robe and flat hat and for so much hugging.

She has a new job: sticking hooks into stinky herring, clipping the short lines onto the long line. Watch the lines go down and then six hours later watch them come up, big white-belly fish taking shape as they swing towards the surface. Maggie's clothesline, Peter says. Like big white panties coming up, and it's for her to unpin them. Bigger than big panties—maybe pillow cases and sheets. Who is Maggie? Peter doesn't know this, just an expression.

Her happiness comes not just from big halibut that will make money for Peter and her. There is the rest to love: sky, waves, gulls with lonesome voices, some fish frying in a pan, a deck to scrub, a movie to watch and forget, mountains far away with snow. And Peter, of course: she wants to be with this man, her Petya, engine oil on his hands and fish oil in the brain.

Yulia is learning about the American enterprise system, quota shares that mean Peter can catch certain pounds of halibut in the part of the ocean called Area 3A. *Enterprising* is when you figure things out, like in science, but for more practical and personal reasons. Peter is always figuring things out, how to make something work, how to use mayonnaise instead of the eggs she somehow forgot at the store. She wants to be enterprising too, and now she has already learned how to run the hydraulics so that Peter can gaff the monster fish. When he was not mad about the eggs he called her "a natural" at baiting hooks and snapping gangions. She felt proud when he praised her "good hands." She is not so confident about knives. It's Peter's job to gut the fish, hers to pack the insides with ice. They will fill the hold this way.

Yes, all the weight of the school year, all the effort she'd made for so long—it falls away until she is like one of the gulls herself. That one, sitting on the water, riding up and over a swell, so lightly, like it is only feathers full of air.

"Dinner," Peter calls through the open doorway. He's fixed sable-fish—black cod, the fishermen call it, although it's not related to cod at all. Butterfish, Peter says the marketing people call it, selling its rich-ness. She doesn't know the Latin, the genus, and maybe she doesn't care. "Like candy," Peter says now, delivering a steamy chunk to his open mouth. He's cooked it his favorite way—marinated in soy and ginger and broiled in the oven.

"Better than candy." Yulia pushes aside a pile of clothing to sit opposite Peter at the galley table.

"Better than sex?"

"I don't think so."

"It's an expression," Peter says. "You like something a lot, you say it's better than sex."

Peter enjoys teaching her American idioms. Already that day: An old man kicked the bucket, he is bending over backwards, don't leave me high and dry. She likes visualizing all these—a person bent like a circle hook, someone on a mudflat with the tide gone out. How is being dead like kicking a bucket?

"You are a wet blanket," she says. "You are spilling beans. *Zamorish chervachka.*"

Peter cocks his head.

"You are not giving enough to eat to the little worm."

"What little worm?"

Yulia shrugs. "In your stomach? It means you eat only a little. Maybe not you. Someone else."

"Definitely not me. I am eating high off the hog. I am the big enchilada."

"I am the fish taco," she says.

"Yes," Peter says. "You are definitely the fish taco."

They're both quiet for a while, rocking in the swell while, down under, their baited hooks are swaying off the bottom, calling in the big halibut. Peter has been thinking about worms, because now he starts to talk about whale falls and what eats them, the ecosystems they support on the ocean floor, new species always being discovered. "*Osedax,*" Peter says. "Bone-eating worms. There's one called the bone-eating snot flower. Not a flower, of course, but a worm that burrows into whale bones and has these sort of pink flowery plumes."

Yulia thinks, what was the chance that this man with rice in his beard would have found a woman as interested as he is in whale falls and worms and likes to talk about them during dinner? Her heart swells a little at the idea of their match and the beauty of whale falls. That dead whales sink into the dark abyss and then feed such amazing collections of creatures that will eventually recycle every bit of flesh and bone back into the living world—well, that is Nature at its most stunning efficiency. She says to Peter, "Such great whale lipids."

Everybody loves whales, but Yulia understands why most of them do not care to learn about worms. Worms do not have economic value or feed species that do. Decomposing whales do not help the whale-watching industry. That is something she learned in her years at university; you had to study something for which there was funding, and funding only came to projects that had economic value. Her professor had told her that over and over again: *You have to say, right here in your abstract and then again in your conclusion and summary, why* Metridia pacifica *is important in the food web. You have to discuss the significance of its rate of growth, its health or decline.* All those words: about copepods making up to eighty percent of metazoan biomass in the marine environment, the link from primary production to upper trophic levels. Trophodynamics. Bioindicators. *Say more, say it explicitly.* Fish and whales and birds eat them. *Yes, fish are the economy. People care about fish.* Her professor pulled out his hair about this. This was not an expression; he literally put his hands in his hair and pulled at it.

Now she cares about fish. Someone is going to give them money for halibut. The fish are in the ocean and belong to Nature, but soon they will be on their boat and belong to Peter and her. That is American enterprise. It is regulated, for sure. They can only take so much, the quota Peter owns, so that the fish make more fish. That is called "sustainable fishing practices."

Peter has gone off to his collection of dog-eared *National Geographics* to find an article he remembers about the Monterey Canyon, with photos of *Osedax* species on whale bones. His muffled voice, coming from the fo'c'sle, is saying "sexual dimorphism."

Yulia takes their plastic plates to the tiny sink and washes them. She is thinking about her professor, who loves all the creatures in the sea. He pulls his hair out when he sees what is happening to the ocean—the "blob" of warm water in the North Pacific, the southern species moving north, the other species diving deeper to find cooler water, the acidification dissolving the shells of his cherished pteropods.

She was supposed to go on his spring research cruise, and now she is one more disappointment to him.

It had simply come to her one day that she was no longer looking forward to more oceanography, in fact did not want to net the same samples again, did not want to count eggs again, did not want to squint into more bouncing microscopes or teach undergraduates the difference between *Neocalanus cristatus* and *Neocalanus flemingeri*. Yes, it is interesting to her what these species are doing, and yes, the time series are very important to understanding what's happening in the ocean, but she is not as excited anymore about doing the same work over and over, while everything on the planet is in a toilet bowl, swirling down.

When Peter returns with the magazines, she says, "I am feeling a little guilted,"

"About the cruise?"

"It is starting in one week."

"It was your idea to come fishing," Peter reminds her. "This is also a good skill, to know how to catch fish, and to run a boat. You'll have many arrows in your quiver."

Yulia will be happy to have arrows in her quiver, whatever that is, but what she doesn't have is a life plan. For a long time she had thought she would take her American education back to Russia. But lately the news from home is not so happy, and her parents said, better to stay in America. She has, right there on the boat with her, applications for several doctoral programs.

"You will never be hungry, if you know how to fish," Peter says.

"Until there aren't any fish," she says.

Peter plants a wet, fish-mouth kiss on her forehead. "You have the very attractive Russian soul. Always suffering."

Yulia puts on warmer clothes and comes back on deck.

"They found us," Peter says, handing her the binoculars. "Sperm whales."

Yulia follows their tilty blows as they advance toward the *Morning Star*. Three, four big whales, one perhaps smaller than the others.

"Oh, crap," Peter says.

"Why oh crap?"

"Oh crap, that's the end of our black cod. You'll see. These guys belong in deeper water, chasing squid. But they've followed us in here over the shelf. Like flies to fish camp." Peter is excited, not in a bad way.

The sky has darkened some, with a cloud pattern she knows is called "mackerel," after a fish with big, shimmery scales. The light on the water shimmers in a similar way, blue and darker blue. Yulia watches the big whales slide alongside them, just boat lengths away. They settle there, long islands of backs catching the slippery light. Their breaths become soft murmurings, like a roomful of dreaming babies.

The only sperm whales Yulia has ever seen are in books--drawings of Moby-Dick bashing his big square head into boats, making them into wood splinters, people falling from the boats with screaming mouths. This is very different. This is a world at rest, even Peter now. She remembers fin whales she saw on her last research cruise, passing under their boat, the same feeling she had, something like what she imagines other people find in their religions. To know there is more than you can understand. And that not everything is about killing, although everything has to eat.

Peter is going on, quietly for Peter, talking about whale intelligence. Yulia is not hearing all of it. She is a scientist; she has learned not to say that any animals are intelligent. Whales have large and specialized brains—that is what science says. They make vocalizations and form social units. They often cooperate when feeding.

Peter and Yulia take a nap, same as the whales. Then, after coffee, it's time to haul gear. Deck lights. Hydraulics. The whales are not close now. Their blows are away, maybe a quarter-mile in front. Peter gaffs the first halibuts aboard, two in the thirty-pound range. A black cod, a halibut, then a dozen empty hooks and a dogfish with eyes like green marbles. Peter shakes that one off. A bigger halibut and a gray cod, a real cod. No more black cod. The whales are still in front, keeping the same distance.

"You see what's happening?" Peter yells to her. "They're one step ahead of us as we pick up the skate. As soon as the line's coming up taut, they're snatching the fish."

"Black cod is their favorite."

"Yes, they're selective. Some guys say they lose halibut to them, too. I don't know. I think this first skate is pretty good for us. I think it's easy to blame bad fishing on a whale."

Peter is shoving another halibut across the deck. Snot is dripping from his nose. "How can you blame whales? We invent technologies to catch fish, the whales invent ways to use the same technology. It's adaptation. You'd do the same thing if you saw a bunch of tasty dishes going by you, like in those sushi restaurants where the little dishes are going around."

Peter talks and talks about whales—killer whales that kill larger whales, humpback whales that sing, beluga whales with necks they can turn to look at you. Now he's a philosopher. "We almost killed the big whales off because we didn't understand what we were doing and what value they might have besides grease and oil. But now they're coming back. You see, it's possible to turn things around."

What Yulia can see is a very big difference between what was simple in the past and what is no longer simple. Stop sticking harpoons and bombs into whales and fewer whales die. Now, nothing has one cause or easy fix. Sometimes her boyfriend can be a simpleton—or in America, what they call an optimist. This is maybe why she loves him. He believes that nothing is impossible.

Peter likes to talk on the marine radio to the other boats. On one channel he talks to his friends, and they share information about where they're fishing. Maybe they lie about what they're catching—or maybe they don't. On other channels, with other fishermen, it's just bullshitting. Now he's telling someone they're running east, trying to leave the whales behind. Let the whales find some other boat to dine with. Now he's telling someone else about ocean acidification. "No, man, this is real. This is happening now. It's chemistry."

Some other fishermen want to argue with him. They tell him they heard that fishing would be shut down to protect some stupid little snail. They know that the real source of acidification is from underwater volcanoes. They insist that acidification is not a problem because climate change is fake science and, besides, everything can adapt.

"Were do you get this shit?" Peter yells at them. "No one's talking about shutting down fisheries. It would be smart to let the science people study the effects, though, and think about managing for resilience. Yes, *resilience*. Like *resilient*. No, I'm not going all dome-headed highbrow! It's a word! Get used to it!"

Peter has always said that one reason he likes being on the boat is that he can always think clearly there. His best ideas come in the motion between sky and sea, in the big hum that is more than engine noise. He turns to Yulia now. "We need to write some of this stuff down. Fact sheets. You know, the chemistry with the molecules and the cycling arrows and the pH scale and rate of change. All that. And about warming, how ocean temperature affects everything, how we're frogs cooking in the pot."

"Yes," she says. "Let's do that!" She is thinking of her sad professor and the others with their papers and slides. They talk to themselves, the bad news about the ocean, the way everything connects, what needs to happen to protect their ocean home. Someone needs to talk to *other* people. Her Petya is a good talker. Frogs she doesn't know about. Whales she does. "Whales for carbon capture," she says. "Iron in their poop."

Peter gives a big sigh, a frowny look. "No poop. Be serious."

"I am *very* serious. I am a marine scientist." Yulia lifts her chin. "Whales can help."

Peter is listening.

She starts with whale falls. They don't just feed worms and other creatures when they die and slowly come apart. Their giant bodies hold tons of carbon, and that carbon can be locked up for a very long time, for centuries. If we protect whales and build up their populations, and some of those whales die and sink to the bottom, that can be effective carbon capture, better than growing trees, according to an analysis she'd read.

"But also, whale poop," she says. "Is full of iron and nitrogen, good for plankton blooms. Phytoplankton makes half of all oxygen and feeds creatures, zooplankton and fish but also whales. What isn't eaten dies and sinks to the bottom ocean. It stays there for hundreds of years. Maybe thousands of years, we don't know. Where there are a lot of whales right now has the most phytoplankton. What does that tell you?"

Peter, in his captain's chair, has wild hair sticking up, sleeves rolled to elbows. His dancing eyes are looking to where the sea and sky meet. He's seeing the future, or *a* future, one with fish and whales and, of course, phytoplankton and copepods—her copepods. She tries to think of an American way to say this—that he is a happy man who believes in a happy future. He is over the rainbow. Maybe he is over the moon. He is a fish in water. Or maybe a bridge over troubled water. That is a song she's heard.

Peter is grabbing his pad of paper. He's making a list. "Educate people. Invent and promote whale-safe fishing techniques. Make government create shipping corridors and speed zones to avoid whales. What else?"

"Stop pollution."

"Stop pollution." He writes it down.

"Include noise pollution."

"Got it. No more seismic explosions, no more military exercises in the gulf."

"Electric boats."

"Yes, convert the fishing fleet to battery-electric and hybrid engines, and alternative fuels. We can do that."

"The ferries too. And sports boats."

Peter continues to write--printing in capitals, underlining, circling, making the big dots he calls bullets.

Yulia is a scientist. Science is essential. Science is methodical and slow. In an emergency, there's not enough time for it. She will be on Peter's bridge, taking care of troubled water. No kicking the can. No steering clear. Not even a *mayday* shouting. There's no waiting for someone else to be the rescue.

"Organize other people," she says. "Fishermen and every other people."

Peter writes it down.[1]

---

1. To find out more see: https://www.greenstories.org.uk/anthol ogy-for-cop27/stories/come-and-help-me/

REFREEZE THE ARCTIC

by Steve Willis

A fter the meeting, we went to the little bar downstairs, an old-fashioned Japanese place, like Midnight Diner. We had been watching and discussing a presentation from the Cambridge Centre for Climate Repair about the melting of the Arctic and a sense of doom filled the air.

The rather dour British Professor had said, "As melting ice caps darken with water, sunlight is no longer being reflected back into space. What we feared for decades is happening. We've tipped over into a positive feedback loop, meaning our ice caps are melting faster and faster. Scarier still is the methane time bomb. Rising temperatures will cause this greenhouse gas, around eighty times more potent than carbon dioxide, to be released from the permafrost and the shallow Siberian Seas, tipping us into jungle planet mode, ending civilization as we know it."

We ordered some beer and fished around disconsolately for solutions. After half an hour, a short, older man with glasses approached me and asked for a word.

'What would YOU do about this, if you could?'

Emboldened by Sapporo, I ran our dream scheme past him. He asked a few questions. We pulled up a map. Sat at the bar and ordered more beer. Coming up to midnight, I'd missed the last train and was wondering where to crash for the night.

Ito San, for that was his name, had gone for a leak, and had urged me to wait.

There were four of us sat at the corner of the bar, waiting and finishing off the wasabi nuts.

When he returned, slightly unsteady on his feet, he sat down and considered each of us in turn, in silence. After a long moment, he said, 'I will pay.'

We started to thank him for the beer and his hospitality, and he said, 'No, no, no. I will pay for your magnificent plan. It is November. Can we have everything in place for February?'

So here we are, in northern Hokkaido. We'd been worrying about the weather forecast, but of course, climate change can bring cold weather forward as well as back. It has been freezing here for two weeks already. It's minus 20 today. The Okhotsk sea ice is due to arrive tomorrow.

All the equipment is set, and we are beyond excitement to start the work. Ito San is here, with his entourage and a camera crew to record the start of the work. The camera crew will remain with us for the two months of planned work. Ito industries have arranged all of the equipment and we have developed a series of scientific experiments which will explore our hypothesis.

The idea is simple. The Arctic ice is melting. In order to help manage climate change, we need to manage the melting of the ice. We will do that by simply making lots more ice – and we will do that by spraying huge volumes of sea water into freezing air and making new sea ice. Ito San has hired us an ice breaking tug, a crew and a series of water cannon, snow machines and other high power pumps with which to do the experiments. Ito San has been remarkably helpful, popping up at unexpected times while we made the arrangements.

He said last week 'This is the most fun I have ever had spending a million dollars – and I can get most of it back as a tax rebate! I'm almost embarrassed to reclaim it from the government!'

We have found that most people have bent over backwards to help us, pleased at the prospect of being involved in something that can actually make a difference to the climate crisis.

We are in Hokkaido because, for two months every year, there is a huge area of sea ice that comes down from the Sea of Okhotsk in Russia, though there is nothing hot about it! The sea ice is not persistent; it melts away completely as the weather warms, which makes it ideal for our trial work – no lasting harm can be done. We will make some areas of thickened ice, marked with food dye, and compare them with the naturally formed ice. This will allow us to calculate the longevity of the thickened ice, and to work out if it really could help in the Arctic.

This is stage 1 of the plan.

Stage 2. We're going to need a bigger boat. Up in Arctic waters, working the whole winter, thickening as much ice as possible and monitoring the new ice with satellites and drones.

The third stage would be a lot more boats and a series of new technologies we have been dreaming up to make thousands of square kilometres of thickened ice. This will help with albedo as well as so many other things.

Stage 4, insanely bold as it is, is to refreeze the high Arctic so that there is as much ice as there was at the end of the last ice age. This is a big man-made cooling block to balance the centuries of man-made heating. This huge reflective shield will be less damaging than the

SRM mini-Pinatubos that have been considered – the earth has had ice shields before, after all, and it will buy time.

Time. A resource we thought we had run out of.

I can't wait to get on that boat.

Ten years on

Murmansk Zeppelin Yard

Good morning. Andrei here. Ready for interview.

Yes, I can hear you. But my hearing is not so good. I will repeat your questions, so I am sure I answer the question you are asking.

Ice? You want to know about the ice? Now is the fire-fighting season, but yes, I can tell you about the ice. Ice is made in several different ways. There are hundreds of ice-hardened tugs which plough their own path through thin ice, spraying water high into the air, like the original trial that was done in Japan. Some are manned and some are big remote-controlled drones. They work in pods, or herds – like whales or walrus – so the broken ones can be recovered.

And there are the hundreds of zeppelins. Big airships. They fly further out with a large submersible pump on a hose which is also a cable and a powerline. Once on site, the pump is dropped through thin ice to act as a weighed but buoyant anchor and the long connecting hose is reeled out. The zeppelin switches propellers over so that they serve as power generators, and this provides electrical energy for the pump. The pump drives a large volume of water, approximately 100 metres back up the pipe and this sprays through freezing air onto ice below, thickening the ice.

The ice gets pretty thick, sometimes ten metres or more, so it can be difficult to get pump back out. To help this, line and top of pump can be electrically heated so that they melt their way out, but as you can imagine, we've lost a lot of pumps and several zeppelins doing this.

These zeppelins and pumps make clusters of large thick, man-made icebergs which last all the way through summer. The icebergs are much more resilient than first season, thin sea ice. We've been steadily increasing the amount of multi-year sea ice.

We have recently started freezing onshore lakes, either with a static pumping buoy on smaller lakes, or with a small zeppelin on bigger lakes. It is important that we find ways to reduce the melting of permafrost and associated methane release – we are in really serious trouble if that happens.

Who am I and where do I work?

I am an engineer working at Murmansk Ice Tug and Zeppelin yard. Not so many of us speak good English here, so I have been volunteered to speak to you. I am 65 years old and have been working on this yard since it opened nearly ten years ago. I came here from Sevastopol as a logistics specialist, supporting the growing fleet of ice-making tugs and the first of the zeppelins.

In this part of the yard, we repair zeppelins that work on ice restoration and firefighting. They work hard, so there are many repairs to do. Every week we receive new zeppelins from the Singapore Equatorial zeppelin yards. It sounds crazy to build zeppelins so far away and send them to the north, but when the wind blows and there is no more room in the hangars for broken zeppelins, we are relieved that there is some place in the world where it is possible to work without high winds. And that place is around the equator, in the doldrum belt.

There is another storm forecast today. I will need to go if the siren sounds.

How many zeppelins are there in Murmansk?

Sometimes many. Sometimes few. Today we have 407 in the wider control area. There are perhaps 2,000 in the big Arctic merry-go-round all together. It depends on the weather. The wind blows mostly from west to east in these northern latitudes. It takes a lot of energy to work back into the wind when it is strong, so the zeppelins move over to the next control station following the wind.

We have one old goose, number 401, that has been around the Arctic Circle five times over course of nine years. She is now dedicated as a parts lifter, so an easy, old lady duty, but still impressive. She has the Volvo lift gas compressor and trim control system which has been very reliable.

They come in three different sizes, which are all similar in design. They are as interchangeable as possible. The small ships like 401 do scouting, hose lifting, parts recovery and sometimes water shuttling. Medium sized craft do anchor handling, medium weightlifting, front line firefighting and the main ice work. These two sizes are all remote controlled. The largest zeppelins have a pilot on board and take crews out into field for ice and fire work. We also use them to get to crash sites to recover parts from zeppelins that have failed to return to base.

How is this operation paid for?

The Murmansk based Arctic Circle operation peat fires work alone prevents around 100 million tonnes of greenhouse gas release each year. Most of the money that funds our work comes from carbon credits created by putting out peat fires and forest fires. It is monitored closely by satellite and calculation done to determine the amount of GHG that would have been released with no control compared to the release with the intervention. There are also albedo credits, from the ice restoration, but they don't raise as much money as the fire fighting. Fire is easier to understand.

How many are lost each year?

Tricky. Twenty or more. We pick up most of the damaged ships and get them back into service, so they don't count. When a zeppelin is on a risky job firefighting, or in heavy weather, a pre-planned crash site is chosen and programmed into onboard control system. This is a tree-free, cleared space with firm enough ground to work and for heavy parts not to sink into the peat. There are hundreds of these planned crash sites around the Arctic. When a zeppelin goes down over the ice, we try get to it before the melt, though we do lose more up there.

Do you go out?

Yes, during spring and summer we are out every week. There is a winters' worth of parts to collect. It is always sad arriving at a crash site, with ribs poking in the air and fabric flapping in the wind. We try to see ourselves as repairers of broken toys, rather than vultures picking over carcasses of mighty steeds, but it is tricky sometimes, especially when there has been a fire on impact and forest has burned.

We recover engines, batteries, the compressor and trim control, lifting gear, hoses and any of the water bags that are still usable. All main parts are waterproof and impact resistant and have a marker buoy on them which helps find sunken pieces and lift them out of the mud and soft permafrost. We often have to call in a small zeppelin to lift and schlurp pieces out of the deep mud before re-strapping and sending the parts back to base. We collect loose fabric, ribs and other parts to keep sites tidy and store material for later pickup.

What is it like out there?

Flying out over the permafrost? It is incredible. So empty. So peaceful. And Taiga, the endless Siberian forest. Mysterious. Mythical. Beautiful. When we land, it is a bit more challenging. After June the mosquitoes are unbelievable. We have to wear mesh hoods to work. I keep thinking 'what do they eat when they can't get Hobbit!' That was a good movie, but not as good as the Russian language original. . We pick our way up to crash sites, and it is like crossing the planet Hoth. We go in spring, so the weather can be rough. We've had to retreat to other control stations many times, and we've even ended up in Alaska after one angry storm chased us north over the Pole.

Who flies the zeppelins?

Zeppelins are large drones, flown by remote control. We have some pilots here – they work from those grey buildings next to the hangers, but there are pilots all around the world. This drone control technology was developed for the military, of course, but is ideal for this work. There is some automated control for transit flights, but for actual firefighting, zeppelins are under direct control by a real pilot. It reduces losses. When the zeppelins are working with ground teams, there is very close control and communication along with several backups to ensure that operations are as safe as possible.

What is the lift gas?

We would wish to use helium for the fleet, but there just isn't enough in world, too rare. And it is too valuable for other things to be used for a rough duty like this. Manned zeppelins are filled with helium, but everything else is hydrogen. To be honest, hydrogen doesn't give too much trouble – even the original zeppelins in the 1900's didn't have many problems and travelled huge distances quite safely. We've only had a few isolated Hindenburg incidents through millions of hours of operation. We've recently started experimenting with steam as a lift gas. I thought it sounded crazy, but now I think we might be able to get it to work. It could be a very useful supplement to existing systems.

How many negative emissions and how does it work?

The whole Arctic Circle operation is approaching one gigatonne per year of negative emissions. A remarkable achievement. A remarkable collaboration.

But we must remember, every single thing we do has a carbon footprint. If we drink a milky coffee together, that is one kilo of CO_2. There is a huge industry making, delivering and serving that product to us. There needs to be a matching industry somewhere that does a negative one kilogram emission to match every single one kilogram emission we make. Can you imagine how vast that industry needs to be? No. Neither can I.

We use two main mechanisms to refreeze the Arctic, latent heat of fusion and albedo enhancement, but it's complicated, and I don't have time to tell you now – my colleague is banging on the window.

The way forward?

So now countries are working more together. Not enough together, but better than before. And not before time. The west is finally building renewables at the proper rate. Hydrocarbon usage is finally falling. At long last.

The eight countries of the Arctic Circle work closely together to fight fires and freeze ice – we have to cooperate, because the prevailing wind from west to east makes it impossible to work in isolation. This ice rebuilding and firefighting operation is now huge, approaching a gigatonne a year of negative or prevented emissions as well as restored albedo, and needs to be at least four times bigger.

Remarkably, peat fire prevention, biochar and ice albedo carbon credits cover much of the cost of the operation. Who would have thought that restoring the planet might be self-funding?

How is a fire fought?

Fighting the forest fires and peat fires is the main work of the zeppelin fleet, in the summer season.

Ah – the siren has sounded. We all have to go out now and tie down the zeppelins. Everyone has to help secure the fleet: cook, priest, bottle washer. Even old engineers like me. There is a big storm coming through that might shut us down for weeks – call me then. I must go now. Speak another day.

Do Svidaniya.[1]

---

1. Interested to know more about climate solutions included? See https://www.greenstories.org.uk/anthology-for-cop27/solutions/refreeze-the-arctic/ and

https://www.greenstories.org.uk/anthology-for-cop27/solutions/refreeze-the-glaciers/

GROUND UP

by Elizabeth Kurucz

"The soil is the great connector of lives, the source and destination of all. It is the healer and restorer and resurrector, by which disease passes into health, age into youth, death into life. Without proper care for it we can have no community, because without proper care for it we can have no life."
~ *Wendell Berry, "The Unsettling of America"*[1]

My oldest kin were in the soil. So many relations, all of them holding tight together, rich, like chocolate cake moistened with beetroot and no need for second helpings.

Dust bowl dirt never wearied this land anymore. It blew over our house for years, a relentless cloud of misery from nearby fields deserted by neighbours who had surrendered to the not so common wisdom of agrochemical companies. These engrained habits were a loan made against future generations that could never be repaid; a thought, a shadow, a plague that passed over us and slowly dissipated. We came to the brink but were spared the ruin of our own topsoil.

---

1. Published by Counterpoint LLC, 2015

The day a defensive lineman broke through our formation and threw me to the ground, tearing the pelvic muscles from my hip bones, I knew it was over. I didn't need to see the x-rays; I could feel that my body was broken for good. The last two operations in my freshman and sophomore years had created a weakness that the surgeon had warned me would never fully heal. He said the best he could do now was to patch me up. He told me to forget about my bowl game dreams and pray that the stitching would heal well enough for me to go early in the draft, but I'd given up on church years earlier and the scouts sniffed it out at the combine.

Undrafted. Cut loose. A washed-up star college quarterback, a has-been whose sorry bones refused to carry him to the professional ranks. It's still painful to recall. The price I paid to end up damaged goods. The realization of what I'd done and where I'd been. A pariah with former teammates and old friends. Everyone steered clear of me, afraid of some voodoo that might infect them too. I was the unhappy ending no one wanted to believe was possible.

Cut off from my supply of adoration and medication, unable to go backward or forward, I had no Plan B, no energy to push against the current trajectory of my life for an uncertain future I wasn't sure I wanted. It took an overdose on opioids laced with fentanyl and the thankful grace of a roommate who called 911 to begin my painful journey of self-discovery and agricultural repair.

The more I think about it these days, the more I realize there was always someone trying to wring one last ounce of something out of me.

Except for Amy.

In my earliest memories, we are playing together in the mud, walking barefoot, letting it squish up high, soft mountains in between our toes. We liked the sticky feeling and the sounds that accompanied us as we hopped our way around the farm. We hid from well-meaning adults who tried in vain to reunite us with our rainboots. When the sun came back out, we were fascinated by deep cracks that had formed on the hard surface and imagined ourselves on another planet. I didn't know why it made my mom cry, but I could tell there was a problem in our paradise.

Later I understood; how this hard shell on the surface of the earth ensured the runoff of the next downpour, setting up the cycle of flood and drought that our community knew so well. It was a time when rain in our county provoked as much grief as celebration; a thirst in the land that a history of bad farming practices guaranteed would never be quenched.

"Jake," Amy sighed, drawing out her response in no particular hurry. "You know I'm just gonna keep telling you this until it sinks in your hard head." I laughed as she knocked playfully on my temple: "you'll realize soon enough that everything you ever needed was right here all along."

She started telling me this in high school, while I was boldly sharing plans for my great escape from Peosta, a town whose proud claim that it was in the 'middle of everywhere' left me unconvinced. I postured with the bravado of a card player who'd been dealt a bad hand and was still going all in. Amy could see right through me. We walked home together then, sometimes holding hands if the feelings were flowing both ways, but never more than that. She had a good nature and good sense. I've never seen anyone prettier; not then or since. She had everything that was going to get in the way of where I wanted to go. One day I slipped through those deep cracks in the ground and rode a river of topsoil out of there, fast.

Amy came to visit me in the hospital, but only once. I pretended to sleep while she cried beside me. I was too ashamed to look at her, for her to see me; to admit what I had become. She whispered one sentence in my ear before she left, pressing a small bag in my hand, and squeezing it tight with her fingers wrapped warmly over mine.

"Jake Hutter, here's the cure for your *solastalgia.*"

I could have grabbed her and kissed her right there. I could have pleaded for her to forgive what I was, how weak and stupid I had been. But I wasn't strong enough then to own up to what I didn't yet understand.

I'm ashamed now to admit that the tremor of excitement I felt holding the pouch was not innocent. I was hoping in my delusion of withdrawal that she had, in a great act of compassion, given me some magical elixir, a tonic that that could erase all my pain in in one clear snort. When she was barely down the hallway, I eagerly tore it open, sniffing hard, agitated, tasting the contents inside. I shook my head and my eyes teared up; the sensation was overpowering; smelling salts that woke me to the purpose of my life.

I stayed up all night, inhaling the aroma of the damp soil, running my fingers through it, placing it on my tongue, letting it roll to the back of my throat and dissolve in my cheek. This was pure stuff, wholesome, organic. There was no contamination from nearby industry, no taste of fertilizer, pesticides, or insecticides to be found. Dark and sumptuous, the smell slightly sweet with the aroma of geosmin, I instantly recognized this native prairie soil. It was taken from the small, undisturbed lot preserved by my great grandad and generations since, unaffected by and unconnected to our modern operations. It had been covered by perennials for thousands of years, before he had arrived with his wagon and family in tow, setting up homestead in Peosta; it was a font of ecological knowledge, an open classroom offering enlightenment for any farmer who cared to pay attention.

I hadn't listened to Amy's advice in those early years or heard the voice of the land. The road out of town had been made easy for me. Exploiting my natural athletic talents was simpler than the alternative; a punishing drama of pretending to make a living amidst the carefully arranged hardships of annual agriculture. It had become a way of life that produced a clear return for agrochemical companies in exchange for a lifetime of servitude from farmers who honoured their exponentially accumulating debts.

At college it was further simplified: physical risk yields instant rewards. Bowls of opioids, like my great-aunt's candy dish, made readily accessible on the desk of my equally accommodating football coach. His comforting assurances justified a regular habit of filling my pockets with a quarterback's little helper, no up-front payment required. There was more relief in those pills than the best protection a 300-pound offensive lineman could offer. I was there after all to contribute, to compete, to help my team. The less I was on the field the less productive I could be. If we didn't win, it hung on my shoulders alone, a heavy burden to carry. The lion's share of glory was channelled my way when we prevailed. My teammates wordlessly accumulated their own lifetime of injuries, as I executed the game plan.

That blissful fog: nothing had compared to it before or since, quickly taking all my pain away on a cloud that never let me touch the ground. On game day when I had to be clean, the cheering crowd carried me through. And those girls; the jam on my sandwich that I greedily devoured. I used them up too, pretending I was their ticket out of nowhere. I suppose I was too high then to remember or to care.

I stirred restlessly for the next 24 hours in a fever of torment and wicked dreams. When I awoke, I felt for the first time in years, a flicker of possibility that came from my heart. I wanted to fan it into a fire before I stood up to argue for my future. I didn't say anything to anyone about it. I suppose I didn't know what could be said. Everything that had been done couldn't be undone. I had no real reason for hope, but reason wasn't my purpose, reason didn't drive me to change my life. It was that word, that one mysterious word that Amy had whispered to me before she left. *Solastalgia.* It was her promise that the soil could cure what ailed me. It was her ability to see my best self, beyond the broken person I'd become.

I would have laughed myself out of the room with those sentimental thoughts when I left for Cedar Rapids after high school, but I didn't judge things so harshly anymore. Experience had taught me that I needed the mercy of idealism more than a shield of cynicism. Amy planted a seed of possibility in a deeper place than I could reach. I let it grow its way toward me. I watered it with an aquifer of my own unshed tears until I felt like I had something inside of me again; something to give.

Time slowed down after that, a gift that offered me the chance to make sense of a journey that had taken me so far away from where I knew now that I needed to be. I tried to recall just when the ties between me and my home had finally severed, the moment where I moved from dreams and plans to the action of exodus. It was a clean break on the surface but a more gradual inner transformation. Amy had been accepted on academic scholarship to the University of Iowa the same year I was recruited to join their football program. I lost touch with her when I decided to move to student housing in Cedar Rapids and she stayed at home to help with the farm. I would see her on campus from time to time as she headed into the Developmental Psychology lab close to our practice facility at the athletic centre. I wanted more from life than a constant reminder of the limits of my prospects, so I kept my head down and my feet moving.

The day I bumped into her, knocking her books from her arms when I turned, laughing, from a crowd of friends scheming to skip class, startled me. It shattered the independent picture of myself I was creating, reflected on my junior year football card; the one where I appeared to be ascending into the clouds with light streaming behind me, some sort of football Jesus, my polished helmet gleaming in the sun.

"Jake," she had said, with surprise and a kind smile. Just my name, no other comments, no 'how are you doing?', no updates from home. I wasn't sure how to respond. On the surface it was nothing, but in the absence of small talk it felt profound, like she was calling me out, calling me home. I had an anxious moment of self-conscious awareness. I thought about how different things might have been if I had allowed myself to be vulnerable in that moment, instead of steeling my heart against any personal epiphanies. Amy looked at me and I felt revealed, seen, right through to my inner core that the armour of my football gear had closely hid.

I helped her to pick up her things, muttering a quick apology as I jogged to catch up with my crew. I remember the look on her face. Not judging, but hurt, or, maybe disappointed, by how bluntly I moved on, barely acknowledging her presence. I shook off the feeling later with my friends at the bar. A few beers, some oxycodone, a couple of percocets. I was riding high above the ground again and thoughts of Amy retreated to some distant corner of my mind.

After that encounter I completely silenced the last bit of her echoing voice that had followed me on the 151-S from Peosta to Cedar Rapids. I blunted it with painkillers and replaced it with adrenaline generated by a deep animosity directed at my enemies on the field, kids from other colleges who were obstacles in the path of where I was headed. No one was going to send me back to that place where I was treated like dirt, a local hick who didn't know shit, someone stupid enough to suffer at the hands of agriculture and never earn a living.

I suppose football gave me a sense of pride, although I can't recall it now. In my senior year I earned the starter spot and played with a furious intensity to ensure I kept it. My coach fed off my rage, converting it into raucous locker room celebrations where I was held up as an example of what any man should aspire to become: focused, heartless, vicious. "Tear his head off and throw it back in his face" was our pre-game chant, breaking out of the huddle to act out our 'eye-for-an-eye' brutality as results piled up in the win column. I took no sacks until the last game that season, my uniform was spotless. Dirt was the great equalizer of all relations and steering clear from it was my chosen path forward.

I don't know exactly why I decided to return to the farm when I was finally released from the hospital. It would have been easier to move somewhere entirely new, to make a fresh start. Was it a sense of unfinished business? A retreat to lick my wounds? The hope that some scrap of a world I once believed in might still remain? The sound of *solastalgia* stirred in my brain, the diagnosis Amy had whispered that night; a kiss on her lips that was waiting to be collected somewhere else.

My dad didn't know much about regenerative systems or permaculture practices and never taught me any of those ways. He'd never cared too much for the plow himself, but it wasn't from a commitment to no-till. When I crawled back home, away from the wreckage of my college dreams, there was an apathy that settled in between us, replacing the eager conversations of my youth; old ambitions sparked by Friday night high school football games that had fuelled our hope of a different future.

"Jake," he would say to me with his shoulders hanging down, burdened by his role as a harbinger of doom. "It's a useless struggle, I tell you. All a farmers' life and money...devoured, gone, eaten up fighting against drought, pestilence, and disease. Truth be told, it's more of a punishment than a way of living."

He didn't speak to me about my plans anymore and in return I didn't pretend to have any. I sat in the dark for the first few months, brooding on what I'd lost, trying to understand why I was there and what to do next. In hindsight I suppose it was my first attempt to listen to the needs of our landscape and to allow our farm to adapt to my new choice of practices.

After weeks of debating my next step, I picked up the phone and called Amy. My fingers dialled her number without thinking; it hadn't changed. I was relieved to hear her answer and eagerly demanded more information.

"*Solastalgia*, Amy, what did you mean? Why did you say that dirt was the cure?"

She was angry.

"Is that what you think I gave you? Dirt? Dirt is soil without life Jake. I didn't give you no bag of dirt."

Her hard reply caught me by surprise.

"And how dare you call me up and ask me the answer for anything? What about, 'how have you been'? What about 'I'm sorry for being such an asshole to you and everyone else I've been treating like nothing more than dirt since I left town.'"

I sat in silence, realizing that she was right. I was so urgently in need of something to preserve myself. I hadn't taken a second to think of anyone else for a very long time.

"I'm sorry Amy, it's just that..."

She interrupted my feeble apology with a swift rebuke.

"All our lives you've come to me for inspiration whenever you need a quick fix; like I'm some font of knowledge or comfort. Then you hide from me when you're hell bent on doing whatever stupid thing you've decided to want next."

Her words stung but I didn't interrupt. I was hearing something that I had never heard before, that I was finally ready to hear.

"I'm not some ideal you have of mother nature or the girl next door; some breast you can burrow in to make everything wholesome and good again. And I'm not here to be a passive, loving mirror reflecting your best image. So, stop running away from me whenever you realize something about yourself you don't like."

"Amy, I'm really sorry."

"Jake, forget sorry. This is much bigger than any apology. You've got to turn your eyes out from your own damn self and see everything that you have around you. I'm a human being with real feelings. We were friends. Call me when you figure that out."

Her voice cracked and I was left alone with a dial tone. I listened to that high pitched sound for over an hour to avoid the pain of silence that I knew would shake my body when I put the receiver back in the base.

I started my new journey that afternoon with some simple research on the computer before I immersed myself in the ecosystem of our farm that would become my best teacher. Solastalgia, it turned out, wasn't so cryptic after all. I only had to look.

A philosopher had come up with the word to describe a special kind of ecological grief, feelings of nostalgia, desolation, and yearning for solace. It was the constant homesickness that I felt even when I was at home, an anxiety that was provoked... because my home environment had been changed or even destroyed.

When my grandad died in my first year of high school, my dad's own best intentions got in between me and my healthy soil relations. Everything my grandad had taught me in those early days on the farm was quickly replaced with my dad's own ideas: a college degree in agribusiness, a football scholarship to pay for it and large-scale production opportunities that would follow. It was as if my grandad's passing had released the pressure built up in our enterprise, the gradual decline in profit and yield over a lifetime of work. In the absence of any viable alternatives, my dad was completely signed up for the modern program: GMOs, nitrogen-based fertilizers, pesticides, fungicides, and herbicides. US farm policy was an invisible hand that firmly shaped my life, more than nature or nurture.

I wasn't like my father, running from the past. I had believed that there was good in my grandad's operations, but he had no vision of how to bring the best of those old days forward to change the future.

It had been naïve, or perhaps more truthfully, ignorant, to think that Amy would take each step with me, that I could use her to do the inner work that needed to be done, all the stuff I didn't want to face up to. She was right to hang up on me, to cut me off from a line to more excuses and delays. I realized that soon after and was grateful for the gift she had given me; a caring nudge in the right direction.

Looking back on it from a clearer vantage point today, I suppose my saving grace was my senses. I liked the smell of dirt and sweat, the communion of working with others who were close to the soil. Even playing football, when the exaltation of a good performance made me feel that I couldn't get further from where I'd come, I knew that I couldn't throw a pass unless my feet were planted firmly on the ground. It seemed to be some intuition of my future survival.

Over the days and years that followed, I grew to realize something Amy already knew when we were back in high school. Football wasn't my dream. It was a compromise, brokered by my father, as a way out of our old life, a vehicle through a dying landscape that was going to hog shit around us all. My dad wanted me to use my physical talents to make my way toward a new future, one where I could run the machinery, but he hadn't counted on me getting ground up in the gears. It helped when I figured that out, to know that I hadn't lost the core of what he and I were both after, only the map of how to get there.

I didn't call on Amy again until I had something to show her, something that would prove I'd really listened. The word she had whispered haunted me for years, it was a companion to my reparations to the soil, my first act of care. It was more than a strong breeze blowing through the farm that carried me back days after that phone call to the place where my granddad's plow once stood. It was...I'm still not sure entirely what it was. But I know that I heard voices, as if there was a crowd in the stadium again, anticipating a Hail Mary pass in the fourth quarter. I knew what I needed to do, the conviction of my own prime directive to care for the land, for people, for justice. There was no workaround, no quick fix. There was no easy dodge to forget the misery I'd felt and that I'd caused. I had to go straight through. I needed to rebuild my soil relations slowly, one small action after another offering proof of the integrity of my choices.

The problem of the plow was that it was the start of all this trouble. It went well back to some early advice from old books and outdated ideas of how to meet nature head on and show it who was boss. To the violent energy that called men to tear up the structure of the soil, to do their own bidding, to ignore the wisdom of the earth, to challenge the intelligence of seeds that knew where to plant themselves, to wipe out perennials that grew naturally under tree crops whose yield was easy and full. An order to annually destroy all of creation in a misguided effort to endlessly increase yield.

This 'agriculture of eradication' that became the neighbourly approach, every living being annihilated until an eerie stillness set across fields that no longer buzzed with pollinators or pests. The deafening silence of a death zone my dad had affectionately referred to as 'the farm'. I threw it out, all of it, that day I hung up the phone with Amy. No till, no chemicals, no assault on ecological rules. It was the purest feeling of longing that filled my heart, desire without any shame. I felt patient and unstoppable. I burned for the land with an unrelenting need, to be close to the earth was my only preoccupation. These amends I made were preparations of a sort, opening myself to receive her love.

This was the reconciliation that took place before the restoration of a devastated landscape. I could sense I was coming through to the straightaway from a long corner I'd been turning for years. The lure of old habits was manageable now, firmly entangled in these carefully established roots. And now this scene I surveyed today, a diversity of perennials: fruit and nut trees, vines, berries, and fungi. A cropping system that was both wild pollinator habitat and conservation practice; the lushness and abundance was staggering. I was no longer trying to outproduce my ecology.

May Basket Day. It was a day filled with simple pleasures and manageable adversities. I put together the traditional Iowan offering of flowers that were meant to be delivered to a neighbour in a carefully arranged hamper. As kids we had served as willing couriers, dropping our gifts to each other, and then running away before the messenger could be seen. I placed the basket on the step and rang Amy's doorbell, retreating around the corner. When she came out for the delivery, I re-appeared before her, standing my ground, hat in hand, asking her to hear me out.

"I've prepared the soil. I've gone as far as I can on my own Amy. I'm asking you now because I still don't have the cure. Can you help me?"

Amy took my hand and led me behind her house, across the short-cut to our farm, to where she had seen me work from season to season, patiently waiting for what she believed in, for what she knew would emerge with time. She stopped in the middle of the landscape that I had carefully rebuilt with the guidance of ecological wisdom and turned toward me.

"The cure is simple Jake. I can't help you alone, but I can help us. The cure...it's not in me, Jake. It's not in you either. It's between us, between all of us; it's in our relations," she smiled, planting herself gently into the damp ground, soil so rich with dark organics it appeared a purplish black.

Her body was a revelation, reclining on the bed that nature had made, the work done by a billion microbes, plants, an ecology that was pulling together effortlessly in the direction we needed to go.

I don't know why I ever fought so hard against such generous help. I just couldn't see it, I suppose. My spirit had been drained by a world that believed in linear pathways, but it was revitalized that night in the cycles of the soil; nature repaired herself and Amy and I followed.

Rain fell, slowly on us at first, then much harder. It absorbed easily into the porous soil that could finally receive its relief. We were heady with delirious anticipation, building from the ground up. The fertility of the earth had returned, and we were in it. [2]

---

2. Interested to know more about climate solutions included? See https://www.greenstories.org.uk/anthology-for-cop27/solutions/sustainable-farming-2/

FRACKERS

by Martin Hastie and Steve Willis

*I*n New South Wales, underneath Burning Mountain, an eternal
flame smoulders. For six thousand years it has been alight, one hundred feet below the sandstone ground. The flame symbolises no religion
nor commemorates anything of any cultural significance. All day and
all night, it burns. If we do not do something about it, it will outlive us
all.

In Arlene's Bar, the mood had been glum even before Mick and
Clive shambled in and brought it down a notch or two further.

'You better not be thinking of driving that pickup home,' said
Arlene as the boys ordered their third beers, the first two having been
dealt with in no more than a few swift gulps. Arlene was a welcoming
hostess and a loyal confidante, but she could adopt the tone of a
fearsome headmistress at will. A sign above the kitchen door read,
'*Complaints must be submitted in triplicate, countersigned by the last
two Popes and their wives...*'

'Nah,' said Mick. 'The old lady said, "Go get Clive, and don't come back 'til you've had a skinful. Me and the dog'll pick you up in the ute come closing time."'

'Your old ute? Is that thing still on the road?'

'Just about. I'm not sure it should be, but we're in the middle of nowhere, what can you do?'

'And your Mother's had her cataract op?'

'Nah,' said Mick. 'I reckon the dog does most of the seeing for the two of them. It growls if she gets too close to the edge and barks if there's a 'roo in the road. But they get about just fine."

The blood abandoned Clive's face at the thought of a hair-raising lift home. However, the more he considered it, the more it seemed like a risk worth taking.

'Well after this week,' he said mournfully, 'I'm past caring anyway.'

'You drilled your last gas gathering well?' said Mick.

'Yup.'

'Not paid off the loan on the rig?'

'Not even close.'

'No better here, either. Our well-services company ships out next week.'

'Back on the scrap heap again?'

'Looks like it.'

The sonorous clunk of the Swiss cow bell above the door shook them from their doleful rumination.

'Thank God for that,' said Arlene. 'What a misery fest! Let's hope it's somebody with good news to share.'

But the newcomer was not somebody with good news to share. It was Donna, Arlene's niece, whose usually cheerful countenance had been replaced with a face like thunder. She had just returned from

Sydney, where an interview for a carbon credit company had ended in sheer frustration.

'Seems they had a preferred candidate all along,' she grumbled, her fingers stretched around the body of a cocktail glass, inside which was her tipple of choice, a red-and-blue Firecracker. 'So why even bother asking me to interview?'

'Tell me about these carbon credits,' said Mick. 'I've always been curious about them. What are the biggest opportunities?'

'Long term, high-permanence carbon credits,' said Donna. 'There's a terrible shortage and they trade for ridiculous prices.'

'What counts as a good carbon credit?'

'Biochar. Mineralisation. Not much else. They both store carbon in the ground for hundreds of years – and improve the soil at the same time. Pretty cool.'

Clive raised his head from its position side-down on the bar.

'So, Donna, here's a thought. Could we get carbon credits if we were able to shut down a long-term source of CO_2?' Mick asked.

'Maybe. Things like that depend on protocols being in place. But there are loads of new ones being written all the time.'

'So could we put out coal seam fires? Like the one that's been burning for thousands of years down the road at Wingen there, at Burning Mountain?'

'I don't know. Maybe, I guess.'

'So,' said Mick, 'spinning off the top of my head...how's this for a plan? We're going drilling. Drilling for carbon credits.'

'What the hell are you talking about?" asked Clive. 'Maybe it's time to call your old mother to pick us up. You've drunk too much already.'

'Hear me out,' said Mick, warming to his theme. 'I've been thinking about this for a while. We drill, right? We're born to drill. So we're going to do some drilling that helps stop unnecessary emissions and helps slow down the climate crisis. It's a crazy job and it seems no one is doing it. But we can.'

Mick moved over to the games area, grabbed some chalk, wiped the darts scoreboard clean and began to doodle illustrations of the plan he was forming. 'We can get hold of some of the unused fracking rigs and go to these sites with thousands of tonnes of water. I reckon if the Macondo well can be blocked – the one on that Deepwater Horizon incident – we can put out coal seam fires. They're much shallower.'

A small crowd began to form, alerted by the fervour of Mick's performance. Spurred on by his audience, he hoisted a leg and pulled himself up on to the pool table.

'It's a perfect job for us.' He raised a pool cue triumphantly aloft. 'It's a directional driller's dream!'

'Hey!' yelled Arlene. 'Get the hell down off the table or you'll pay for a new one.'

'Sorry,' said Mick, climbing down. 'Got a little carried away there.'

'Yeah, yeah,' said Clive. 'It all sounds very lovely and everything, but no one's been putting out these fires for ever. Why now?'

'Because world-wide they release 400 million tonnes of CO_2 every year. For no good reason. There's no gain, no economic benefit. They just burn because it's not worth anyone's while to put them out. So we'll drill these wells from the side into the bottom of the seams, store up a load of water – truck it in if necessary – and then big fracking pumps will push in masses of water to flood the bottom of the seam. They'll make a load of steam which will gradually cool down the coal, push out the air and help it go out. For the tough wells, we'll add a load of liquid nitrogen or CO_2 if necessary.'

Clive remained sceptical. 'And who's gonna pay for all this?'

'Right... We get one of these smart climate consultancy crews to write us a set of fancy carbon credit protocols. Is that feasible, Donna?'

'Sure. The really good credits earn $100 per tonne or more, but even a cheap one might be $5 or $10. There's a global shortage of decent long term permanent carbon credits. So many companies have committed to net zero with no idea of how it's going to be achieved.'

'For our purposes,' continued Mick, 'some of the larger sites are doing hundreds of thousands of tonnes per year for decades. Pointless, massive, endless fires releasing CO_2 and methane releases for absolutely no positive purposes – crazy. At $10 per tonne for ten years of avoided emissions, each site might be worth tens of millions of bucks. That's more than we earn on a conventional fracking job. We get paid for putting out coal seam fires and preventing unnecessary emissions. Avoided emissions like that are surely almost as good as sequestering CO_2 captured from the air? We'll start with the smaller jobs to learn the necessary skills and extend to progressively larger jobs. We'll use satellites to find the sites and assess the emissions and small local seismic to assess the ground.'

He could tell that Clive was coming round to the idea, his friend's face beginning to contort itself into a vision of intrigue and contemplation.

'We can do this,' said Clive, banging his fist onto the bar for emphasis. 'We can get all the down hole temperature tools and other fancy oil field gear. And here's an interesting trick we can try – we can dissolve CO_2 in the water at high pressure. Although it flashes in the seam, the inert CO_2 will really help snuff out the fire. We can totally do this!'

Mick grabbed a beer mat and asked Arlene for a pen.

'Here's a thought. When I was younger, I was part of a start-up company. We followed a book called 'The Beermat Entrepreneur.'

So what's say we do the same thing this time. We've got the four core founders: Arlene, bar owner – you can be our CFO. Me – sales and commercial. Clive – drilling and technical. Donna – carbon credits.'

He scribbled his thoughts down onto the beer mat and laid in on the bar for the other three key players to see.

Find coal seam fires

Set up a carbon credit route

Find a backer

Hire rig teams or use ours

Send experts to site

Size CO_2 leak with GHGSat

Put out fires

Claim Carbon Credits

Repeat.

'We can give ourselves six months to find a backer to fund the operation,' said Clive. 'It doesn't have to happen overnight.'

'As you know, I don't give credit,' said Arlene, 'but as we're now partners, I'll let you run a food tab at the bar.'

'We can aim to work eight hours a day,' said Clive, 'whenever suits, but with some core hours when we're together to encourage us to actually do some work rather than mess about all day.'

'Great idea! You boys can come here to the bar, 10 til 12, have lunch here. Only from the healthier option menu, though – you could both stand to lose a few pounds. You can have the big table in the window facing the road. No one usually sits there in the day anyway.'

"So now we've got an office, lunch and working hours, almost like a regular job.'

'Just need a school bus,' said Clive.

'No worries,' said Mick. 'There's a pile of old bikes in our barn we can use. We don't even have to buy gas.'

More drinks were poured as they began to thrash out the details. Arlene slid newly refilled glasses across the bar in quick succession, Firecrackers for Donna, beers for Mick and Clive.

'When I was in college,' said Donna, 'we ran a team through. They had a great boot camp programme which took us through all the basic stages and questions for starting a company and bringing on a climate solution. This ticks a lot of the boxes.'

'Is it still going?' asked Clive. 'And isn't it just for students?'

'Not at all,' said Donna. 'There were some ancient teams on the programme.' She looked at Mick and Clive and hurriedly added, 'No offence. And yes – not only is it still going, but submissions for the next round close in six weeks!'

'So I guess the key question is how big will the climate impact be?' wondered Donna. 'In the cold light of day, most of the solutions submitted to these things are next to pointless. Sorry if that sounds a bit harsh, but it's true.'

'We could reach the gigatonne scale,' said Clive, his excitement increasing by the second. 'I'm convinced of it. If there really is 400 million tonnes of CO_2 released from coal seam fires, we could aim to do a steadily growing percentage of that amount. It might not be easy to hit a gigatonne a year, but I can certainly imagine a cumulative gigatonne, no problem at all.'

'So what do we need to cover in our application, Donna?" asked Mick.

'Beachheads, customer discovery, 'The Deal', what's the process, financials, potential size of the market, job and social impact, technology potential and the quality of the pitch.'

'Not much then!' said Arlene. 'Maybe I should pour some more drinks.'

'We can do it,' said Clive. 'I know we can do it. The beachhead would be coal seam fires here in Oz, then fires in Indonesia which isn't so far, and then the rest of the world using partner teams.'

'The Deal is always a tricky one,' said Donna. 'But for this it might be 'stopping pointless CO_2 emissions for high quality carbon credits.'

'So all we need is a name,' said Mick.

Donna's eureka moment came as she took a sip of her Firecracker. She cried out 'Fire Frackers!'

And that was where it all began.

A few more rounds were drunk in celebration. Nobody could remember a time when Arlene's Bar had been so lively and buoyant. Arlene astonished everyone by announcing that drinks were on the house. Eventually, though, even Mick and Clive reached their limit.

'Look at the time,' said Mick. 'Shall I call my old mother to pick us up?'

'You know,' said Clive, 'I was completely downhearted when I came in, and now I feel on top of the world. I just can't wait until tomorrow so we can get started.'

He downed the last of his remaining drink.

'So I think, all things considered, it might be better if we ordered a taxi.'

If we can extinguish an eternal flame, we can achieve anything.[1]

---

1. Interested to know more about climate solutions included? See https://www.greenstories.org.uk/anthology-for-cop27/solutions/coal-seam-firefighting-2/

THE ASSASSIN

by D.A. Baden

*T*his is a stand-alone story that draws on two characters from the novel Habitat Man

SARAH

Sarah guessed who the caller was before she looked at her phone. On the day she'd achieved her life's ambition, of course the person she missed most would come calling.

'Congratulations,' said her partner – ex partner's – voice on the phone. The tone belied the sentiment.

'Thanks,' said Sarah, cradling the phone to her ear. She paused, wondering what to say. This was new territory – were they now friends? Her feelings were still too raw for that.

'You got your way then. Calling them citizen juries, not assemblies?'

'That's because they now have full legislative authority. This will be a game changer for the climate crisis.' Sarah couldn't help the excitement creeping into her voice. A mistake.

'Let's hope they work. You've sacrificed enough to get this far.'

'I sacrificed us, you mean?'

'Yes.'

The words hurt. She wanted to blurt out a stream of lies just to get her back. Lies like, I'll be around more, there will be time for a family after all. But she'd be spending even more time away, immersed in closed rooms, shepherding groups towards climate solutions that might just save humanity.

'It's not just about ambition. I'm trying to—'

'Save the planet, I know. Anything I asked of you, it's my selfish demands getting in the way of you saving the bloody world.'

'That's not how I feel, please...' Sarah pleaded, not even sure what she was asking for. 'This will make the difference. Don't you see? Citizens' juries now have real power.'

'As will you.'

'Don't be like that.' This was why they'd split up. This constant implication that she was in it for the glory.

'Just make it work. That will be our consolation.' There was a click and nothing.

Sarah put her head in her hands and slumped in her chair. She snapped back upright when her colleague appeared at the door, beaming.

'Have you seen the social media?' he asked.

'Is it good?'

'Mental!'

'Everyone's desperate for hope,' Sarah said.

'After the fiascos in politics, they reckon that this might be the silver bullet.'

'No pressure then!' she said wryly.

'Have you sent out all the summons?'

'Yup,' said Sarah.

'I got you an auditor who can keep track of the costs and benefits of each decision.'

'Have you sourced a knitter?'

'No, I got you a meditation specialist.'

'I put in for the knitter,' she protested.

A research team had funds to compare different formats of juries to hone the process, but Sarah hadn't been convinced of the meditation one.

'You want to be on the winning team, Sarah. Mindfulness, meditation, that's where it's at.'

'The conservative types will see a guy in an orange robe and dismiss it as a 'woke' thing.'

'Don't be ridiculous, they'd dress normally. And everyone's into it these days.'

'My mother calls the Buddhist refill shop 'that religious hippy place'.'

'She's not typical.'

'You only need one like that on the jury to sabotage it. I can't risk it. Crafts have a track record in creating a calm, conversational environment.'

'Yes, in mental institutions. But I guess it could get quite mental in there.' He grinned as he left. 'I'll sort you a knitter.'

Sarah put her head back in her hands and made a vow. Whatever it took, she'd make this work. She'd sent out twenty invitations to a carefully chosen sample – a mix of age, gender, ethnicity and social class, but she'd take the first five who responded. She wanted the keen ones.

STEVE

Steve barely glanced at the summons. He was trying to stop his wife from leaving.

'Ste-efff.' He lingered over the name. Steve and Stef. He'd played on her delight at the alliteration when they'd first started out. He'd not been in the market for an English Major – he was foremost a practical man, but he'd spotted a softness in her. He'd gone with his gut instinct and it had paid off. She was an asset. 'Don't leave.' His voice was beseeching but gave no ground.

'You only think about yourself.' She unfolded the crumpled jury summons. 'You wouldn't dream of attending, would you? Not unless there's something in it for you.'

He was about to protest when his son entered the kitchen, his brother hovering close behind. 'Can we have a lift?'

'For the last time, no!' roared Steve.

They retreated rapidly into the hall.

Steve saw the emotion leave Stef's eyes and knew he'd just blown it. He'd thought the organic farm thing had been the tipping point, but it was the bloody kids.

'I don't want to lose you,' he begged.

'Course you don't. You do very well out of me.'

'Look, I'll go to the citizen jury thing. I wanted to anyway, but you said I don't spend enough time with you.' He grabbed the summons and signed it.

'Good.' Stef put the form in the Freepost envelope. 'I'll post it on my way out. It might provide distraction for you when we've gone.'

Steve glared at his sons as they followed their mother out. It was their fault. He'd worked his way up the hard way, but they hung around, doing nothing, always wanting something. Can I have this? Can I have that? Take me here, take us there. Bloody scroungers, the pair of them, and now he'd committed to the citizens' jury. She was right about one thing, though. He'd find a way to get something out of it.

DEVANIKA

Devanika scrolled through her phone frantically as her husband drove them back from the hospital. The nurse's words still rang in her ears. 'It's not your fault,' she'd said. 'We're seeing more fertility issues each year. It's the build-up of toxins in the environment, I'm sure.'

Her husband was talking about trying again, about whether they could afford it, but she tuned him out. First she needed to know if the nurse was just being kind.

She typed in environmental toxins and infertility, and clicked on the article[1] that came up.

'The nurse was right,' Devanika cut her husband off mid-sentence. 'This is what it says: *metals and chemicals in air, water, food, and health-and-beauty aids are damaging fertility in many ways. These toxicants are causing men to experience relentlessly decreasing sperm count and function while women are suffering progressively worse anovulation, impaired implantation, and loss of fetal viability.*'

When they arrived home, she waved away offers of food and turned on her PC. She needed a bigger screen. The take-home message was clear. While each chemical on its own passed safety tests, the little research that existed on the likely combined effects was alarming. Car exhaust, pesticides in food, toxins in cleaning products, endocrine disruptors in beauty products, chemicals used in water-proofing and fire-retardant materials, and contamination of water supplies by agricultural run-off. Together, the effects were synergistic, producing a combined effect much greater than the sum of their parts. Her grief turned to fury and then to action. She wrote to the local council demanding they follow the example of numerous other local author-

---

1. https://www.ncbi.nlm.nih.gov/pmc/articles/PMC6396757/

ities to become pesticide-free, emailed each company whose products contained toxins, harassed her MP asking for greater regulation, but it wasn't enough. When the invitation to the citizens' jury came, she accepted it immediately. Finally, some real power.

BARRY

It had been another frantic day. He'd not even had time for a shit. It was a human right, for God's sake! He should probably visit the bathroom before he set off for work as there were precious few opportunities for delivery drivers. But after so many frustrated attempts with one kid or other demanding attention every time he sat down, it had gone back in. Barry checked the clock. He had ten minutes to sign the anniversary card, put all the toys away, and get ready for work.

'Millie, do you have my pen, love?'

'Nope.' She waved a tiny paintbrush at him.

'Put that away now before mummy gets home.'

'Wanna finish my picture.'

He should look at her efforts and say something nice but he didn't want the precious moments between his wife coming home and him leaving to be spent clearing up. Since they'd both been forced to take on extra shifts to pay the bills, they barely saw each other. He gazed at a photo of the two of them laughing into the camera, remembering back to the days when she'd come home, he'd remove her nurse's uniform and they'd go giggling straight to bed.

The baby was asleep in the bouncy chair. Perhaps he could get the kids to clear up and stay out of their hair while they just grabbed ten minutes. It was their anniversary after all.

'Tom!' he shouted at the ceiling. 'Clear up your mess, now!'

There was a thudding of small feet, then the projectile that was his son skidded into the room knocking the baby's drink over the card and Millie's picture.

Millie shrieked, setting off the baby who joined in.

Barry shoved a dummy in the baby's mouth and frantically mopped up the liquid, but it was too late. The card was ruined. He chucked it in the bin along with Millie's sodden painting, ignoring her cries.

'Come on, who can put their stuff away fastest?'

It worked. Millie forgot her picture and grabbed her paints and paper and sparkly glitter and shoved it in the cupboard. Tom threw in his football and Lego star ship. Barry picked up the baby walker and hesitated – the cupboard already looked precariously full. He heard a car pull up and rammed it in on top of the scooter and shut the door.

'Hiya lovelies. I'm home.'

The baby was peaceful again, dummy in mouth, rocking herself back to sleep with one little foot in the bouncy chair. There was a still a chance.

'Kids,' Barry hissed. They drew close, intrigued by his air of secrecy. 'Quick, let's play hide and seek. If you hide really well, I bet we can fool Mummy for at least ten minutes. I'll go upstairs and you hide down here. Let's see who can stay hidden for the longest.'

They nodded, and Barry ran into the hall and shut the door behind him.

'We have ten minutes,' he whispered in her ear.

'We can't!'

'It's our anniversary.'

He watched her, his heart full of love as she considered, then a dimple appeared in her left cheek, and she giggled. 'Come on then.'

As Barry mounted the stairs, he had a horrible thought.

'Don't open the cupboard door!' he shouted suddenly.

Crash!

They ran into the sitting room to find it strewn with a cupboard full of stuff, and Millie crying, rubbing her head where the baby walker had landed.

It took every ounce of self-control to bite back the barrage of swear words. All he wanted was a moment with his bloody wife, for God's sake. He forced a smile and allowed Millie to sob on his shoulder while he shushed her. He loved them more than he could say, but he didn't know how much longer he could go on like this.

The summons arrived as he was rushing out the door for work. He thrust it in his pocket and read it later while waiting in a traffic jam. He read only as far as 'free childcare provided' before he ticked yes.

NAOMI

Naomi heard the doorbell and rushed down, wireless earbuds in place, to pick up her parcels.

'It's just some storage boxes and a couple of decluttering books.'

She nodded at the delivery man without seeing him and grabbed the large package with the smaller package on top.

'Is it mad that I have three books on minimalism?' she laughed and shut the door.

'I know, sis, but I needed to cheer myself up.'

Naomi lugged the parcels into a living room, still talking.

'No, it's not just the breakup. Well, it is obviously, but the good thing is I have more space now.' She looked round for somewhere to put the boxes.

'Well, someone complained to my company about misleading blurb on our skin care products... I know!... It's not fair. Bloody customers.' She laughed. 'I suppose it's not the attitude for a marketing exec!'

Naomi gave up and lugged the parcels upstairs.

'I'd love you to come down and cheer me up, but...' She opened a bedroom door and shoved the parcel on the bed along with all the others. 'It's just I haven't sorted out the spare room yet... Okay... yes... look forget it, you're not telling me anything I don't know. Bye.'

Naomi ended the call. With her job in jeopardy, she didn't need grief from her sister, however well-meaning. Maybe the new storage boxes would do the trick. She pulled them out of the box. They were fine, if not as great as they'd looked on screen. She could pack away some of her stuff in them, but there remained the problem of where they'd fit. Her phone rang, and she answered.

'...It's fine, love. I'm sorry too. I'm just worried about my job...'

Naomi wondered into her kitchen and poured herself a gin and tonic, adding ice cubes.

'... Yes that's my new ice-dispenser you're hearing... I was glad when a shelf split so I could get a new fridge... No the old one came with the flat, it was six years old... Trouble is, the platinum finish doesn't match my appliances, so I'll have to replace them too... At least I don't have to put up with any more nagging about spending.' Naomi noticed a brown envelope partially hidden under a pile of brochures and opened it. 'No, I am upset. It's such a pain having to find someone new... No, I'm done with dating apps.' Naomi paused as she took in what she was reading.

'You'll never guess what... I've been invited to be on a citizens' jury... You think I should?... might meet some interesting people... And my job would be obliged to give me time off... You're right, a chance to lie low for a bit.'

Naomi grabbed a ballpoint from a deluxe leather desk pen holder and signed it.

JASON

Jason enjoyed his weekly outing at the refill shop. He rarely went out these days, but the Rice Up cooperative run by the local Buddhist group was cheap and had a friendly, non-judgemental feel. He filled up his containers with a week's worth of red lentils and brown rice.

He hung back when he heard an angry-sounding South Asian lady berate the staff for running out of organic wheat bran. The excuse that they'd just lost their supplier wasn't cutting any ice. He felt his anxiety mount and wished she'd shut up and go. She was spoiling the vibe. Eventually she went, and it was safe to pay and leave.

Jason detoured home via the house that left home-grown produce out when there was a glut. Today there was a box of onions and peppers, and a note saying *please eat these before they go to waste*. He packed a few in his backpack. It almost made him feel like a hero for making use of them.

When he got to his bedsit, he rinsed the lentils, then put them onto boil. He added water to a pan full of brown rice. He made loads so he could reheat during the week. He chopped the peppers and onions and fried them. He sprinkled in garam masala and turmeric from large bags bought cheaply from the international grocer down the road. He drained the lentils and stirred them into the onions and peppers.

He was dishing up when he heard the letterbox. A brown envelope. He scanned it in a panic, then rang his mum.

'I've got to go to a citizens' jury. I've been summoned.'

'Do you have to attend?'

'I dunno.' Jason studied the form. 'There's a lot to read.'

'Maybe you should go. Get out a bit. See the doc, get some more meds,' she said.

'Shall I sign it then?'

'Yes, do you good.'

He obediently signed the form.

There was a pause.

'You know my bedsit's really small?' he said.

'Yes.'

'Now you've some more space, can I store—?'

'No.' Her voice was sad.

There was a moment's silence.

Jason ended the call, sat on his bed and wept.

Thirty minutes later, he filled his bong with grass, and got himself high. He ate a bowl of lentils and rice, turned on his gaming PC and played Call of Duty for six hours solid.

NEEDLES

Needles knitted in the passenger seat as her daughter-in-law drove back from the supermarket.

'Do you have to keep doing that?'

'The guerrilla knitters are working on covers for the benches in the underground to make it more cosy. We're an underground movement,' Needles cackled at her own joke, but got no response from the driving seat.

As they pulled up in the drive, Needles turned to her grandson in the back. 'In my day, after each journey, we'd have to scrape the windscreen clean of all the insects.'

'Yuck!'

'No! It's a good thing.'

Her grandson jumped out of the car and helped her out of the passenger seat. He was a lovely boy.

'What do you see on this hedge, darlin'?' she asked him.

'Nothing.'

'Exactly! This hawthorn should be alive with bees. The insect world is what holds us all together. It's like the stitches in me knitting. They go, and it all unravels. It's where your food comes from, sweety.'

He laughed, humouring her and swung a Sainsbury's shopping bag. 'It comes from the supermarket, Grandma.'

'I fear for you young people. I really do. What do they teach you nowadays?'

'Maths, English, Drama, I'll be doing business studies for my GCSEs.'

'Well, you'd better get on with it then,' said his mum. She turned to Needles. 'The struggles I have getting him to do his homework.'

'It's a waste of time,' declared Needles. 'With what's coming up, you need to learn how to survive, my son. With the world heating up and pesticides killin' off all life, you need to be ready.'

He looked back at her, wide eyed with fear.

'Shut it now,' snapped her daughter-in-law, furious. 'Don't go giving him that eco-anxiety.'

'But if he's got the knowledge and skills, he don't need to be scared. That's the point I'm making, love,' said Needles.

'He needs good exam results, a good job. I don't need you butting in, telling him it's all a waste of time.'

'I just want to prepare him for the future.'

'Oh yeah, by telling him to chuck in his education?'

'But love—'

'No forget it, I've had enough. I'm not having you fill his head with fear and nonsense. You got no idea how hard I work trying to get him to do his homework and you undermine it in a minute. He don't need no encouragement to skive off.'

Needles watched her grandson escape quickly into the house with the shopping. He hated conflict. He was such a sweet-natured lad. Not like his mum. Needles was desperate to protect him from the future. She'd do all she could to help him learn the skills he'd need.

It took a moment for her to take in what her daughter-in-law was telling her.

'It's best you don't see him anymore.'

'What? No!'

'You're a bad influence.'

Needles leant against the car in shock. 'I'd do anything to protect that darling boy,' she said in a quavering voice.

Her daughter-in-law's pursed mouth left no room for argument.

'Anything,' Needles repeated.

DAY 1. WELCOME

Lincoln, Gandhi, Malcolm X, Martin Luther King, John Lennon
  The world is as it is because the nice guys get assassinated

Sarah tried to concentrate on her notes, but couldn't help wondering how they were responding to the film next door. She'd watched 'Breaking Boundaries' many times, and she knew exactly what they'd be seeing. She heard the familiar, expert voice of David Attenborough faintly through the door, calmly narrating the possibility of the end of the world as we know it. Explaining the meaning of tipping points – a boulder on a hill that tips over and then can't be put back. Glaciologists, ecologists, chemists, all shared their knowledge and their hopes and fears. She heard the restraint in their voices, the effort it was costing them not to break down and just plead with the viewing public. Listen. Act. Now! But they stayed professional, letting the facts speak for themselves. It went quiet. The final chilling graphic –

an image of a mass of people marching relentlessly on, towards the dangerous unknown.

She put her papers away and braced herself for the onslaught as the door burst open and they tumbled white-faced and ranting the room. She ushered them towards their places at an oval table. Somehow, she had to turn this alarm into effective policy making. But first she had to get a word in.

'Why aren't we doing anything?'

'I didn't know.'

'What do you think Greta meant when she said our house was on fire?'

'But we haven't acted like our house is on fire.'

'That's the point.'

'What about my children?'

'My grandson. He won't cope.'

'Bloody leaders, they'll just run off to their country houses.

'Why haven't they done anything?'

'It falls outside the electoral cycle, that's why.'

This was her chance. 'You're r

ight.' Sarah smiled at the South Asian lady. 'The shortcoming of our current system is that it tends towards short-term decision-making, meaning existential risks such as climate change are unaddressed. That's why you have been invited to be part of this citizens' jury. This is your chance to direct policy.'

The group nodded, settling down, and Sarah continued. 'We have two aims. The most important is to enable participation in decision-making and agenda-setting by the very people who will be living with the consequences. The second is to explore the relative effectiveness of different styles and sizes of citizens' juries. For this one, we drew upon research indicating that craft-making induces an atmosphere conducive to peaceful and productive conversations.' Sarah ignored the dismissive snort from the smart-suited man and introduced the knitter who was sitting beside her. 'This is—'

'They call me Needles,' said the old lady, bringing out knitting needles and a ball of wool. 'I'll be knitting a jumper for my grandson with recycled wool.' She began to knit and the rhythmic click-clack of the needles immediately imparted a cosy atmosphere into the room.

'To my left is Andrew,' Sarah indicated a tall, smooth-faced man who sat in front of a whiteboard.

He nodded around the table. 'I audit carbon offset projects and my role is to assess the social, environmental and economic implications of various policies discussed, with particular emphasis on carbon savings.'

Sarah picked up her spiel. 'Over the next few days, various experts will present policies to address the climate crisis, supplemented by data from research studies. Your job is to sift through these and decide which to progress.'

Sarah paused as a scruffily dressed young man sloped in, smelling strongly of weed.

'Sorry I'm late,' he muttered, sliding into the chair by the window.

'I want you to take this seriously.' She fixed her gaze on the young man. 'You don't just advise, what you decide will be acted upon.' Her gaze swept around the room. 'There is real power here.' She noticed the smart-suited man sit up and pay attention.

'What's your name?' she asked him.

'We already did this,' he said impatiently. 'I'm Steve. This lovely lady to my right is Naomi and the Indian lady next to her is Dekanovi.'

'South Asian is the term. I'm not from India and my name is Devanika.'

Steve smiled and licked his lips. He'd enjoy taking that one down. Naomi was quite attractive underneath the makeup. Lots of jewellery but no wedding ring. He could have her, he decided. The guys looked to be no challenge, either. Barry, the nice-looking chap at the end who kept going on about his kids, was probably a seething mass of resentment underneath. Nice guys usually were, and he'd keep that stoked. The last guy was clearly a stoner. This jury was his for the taking.

'Well Steve, what do you do?' Sarah asked.

'I'm a farmer.'

'You should have been at the last one. We covered sustainable agriculture,' said Sarah.

'I'd have told you there's no point unless you make it worthwhile. Farmers want to turn a profit like everyone else.' The rest of the group glared at Steve, who shrugged. 'I took over an organic farm, and it just didn't pay, so I returned to traditional methods.'

'Hedgerows for biodiversity and crop rotation to regenerate the soil?' asked Sarah.

'Pesticides and artificial fertilizer.'

'For God's sake,' burst out Devanika. 'We're looking for climate solutions and this joker actively shuts down a working organic farm?'

Jason jumped. Her angry voice rang a bell.

Steve smiled, pleased to have rattled her.

'I suppose you use the no-dig method, though?' Sarah asked, hoping to smooth things over. 'It's more environmentally friendly, and it saves money as you're not dragging a plough across the ground.'

'I stick to the plough.'

'Why would you do that?' asked Devanika, outraged.

How could he explain? There was something about the huge blades cutting into the earth and churning up the ground that gave him a thrill. Dopamine buzz, they'd probably call it. The same feeling he got when he put his foot down on the gas and felt his car's huge engine surge underneath him. It was the sense of domination, of control.

'Basically, organic farming is gay,' he declared. He flicked a glance at the auditor to see if there'd be a reaction. He reckoned he'd got the measure of everyone except him, but Andrew's blank expression gave nothing away. Sarah's face had hardened though. He stored the observation away for future use.

'And you?' Sarah addressed the tired-looking man at the far end of the table.

'I'm Barry. I have three kids, me and my wife both work shifts, so mostly I'm looking after kids or delivering parcels. It's them I worry for.'

'I worry about my grandson,' said Needles, as she knitted. 'He won't cope when it all goes tits up, that's fer sure. Don't you care about your kids?' She pointed her needles at Steve.

'They do all right out of me. What about you ladies?'

Naomi shrugged, uneasily aware the clock was ticking. She'd better get on with it, but there were so many other pressing things first.

Devanika shook her head curtly.

'I bet you're one of those birth strike women, refusing to breed because of the climate breakdown,' said Steve.

'None of your business why I don't have children,' Devanika snapped at him.

'Well, this citizens' jury is my baby,' said Sarah. 'And it's a climate solution in itself. If anything is going to change our world, it's going to be who makes the decisions and on what basis. So I'll be making sure it grows up smoothly.' She flashed a smile round the group, which had a hint of steel in it when she got to Steve. She turned to the well-groomed lady next to him. 'Naomi, what do you do?'

'I'm in skin and cosmetics marketing, and actually seventy-eight percent of our customers reported they'd pay more for a sustainable product.'

'My mother said her skin and hair was never as lovely as when she had to stop using products during the war,' Needles contributed as she knitted. 'Nature knows best.'

'She's right,' said Devanika. 'Some chemicals in these products are basically hormone disruptors.'

Naomi looked at her sharply. That was the phrase used in the letter of complaint to her boss.

'I don't use a thing on my skin and look at me,' said Needles.

Her skin was lined as hell, thought Naomi, but then again, she looked to be at least seventy.

'I'm eighty five,' Needles added, as if reading her thoughts.

'And can you introduce yourself?' Sarah addressed the latecomer, who was avoiding her gaze. 'Jason isn't it?'

'Er yeah, that's me.'

'And what do you do?'

He shrugged. 'Nothing.'

'How do you live?' Barry asked.

'On taxpayer's money,' said Steve.

'I suffer from mental health problems. That's why I can't work,' said Jason. He regretted coming already. He knew they'd be judgmental.

'Here, love, have some knitting.' Needles pulled out some needles and wool from her bag and offered them to him. He shook his head. 'It will calm you,' she insisted.

Sarah sighed. The knitting was supposed to provide a relaxed atmosphere, not take over. Thankfully, Steve chipped in.

'I know you all think I don't give a damn, but I'm not one of those climate deniers, for God's sake. I'm a realist, not an idiot. Can we get started so we can get out of here alive?'

The assassin hid a smile.

DAY 2. CARBON OFFSETS

Stage one. Success. No one has noticed the weapon.

'Countries and businesses are using carbon offsets to meet their net zero targets,' the expert was explaining.

Steve had closed down the proposal for personal carbon allowances yesterday without a hitch, but today's carbon offsetting proposal was voluntary, so no threat. He eyed up Naomi instead and allowed his mind to wander.

Jason slid his phone out from his pocket and loaded up Candy Crush.

Naomi wondered if it would be appropriate to ask Andrew about his skincare regime. His face was unlined but his eyes seemed old. Maybe his skin was so smooth due to his lack of facial expressions, although he didn't look like a guy who'd Botox. Steve caught her eye and winked. She gave a half smile and looked away. Unlike Andrew, he was easy to read.

Barry also wasn't listening. He was seething. 'How come he gets to keep his phone?' he burst out suddenly.

'I've got special needs,' said Jason.

'I've got kids, and I wasn't allowed.'

'Jason, please,' Sarah shook her head at him, 'and Barry, if there are any problems, the front desk have instructions to let you know. But if you feel you really need it?'

'No, it's a relief to get away from them to be honest,' said Barry, happy once Jason put his phone away.

Sarah nodded at carbon offset man and he continued his spiel. 'Cutting down on emissions on its own won't be enough. We must also take carbon out of the atmosphere. Business and governments have money that we can harness towards carbon sequestration projects.'

Devanika put her hand up. 'So they chop down an irreplaceable old-growth forest to mine a ton of stuff, then plant a mono-culture in some remote area just to tick a carbon offset box?'

'We don't deny some of that goes on, but this app is much more rigorous. This is where our auditors are crucial,' he nodded towards Andrew. 'We only include carbon offset projects with triple A accreditation based on key criteria. That is, they don't solve one problem by causing another, have been checked for unintended consequences, and are genuine carbon removal, not just cutting down on emissions.'

Devanika nodded, satisfied.

'It also applies at the individual, consumer level,' he continued. 'This app brings together those who want to offset their carbon footprint with carbon removal projects that require investment. Your offset money may reforest an area or contribute to direct air carbon capture and storage.'

He passed iPads round the group. 'The app is preloaded, so have a play.'

Needles shook her head when he got to her. 'Don't worry, love, I'm knitting. I'll just listen.'

Carbon offset man looked around with satisfaction as the group scrolled down. Jason wondered if he'd get away with returning to his game, but Sarah was looking at him, seeming to read his mind.

'Each carbon credit removes one tonne of carbon from the atmosphere. You can also set up a profile, and type in what you consume and it will let you know how far over your allowable carbon footprint you are.'

'Didn't we do this on the first day?' Barry asked.

'No, that was personal carbon allowances,' said Andrew.

'This is different. These carbon credits and the app operate in the voluntary carbon market,' the man explained. 'This allows you to estimate the carbon footprint of what you consume so you can see how much to offset. We hope to partner with all major supermarkets, retailers, energy providers, etc. so you can do this at the point of each purchase automatically.'

'Can you offset travel?' asked Devanika.

'Yes, that's one of the most popular things to offset. Click on the offset calculator and type in flights.'

Devanika tapped in a flight from London to Dhaka. It was nearly three tonnes. She clicked on the offset button and was faced with a list of different projects of varying costs, ranging from twenty to eighty pounds. 'How do I know which project is best?'

'You can choose based on your values. Many have additional benefits. We have a peatland restoration project in Indonesia that not only prevents carbon loss, but improves biodiversity and also the quality of life for indigenous people.'

'Cool, it would make me feel less guilty when I visit my family.'

'I like this menu tab,' said Steve. 'Say I was on a date with someone like you who'd want me to eat lentils,' he nodded over at Devanika, 'I could still have a steak, plant some trees in Kenya with a quick swipe and be done.'

'I wouldn't go on a date with you,' retorted Devanika.

'Steady on love, I wasn't asking. You're not my type.' Steve smirked round the room.

'Anyway, you can't offset the animal's suffering,' Devanika bit back.

'I can if I'm having a good time. But then I'd have to go with Naomi.' Steve laughed, and nudged Naomi. 'What do you think?'

Naomi thought he was being a dick. Although she couldn't help feeling a little flattered at his attention. He was handsome and clearly well-off. Shame he was so slimy.

'Won't people just do more of this stuff if they offset it?' said Needles. 'All these folk giving up flying and going vegan, maybe if they could just offset, they'd stop cutting down.'

Andrew stepped in before the carbon offset man could speak. 'We have studies here on the extent of rebound effect. We'll factor that in when we assess the impact potential.'

Naomi put her hand up. 'I don't want to sound selfish or anything, but would people offset if they didn't have to?'

The carbon offset man responded quickly, 'we're hoping to create an expectation, a kind of social pressure, like a service charge at a restaurant. You'd look pretty bad if you didn't tip.'

Naomi was unconvinced. For all her high salary, her credit cards were maxed to the limit. She wouldn't pay more than she had to. Not unless someone was watching.

Barry nodded. 'It's all right for those with money, but we can only afford to go on holiday once every few years. Why should I pay extra if people who don't give a damn do nothing?' He glanced at Jason.

'Don't look at me, look at the guy who gave up his organic farm!' cried Jason. 'My carbon footprint is tiny compared to you lot. I can't afford most of this stuff anyway.'

Jason was right, but he still pissed Barry off. At least Steve worked for a living.

'If I'd have got some offset money, then I might have stuck with the organic farm,' Steve declared.

He had a point, thought Sarah. The last citizens' jury had discovered that some farmers weren't keen to take on extra costs, such as adding supplements to cow feed to reduce methane or planting hedgerows for biodiversity. She looked at her watch. Time to wrap up.

'Let's get to the figures, now,' she nodded at Andrew.

Before he could stand, carbon offset man bounded up and wrote 300,000,000 on the whiteboard under tonnes saved.

Andrew raised his eyebrows. 'That's a lot.'

'I know,' carbon offset man agreed, pleased.

'Based on what assumptions?'

'That we all sign up to the app and offset any carbon emissions over our personalised allowable carbon footprint.'

'All sign up? To the voluntary scheme?' Andrew said.

'Please don't write them off,' carbon offset man pleaded. 'You saw the figures. The Greenland ice cap is losing ten thousand cubic meters of water per second. It won't stop now, even if we stop all emissions. It's past its tipping point – we need to actively remove carbon. It's now going to warm faster and faster, so we need to cool faster and faster.'

'But it's such a nice day outside,' said Naomi, 'it just doesn't seem real.'

'California, Australia, half of Southern Europe is literally on fire as we speak. Even the bloody Arctic is on fire!' he cried.

The rest of the room avoided his eyes as he spoke, uncomfortable at his emotion. He was right, but they were all thinking the same. Naomi was the one to finally say it.

'The thing is I do care, but why should I give up what I like, or pay extra for it, unless everyone else does? It will make almost no difference to the planet but make a lot to me.'

Carbon offset man shrugged helplessly.

Andrew got the eraser and rubbed out four of the eight zeros.

The click-clack of needles accompanied the sad shuffling of papers and click of the door as carbon offset man left the room.

Stage two. Decide upon target

DAY 3. THE SHARING ECONOMY

I owe it to the next generation

The library lady's introduction was lost on Barry. His mind was elsewhere, worrying if the child minder was coping.

'Hi there! Do you have kids?' Oh no, she was looking at him.

'Erm, yes. Three.'

'I bet you have tons of stuff everywhere?'

'God yes! You take your life in your hands opening the cupboard,' Barry said.

'Really! What's in there?'

She looked genuinely interested, so he answered. 'Well, there's the kid's toys. Sports stuff, the tent, some tools right at the back we can't get to. An easel from Millie's painting craze. A bread maker we never use, but my wife wants to keep in case she gets time to get back into it. Her sewing machine, ditto. Bike rack – actually I've no idea where that went. We looked for it the other day and couldn't find it.'

The library of things lady nodded her head sympathetically. 'I'm sure we all have cupboards like that.'

'You don't know the half of it,' Naomi thought to herself.

'Imagine,' said the lady, 'if you could clear out everything in your attic, sheds and cupboards that you only use now and then, but get access to it anytime you wanted?'

'I'd love that,' said Barry, hooked.

'Well, that's the principle behind the library of things. The most popular items are the ones you talked about – toys and items that are rarely used. We find gardening tools such as strimmers are popular, carpet cleaners, kitchen items. Fun stuff too, like party gear, golf clubs, instruments, games.'

'Do you have old consoles?' Jason asked.

'Yes, they're very popular, Nintendo, Atari—'

'And games? Like do you have Super Mario brothers?'

'Yes we do.'

'Sick.' Jason was in ecstasy. How totally brilliant would that be? He'd had to chuck all his old consoles out when he moved to his tiny bedsit, and his mum had flatly refused to store them.

'So how does it work? Can you just like borrow what you want for free like a library?' Barry asked.

'There are several models. Some have a small per item fee, but ultimately we'd like to go for a subscription model with a monthly fee.'

'A Spotify of stuff?' suggested Jason.

'Exactly. Our aim is to have libraries of things in every neighbourhood, within five minutes of most homes, kind of like your local shop. Different membership options would allow different levels of borrowing.'

'How much?' asked Jason.

'It depends on economies of scale. If it takes off, then we can operate more cheaply, so basic membership, borrowing up to three items a month for up to a week each, for around £10. For silver you can reserve and borrow for longer.'

Barry was more excited than he'd been for a long time, but one thing worried him. 'What if you borrowed something and broke it? Stuff gets broken all the time in our house.'

'We'd be delighted,' said the library lady.

'Huh?' He couldn't believe his ears.

'No, I mean it. We want to avoid waste – so much is hardly used before it's thrown away. If you used it enough to wear it out, that's' brilliant.'

'This might be a good time to share some of research.' Andrew walked round the table, handing out fact sheets. 'This study reports that drills are typically used only 18 minutes a year and emissions from their use are just two percent of the total emissions, the rest coming from their manufacture, distribution and disposal.'

Devanika looked up at him as he dropped the fact sheet in front of her. He looked away quickly when she met his eye.

She was sure she'd seen him somewhere before, but in a different context. She didn't trust his studied neutrality. Never mind, it would come to her.

'Trust me, we don't have trouble with getting items. We have too much, just like you,' library lady continued. 'We often get entire households of stuff donated to us when someone's parents die or move to a care home and have no use for it. Our issue is the time taken to sift through it all. We keep what's in good condition, other items we may repair.'

Barry imagined his house with no clutter. No more clambering over boxes or hunting for things. They could borrow a guitar, Tom was dying to learn but they couldn't afford it and it was almost certain he'd get bored after a few days. Same with a tennis racket for Millie. Once all the shite was gone and they could actually see the floor, they could even borrow a carpet cleaner. This had got his vote.

Naomi raised a hand. 'Won't it all be kind of dirty and smelly?'

Barry and Jason glared at her.

Two targets – could I do both?

Needles chimed in, knitting away. 'Dirt, my dear, is good for you. All this hygiene business, it's more of your marketing, my love, creating fear of germs to sell cleaning products. No one had allergies in my day when we bathed once a week.'

'It's true,' Barry spoke rapidly, fearful she'd vote against it. 'All this antibacterial cleaning – you're killing the good bacteria they say.'

Steve nodded. 'Yep, I'm a farmer and I never get sick. Come and visit,' he nudged Naomi, who looked unconvinced.

'Obviously we clean items,' continued the library lady, 'but our aspiration is to extend the idea of borrowing over buying to everything and for everybody. We want to create a gold card option too that allows trusted borrowers to access luxury items.'

'What like?' asked Naomi and Steve in unison.

'Art, expensive jewellery, boats even. Yachts, for example, are typically unused for all but a few weeks a year. This way, you'd be relieved of the upkeep, the insurance and repair costs, and yet could access the boat when you wanted to.'

'Where do I sign?' asked Steve, nudging Naomi, who nodded in agreement.

'We don't have such options currently, this is just to fire your imaginations of how far the library of things model could extend if properly funded.'

'Oh,' Naomi felt deflated.

Andrew returned to the whiteboard. 'Your last report indicates that £150,000 was saved collectively by borrowers?'

'Yes, this is a much more equitable way to allocate resources,' said the lady.

Andrew added a tick by the social justice column. 'And you saved 88 tonnes of emissions.' His marker hovered under the environmental benefit column.

'The manufacture and transport of goods also gives rise to issues such as deforestation, loss of habitat, loss of biodiversity, pollution, and toxic waste,' she added.

'Indeed. But we need to save millions of tonnes.'

Sarah sat up. This was where they got down to the nitty gritty. She reminded herself that she mustn't interfere. Observation only.

'No, but this is just as it is. If we got more resources, well, look.' The library lady thrust a sheet at him. 'We reckon we can save seventy million tonnes.'

Andrew scanned the figures in front of him, shaking his head. 'These figures are very high. What kind of uptake were you assuming?'

'If everyone was a member, and we all switched from buying to borrowing. We could do an app too.'

Andrew got out his calculator. 'You currently have five thousand borrowers in the Greater London area with a population of ten million. That's a fraction of a percent.'

Needles knitted steadily, watching the library lady squirm under Andrew's questioning.

'No, but the point is, if it got supported and promoted.'

'Your library already has free space from the local authority, a grant, and relies on volunteers. What more were you hoping for?'

Barry wasn't going to let his dream die. 'What if there was a law that every area had to have one?'

'Don't be ridiculous,' Steve scoffed.

'Many neighbourhoods have libraries run by the government as a public service,' said Needles. 'Just for books, though.'

'Yes exactly, a public service,' echoed the lady, grateful for the support.

'And it's about resilience, isn't it?' commented Needles. 'You can't always rely on the infrastructure. Supply chains break down – local stuff for local people.'

'Even if everyone had a library of things nearby doesn't mean they'd use it,' said Naomi.

Sarah repressed an unexpected flash of anger. She reminded herself it wasn't Naomi's fault that she'd given up everything for this. Her own heartbreak was just heightening her responses. After all, she'd come across plenty like Naomi in previous Citizen Assemblies. Those who went around claiming they didn't know, proclaimed great concern but shot down any idea that limited their freedom to consume. But then it hadn't mattered so much. Governments were supposed to follow up on suggestions, but few actually had. This citizen's jury though was the real thing, the stakes were high and she was struggling to retain a professional neutrality.

'Let's take a poll,' suggested Andrew. 'How many here would use a library of things if it were nearby?'

Barry had his hand up straightaway, as did Jason.

Devanika was conflicted. She'd decided to vote for it on the social justice angle, but would she use it? Habits were hard to break. She bought books all the time. It never occurred to her to check the library.'

Needles didn't pause knitting but nodded her head vigorously. 'I'd use it every time my grandson came to visit. Before it would have been for the toys, now he'd be wanting to try out a guitar or computer game.'

'Jason would have nabbed them,' said Steve.

'I'd want the guitar for my son,' said Barry immediately. He'd be buggered if layabout Jason took the guitar when his son wanted it.

'Our research shows that eighty percent of household items get used less than once a month. With broad membership, there'd be plenty for everyone,' the lady insisted.

'That's the thing though, isn't it,' said Steve. 'On a sunny day, everyone would want the barbecue.'

'You can reserve items,' assured the lady.

'But then you have to think ahead,' said Naomi. 'This is why it's not going to work. You got your own stuff, you know it's there, you don't have to worry.'

'But I can't even find things half the time among the clutter,' said Barry.

Naomi shook her head, but a part of her knew he was right. How many times had she bought something new she already had, just couldn't be bothered to look for?

Andrew added a column marked 'take-up' to the whiteboard.

Look at him hovering over the board like a God, our fate in his hands.

He wrote 'assume one percent take up' and wrote the figure on the board. Andrew remained impassive, his back to the group, as everyone spoke at once.

'But we had three out of six. That's fifty percent!'

'That's harsh.'

'You had 0.05 percent take-up in a real life sample. One percent is generous.'

'What about my games?'

'You're making a big mistake young man.'

'Sorry, but I just wouldn't use it.'

Sarah willed her mouth shut and waited until the din subsided and only the steady click-clack of needles remained.

DAY 4. ON-DEMAND BUSES

Everyone dismisses me, but I'll show them.

Sarah marvelled at the man's patience as he tried to explain the principle of demand-led transport to Needles.

'On-demand buses come when you call them,' he explained again.

'How can they?' Needles repeated.

'Forget checking out the bus timetable and waiting at a bus stop for a bus that always goes to the same place. With demand-led transport, you say where you are and where you want to go.'

'But how?'

'You download the app.'

'What's an app, my dear?'

'It's an application, like a piece of software.' He leaned over and showed Needles his phone.

Needles waved him away with her needles. 'Forget it sweety, I don't have me glasses.'

'I don't get it either,' said Jason. 'Say I want to go to a doctor's appointment in Bitterne, but the people on the bus want to go in the other direction?'

'There will be lots of buses and they'll learn typical patterns and the algorithm will—'

'What's an algorithm?' interrupted Needles.

'It's a way of determining the routes in response to bookings using advanced computation. The algorithm matches demand in real time to what buses are where. The system tells the person when the next bus will be and where to meet it. It doesn't even have to be an actual bus stop. It could be by a corner shop near you. It will show you on the screen where to go.'

'What screen?'

Barry caught Devanika's eye, and they both grinned.

'You can ring in, if you don't have the app,' bus man continued. 'Say where you want to go and someone will tell you where to stand so it can pick you up.'

Needles shook her head, confused.

Sarah took pity on him. 'What does everyone else think?'

'I couldn't manage my kids on a bus. It's enough hassle just getting them all in the car,' said Barry.

'Demand-led buses are especially useful in rural areas, where you get just one or two buses a day, if that,' said the man.

'You can say that again,' said Steve. 'This would be good for my business. I can never get enough workers for harvest time. The youngsters up for that kind of summer work can't get to the farm, and cabs are too expensive.'

'Probably below minimum wage,' muttered Devanika.

Steve ignored her. If this took off in his area, he might even get his family back.

Bus man lit up, glad to have found an ally. 'And the algorithm would quickly learn the pattern of commuting and adjust the frequency and routes as needed.'

'I can see it's good for people with no car, especially in rural areas, but it won't replace car ownership,' said Barry.

'Might be handy though for when you want a drink,' Devanika said.

Steve nodded. 'Then you don't have to choose between having a few whiskies after work or carting your kids from place to place, because there's no public transport.'

'I'm guessing you chose whiskey,' commented Devanika.

Steve controlled the surge of anger that coursed through his blood. Obviously he'd chosen whiskey. After working all day, it was his right. But they'd had no right to leave. They were his kids.

'I couldn't give up my car, though,' said Devanika.

'So much for our climate champion,' said Steve.

'Actually, I have a car share app, so when I'm not using it, others can borrow it,' said Devanika.

'Do you make a lot of money?' asked Naomi.

'Let's not get off topic,' Steve glared at Devanika.

'I made three hundred last month.'

Naomi made a note to follow up. She might have to consider something like that.

'That would be good for me too,' added Jason. 'I'd borrow one when I need to go out of town.'

'The on-demand bus app will do that,' bus man told Jason.

'But this car share app exists now, and your bus thingy doesn't exist yet here,' said Jason.

'It will if you all support it and see its potential,' he insisted. 'The goal is to switch from private transport and everyone having their own car to demand-led buses.'

'But will people go for it?' asked Naomi. 'No offense, but buses are a bit grubby.'

'You and your dirt!' said Needles. 'Too good to travel with us plebs is that it?'

'No,' she lied. 'It's just having your own car is more convenient, especially if you've got a lot of stuff, and like your own space. I'm going to get an electric soon anyway, soon as I can afford it.'

'I've got an EV and an SUV,' said Steve.

'That just won't do,' protested bus man. 'Just making an EV incurs environmental costs, and these don't pay back until you've driven 25,000 miles. Cars have huge embedded carbon and use limited resources. The solution isn't to get an additional EV or even swap, it's to give up private transport and have an extensive, high-frequency, efficient, clean,' he looked at Naomi, 'demand-led public transport system.' He turned to Steve. 'In rural areas like yours especially, can you imagine what a difference it would make?'

'No point asking him,' spat Devanika. 'This is the guy whose agricultural runoff pollutes our rivers, causing a public health hazard.'

Steve was startled by her vindictive tone.

'Don't take any notice of 'Dev', I like this idea.'

'Dev's a boy's name. It's Devanika... Stef!'

'Don't call me Stef,' he snapped.

'Why not Stef! Don't you like being called Stef?'

'Stop it!'

'Stop what? Stef!'

'That's my wife's name!' he shouted, enraged.

Naomi looked at him, surprised. 'Wife?'

'Ex then. She ran off with the organic farmer.'

'Was that before or after you changed the farm?' Devanika asked.

'None of your business,' he snarled, furious at having lost his cool.

'No really, we're all interested. Did you overturn the organic farm as revenge for him running off with your wife, or did she run off with the organic farmer because she was so disgusted by you?'

The click-clack of knitting was a metronome, breaking the silence as all eyes turned to Steve. His charming manner had disappeared, and his eyes were ice cold as he regarded Devanika.

Sarah stood up and clapped her hand to break the tension. 'Shall we assess the impacts now, Andrew?'

Andrew took his place by the board.

'Transportation accounts for more greenhouse gas emissions than any other industry, with personal cars being the primary culprit,' bus man said as he handed Andrew a report. 'So for the UK, replacing individual cars with on-demand buses would save forty million tonnes of carbon emissions.'

'We can calculate savings from using public transport rather than individual vehicles,' said Andrew, 'but to get to millions of tonnes of savings, people need to give up their private car. Is there any evidence of this happening?'

'Not yet, but, if we can get uptake of even ten percent rather than just one percent, the service gets exponentially more convenient as more buses run. At that point, it really wouldn't make much sense running your own car, and the cost of the app also gets cheaper as more sign up. Few Londoners run their own car, for example, due to the convenience of public transport.'

'Are there any areas where take-up has gone over one percent?'

'For God's sake, give the man a break,' interrupted Steve. 'It's a good scheme.'

'Yes,' agreed bus man. 'Imagine, everybody. Imagine a world where roads aren't narrowed by endless parked cars. No having to worry about parking, or drinking and driving, or having to concentrate. No more being stuck in traffic jams, no more road rage. Goodbye to all those exhaust fumes. No car tax or car insurance or worrying about MOTs or the next hike in fuel prices. And think of the carbon savings. It would make such a difference to all our lives and our beautiful planet if we all ditched our cars and signed up to the app.'

'If...' said Andrew and turned to the board.

Bus man's evangelical glow disappeared as Andrew wrote a number on the whiteboard.

I have chosen.

DAY 5. RIGHT TO REPAIR

I must do what is necessary

'Back in the seventies, appliances were expensive, and most people rented them. We repaired televisions rather than throw them away. A fridge from the sixties was built to last sixty plus years, whereas today not more than twenty. We're not shown how to properly use, maintain, or even clean appliances to extend their life.'

Naomi wished the repair man would shut up. Let's face it, no one was interested in mending stuff. Nothing could replace the thrill of buying new. She gazed round the room.

Needles was knitting and nodding. Devanika was paying attention. Barry looked sleepy. Jason was staring at Andrew, seemingly in a trance. She avoided looking at Steve, who kept trying to catch her eye.

Jason was trying to work out how old Andrew was. His calm air reminded him of his dad. A wave of emotion rose in him, stopping his breath for a moment. Stay calm. Ride it out. It's just the hash cookie kicking in.

'Extending the lifetime of smart phones from 3 to 10 years would save 6.2 million tonnes annually by 2030 – a 42% reduction on the overall footprint of the products.'

As the repair man spoke, Andrew jotted down the numbers, uncomfortably aware of Jason's eyes upon him. Had he guessed that Andrew wasn't all he seemed?

'Producing a smart phone requires 12000 liters of water. It contains 75 grams of metal, which means drilling through 6 kg of ore, and emits

7 kg of emissions while it's being produced, 300 times the weight of the phone itself. So it's not just the water, it's all the resources and energy going into making them.'

A ray of light shone a spotlight on the brand new iPhone peeking out of Naomi's bag. 'I always recycle my old phones,' she said defensively, looking round.

'Recycling isn't the issue,' the man explained. 'You can't get back all the materials in a product. Repairing means we don't have to keep making products and causing these environmental impacts. Recycling is the last resort after being repaired and used and reused and worn out.'

'This is sounding a lot like the library of things proposal,' said Naomi.

'Very perceptive,' agreed the repair man. 'Most libraries of things have an associated repair café as the principles are the same. Avoiding waste, extending the life of a product.'

'You modern folk, you just chuck stuff away without a second thought,' said Needles.

'The thing is Granny, that stuff is cheap and time is precious,' said Steve. 'I'd rather be playing a round of golf than huddled over some workbench with a screwdriver.'

'I took the kids to a repair café once, as we had so much broken stuff, but the kids got bored waiting. To be honest, I just don't have time,' Barry said.

Needles gazed at him sternly. 'You say you love your kids, young man. You keep going on about them and how scared you are for their future.'

'I'm bloody terrified. I saw the film too.'

'We've got to help our young people prepare. My grandson don't even know food comes from the ground. He couldn't tell a screwdriver from a piece of string.' Needles knitted furiously, shaking her head. 'I told him, forget about your exams sweety, they ain't going to help yer. His mum won't let me see him now cos she don't like what I have to say. But he's so vulnerable, he wouldn't have a clue, the sweet babe. He needs to be taught don't he?'

Barry jumped as a needle was pointed at his face.

'As their father, you should know how to repair things and show your children.'

'My dad used to show me how to repair stuff,' said Jason.

'I also need to fix the fence, sort the tap, help Millie more with her homework, and sell everything we don't need on eBay so I can pay the energy bill,' snapped Barry.

'It's easier just to buy new, isn't it?' Naomi appealed to the group. 'You get the latest thing with instructions and guarantee. All nicely wrapped and shiny.'

'Colonialism rules supreme,' said Devanika. 'We enjoy our latest smart phone and let the developing countries deal with the toxic waste.'

'When was the last time you repaired your phone, Dev?' Steve asked. Naomi shot him a grateful look.

'It's Devanika!'

'You didn't answer the question.' Steve smirked at Naomi, pleased with himself. Now Naomi saw him as her protector. And he'd put down the snooty cow. Two birds with one stone.

The repair man jumped in. 'You made a good point, Devanika. E-waste is increasing rapidly all over the globe and poses significant hazards. The toxic materials, heavy metals and acids leak into the soil and contaminate water supplies. You see increased prevalence of cancer and birth defects in surrounding communities. Children are especially vulnerable, affecting brain function and development.'

'It's capitalism. The manufacturers design products not to last because that's the most profitable business model,' said Devanika.

'Again, you have hit the nail on the head. Planned obsolescence is what they call it.'

'What are you going to do? You can't exactly pass a law about it?' scoffed Steve.

'You can actually,' he countered. 'The EU have proposed a ban on it, and many countries have implemented a right to repair policy. France, for example, requires manufacturers to display the repairability of a product for consumers and make parts available.'

'I took my radio alarm back and they wouldn't repair it,' said Needles.

'We advocate removing VAT on repair,' repair man said. It's one of the few things manufacturers and the right to repair movement agree on.'

'Said it would be easier to buy new,' Needles continued. '"Young man," I said to him, "this isn't even twenty-five years old, and you want me to chuck it away?"'

Naomi snorted involuntarily. Steve laughed, Devanika shared a sideways smile at Barry, and Jason collapsed into giggles.

'Yes, just like you, young man. He laughed in my face,' said Needles.

You've got no idea what's coming.

'Well, it isn't so funny,' the repair man insisted. 'Sorry to get heavy, but we all saw the same video. These figures matter. Over 200 million smart phones are sold every year in Europe. That's nearly 7 every second. Each time one of these phones is made, it creates between 40 and 80 kilograms of CO_2.'

The anxiety of his tone and the increasing speed of the knitting needles created a panicked hush as everyone remembered day one and the video.

'It's urgent, people. Repair and reuse are the key. Recycling is a copout. The future of our planet depends upon it.'

Jason looked up, red-eyed. 'This is getting heavy. I gotta watch my mental health.'

'That's cos you're off your face, mate,' Barry remarked.

Sarah looked over, surprised. She'd have expected such a comment from Steve rather than Barry.

Barry was also surprised at himself, but the idea that Jason had time to loll about smoking dope, playing guitar and computer games while he didn't have time to teach his kids was too much.

'I'd vote for a repair café alongside those Libraries of Things,' he conceded.

'The thing is, even if there are repair cafés, doesn't mean we'd use them,' said Naomi.

'It's true. Although we all should repair, most of us don't know how, or have the time to learn,' added Devanika.

'That's why crafts are so important,' said Needles waving her knitting in the air.

'I'm good with my hands.' Steve leered at Naomi, who looked away.

'YouTube videos show you how to repair things,' said Jason.

'And what if the internet goes down and you don't have Google?' Needles stared at each of them in turn. 'You'll rue the day. Don't say I didn't warn you.'

'Needles is right,' said the repair guy. 'Back in the day, the three R's meant reading, reckoning and repair. It should be taught in schools.'

'I loved design and technology,' said Jason wistfully. 'It was the only thing I was any good at, but then they stopped running it.'

'People report immense satisfaction and empowerment when they learn how to do something for themselves,' said repair man.

'We were without Google last year,' said Naomi, suddenly coming to life. 'For five days. I was up in Scotland with my sister during the blackout. We couldn't get television, and everything had run out of charge, so we worked out how to repair the torch and then managed to repair the old transistor radio. It was actually amazing.'

Repair man lit up encouraged. 'Exactly! Yes! Now just imagine if our culture changed. What if, instead of having the marketing and money people calling the shots, getting us to buy, buy, buy, how about we value what we have? If we consider everything as precious as gold and throw nothing away, but repair and re-use? Preserve our precious world instead of trashing it? The repairers would be the new elite, valued as they should be.'

Jason beamed, the dream of a world where he felt useful hovering like a mirage on the horizon.

Steve tutted. 'You just lost Naomi, mate. She's in marketing.'

Repair man looked at Naomi, gutted. It was true. She was now shaking her head.

Sarah also felt an unexpected jolt of disappointment. She reminded herself of her training: be aware of your own biases. Don't let hidden emotions and assumptions hi-jack the process. She forced herself to examine why tears were pricking the back of her eyes. Naomi reminded her of her ex. That was it. The time her ex had admitted that she shared Sarah's concerns about climate change and Sarah had felt a resurgence of hope that they could work. But then she'd spoiled it all, calling Sarah grandiose for wanting to save the world, accusing her of having a saviour complex. Her girlfriend had basically medicalised her concerns. Treating a behavioural response that was absolutely necessary for the survival of all humanity as if it were a disease. It was the ultimate fucking gaslighting. Sarah had known then in her heart that she had to jettison her, but she hadn't acknowledged until now how angry that had made her.

Sarah looked around for solace and found it in Jason. He'd come out of his shell and was chatting to Andrew about how his dad had taught him to work with his hands, not just fixing stuff, but DIY and cooking. She was pleased and surprised. She'd assumed he'd be the ready meal type. Maybe there was more to him that met the eye.

Are we ready to get some figures on the board?' asked Andrew. 'Although I suspect we may have the same issue as with the library of things.' Andrew tried not to show his alarm when he saw Jason's smile abruptly replaced by a suspicious glare. The click-clack of knitting needles seemed to quicken, then quieten back down.

Not yet.

DAY 6. PERSONAL CARBON ALLOWANCES

Remember why you're doing this.

Sarah tried not to show how nervous she was. It was the final session of the citizens' jury and things were heating up, both metaphorically and literally. The room was hot, Naomi looked stressed, and Steve was challenging everything she said. Jason was breathing hard and wiping his brow. Even the ever-calm Andrew looked on edge.

'First, we need to go back to personal carbon allowances, then we'll make our final decision,' Sarah insisted again.

'PCAs are out. Carbon offsets are just an extra business cost. On-demand buses will actually be good for business. Workers can get to my farm for a start.' Steve sat back, his point made.

'You're not going to let him get away with this, are you?' demanded Devanika.

'Don't worry,' said Sarah. 'We'll cover personal carbon allowances before we take a vote.'

'They're an infringement of basic liberty. I'm a businessman, not a hypocrite. Unlike you lot, I'm not pretending to be something I'm not.' Steve looked meaningfully around the group.

Hold your nerve, Andrew told himself. Don't sabotage everything now by telling them who you really are.

Needles was worried too. Did Steve mean her? She'd got away so far without giving her real name.

I must do it now, before I'm unveiled.

The sound of knitting paused, creating an ominous silence.

Andrew saw Needles staring at him and panicked. He pulled Sarah aside and muttered urgently in her ear.

'What?' Sarah gazed at him in shock. She was prepared for everything, but not this.

'I thought you were doing the meditation one, but then you introduced the knitter, so I kept quiet,' he whispered.

The group shifted, sensing something was being kept from them.

'You can't say anything now. It's too risky,' Sarah hissed back.

'I thought these proceedings were supposed to be a hundred percent transparent,' commented Steve.

Sarah sighed. She nodded at Andrew.

He stood up. 'My name isn't Andrew, although I am an auditor. I'm a Buddhist and my given name is Samudrapati. I am sworn to a life of compassion for all living things. I reverted to my original name for fear you'd make assumptions about my independence in this process.

But as Steve has already questioned this, I judged it was better to speak up.'

The click-click of needles resumed.

He sat down and looked hopefully round the group. 'I hope this hasn't prejudiced you against me.'

They shook their heads uncertainly, but Sarah didn't like the smirk on Steve's face. Andrew had just handed him a gift and she had no doubt he'd use it.

'Well, thanks for that, Andrew, or should I call you your other name?' Sarah shook her head slightly.

'Er no, Andrew's fine.' Best not push his luck.

'Let's get back to where we were, then. Naomi, you look worried. Any thoughts?'

'You liked the library of things idea a bit, didn't you?' said Barry.

She looked doubtful.

'You fancied the gold card option, didn't you love, where you could borrow yachts and such?' Steve suggested. Naomi let the endearment pass and gave a small nod. She didn't have it in her to resist.

'We see alike on these matters,' Steve declared to the group.

Naomi sighed. 'Yes, but realistically, it would never get to that level, would it?'

'I like the repair cafés,' said Jason.

'Me too,' said Needles.

'Aren't you supposed to just knit?' asked Steve.

You all think I don't count.

'Didn't you like the repair one?' Jason asked Naomi. 'You lit up when you talked about repairing the radio during the blackout.' Jason saw her smile as she remembered. 'I know what you mean, it's really satisfying fixing stuff, isn't it?'

'Yes, it was,' Naomi agreed, 'but I know that I wouldn't have done it if I didn't have to. I'd just buy something new.'

'If demand-led buses get proper support and take off, the private sector will get involved and do smart buses, they won't all be grubby,' said Steve.

'They'll only get high demand if people give up their cars and no one's going to do that,' said Naomi.

'Naomi doesn't like anything,' said Needles.

'Why does everyone make me have to be the bad guy? I only say what you all think. It's not fair.' Naomi was out of sorts, and it wasn't just the jury. She'd gone overboard on the shopping channel and now she had to pay for it. She could send it all back, but it was such an effort to parcel everything up again. It was all such a struggle.

'Don't worry,' said Steve, 'I'll take care of you, love.' He put his arm round her and she was enveloped in his aftershave. It smelled reassuringly expensive. To her shame, Naomi couldn't help thinking how nice it would be to be taken care of for a while.

Steve noticed that she didn't pull away. He'd have her tonight, he decided. But she was wrong if she thought he'd take care of her. She'd be a one-nighter.

'I don't want to always feel guilty,' she said.

'No one's trying to make you feel bad,' soothed Devanika. 'I feel guilty all the time, too.'

'And me,' added Barry.

'But it's as you say. You have said no to everything,' said Needles, knitting briskly.

Naomi looked over. Had the needles always been that sharp?

'We haven't fully discussed personal carbon allowances,' said Sarah. 'We do this properly or not at all.'

'Not at all then.' Steve didn't try to hide his irritation. He'd shut that down on day one. He wasn't expecting it to come back and bite him on the arse.

'This is not your jury!' Sarah glared at him through narrowed eyes. 'This is my baby, and we'll discuss PCAs.'

He threw himself back in the chair, hands up. 'Whoa. Steady on lady, keep your hair on.'

'Let me recap.' Sarah nodded at Andrew, who stood up and wrote PCA on the whiteboard. 'We need to limit global temperature rise to 1.5 degrees Celsius, and this requires immediate and extensive reductions in greenhouse gas emissions. There are several versions of this idea, but the key aspect is that Government sets a personal and equal cap on emissions so everyone would receive the same carbon allowance.'

The click-clack of knitting seemed to echo each statement. Steve tapped his fingers on the table impatiently.

'Once your allowance runs out, consumption would become much more expensive. Those who don't use up their allowance can sell their remainder on the personal carbon market. This benefits less well off or greener people and encourages people to reduce their carbon footprint. For example, by insulating their homes or using more energy-efficient transportation.'

Barry put his hand up. 'How would it affect medium to low-income households?'

'Good question. It's been calculated that 71% of low-income households would be better off under PCAs,' said Sarah.

'Yay!' Jason went to high five Barry, who ignored him.

'And high-income households?' asked Steve.

'It's likely that you'd need to pay more than you usually would, depending on how much you went over your allowance. It acts as a very progressive form of taxation.'

Andrew ticked the social justice column.

'That's not social justice!' cried Devanika. 'The poor won't be paid off with a bit of money while the rich buy up all the carbon credits and continue to trash the planet.'

'I'll take the dosh. I'm not proud,' said Barry.

'Have a ration, like during the war,' said Needles.

Devanika nodded.

'The strict version does indeed act like a ration on high-carbon consumption,' said Sarah.

'That's an infringement of our liberty. There's no point my having money if I can't spend it,' protested Steve.

'No,' agreed Devanika, satisfied.

'I worked hard for my money,' said Steve.

'I bet you inherited it,' said Barry.

'I worked my way up from nothing.'

'Oh God, they're the worst. I did, so anyone can.'

'Don't worry, the rich will have to pay for their excess consumption,' Sarah reassured Devanika. 'Some versions add a premium that goes towards carbon removal projects, in addition to paying lower consumers for their carbon credits.'

'What about kids?' Barry asked.

'Just like money, you can apply for extra, like you do with child benefit and the disability allowance. If you vote for PCAs, a follow-up citizens' jury will decide the details.'

'It's total lunacy,' Steve adopted his most authoritative tone. 'There will be a black market instantly, fraud and all the rest.'

'It's the same with money. Just because people evade tax and engage in financial fraud, we don't not have money,' said Devanika.

Barry looked worried. 'The thing is my kids, they won't eat vegetables. Millie won't eat anything but beefburgers. The kids are too stressy to get on a bus.'

'Stop moaning about your children. You're lucky to have them,' said Devanika.

'I love my kids. I'd do anything for them,' protested Barry.

'Well, it doesn't sound like it. You've not gone for anything that hasn't suited you.'

'Don't make me feel bad. I don't ever stop, and it's still not enough. This time away has been bliss. They paid my employer, sorted a child-minder. It's the first break I've had since they were born. You just swan around saying 'I'll pay my carbon offset' or 'I might jump on a bus' as if it's not a ton of hassle. And there's Jason,' he mimicked Jason's slow drawl, 'I'll just take time out from strumming my guitar to have a little tinker and repair something.' Why the hell should I? There's enough on my plate already. You like kids so much. You babysit and I'll take some of that carbon offset money to take my missus out for dinner cos that's not something we've done since the kids arrived.'

'Okay,' said Devanika.

'What?'

'I'll look after your kids while you go out.'

'That shut you up,' said Steve. 'Thank God.'

'Oh! Well, thanks! I'll take the bus to the vegan restaurant, just to show willing like. I heard it's pretty good, actually.'

The steady sound of knitting filled the brief pause.

'Anyway,' continued Barry, 'I just wanted to ask how life would change, like how drastic it would be?'

'A lot of changes you'd hardly notice,' said Sarah. 'A quick win is to use less hot water as that uses most energy, so launder and shower less and at lower temperatures. If you've got a dog or cat, you can switch to insect-based pet food which has a lower carbon footprint. Buy clothes second hand, do fashion swaps. None of this should affect your quality of life. In fact, you'd save time and money.'

'Could you still fly?' Naomi asked.

'There are exciting new developments that just need more investment, such as converting factory CO_2 emissions and municipal waste into aviation fuel,' said Andrew. 'If people can no longer afford conventionally fuelled flights than you can be sure that investment to explore these more sustainable options will come flooding in.'

'But in the meantime, if you want to go on your summer holiday, you just have to cut right back on your other areas or pay a lot more for the privilege than you do currently,' said Sarah.

Steve had decided to say nothing and let the others argue for him, but Naomi just shrugged.

She wasn't as upset as she'd expected. Holidays weren't what they were. What with seas full of plastic, queues at airports, worries about Covid. Plus, that feeling of being judged. It wasn't worth the effort anymore.

'Wake up, people,' Steve said. 'They'll start the PCA low at first and then tighten it like a screw.'

Needles paused her knitting almost like a stenographer taking proceedings, watching Sarah intently as if for a cue. The knitting resumed as Sarah spoke.

'That's the plan, yes.' Sarah gazed at the group and spoke softly. 'Remember day one and the film we all saw?'

She looked at Needles, who'd slowed her knitting down to a sorrowful clicking. No, she wasn't imagining it. It was like the soundtrack in a nature documentary. It had been especially 'clicky' during Steve's outbursts, brisk and almost accusing with Naomi earlier.

'We'll start easy to give the market and business time to adjust, and then we will set the PCA at the level determined by climate scientists. In stage one, PCAs will apply to personal transport and energy use only, then broaden to include food and material goods. Andrew, can you show us the figures for all the ideas we discussed so far?'

He nodded and wrote emissions savings at the top and listed the solutions down the side. He consulted his notes and created several columns: uptake at 1%, uptake at 10%, uptake at 50%. Under the first column he listed the figures arrived at previously, numbers that had left each presenter disheartened.

'You can see,' he explained, 'none of these solutions obtained even one percent take up. In fact, between them. they struggled to reach one million tonnes. We expect that with the PCAs with the financial incentive to stay below your allowance, we'd easily reach ten percent take up for libraries of things, repair cafes and demand-led buses. Emissions savings would go up exponentially. Remember that it's not enough just to reduce our emissions, we've left it too late for that, tipping points have been passed. So, like the carbon offset project, it funnels money into carbon removal projects.'

He consulted his report and wrote new figures up on the board. Everyone gasped as they all increased by several zeroes.

'Now, once the PCAs are reduced to the level required in the second phase, we anticipate few people would run their own car.' The number next to demand-led buses increased to forty million tonnes.

'In the second stage, embedded carbon would be included in the calculations, increasing the advantages of borrowing and repair over buying new.' The pen made a slight squeak as the numbers went up to sixty million for the repair cafes and libraries of things respectively.

'Surely not that many people would go to musty libraries?' asked Naomi.

'It's not just libraries. As buying new goods uses up carbon allowances, your fancy department stores would swap their toy, fashion and games departments for subscription services. You'd be more likely to buy your dad a year's membership to the sports department than a new set of golf clubs,' he said. 'There would be apps developing and expanding, like there are already, to swap fashion and games. You'd borrow and return.'

'An Amazon of borrowing?' suggested Jason.

'Probably,' said Andrew.

Naomi nodded, mouth open, trying to process what she was hearing.

He turned again to the whiteboard. 'We can add an estimated extra sixty million tonnes for the spillover effects as there'd be increased incentives towards home insulation, businesses would invest in low-carbon technology and so on.' He nodded at Steve. 'For example, adopting sustainable farming methods would lower the carbon footprint of your produce, enabling you to reach a wider market.'

Steve maintained a stony expression.

Jason whistled through his teeth as the number increased to 220 million tonnes.

'Oh my God! It's the only thing that will get us there,' breathed Barry.

Sarah observed their expressions – inquiring, concerned, hopeful, calculating. The knitting sounded almost jaunty. If they got this through, her sacrifices would have been worth it.

Steve thought quickly. They'd be expecting him to play the personal liberty card, but even he could see it didn't stack up against the survival of humanity. The one who kept their cool would win.

'The trouble is,' said Steve smoothly, 'that as the economy nose-dives due to the drop in consumption, business won't have money to invest in anything. Something mister Darly Llama here wouldn't understand, being against material values and all that. There'll be a huge recession, people will protest and we'll be rushing back to normal as fast as we can.'

Naomi nodded.

Andrew responded in the same reasonable tone. 'That's because a recession is defined as a drop in the gross domestic product – that is, retail sales and manufacturing go down. Let's do a thought experiment. Imagine everyone could get access to what they want without having to buy anything new, so they didn't need to work so hard.' He was pleased to see that they all looked thoughtful, except for Steve. 'Well-being has gone up, but GDP, gross domestic product has gone down. Recession is just a word. Does it actually matter if consumption has gone down if well-being has gone up?'

'Then why is everyone chasing economic growth?' asked Barry.

'Habit.'

'But what about jobs?' parried Steve.

'You said yourself, PCAs generate bureaucracy. There'll be no shortage of work, and repairing stuff takes time,' said Andrew.

'I'd volunteer at a repair cafe,' said Jason.

Andrew smiled at him, the first time a proper expression had crossed his face. 'They'd be doing very well under PCAs. They could afford to pay you.'

'Nah, too much pressure if I'm employed. Anyway, I'd get lots of dosh from selling my spare carbon credits.'

'Our last citizens' jury decided that switching from the GDP as our key metric of success to a well-being index was a crucial climate solution,' Sarah added. 'Then we could change the conversation from what's good for the economy to what's good for us. The assumption that they are the same thing no longer holds up.'

Steve was down to his last card. He leaned forward 'Wake up everybody! This is a brainwashing exercise. Do we want a religious nut guiding our thoughts?' He nodded towards Andrew.

'He did lie about who he was,' Devanika said slowly. 'In fact, I know where I've seen you before. At the refill shop, in your orange robes.'

Sarah was dismayed. This is what she'd been afraid of.

'They've kept us in this room, away from outside influences, parted from our phones, like some kind of cult,' said Steve.

Buddhism was hardly a cult, but to argue the case was to play into his hands.

The room suddenly felt hot and oppressive. Sarah kicked herself. She'd known there was more to Andrew than met the eye. His unnatural calmness for a start. She had chosen not to probe. This was her fault. The planet's future... no the planet would be just fine – humanity's future was in the balance and she'd failed it due to lack of due diligence.

'Don't you care?' she asked Steve suddenly.

Steve donned the expected expression. It amazed him why everyone played this game.

'Yes I do. I care a lot.'

They both knew that if she challenged his statement, she'd just look cynical and aggressive.

The click-clack of knitting had taken on an edgy note. Jason was breathing heavily. Naomi, for all her smart clothes and makeup, looked strangely vulnerable.

Sarah noticed the sun was now shining into Jason's eyes. 'Can you close the blinds, please Andrew?' She couldn't help her clipped tone.

There was so much at stake and his confession had given Steve a way in.

'It's Samudrapati,' he said suddenly. They had nothing to lose now. Time to stop hiding who he was and use it. 'Can we use the courtyard garden out the back?' he asked Sarah.

She looked at him in surprise. His face had lost that deadpan look and come alive with wisdom and a certain authority. The sun's rays blazing in through the window lit up his head like a halo. A change of scene might just save them.

'Great idea!'

'We'll head outside now for a mindfulness exercise.'

Steve snorted. 'Here we go.'

'This is a process used by EU officials working on climate change policy. They've found it improves consensus building,' Samudrapati responded calmly.

Steve remained sat, his arms folded. Sarah nodded towards Jason, who was now hyperventilating.

'Come on,' she said firmly. 'Leave everything here.'

'What about my knitting?' said Needles.

Samudrapati shook his head and opened the door.

Steve reluctantly joined the group as they shuffled out. Needles quickly shoved her knitting in a pocket. Sarah closed the door after them and locked it. Samudrapati led the group round the corner and out a back door into a walled courtyard garden. It had a tiny lawn and benches surrounding a central oak tree.

Jason collapsed on a bench, breathing hard. Everyone stood around staring at him, concerned.

'Don't crowd him,' said Samudrapati. 'Find a bench and give him some space.'

'Sorry, when it gets hot, I get anxious. My—' he gulped, 'my dad. He had a heart attack on holiday. They said it was the heat. Sorry.'

'No need to apologize.' Samudrapati's warm eyes were compassionate. 'We'll sit quietly for a while. You too, Sarah.'

Sarah decided to trust him and relaxed into the bench.

'You can close your eyes if you wish, or look around you. Let your mind be still. It might help to count your breaths, in... one... out... two.'

Gradually, Jason's breathing slowed.

'Thoughts will come,' intoned Samudrapati, 'but just imagine them like puffs of white clouds across a clear blue sky.'

Jason gazed up into the tree. Glimpses of sky were visible through the foliage. Sunlight sparkled through the leaves.

'You've all had a lot to process, so I'll stop talking and we'll just sit for five minutes.'

Sarah breathed a sigh of relief. The sound of birdsong had replaced the click-clack of knitting and the peace of the garden was working its magic.

Devanika closed her eyes and counted her breaths as suggested.

Steve's thoughts were less peaceful. One thing stood out for him. If they adopted PCAs, the organic farmer would win. His jaw tightened.

Needles considered the personal carbon allowances. There was hope yet for her grandson if they got these through. Would she get extra for her cats? If not, it would be a small price to pay. She'd try out that insect-based cat food.

Naomi gazed at the oak. It was magnificent in its raw beauty. Strong, rooted, branching out in glorious symmetry. Its leaves shimmering green against the vivid blue sky. She thought of all the cardboard boxes piling up in her spare room.

Barry was feeling guilty. He'd been irritated at the pride in Jason's voice when he'd talked about his dad showing him how to repair things. He'd thought Jason was having a pop at him for not teaching his kids. He'd got it so wrong.

'That's five minutes,' Samudrapati's voice was like liquid honey, 'would anyone like to share their experience?'

'Hearing nature all around, well it reminded me what we have to lose,' said Devanika.

'Rubbish,' scoffed Steve, 'it made me realize that the world is just fine!'

'Listen,' said Sarah. 'What do you hear?'

The soft coo of a wood pigeon, a silence, then the tuneful melody of the garden robin, looking at them sideways from the wall.

'A few years ago, you'd also hear the hum of bees on the honeysuckle,' said Sarah.

The robin drew its song to a close, and the silence seemed loud all of a sudden.

'There's one!' Jason pointed in excitement at a lone bee and everyone breathed out in relief.

'I like the idea of a world where we take care of stuff,' Barry murmured.

'It shouldn't be such an alien concept, I suppose,' Devanika agreed.

'We don't want you to take care of stuff,' said Naomi. 'We just want you to buy. We don't care what happens to it after that.'

'It's called business, it's the economy. It's a good thing,' Steve said, putting his hand on hers.

'Do you think it's a good thing?' Needles demanded, peering at Naomi.

Naomi reeled a little under her gaze. The old lady seemed suddenly intense without the knitting.

'It's just marketing.' Naomi thought of the video they'd seen. The horrifying picture of humans marching towards their own destruction like automatons. The image hadn't left her all week. It was too close to home. The unpaid bills, cupboards full of things, boxes everywhere. She'd splashed out on an extra bedroom so her friends could stay, but she could barely squeeze in there now herself. She knew the party was over and it was time to pay the bill. It was almost a relief to admit it. But she didn't know if she could pay.

She shook her head slowly.

Steve saw it all slipping away from him. He was losing his key ally. 'But didn't you say your customers prefer sustainable products?' he asked desperately.

'We take the same product, put it in a brown cardboard container instead of a shiny plastic box and charge twice as much for half the quantity.'

'That's greenwash!' cried Devanika.

Naomi nodded. 'I've made up test results for skin care, saying ninety percent say this or that. Although, it's strange, even though I was inventing them, I still kind of believed it.'

'I'd do anything for my grandson,' said Needles, seemingly apropos of nothing.

'If we vote for this, will it really happen?' Naomi asked.

'Yes,' said Sarah.

Naomi started to weep.

Tears won't help you, love.

'It won't be that bad, reassured Sarah. 'With everyone on board, it won't be long before you get your Gold Card membership for the library of things. You might even get to borrow a yacht! You can gad about by bus wherever and whenever at hardly any cost and rural economies will be transformed. Life will be cheaper. You'll gain in confidence as you learn to value your stuff, learn how to maintain it, and how to sew and repair. You'll have space in your homes. Picture the roads with no parked cars, no traffic jams. You'll have more time to take slow transport, you'll still have holidays. And you won't need to be resentful of others who aren't doing their bit, or guilty for wanting a beefburger because you will have your own allotted carbon allowance that is yours to do as you like with. Be green and richer or high-consuming and pay the full cost and a bit more for luck.'

Naomi gazed up at her through red-rimmed eyes. 'What's the catch?' she whispered.

Oh, she's in. I nearly made another mistake.

'We all have to agree. It has to be unanimous,' said Sarah.

Everyone looked at Steve.

He shook his head. 'Like I said, it's bureaucratic and costly.'

'So what, if it's necessary?' hissed Barry. Sarah had said he'd be better off under PCAs and he needed a break. The thought of returning to his punishing schedule wore him out just thinking of it.

The others nodded in agreement.

'That's what Churchill said, weren't it? You gotta do what's necessary,' said Needles.

Maybe I shouldn't...

'It's always the same,' muttered Barry, furiously. His resentment previously aimed at Jason transferred itself suddenly to Steve. 'The loud-mouthed rich bastards and vested interests kick up a stink the moment anything hits their pockets.'

'Global warming, that's more heatwaves, that's what they said, isn't it?' Jason cried suddenly. He rounded on Steve. 'A heatwave killed my dad,' he shouted. 'He was only 45. He was a really good bloke.'

Steve was 46. 'Look around you, we're fine,' he blustered, suddenly feeling hot. Then Devanika was in his face.

'My baby died,' she hissed. 'Probably due to nitrates from excessive use of fertilizers. Like from farms like yours.'

Before he could protest the ridiculousness of the statement, Sarah was staring intently into his eyes.

'This citizens' jury is my baby,' she said in an ominously quiet tone.

'Our baby,' Devanika was back in his face.

'And I'll protect it as viciously as any mother would protect her cub,' Sarah said quietly.

'In the rest of the world, rich white power-hungry leaders might make the decisions,' Devanika jabbed a finger at Steve.

'But in this citizens' jury, with expert input, and a calm, reflective environment, people will choose what's best for them,' Sarah said with an air of finality.

Naomi wrenched her hand from under Steve's grip. She wanted this. She wanted it desperately and right now.

'Make me,' said Steve.

Oh yes!

'Aiyee!' cried Steve as the needles penetrated his flesh.

Back inside, the police had finished taking witness statements. They were uncertain what to arrest the old lady for. She insisted her needles had just 'slipped.' Everyone else had stated that it had all occurred so fast that no one could be sure what had happened. Hard to believe, bearing in mind she was 85.

The only thing there was full agreement on was that at the moment the needles penetrated his flesh she had cried, 'this is for my Grandson.' However, the old lady insisted she'd meant the jumper she was knitting and was nothing to do with that fact that the victim had failed to vote for something called Personal Carbon Allowances which would save humanity from extinction.

The victim was finally carried out on the stretcher, two knitting needles still protruding from his torso. The police officers heard that the knitter had been recruited to provide a peaceful atmosphere to negotiations.[2]

Interested to know more about climate solutions included? See

---

2. Interested to know more about climate solutions included? See https://www.greenstories.org.uk/anthology-for-cop27/stories/the-assassin/

OUR SHARED STORM

by Andrew Dana Hudson

*T*his is an excerpt from Our Shared Storm: A Novel of Five Climate Futures by Andrew Dana Hudson, published 2022 by Fordham University Press

Diya hated talking to rich people, but she was good at it. She was one herself, or had been, though that sense of isolated entitlement never quite leaves you, she feared. The lingering rich needed most to be made to feel that they were winning, in charge, going of their own free will, even as the sea overtook them. So, that's what Diya offered them.

"This, my esteemed friends, is the kind of glory your money can buy."

Diya stood at the prow, shouting to be heard over the wind and the waves and the low hum of the sail yacht's electric control motor. Her audience sat on cushioned benches bolted to the deck of the boat. They drank mimosas and wore gold 'VIP' badges which glinted in the summer sun, an ego-stroking touch Diya was particularly fond of.

She waved at the octagonal structure looming ahead of them. It looked impressively industrial, in that very 20th century way. But was also draped with greenery, vertical crops hanging in sheets from four of the sides. Around the structure the open ocean was broken by smaller works – a farming flotilla of rafts and buoys, beneath which hung yet more crops: kelp, scallops, mussels, fish traps, and soil bags growing a dozen kinds of artisanal aquatic vegetables. It was one of the more impressive offshore agriculture projects in the region, providing significant fish protein to nearby Buenos Aires and helping reduce local acidification levels in the surrounding waters. But Diya wanted to keep her audience's attention on the rig.

"The platform you see before you began life at a shipyard in Itaguaí, Brazil, at the cusp of the Transition Era," Diya continued. "It was destined to be an offshore oil drilling rig pulling toxic hydrocarbons out of the Argentine Basin, at the behest of a hungry market and hungrier investors. But we have found a better use for it. Mr. Campbell?"

Her audience turned to Noah, who grabbed hold of a rope and hauled himself up to stand unsteadily beside her. She had brought Noah along to explain the technical details of the storage project, but also to remind her guests of the powerful unions they might come up against if they said no. She would be the carrot, Noah would play the stick.

"Far below us, under the ocean floor, is a large, porous formation of sedimentary rock," Noah explained. "Right now those pores are filled with saline – salt water. With robots and special concrete-setting microbes, we have fashioned that formation into one of the world's first carbon waste reservoirs. Carbon dioxide is transported here in a flexible undersea pipeline from an air capture plant tethered to the offshore wind and solar farm a few dozen klicks further out. Here it is pumped down into the reservoir, where it forces the saline out into the ocean and pretty much stays put. The technical details are obviously more complicated, but I promise you the chemistry is too boring to be worth getting into. The gist of it is, we take clean energy, use it to fix waste carbon out of the atmosphere, then put that sky trash more or less back where it came from – underground, where it contributes to neither radiative forcing nor ocean acidification. Questions?"

"Why do all this, instead of planting more trees?" asked a man with thick plastic sunglasses – showy and expensive given the limits on non-essential plastic manufacturing.

"As I understand it," Noah said, "that's an ongoing debate at the COP – the balance of these strategies, anyway. But one answer is nutrient bottlenecks. We've got a lot of waste carbon, but that's not true of everything we'd need to do huge amounts of afforestation. Another is land, which people don't always want to give up to plant carbon dark forests. Plus, because of the sensitivity of weather systems, if you plant a new forest in one spot, it can reduce sequestration in a neighboring area. A third answer is time. Industrial air capture works somewhat faster than trees mature.

"And finally, when trees eventually die, they release much of the carbon they captured back into the air – usually on a shorter time-frame than we are looking for with carbon storage. That's fine when you're working at scale. You count the forest, not the trees, as it were. Still, forests catch fire, trees burn, and then you're set way back on your drawdown. Living systems take a very different kind of management. Nothing wrong with that, but we think it's better to put as big a chunk of the problem as we can away for good, and not all in the tree planting basket."

"Why the pipeline?" someone else called out. "Why not just do the capture right here?"

"Eventually, yes, we hope to incorporate generation, capture, and disposal all into the same facilities. But right now these pieces are largely being built out in a modular way while the carbon trades find their feet. The other reason is that we might want to pipe CO2 in from other sites, depending on the eventual capacity of the reservoir and where the solar surplus shakes out."

"You don't *know* the capacity of the formation?" A bottle blonde in the back raised a skeptical eyebrow. She wore a high-fashion version of the jumpsuits coming out of the new European clothing provision houses – a statement of either scorn or envy for the empowered masses, Diya didn't know which.

"It's hard to know anything for sure about anything that far underground," Noah said, unfazed. "This isn't some big cave we've dug. We're talking about rocks, under more rocks, under the ocean. But we have sensors, we know where the carbon goes and whether it stays there. The biggest challenge now is building an organization that can ensure the integrity of those sensors and the data coming from them, and be financially responsible for any leaks that occur over the minimum time we want the carbon to stay put. Say about 500 years. Which, I guess, is where you all come in."

Diya took the prow again.

"Esteemed friends, you know I have brought you here today to show you the vital work funded by the Planetary Trust. This is but one of hundreds of beautiful, state-of-the-art storage sites we are building. They are true marvels, a great gift to all the world and every living thing in it, and to a hundred generations yet to be born. We are also funding a great deal of the aforementioned afforestation, and countless other projects that benefit the planet as a whole. But when something benefits me, I pay for it. When something benefits a city or a nation, that city or nation pays for it. Who pays for something that benefits everyone? We need a new kind of institution, one whose mandate is both broad and long. That is why most of the parties to the UNFCCC individually – soon to be followed by the UN as a whole – have instituted a global wealth tax that pays into the Planetary Trust."

The mention of taxes made the crowd shift uncomfortably.

"I know, I know," Diya said, giving them a knowing smile. "A topic sure to ruin an otherwise lovely day out on the yacht. That's why I'm here to offer you an alternative. All of you control significant private assets, and while your investments have been smart, much needed, even world changing, we now have ever more data showing that private mobilizations of capital are deeply inefficient for achieving long-term climate stability.

"We need to put the world's capital into the hands of the Planetary Trust if we are going to build projects like the platform you see before you and operate them for the next five hundred or one thousand years. And we need that money fast, because, esteemed friends – we are still up against it. The storm our fine host city experienced this week is a reminder of the tipped-over world we are desperately trying to right. Every year that passes with this much carbon in the air continues our planet's slide toward the hothouse. We need every resource available to us to build the removal industry at scale and at speed!"

At this Diya stepped down from her perch and took up a champagne flute of mimosa. She held it up, as if making a toast.

"My most esteemed friends, today I ask you to make this possible. Hand over your assets to the Planetary Trust, so that we might accelerate our plans and stabilize the world. Why wait for the wealth tax to siphon them away year by year? I know, as well as any of you, the burden of these vast, clunky masses of capital. Masses that many of us never asked to be charged with keeping. They are in their own ways as toxic as the oil this rig had once been built to dig up. Relieve yourselves of them, put them to better use. And in return, you will be cared for all your life, with freedom to go and live as you please, a citizen of every country party to the Trust. You will be honored forever on these monuments for your generosity. You can build us a stable climate future. And if we can do this, we can do asteroids! We can handle the many dangers that lurk in deep time. The Planetary Trust can ensure a prosperous human future where your names will be remembered!"

She swept back up to the prow and pointed at one of the massive struts lifting the platform above the water, which had just come into view. On it were freshly carved names – famous names of ultrarich people Diya had already talked out of their fortunes. Diya raised a toast once more.

"To you! May your names be honored for a hundred generations!"

She drank. Many of the others drank with her. Those who did not glanced away, not able to meet her eye. She'd get them too, soon enough.

Diya's speech was done. She did not mention how paltry the perks and pensions and honors were compared with the titanic sums they'd be giving over to voluntary democratization. She did not mention the increasing legal precedent for holding the megarich accountable for what their investment portfolios paid for in terms of fossil extraction, deforestation, ecosystem damage, and political dithering. The Hague's climate trials had a momentum all their own now, with prosecutors always hungry for new enemies to feed into the environmental justice maw. She did not mention what she would hint at later, in private conversations: that the best way to avoid a dangerous audit was to just give their money up now, after which prosecutors would look the other way. She did not mention that the unions Noah was representing were clamoring for the Trust to move forward with more hostile expropriations of such "stuck capital."

Noah caught up with her on the ride back.

"Heckuva pitch," he said. "If I were a lonely, anxious billionaire, I'd be jumping to give you my money. Though, it leaves a sour taste in my mouth, seeing their egos stroked like this. They are my class enemies, after all."

"There's only brief catharsis in seeing your enemies humiliated," Diya said. "Letting your enemies save face, however, can prevent them from becoming your enemies again. Noah, understand, these people used to basically run the world. Now we are, shall we say, laying them off from that position. Today's theatrics are just the difference between saying 'you're fired' and saying 'we're letting you go.' If that difference helps them shuffle quietly into the night, I say we let them have their dignity."

"Still, it rankles. Why should some rich assholes get their names on that strut, instead of the workers who actually built the thing?"

"Because the world isn't fair, Noah. Not just yet, anyway."[1]

---

1. Interested to know more about climate solutions included? See https://www.greenstories.org.uk/anthology-for-cop27/solutions/carbon-dioxide-removal/

DRAMBERS

by Kim Stanley Robinson

*T*his is chapter 22 from the Ministry for the Future: a novel that
imagines a Ministry for the Future set up by the United Nations
to address the climate crisis. Reprinted with permission from Hachette
Book Group.

Adele Elia and Bob Wharton were at a meeting of the Scientific
Committee for Antarctic Research, an international scientific organization formed to coordinate Antarctic research after the 1956 International Geophysical Year and the 1959 signing of the Antarctic
Treaty. Over the years SCAR had become one of the main de fac-
to governments of Antarctica, along with the US National Science
Foundation and the British and other national Antarctic research
programs, especially Argentina's and Chile's. The SCAR meeting was
in Geneva this year, so it had been a morning's train ride for Adele and
Bob, who during their work in the ministry had become friends.

Now they sat looking out at the lake from a bar on the second
story of the meeting's hotel. Out the window beside their table they
could see the famous fountain launch its spire of water into the air.
To the south a stupendous set of thunderheads, as solid as the marble
tabletops in their bar, lofted high over the Mont Blanc massif. They

were enjoying this view and their drinks when they were approached by an American glaciologist they knew named Pete Griffen. Griffen was pulling by the arm another man they didn't know, whom Pete introduced as Slawek, another glaciologist. Adele and Slawek had read some of each other's papers, and even attended some of the same meetings of the AGU, but until now had never met.

A waiter appeared with a tray of drinks that Griffen had ordered: four snifters of Drambuie, and a carafe of water with water glasses. "Ah, Drambers," Adele said with a little Gallic smile. This liqueur was what Kiwis always drank in the Dry Valleys, they informed Bob as they took their first sips. When Bob made a face as he tasted it, Griffen explained that long ago a ship filled with cases of the weird sweet stuff had been stranded in Lyttelton when its shipping company went bankrupt, and the cases had been warehoused there and over the years sent south for cheap, year after year. So they drank a toast to the Dry Valleys and settled into their chairs.

When asked, Slawek said he had spent five years all told in the Dry Valleys, and Adele countered that she had spent eight years living on glaciers; Pete grinned and topped them both with twelve years total on the Ice. They quickly pointed out that he was older and so had an advantage, which he agreed to immediately. Slawek said he had become a glaciologist to indulge his introverted personality while still holding down a job, and Adele laughed and nodded.

"A lot of us are that way," she said.

"Not me!" Pete declared. "I like to party, but really the best parties are on the Ice." He rotated his hand at Slawek as if coaxing him. "Come on, Slawek, tell these guys your idea. I think they need to hear it."

Slawek frowned uncomfortably, but said, "You all heard the new data in there today."

They agreed they had.

"Sea level will rise so fast, the world is fucked."

It couldn't be denied, the others agreed. The data were clear.

"So," Pete prompted Slawek, "I've heard some people suggesting we just pump all the melted ice back up onto the polar plateau, right?"

Bob shook his head at hearing this. It was an old idea, he said, studied by the Potsdam Institute at one point, and the conclusions of their study had been bleak; the amount of electrical power needed to pump that much water up onto the east Antarctic ice cap came to about seven percent of all the electricity generated by all of global civilization. "It's too energy intensive," Bob concluded.

Slawek snorted. "Energy is the least of it. Since one percent of all electricity created is burned to make bitcoins, seven percent for saving sea level could be seen as a deal. But the physical problems are the stoppers. Have you run the numbers?"

"No?"

"Say sea level goes up one centimeter. That's three thousand six hundred cubic kilometers of water."

Adele and Bob glanced at each other, startled. Griffen was just smiling.

Slawek saw their look and nodded. "Right. It's six hundred times as much as all the oil pumped every year. Building the infrastructure to do that would not be feasible. And it would have to be clean energy pumping it, or you'd be emitting more carbon. That much clean energy would take ten million windmills, Potsdam said. And the water would have to be moved in pipes, and that's more pipe than has ever been made. And last but worst, the water has to freeze when it gets up there. Say a meter deep per year, I don't think you could go any deeper without problems— that means about half of eastern Antarctica.'"

"So it's too much in every way," Adele noted.

They drank more Drambers while they pondered it. Griffen said, "Come on, Slawek, get to your idea. Tell them."

Slawek nodded. "Reality of problem is that glaciers are sliding into the sea ten times faster than before."

"Yes."

"So, the reason for that is there's more meltwater created on the ice surface every summer, because of global warming. That water runs down moulins until it reaches the undersides of the glaciers, and there it has nowhere else to go. So it lifts up the ice a bit. It lubricates the ice flow over the rock beds. The ice used to be in contact with the rock bed, at least in some places, and usually in most places. The ice is so heavy it used to crush out everything under it. It bottomed out. Kilometer thick, that's a big weight. So the glacier scraped down its bed right on the rock, bottomed out, ice to rock. Even sometimes frozen to rock. Stuck. A good percentage of glacial movement at that point was viscous deformation of the ice downhill, not sliding at all."

Adele and Pete were nodding at this. Adele was beginning to look thoughtful, Griffen was grinning outright. "And so?" Bob said.

Slawek hesitated and Griffen said, "Come on!"

"Okay. You pump that water out from under the glaciers. Melt drillholes like we already do there when we check out subglacial lakes, or to get through the ice shelves. Technology is well known, and pretty easy. Pump up the water from under the glaciers, and actually, the weight of the ice on it will cause that water to come up a well hole ninety percent of the way, just from pressure of all that weight. Then you pump it up the rest of the way, pipe it away from the glacier onto some stable ice nearby."

"How much water would that be?" Bob asked.

"All the glaciers together, maybe sixty cubic kilometers. It's still a lot, but it's not three thousand six hundred."

"Or three hundred and sixty thousand!" Adele added. "Which is what a single meter rise in sea level would be."

"Right. Also, the meltwater at the bottom of the glaciers is really from three sources. Surface water draining down moulins is the new stuff. Then geothermal energy melts a little bit of the glacier's bottom from below, as always. It never melted much before, except over certain hot spots, but a little. Third source is the shear heat created by ice moving downstream, the friction of that movement. So. Geothermal in most places raises the temperature at the bottom of the glacier to about zero degrees, while up on the surface it can be as cold as forty below. So normally the heat from geothermal mostly diffuses up through the ice, it dissipates like that and so the ice on bottom stays frozen. Just barely, but normally it does. But now, the moulin water drains down there and lubricates a little, then as glacier speeds up going down its bed, the shear heat down there increases, so more heat, more melting, more speed. But if you suck the bottom water out and slow the glacier back down, it won't shear as much, and you won't get that friction melt. My modeling suggests that if you pump out about a third to a half of the water underneath the glaciers, you get them to slow down enough to reduce their shear heat also, and that water doesn't appear in the first place. The glaciers cool down, bottom out, refreeze to the rock, go back to their old speed. So you only need to pump out something like thirty cubic kilometers, from under the biggest glaciers in Antarctica and Greenland."

"How many glaciers?" Pete asked.

"Say the hundred biggest. It's not so bad."

"How many pumps per glacier would you need?" Bob asked.

"Who knows? It would be different for each, I'm sure. Would be an experiment you'd have to keep trying."

"Expensive," Bob noted.

"Compared to what?" Pete exclaimed.

Adele laughed. "Jurgen said a quadrillion dollars."

Slawek nodded, mouth pursed solemnly. "This would cost less."

They all laughed. Adele said to him, "So, Slawek, why didn't you bring this up at the session today? It was about this acceleration of glaciers."

Slawek quickly shook his head. "Not my thing. A scientist gets into geoengineering, they're not a scientist anymore, they're a politician. Get hate mail, rocks through window, no one takes their real work seriously, all that. I'm not ready for that kind of career change. I just want to get back on the Ice while I can still get PQ'ed."

"But the fate of civilization," Bob suggested.

Slawek shrugged. "That's your job, right? So I thought I'd mention it. Or really, Pete thought I'd mention it."

"Thanks, Slawek," Pete said. "You are a true glaciologist."

"I am."

"I think we should drink another round of Drambers to celebrate that."

"Me too." [1]

---

1. Interested to know more about climate solutions included? See

https://www.greenstories.org.uk/anthology-for-cop27/solutions/refreeze-the-arctic/

https://www.greenstories.org.uk/anthology-for-cop27/solutions/refreeze-the-glaciers/

SUCK IT UP

by Brian Adams

Kristy was on winter break from her freshman year in college. She was doing her usual late December gig – selling Christmas trees at the vacant lot next to Saint John Cantius Church, something she'd done every year since she was a tween. Her Grandpa Joe had a Christmas tree farm in the heart of the Berkshires, and, every December, he'd load up his truck with freshly cut Fraser and Balsam firs, drive down into the Valley, and set up shop.

Kristy loved selling trees. She'd dress as one of Santa's elves: a dark green dress the color of a Frasier fir, with a red ruffle, painted buttons that resembled peppermints, a wide black belt, and red and white striped leggings. She'd arrange a garland of cut greens in her hair, and, when not helping customers, she'd dance to cheesy Christmas music blasted from a boombox.

She had just hoisted a fragrant fir onto the roof rack of a young couple's car and was tying it down with twine when, lo and behold, who should pull into the parking lot but Colin.

The two hadn't seen each other since they were back home on winter break. Kristy had gone to the University of Massachusetts, majoring in Environmental Science with a minor in Feminist Studies, while Colin had headed four hours north to the University of Vermont to study Environmental Engineering. They'd texted throughout the semester, face-timed each other now and then to butt heads over their college eco-agendas, but that was about it.

"Oh. My. God!" Kristy said as Colin slowly emerged from his car. "What the hell are you doing here?"

"Merry Christmas to you too," Colin said. "You mind giving me a hand with this thing?" Colin opened the trunk of his car and began pulling out a large, bulky contraption.

* * *

Colin and Kristy had bent over backwards to one-up each other on climate change issues since high school. Claws out, fangs bared, the fur flew at those Environmental Club meetings, the dynamic duo's dramatic attempts to out-do each other with over-the-top eco-actions legendary.

"Mother Nature knows best!" Kristy had argued. "Let's plant a hundred trees next to the parking lot."

"Trees?" Colin scoffed, shaking his head and rolling his eyes. "How about we transform the parking lot into an enormous solar array. Let's build a six hundred kilowatt car port!"

"Car port?" Kristy had pounded her fist on the table and wagged her finger menacingly at Colin. "Screw the cars! It's walk, bike or ride the bus! Let's ban cars all together."

Followed by yet another condescending eye roll from Colin. "Earth to Kristy! We're Americans – we drive. It's who we are. It's what we do. The solution is electric vehicles and charging stations everywhere!"

Colin's eyes were chestnut brown with the longest of lashes, and, when he smiled, they twinkled, they sparkled, they danced. But all that was irrelevant. No matter what Colin's eyes did, he was still a royal pain in the ass.

"Technology is not going to save us!" Kristy said. "Have you ever considered that less might be more? Maybe we need to take a giant step backwards and - "

"Sit on our hands while your trees catch fire?"

On and on it went. Nature versus technology. Colin and Kristy were both climate activists, but their solutions to the climate crisis seemed light-years apart.

* * *

"Let me guess," Kristy said, helping to unwedge the awkward object out of Colin's car and finagle it upright onto its stand. "A modern art sculpture? Or just some random detritus you scavenged from a junkyard?"

"It's a Christmas tree," Colin answered. "Do you mind if I set it up here?"

Kristy wrinkled her nose. "Seriously, Colin. What the hell is this thing and why is it in my Christmas tree lot?"

Colin's 'tree' stood six feet high, with a flat circle-shaped base and a pointy tip on the top. It didn't have leaves or branches, but instead flat plastic discs measuring four feet in diameter at the bottom, and a foot at the top. Each disc was stacked two inches apart, one on top of another, like a stack of records, allowing air to easily pass through. A rod in the middle served as the 'trunk', and the discs fanned out from it.

Colin took a step closer to Kristy, gently reached up, twirled the garland in her hair, and breathed in deeply.

"Yum! I wonder if there's a way to get my tree to smell as delicious as that?"

"Your *tree*?"

"Well, my tree that isn't a tree. Sort of like a fake tree. Only not."

"Wow, Colin. That's so helpful. Now I totally get it." Kristy did her best to roll her eyes, but couldn't pull it off nearly as well as Colin. "I'll be right back."

Turning to help another customer hoist a real tree into the back of their pickup truck, she could feel Colin's eyes on her. She wasn't sure whether to be annoyed, flattered, or simply amused, but she was quite sure he'd never looked at her like that in high school. She'd been too busy battling with him over their respective solutions to the climate crisis to think about him as anything more than a friendly rival.

Neither Kristy nor Colin had ever been involved in a real relationship, or, for that matter, even a fake one. Their first year away from home had offered plenty of dating opportunities, but romantic connections had never been there. Now, seeing Colin again after a semester away, Kristy paused for a moment to catch her breath. She couldn't remember the boy ever looking this good.

She returned to find Colin adjusting the discs on his tree. "My Gramps will be back any minute," Kristy told him. "If I can't explain to him what this hunk of junk is, you'll be packing its trunk back into your trunk."

Colin smiled. "You always had a way with words," he told her.

"Most of them insults hurled at you!" Kristy reached over and tugged on one of the discs. "Now tell me what the hell this thing is?"

"I thought you'd never ask! It's my first-year engineering project. A mechanical carbon-capturing tree. You know how real trees take carbon dioxide out of the air, right?"

Kristy whacked Colin on his arm. "Seriously? Are you actually going to mansplain photosynthesis to me? You do remember the Day of the Lorax, right?"

Senior year in high school Kristy had organized a wildly successful tree planting party. Oaks, maples, mulberry, and sweet gum now lined the school's parking lot. It was something she was incredibly proud of.

"Whatever," Colin countered. "My mechanical tree does what real trees do. It removes carbon dioxide out of the atmosphere. It's a CO_2 trap. See these discs?" Colin knelt down reverently and peered between them. "They're coated with a chemical resin that absorbs CO_2. Air flows between the discs and carbon dioxide passively sticks to the resin. You remove the CO_2 using water and heat, and then the tree goes back to sponging up more CO_2. Enough of these trees could remove tonnes of carbon."

"You've gotta be kidding me!" Kristy scoffed. "Your solution to climate change is to make fake trees rather than planting millions more real trees instead?" Kristy gestured to the Christmas trees behind her. "Am I missing something? If the goal is to take carbon out of the atmosphere, we've got the nature-based solution right here."

Colin rolled his eyes. "Cutting down trees?"

"For every single tree my Gramps cuts down, he plants two new ones."

Interrupting their bickering, a tall, pencil thin man wearing an enormously oversized Santa Claus hat, strode toward them.

"This is so not my day!" Kristy groaned. "As if I don't have my hands full with you, here comes Santa to give me even more shit about cutting down trees."

"Wait. You know this guy?"

"Unfortunately. He's a regular."

"You better watch your step!" Colin teased. "Diss Santa. and you'll only get coal for Christmas!"

"Shut up, Colin. I can out tree hug just about anyone, but this tree hugging Santa is just what you were in high school!"

"A pain in your - "

"Exactly!"

Santa approached the two, glaring at the rows of freshly cut trees.

"You've got an accomplice with you!" he snorted, wagging his finger at Kristy. "Yet another lackey doing your dirty work. Killing trees! Both of you should be ashamed."

"Whoa, bro," Colin answered defensively. "This is her gig, not mine!"

Kristy wagged her finger right back at the man. "Chill, Santa! Remember what I told you: for every one tree cut, two are planted."

Santa remained unimpressed. "It's still a crime."

"It's not a crime, it's a crop. Does harvesting flowers make you a murderer? Remember, no farms, and you'd be naked, hungry and sober."

"Not to mention Christmas treeless," Colin added.

"Exactly. And put this in your pipe and smoke it, Santa," Kristy continued, staring Santa down. "Folks bring their trees back to the farm after Christmas, we feed them to my Grandma's goats, and voila! Trees to cheese!"

"I'm vegan," Santa continued.

"Enough!" Colin commanded, briefly considering twirling Santa's hat the way he had twirled Kristy's garland before thinking better of it. "We get it, all right? But it's almost Christmas. Give us a break."

Kristy couldn't help but notice Colin's use of the words "we" and "us".

"I'll be back," Santa said.

Kristy exaggeratedly scratched her nose with her middle finger. "I'm sure you will. Merry Christmas!"

Santa turned, and, with a "humph" rather than a "ho ho ho", headed back to his car.

"Weird dude," Colin said, watching him go.

"That's an understatement. I can't figure out what his schtick is. Shut down my Gramp's business? If he was that much of an environmentalist, wouldn't you think he'd have more pressing issues to deal with?"

"Maybe he's into you."

"Eww! Gross!"

"You are dressed as an elf. I can see why - "

Kristy felt herself turning red. "Colin! Stop! Now where were we before we were so rudely interrupted?"

"Going at it over the usual," Colin answered. "Just like in high school." He reached into his pocket and pulled out his phone to check an incoming text. "Damn. I gotta go."

"Hot date?" Kristy asked.

"Not quite. My sister needs a ride to her dance rehearsal. She's the Sugar Plum Fairy in the Nutcracker. You mind if I leave Sponge Bob in the shed? It locks, right? Maybe I could come back tomorrow with a flyer to pass out to people."

"Sponge Bob?"

"His full name is Sponge Bob Suck It Up, but you can call him Spongy."

Kristy humphed. "I'm surprised it's a boy tree. It's usually left to us girls to clean up the mess you boys make."

"Tomorrow?" Colin asked, ignoring her social commentary.

Kristy shrugged her shoulders. "Why not?" she answered, her feelings all over the map.

* * *

"Here's another fun fact about Spongy," Colin said. "For every pound of CO_2 a real tree sucks out of the atmosphere, my tree, scaled to a much larger size, will suck out a thousand pounds. They're that much more efficient at removing carbon dioxide than real trees."

Following a sleepless night, visions of Colin as the Nutcracker dancing in her head, Kristy remained just as skeptical. After Kristy's grandpa had given the okay, Colin had dragged his tree out of the shed and set it back up in the lot. "A plastic mechanical tree? Sounds to me like another high-tech climate change silver bullet wannabe that will never perform the way it was supposed to. Meanwhile someone, probably an already obscenely rich old white guy, is going to make a shit ton of money from this thing whether it works or not. How much will this sucker cost?"

"Don't be rude. His name is Spongy not Sucker."

"How much?"

"Once production is ramped up, the goal is to get the big ones down to twenty thousand or something."

"Twenty thousand dollars? Are you kidding me? At U. Mass this semester we began rewilding the campus golf course, converting it back into a forest. With twenty thousand dollars we planted five hundred trees. Oh wait. I forgot. There's no money to be made in planting trees, is there? Here we are, deforesting the planet, and rather than reforesting with real trees you'd rather some capitalist fat cat engineer plant your designer boutique fake ones instead? Do you really think that's going to deescalate the climate crisis?"

"Back off, Kristy! If we're going to solve this climate catastrophe it's not enough to just stop burning fossil fuels. We have to remove tonnes of the carbon dioxide already in the atmosphere. Otherwise we're totally screwed. And, whether you like it or not, that's where technology comes in. Where are we at now? 410 parts per million or something?"

"More like 420," Kristy answered. "Santa must be freaking. We keep this shit up and the North Pole will be ice free in no time. Where will Santa live then? And please, for the love of Rudolph, don't tell me he'll move in with me. I'm having enough trouble with my roommate as it is. Plus, how am I supposed to sell Christmas trees if there's no Christmas?"

"Dang!" Colin smiled, relieved that Kristy had lightened up a little, if you could call contemplating a post-Santa world lightening up. "Not a holly jolly thing to think about, is it?"

"I know, right? It's freaking me out."

"You and me both. But think about it; bigger versions of my trees could remove one tonne of carbon dioxide a day. Deployed on a massive scale, imagine what 100 million of these could do."

Kristy reached over and lightly tapped one of the discs. "That's a hell of a lot of fake trees, Colin. Where will all that money to build them come from? And where are you going to put them all? Not to beat a dead horse - "

"Or a reindeer - "

"But you're barking up the wrong tree with this. Mother Nature knows best, and her real carbon sponges are my go-to gals."

Colin reached down and wiped a dusty disc with his handkerchief. "Engineers know a thing or two as well, hence my fake one." He put his arm around his tree and gave it a hug. "And, not to brag, but it *was* my idea to make Sponge Bob in the shape of a Christmas tree. I was thinking of you when I came up with the idea."

"Me? No way." Kristy turned to hide her face from Colin. Once again, she was sure her cheeks were as red as Rudolph's nose.

"Yeah, you. Every year you sell these Christmas trees, right? And I thought, hey, why not turn Sponge Bob into a holiday tree? It's just a prototype and all, but it could get people super stoked about this epic idea of carbon-capturing mechanical trees."

"You're planning on selling these?" Kristy asked.

"Way too early for that. Lots of kinks still to be worked out. I convinced my professor to let me take Sponge Bob home for break, hoping I could show you. I wanted to . . ." Colin's voice trailed off.

Kristy shook her head. "Convince me that mechanical trees are better than real ones?"

"Actually, I was going to say impress you."

As much as she tried to hide it, Kristy couldn't help but smile. It was true there were enormous differences on the paths each were taking, but their destination was the same – a world free from climate catastrophe. And now, here was Colin, dragging out his mechanical tree to impress her? She blinked her eyes. Was this the same boy she had butted heads with so often in high school?

"The point is not to replace real trees," Colin continued, looking down and scuffling his feet. "That would totally suck. The point is to supplement trees. And the mechanical tree we made is not the only show in town. There are all sorts of sweet ideas out there for carbon capture. Wanna hear the other Christmas carbon sponge idea I'm working on?"

Kristy gave Colin the stop sign. "Hold that thought, I've got to help this couple out. Do you mind seeing if that woman standing by the Balsams needs a hand?" Christy motioned to a young woman affectionately stroking a real tree.

"I'm on it, boss!" Colin scurried over to help the customer.

It was a few quick minutes later when Kristy rejoined Colin at the corner of the lot.

"You getting ready to take off?" she asked, the disappointment in her voice apparent.

Colin looked confused. "What are you talking about?"

"Your tree. Did you load it into your car? I thought you wanted to show it off some more?"

Colin frantically looked around. In a lot full of real trees, his fake one was nowhere in sight.

"What the heck? Where did it go?"

They turned to see Santa backing his classic Mercury Comet out of the lot, Colin's tree dangling out of Comet's open trunk. Kristy grabbed a Balsam branch from a pail of water, leapt in front of the vehicle, and waved her branch menacingly.

"Stop!" she yelled. "Turn the engine off! Release Spongy right now and no one gets hurt!"

Santa rolled down the window. "Spongy? What the heck are you talking about?"

"That mechanical tree you're stealing from us. Offload it. Now!"

"Whoa!" Santa said. "I overheard you and your boyfriend bickering about this unnatural piece of junk, and I thought I'd do you a favor and haul it away. Cutting down real trees is bad enough, but planting fake ones? I don't think so!"

Colin joined Kristy, branch in hand as well.

"This piece of 'junk' just might be the very thing that helps save the planet!" Kristy answered. She and Colin quickly scooted to the back of the Comet and hauled the tree out. Then Kristy returned to the open car window.

"Listen Santa, unless you have presents to give rather than a tree to take, you need to take off. No need to come back. Comprende?"

* * *

"Holy crap!" Colin grinned, re-righting the tree in its stand as Santa and Comet high-tailed it down the street. "That was intense! Girl, you got right in Santa's face! Thanks for saving the day!"

"Anytime. The dude's no Saint Nick, that's for sure. More like Saint Dick. It's not often I get to liberate a Sponge Bob Suck It Up fake tree from a rogue Santa. Anyway, you were saying you had another carbon sponge project that might also need rescuing?"

Colin hesitated before answering. "Mistletoe. Carbon-capture mistletoe."

"Mistletoe?" Kristy gave Colin a look. "The plant you . . ."

"Kiss under. Exactly. I'm envisioning a string of carbon-capturing resin infused discs that you hang over your doorway. And every time someone walked under it, you'd get to . . ." There was an awkward beat as Colin stared at Kristy.

"Kiss them?" Kristy answered, meeting Colin's eyes.

"Exactly."

"Wow! That would literally take their breath away." Not that Kristy needed mistletoe to do that. Just being around Colin was making it hard to breathe.

Colin laughed. "Looks like you've got another customer." A young couple, not all that much older than Kristy and Colin, were strolling down the aisle of trees, arm in arm, their eyes twinkling away. "If you want, I can stay and help put trees on the cars."

"I'd like that," Kristy said.

"And I was thinking that, maybe, when we're done here, we could, I don't know . . ." Another awkward beat. "Do something?"

Kristy caught her breath.

"Something like . . .?"

"I don't know. How about a hike?"

"Through a real forest or a fake one?" Kristy asked.

Colin laughed.

"My Gramps has 120 acres on his farm," Kristy continued. "There's a great trail that winds its way through an evergreen forest with awesome views of the Valley. No mechanical trees in sight, but lots of real ones. We could do a little shinrin-yoku."

"Shinrin what who?"

"Yoku. Japanese for forest bathing. Absorbing the forest atmosphere. Good for the body. Good for the soul."

Colin reached over and fist bumped Kristy. "Perfect. Can I bring Sponge Bob?"

"No!"

Colin laughed. "Dang. But who knows, maybe we'll get lucky and . . ." Colin hesitated again. It was his turn to blush.

"Find some real mistletoe?" Kristy offered, seizing the bull by its horns, the tree by its branches, or, who knows, maybe even Sponge Bob Suck It Up by its resin infused discs.

"Exactly!" Colin answered, his eyes doing their magical thing.[1]

---

1. Interested to know more about climate solutions included? See https://www.greenstories.org.uk/anthology-for-cop27/stories/suck-it-up/

MANGROVE MAJ

by Martin Hastie

These things creep up on you without you noticing. One minute, there you are minding your own oil-trading business, racking up the millions (and the rest!) in your numbered bank accounts, feted by fawning industry admirers and sycophantic media hangers-on. Then, before you know it, all of a sudden you are Mr. Unpopular, a leper bell around your neck, featuring at number seven in The Guardian's much-trumpeted list of the *Top Ten Existential Threats to the Global Environment*.

It would be fanciful to suggest that my origins were humble – a first-rate if rather troubled education at Lancing College, a knight-of-the-realm father rubbing shoulders with ministers and minor royals. (Papa was, rather unfortunately, disgraced in later life, but the point still stands.) When you exist only in these rarefied *environs*, the advantages that you have over others are neither apparent nor of any particular concern. Indeed, the first time I read an opinion piece accusing me of being posh and overprivileged, I almost spat out my 1969 Louis Roeder Cristal Millesime Brut. Later in life, though, even

I had to appreciate that such a charge is difficult to counter when you happen to be in possession of your very own island.

As islands go, it was never much to write home about. Small, scrubby, over-grazed with stringy goats. It was really neither use nor ornament. The island's one redeeming feature was the not-quite-golden beach on its south-facing shoreline, and in those early days, my darling wife, Jeane, and I spent many a sun-kissed afternoon seduced by the lapping waves, surrounded almost entirely by unspoilt nature, feeling as though the world was ours alone. Jeane could happily idle away countless hours watching tiny sand crabs scuttling from hole to hole like batters sprinting between bases, while I liked to cheer on the mudskippers as they used their minuscule but powerful forelimbs to hoist themselves through the thick gluey sludge beneath the jetty. It often gave me cause to ponder whether these extraordinary creatures were observing me just as I them, peering up through inquisitive eyes and wondering what on earth is this peculiar man staring at?

My fortune, as I mentioned, came from oil, amassed via a combination of good luck and fortuitous timing, a smattering of expertise and a dedication to the job that very nearly killed me. Aged just forty-four, my heart decided it had had more than enough of my work-work-work lifestyle and tried its best to condemn me to an early grave. Somehow, to even my doctors' amazement, I pulled through. Jeane's immense relief was tempered by the fact that my first act upon opening my eyes in the Intensive Care Unit was to ask if I'd missed any important messages from the office. She was also a little nonplussed by my referring, tongue-in-cheek, to my revival as 'the Resurrection'. But I think, all in all, she was glad to have me back.

I am not a man of any great religious conviction. Agnosticism runs through my family like male pattern baldness. In his early seventies, my father collapsed and died on the pavement outside the village Post

Office. Thereafter, my equally nonreligious mother, who had stood by Papa after both his financial and infidelity scandals, said a quiet little prayer every time she passed that gleaming red postbox. It struck me as unlikely that my father's spirit should choose to haunt the very place where his life was cut short. Having said that, given his disdain for the shoddy customer service he always complained of receiving there and his willingness to hold a grudge, I wouldn't put it past the old devil to be hanging around and putting the willies up the counter staff. In any case, it brought my mother some much-needed solace throughout her final years, and that was all that really mattered.

Love is an incredible thing. When Jeane started giving her speeches, the situation caused much consternation among my peers. 'She must be such an embarrassment to you.' 'She's going to give you another heart-attack at this rate.' And it was true – at first it did cause a tremendous degree of difficulty. The environmental concerns she was espousing were entirely at odds with the practices necessary for my businesses to function. It would be untrue to say that I felt no guilt about the damage my companies were causing around the world, but I found myself able to blank it all out, to pretend it wasn't happening. In those days, I wouldn't have known a mangrove terrace from a palm oil plantation. It makes you wonder why she married me – it was certainly never about the money. I suppose it must have been love.

From the beginning, I admired Jeane's freedom of spirit. On our very first date, I can vividly remember her outlining her ambitions to help save the northern white rhinoceros from extinction, speaking with rare passion, beguiling me with that delightful, soft Scottish accent that brought the blood to my cheeks and weakened my knees. It was clear from the first time she stood at a podium that she was a born orator. Watching her address the delegates at COP 20 in Lima, I could see that she held her audience rapt throughout. They were spellbound by her performance, dazzled by her words. Our daughter, Sarah Jane, was beyond proud. Alistair, a bit younger and still in those awkward teenage years, was horrified. Me? Well, I suppose it should have irked me that she was, essentially, trying to bring down my industry. But she wasn't really, of course – her speeches simply stressed the need to adapt to a changing world. Either way, I couldn't take my eyes off her in that long baggy grey dress and those heavy black Dr. Martens.

At first, as is the way of these things, Jeane received far worse press than I did. She was categorised as a tree-hugging do-gooder (as if these are bad things). But then came the Guardian article naming me Public Enemy Number 7, which was a watershed moment and no mistake. Naturally, the write-up mentioned Jeane – in fact, it was quite clear that her activism was the only reason I was featured at all. It gave the picture editor an opportunity to insert a photograph of her beautiful face into the newspaper – much better for business than my ugly mug. After that, the tabloids latched onto us. Overnight I went from being the distinguished oil magnate Oliver Frankland to *Oily Olly*, while she, of course, was dubbed *Green Jeane*. It caused some friction, I won't lie, but not as much as you might think. Perhaps it was my near-death experience, or maybe it was Jeane's remarkable powers of persuasion, but something had changed and I was starting, slowly but surely, to edge towards her way of thinking.

At the COP 20 meeting, Jeane had grown friendly with Majid, a curious man of astonishing intellect from Abu Dhabi who was better known, it transpired, as Mangrove Maj. He's large and barrel-chested, intense but exuberant, and his entire bulky frame shakes whenever he laughs, which is often. Jeane was bowled over by his enthusiasm and knowledge and was keen for me to meet him. It soon became apparent why.

'He's looking for someone who owns an island. I mean, that's ridiculous, isn't it? That's us!'

Some strange providence must have brought us all together, that's all I could think. A man on the lookout for somebody who owns an island happens to find themselves chatting to just such a person. I can't imagine that sort of thing happens every day.

'It's not like we even do anything with the island anymore.'

She was right, of course. There had been a time when we had entertained the great and the good (and the utterly appalling), but age and misanthropy had caught up with me and I no longer had much desire to play mine host. Coastal erosion had set in anyway – a result of increasing storms, and I'd accepted a chunk of it might one day be lost to sea rise.

'Just say you'll speak to him,' she badgered me, over and over, until I eventually made room in my busy schedule for a call. And thank God I did. Speaking to Mangrove Maj changed my life. I can only hope it's going to eventually change millions of other lives, too.

'Have you ever heard of mangrove terraces?' he asked me after a few strained pleasantries.

'Yes, I think so – it's a golf resort in Barbados,' I replied, half-joking. Of course I hadn't heard of mangrove terraces.

'Well, strap yourself in,' he said. I could sense the smile in his voice. 'You're about to hear *absolutely everything* about them.'

I don't think he stopped talking again for around forty-five minutes. Their carbon-capturing potential, how they can protect against storm surges, increasing resilience of coastal areas to climate change.

We started work almost immediately. In the beginning, securing funding proved difficult. I pumped a million dollars in to start things off, as no one else would touch this outlandish idea, this absurd novelty. The tiny start-up team delivered, three months late, a large submersible pump, 500kW of solar panels, two kilometres of plastic pipe, the connectors, a supervisor (appointed directly by Mangrove Maj), fifty litres of sun cream, thirty sun hats and ten Indonesian labourers. Oh, and twenty thousand mangrove seedlings. They spent three months laying pipe, building berms, pumping water and, eventually, planting mangroves. The mangroves were laid out not in coastal waters, as is almost always the case, but in terraces, like rice.

Environmentally, intentionally salting dry land was a little dubious, but it was a private island so that was much less of a problem. An unforgiving tropical storm led to flash floods that washed away some of the mangroves, but they flowed down the gullies and were collected in the grid at the bottom. Large seedlings were replanted the following day, and, luckily, mangroves grow rather quickly. After a year, most were doing well, and the 'salty forest' was coming along nicely. The terraces were watered with sea water, which was pumped up from the beach using solar power and distributed through small trenches designed by an old rice farmer in Bali with whom Mangrove Maj had become acquainted while he was over there for COP 13. The old man's trenches worked beautifully.

There had been concerns about the goats, but it seemed that they weren't partial to ready salted leaves and they mostly left the seedlings alone. After the third year, a trial batch of prawns was added to some of the terrace pools near the sea. This was particularly good news for me – Jeane and I ate prawns on our first date and they subsequently became 'our thing', so I was devastated to learn that they were an environmental disaster area. Mangrove Maj explained to me that it's the trawling that causes the damage, comparing it to picking strawberries with a bulldozer. But these prawns fared really rather well and were harvested by opening the sluice gate, flushing the pond with sea water and catching them in a simple net in the gully. Gravity did most of the work. Sold at the local fish market, the prawns were snapped up in ten minutes flat like hot tickets to the Philharmonic. All of the ponds now have prawns and/or fish, and the unbothered aquaponics system reduces the feed that they require. It seems to help the trees, as well. Seafood has been a major part of the revenue for the project, particularly in the early stages.

After the fourth year, a small crop of wood was taken from the largest trees. This wood was made into biochar using a homemade kiln on the beach. Not so efficient, but easy to use. The biochar was soaked in chicken manure, left to dry in the sun and then added to the fallow ponds and the new seedling areas. It works a treat, though the chicken manure job was not the most popular. It's rather more popular now, though, as it pays double. After six years, and five rounds of expansion, the first serious coppicing was done by a local team hired from a nearby island. They cut strips through the forest, only harvesting a third of the trees, and hauled the wood down to the beach with a jury-rigged zip wire and a winch – a system that has grown ever more streamlined with each repetition. The brash was turned into biochar on the island as before, and the three hundred tonnes of logs were taken to a gathering yard in the nearest major port. To transport these small shipments, fabulous little wooden coasters called pinisis, halfway between a dhow and a pirate ship and a real blast from the past, were deployed.

The coppicing grows beautiful straight poles. Ridiculously straight, like massive broom handles. The poles are used for tents and canvas structures of various sizes, and as they are wood, they are easy to work with and still reassuringly natural.

To avoid them being used for firewood, to prevent rot, mould, insects and to extend their life, they are pressure treated with Borax, like the beautiful bamboo school in Bali. Because the poles now last for years, it is recognised as a form of carbon sequestration with massive added social benefits. This generates further income with new so-called social credits as well as carbon credits.

There is an ongoing debate about whether the poles or the biochar is most efficient, and there are arguments for both sides. No doubt there will be for many years to come. Both systems are making a positive contribution in slightly different ways.

Now, after seven years, the island is 50% salty forest and 50% what it was before. The ready salted goats were sold a couple of years ago. The whole island has bounced back, with a surprising variety of plants, animals and birds. Islands are always a bit narrow in terms of the wildlife they can host, but in this case, it has been made up for by a bold abundance. There is a surfeit of fascinating little birds and a cracking selection of insects.

We worked hard, carefully choosing watersheds and checking aquifers, to ensure that the seawater does not damage anything that would be better left undisturbed. Most of the mangrove wood is made into biochar for both local use and export. We have, I think, thought of everything.

And yet, I can sense you thinking, there appears to have been a media blackout about all of this. Where is the Guardian article slapping you on the back for this monumental achievement and celebrating your Damascene transformation from ecological pantomime villain to spearhead of the upcoming mangrove terrace revolution?

Well the project is still, as we speak, top secret.

In fact, beyond knowing that I had agreed to talk to Mangrove Maj, even Jeane knew nothing about any of this. A brain tumour – swift, merciless, devastating – stole her away from me three days before that initial conversation. It is, perhaps, poetic that my greatest triumph is also my greatest tragedy. You will have read the various obituaries at the time, of course. Universally glowing, as befits. Even those rags that had vilified her in life deified her in death. *'Green Jeane' didn't quite live long enough to change the world,'* read the tribute in The Telegraph, *'but she laid a path so that others might.'* Sarah Jane has, of course, followed in her mother's footsteps. Our hugely talented daughter's debut book takes pride of place on my bookcase and is always prominently displayed in the background whenever I have a Zoom meeting. Alistair runs half-marathons to raise money for environmental causes in his mother's name.

The truth is, I can take no credit for any of this. She changed everything. Well, she and Mangrove Maj, of course. He told me that he intentionally sought Jeane out at COP 20 because he'd read that we owned an island. He also told me that it was the best thing he ever did.

Although I can no longer quite face eating them, Jeane has opened up a world where people can munch prawns, guilt-free, to their heart's content (unless they're vegans, of course.)

I still see her radiant smile in the faces of the grandchildren she never knew. And that's what matters, isn't it? Yes, I'll always wish I'd acted sooner. And yes, I'll never quite shake the feeling that I took her for granted. But we'll all be gone one day. What we're working for, what we're fighting for, isn't for us. It's for those future generations yet to be born. That's why we're sequestering carbon, installing seawalls, helping wildlife to prosper. That's what it's all about.

Next week, we're going public. It's finally time. We wanted to prove beyond any doubt that this could really work over a sustained period. For the rest of the coastal mangrove terrace industry, our worked example will help to secure funding for other sites around the world. The potential is *unimaginable*.

Meanwhile, Mangrove Maj has made it clear that he wants no publicity. When the media circus hits town, he'll be lying low, working on yet more pioneering ideas of how we can make the mangrove terraces even more effective. And me? I'll be where I usually am these days: on the south-facing shoreline, watching those incredible nippy sand crabs as they race back-and-forth across the not-quite-golden sand, saying a quiet little prayer.[1]

---

1. Interested to know more about climate solutions included? See https://www.greenstories.org.uk/anthology-for-cop27/stories/mangrove-maj/

PROJECT SLOWDOWN

by Kim Stanley Robinson

T *his is chapter 93 from the Ministry for the Future: a novel that imagines a Ministry for the Future set up by the United Nations to address the climate crisis. Reprinted with permission from Hachette Book Group.*

Project Slowdown had been active for a decade, and the thirty largest glaciers on the planet, all of them in Antarctica and Greenland, had seen expeditions to their crux points where wells had been melted through their ice and the meltwater under them pumped to the surface and spread to refreeze as near the pumping wells as was convenient. Our team had been involved with the Weddell Sea area effort, which was particularly complicated, as a dispersed fan of glaciers and ice streams had fed into the Filchner Ice Shelf and the Ronne Ice Shelf in a way that was difficult to deal with. The landforms under the ice resembled a half bowl, not steep enough to easily identify the places upstream where glacial input was fastest. But we had done the best we could with that, and drilled 327 wells over a five-year period, focusing on the crux points we could find and hoping for the best.

It wouldn't have been possible without the navies of the United States, Russia, and England. They let a little village of their aircraft carriers freeze into the sea ice and overwinter in the Weddell Sea, and from these carriers we were able to keep the work going year round, and supply the land bases that were set on the ice of the Ronne and Filchner. Fleets of helicopters kept these camps supplied, and helped to move camps from drill site to drill site. Something like ten billion dollars was spent on the effort just in our zone alone. Such a deal, as Pete Griffen used to say. A lot of us had worked with him back in the day, and he was often remembered.

All good. Only four deaths, including his, all from accidents, and three of those accidents resulting from stupid decisions, including his. The other death, weather. Pretty good. Because Antarctica will kill you fast. And none of the deaths were people on our team, although we never said that of course. But it was a comfort, given what had happened to Pete. No one in my group wanted anything like that to happen to us.

So; ten years in Antarctica, with good work to do, and no more grant applications either. Papers got written, science got done, but mostly it was engineering the drills and pumps and dispersion technologies. There were papers to be had there too, even if it wasn't exactly what we had gone down there for. Actually the glaciologists were getting data like never before, especially structures of ice and fl ow histories, and most of all, bottom studies. For sure no one had ever had the kind of information about glacial ice/glacial bed interactions that we have now! If we had been doing that research only for its own sake, it would have taken centuries to learn what we've learned. But we had an ulterior motive, an overriding concern.

So, at the end of the season, we were flown into the middle of the Recovery Glacier, where we had drilled a double line of wells five years before. One of the lines was reporting that all its pumps had stopped.

Helo on up to a pretty dramatic campsite, on a flat section of the glacier between icefalls upstream and down, with the Shackleton Range bulking just to the north of us, forming the higher half of the glacier's sidewalls. Lateral shear at the glacier's margin was a shatter zone of turquoise seracs, so tall and violently sharded that it looked like a zone of broken glass skyscrapers. You never get used to helo rides in Antarctica. Not even the helo pilots get used to it.

Out on the flat we went to the wells that were reported as stopped. We had drilled these long before, back at the beginning, and now it was a familiar thing to check them out. Everything looked okay on the surface, and it wasn't the monitoring system. Very quickly the problem noticed by the automatic monitoring was confirmed, pump by pump, just by looking in the exit pipes and seeing nothing there. The closer to the center of the glacier the holes were, the less water they were pumping. Most were pumping nothing at all.

We were moving around on skis, and roped together, just in case the crevasse-free route between the wells had cracked in the years since someone had been there. There were no crevasses, so we flagged the new route, then got on the snowmobiles and tested the route to be sure. No fooling around in our team.

The wells were in the usual line cross-glacier. Tall pole with transponder and meteorological box, tattered red flag on top. Under that a squat orange insulated plywood box covering the wellhead, a very small shed in effect, heated by solar panels set next to it. The pipeline was lime green, crusted with gray rime. It pumped the water south, up to a hill beyond the south bank of the glacier, joining a big pipeline there, which took a feed from all the pumps in the area.

We got the door to open, and went into the hut covering the well-head. Nice and warm in there. Dark even with the lights on, after the glare outside. Wind keening around the sides of the thing. Nice and cozy; it had to be kept above freezing. Checked the gauges; no water coming up. We opened the hatch on the well cap, fed a snake camera down the hole. The snake's reel was so big a snowmobile had had to haul it here on a sled of its own; two kilometers of snake on one big wheel.

Down went the camera. We stared at the screen. It was like doing a colonoscopy of an exceptionally simple colon. Or probably it's more like the cameras that plumbers use to check out a sewer line. No water in the hole, even two hundred meters down; this was a sign something was wrong, because when a hole is open from the bottom of a glacier to its top, the weight of the ice pushes water up the hole most of the way. But here we were looking far down the hole, and no water.

Got to be blocked, someone said.

Yes but where?

Eventually we got to the bottom of the hole; no water at any point along the way.

Hey you know what? This glacier has bottomed out. There's just no more water to pump!

So it will slow down now.

For sure.

How soon will we know?

Couple years. Although we should see it right away too. But we'll need a few years to be sure it's really happened.

Wow. So we did it.

Yep.

There would be maintenance drilling, of course. And the glaciers would still be sliding down into the sea under their own weight, at their old slower speed, so every decade or so they would have to be redrilled upstream a ways from the current holes. There were going to be lots of people working down here for the foreseeable future— maybe decades, maybe forever. A rather glorious prospect, we all agreed, after thawing out and getting into the dining hut, standing high on its big sled runners.

Little windows on the south side of the hut gave a view of the Shackleton Range, oddly named, as he never got near this place. Possibly it was near where his proposed cross-Antarctic route would have gone, but when the *Endurance* got caught in the ice and crushed, all that plan had to be scrapped, and they had set about the very absorbing project of trying to survive. We toasted him that day, and promised his ghost we would try to do the same. Drop Plan A when the whole thing goes smash, enact Plan B, which was this: survive! You just do what you have to, in an ongoing improvisation, and survive if you can. We toasted his rugged black-cliffed mountains, rearing up into the low sky south of us. We were 650 meters above sea level, and ready for food and drink. Another great day in Antarctica, saving the world.[1]

1. Interested to know more about climate solutions included? See https://www.greenstories.org.uk/anthology-for-cop27/solutions/refreeze-the-arctic/

https://www.greenstories.org.uk/anthology-for-cop27/solutions/refreeze-the-glaciers/

THE CARETAKER

by Matthew Hanson-Kahn

Is it a disco light show, an aurora, or am I now fuzzy in the head? Is it just another moment of ever more frequent absent mindedness, the slip of the ageing mind where my brain skids on a banana skin, dumping me somewhere new, somewhere unexpected? Is that where I am, imagining this bioluminescence? Am I living a waking dream, transporting me to the giddy days of childhood, when the reef was ablaze? I give myself a mental pinch, to jolt myself to reality, but the lights are still here, not as bright as the extinguished lights of my youth, but they are here, nonetheless. I marvel at the oceanic fireflies, a seabed 5th of November. If it is a dream, then let me sleep forever.

Corals are very old animals, and when I say old, I don't mean creaky boned. Press a shiny coin into your hands granny old; I mean, beyond the limits of our imagination, old. Think of The Colossus of Rhodes or the Pyramids. 4,650 years old; now multiply that roughly 200,000 times and that's what I mean by old. That is when coral first appeared in our oceans, creeping, colonising, along with their wobbly, transparent cousins jellyfish. They are neon light show pleasing, or rather the animals that inhabit the coral, radiating blues, purples, greens, reds and pinks, a gay rainbow of ocean fauna. Little animals with the appearance of nettles, hedgehog backs, bathroom sponges and dermatitis; these polyps terraform the ocean floor.

In my childhood coral was abundant, perhaps 500 types if I counted them all, plentiful loaves and fishes. Talking of fishes the coral sustained maybe a 1,000 reef fish, though I was barely conscious of their darting, skulking or marauding presence. I swam, I dived, I harvested, and they were there, ubiquitous. I didn't bat an eyelid. This array of life and colour was the backdrop to my youth, its permanence unquestioned.

At first it was fishing. Spears, nets and baskets, scooping as much of the sea's rich harvest as was possible. Sad, but no tragedy, people need to live, sustainability the key, as the fish stock and coral bounced back. Then in early adulthood I witnessed bigger nets scooping thousands of fish in one greedy swoop and anchors crashing through coral, a wrecking ball to an increasingly decrepit old house. Still, the oceans coped although fish stock wobbled, and the coral struggled to repair, sticking plasters to a growing wound.

I sensed we would survive, but as I moved through my middle-aged years, my naivete, that faith and trust in the good, or at least common sense of humankind, was sorely exposed. Vast nets dredged the ocean floor, ripping apart the reef. I went down in the fifth, a combination of punches battering my head and torso. Winded, I climbed to my feet, ready to recover. Then in the eighth came a series of concussive blows, as nutrients and pesticides from land runoff decreased the oxygen in the shallow coastal waters. I gasped for air and fought to survive through the onslaught as algae covered the surface, feeding off the rich nutrients. The fields of seagrass and plants that I remembered withered, and with them the fish and crustaceans. Even then, I still believed I could survive the fight, hanging on for dear life to stop the relentless body blows. Then came the assault from which I could never recover, climate change, that one two to the body and with it the uppercut of rising ocean temperatures. I hit the canvas, Ali felling Richard Dunn again and again. But this time I wasn't going to make the count. I couldn't hear the shouts from my corner. My legs had gone and with them my spirit, and my fight to survive.

That was it. The multiple assaults had left the ocean scarred and lifeless. So I dived. I swam amongst the scarred wreckage of the reef, scattered and lifeless, the grim reaper's harvest complete. Gone was the forest of seagrass, leaving an underwater desert of pale-yellow sand stretching towards the darkness. Deserts hold little life and this was no exception. The occasional lone fish that had lost its way, or perhaps working on instinct, remembering more abundant times. I dreamed at night of the olden times, where the reef put on a show of colourful glitz, the backdrop to an all singing, all dancing cabaret of colourful sea creatures. Each day a party, each day a riot. I was young and times were good. But now, as I enter my older years, my memory is jaded, my limbs stiffen, my eyesight fails, and it is a blessing that I have little appetite, as food is scarce. Each day is a living nightmare, as I patrol the desert searching for something, anything, that will give me hope.

Back when I was young, something peculiar occurred. It was a hurricane, not unusual for this part of the world, but this one was a beast and it invaded my sanctuary. So much so that land became an extension of the sea. It began with the sun heating the ocean to a bath time warmth, the type that caresses you all over. Condensation ascended, crashing into cold air above; the air swirled as they conjoined. The greater the condensation, the more violent the meeting, and the air moved faster, whipping up storm force winds that heltered and skeltered around the central calm eye.

Then it moved landwards. Beneath the ocean there was calm, while above was energy and turbulence, a duck treading water inversely. At landfall, the wind ripped at structures and vegetation, prizing its fingers into gaps, finding weakness and tearing what it could from its mooring, lifting it high and hurling like a champion's discus. What remained after this violent assault would then be subjected to worse. You can hide from the wind, somewhere secure, hatches battened, doors bolted, but you can't run from the water. If you conceal yourself, it will find you curled up in your hide and seek corner. All is submerged head to toe, brine pickled cucumbers drowned in dill. My first realisation was being swept up the coast, across the beachfront. Timber huts flattened like matchwood, the beachside bar turned to kindling. Then I was washed along streets, across lawns and a surge took me up to a suburban front door, where it knocked once, then crashed through the sturdy structure as if it was a net curtain. I sprawled on my back along the hallway, into the kitchen where I swirled in a vortex for seconds before being vomited out of the backdoor.

Hurricane, typhoon, cyclone, call it what you want. You can even name it Katrina or Franklin, but this isn't what determines the destructive force of the beast. I witnessed the destruction of crops, the death of livestock, land changed forever. Buildings collapsed and people fled the storm surge, not returning to a land that could no longer support them.

Now empty villages stand where there were once thriving fishing communities. With no reef for protection, the coast floods changed from fertility to salinity. This attitude of take take take and screw the future has done just that; a brief moment of abundance followed by wasteland.

My continuous patrolling of this once abundant shoreline now turned to waste, akin to the Marie Celeste, floating aimlessly. Nameless passengers with no destination, all life long since perished. Venturing to a part of the shoreline that I haven't visited for a while in hope, I struggle, wheezing, muscles stiff, limbs that ache, everywhere another jag, a sharp stick to the ribcage, a dull thud to the spine. It seems the years have finally caught up with me and everything beneath the waves is misty. The fog of my eyes, the creak of my body makes searching that bit harder. Then a something catches my eye, an irregular structure on the barren floor of the ocean. Turning to investigate, I see a wooden frame and attached young polyps of coral. Through my blurred vision, I see the beginnings of life. A nursery of toddlers has been magically transported to the seabed. My excitement dulls the pain, soothes the limbs, and I continue. Another frame, this one nearly covered with coral. I see blue, pink, green. I had forgotten its beauty and around it, the beginnings of snails, fish, life. I swim further and first I am greeted by sporadic fish, then a clump of coral, and another, and another, an ocean garden replanted.

Perhaps there are more further on, but I am tired and turn away. The exhilaration, the extra distance, has exhausted me more than I think, so I barely notice the small boat draw alongside, the powerful hands that lift me out of the water.

"Hey what we got? Come on, old boy let's have a look at you." Placed onto the deck, hands turn me feeling my limbs, stroking my forehead, checking a patient at the doctor's surgery. "How old do you reckon this fella is?"

"Maybe 50 years. He's been around the block, that's for sure."

"He was probably here before the reef was decimated."

"Yeah, amazing that he's still alive. Here, I'll just tag him and we'll put him back."

"That's so cool, perhaps we'll see more turtles now that we're re-planting the reef."

"Yeah, let's put him back in." I feel hands lower me over the side of the boat and gently into the water. "See ya fella."

"Yeah, and good luck." The boat doesn't move as I swim slowly away. They are loath to let me go and I feel the affection in their distant gaze. I hear the engine as the boat heads away towards the fledgling reef. They are now the caretakers and I know that, in their hands, I might once again dive in rainbow seas teeming with life. [1]

---

1. Interested to know more about climate solutions included?
   See https://www.greenstories.org.uk/anthology-for-cop27/solutions/coral-planting/

MOSTLY FOR YOU

by Jenni Clarke

Miriam stared into her morning coffee. Last night's date was the best and the worst she'd ever experienced. She was never dating again.

Jerry was a feast for the eyes and mind. She couldn't remember how many topics they'd discussed, only that he'd listened to her opinions as if they mattered rather than bulldozing through her words. It felt like she'd known him forever.

She swiped a tear from her cheek in annoyance. One evening with a man was not worth heartache, and yet she was crying into her coffee, stomach too knotted to eat, brain rehashing everything.

Miriam's flatmate thumped her shoulder

'Girl, why are you still here? You'll be late for work.'

Miriam glanced at the clock on the wall and swore. Her first client was a dragon, but she paid well. She couldn't lose this job mooning over a man she'd just met.

'You best cough up later, girl.'

Miriam grabbed her keys. 'Sure, I will. Pizza and beer? My treat.' She hurried down the stairs.

Her little car coughed into life and Miriam thanked the car gods. She wished she could afford a new one. Her blue beast drank fuel and spat out more nasties than she was happy with, but the rising living costs meant her meagre savings were melting away like an ice cube on a hot bonnet.

'Oh, come on,' she shouted at the slow driver in front. 'You could get a bus through there.' She slapped her hands on the wheel, tension building through her body. One minute late, and she'd lose money. One minute.

A gap in the traffic allowed her to risk overtaking, although it meant giving the other driver heart palpitations. A horn blared behind her, but she zipped away, almost running a red light before swerving into the avenue and slamming her brakes on to avoid hitting Buster. Killing her client's pet would not be a good idea, even if it meant less cleaner for her.

Miriam parked in the driveway with seconds to spare, but still had to grab her cleaning equipment and hurry to the back of the house and through the utility door, ready to blast away any dirt or germs. She never skimped on the products she used, but after last night, she shuddered at the amount of harsh chemicals in her box.

Her client's scowl and tapping foot told her all her efforts had been in vain. It didn't matter how strong or expensive her cleaning products were, it would not be good enough. She was late. There would be a speck of dust somewhere, a smear on a mirror, or an imagined crumb wedged in a corner. A reduction would be demanded, and one rule of being a self-employed cleaner was you never argued with your client.

Miriam dumped pizza and two opened beers onto the table in front of Rose and flopped onto the sofa.

'Spill, girl,' Rose said, grabbing a slice and waving it in Miriam's face. 'And don't skimp on the details or fob me with nothings. I saw your glum this morning.'

Miriam laughed. 'Great date, hottie, conversation, no awkwardness, perfect, disaster.'

Rose picked up both beers and held them out of Miriam's reach.

'Okay. He was lovely, we chatted about everything, and he listened. Can you imagine? He didn't steer the conversation back to himself or football. He listened. And his big brown eyes that saw me and didn't judge, well I guess they did in the end, and he has gorgeous hair, natural, you know and sort of flopping in his eyes.' She stopped as Rose passed her a bottle and laughed.

'You dated a puppy, girl?'

'Ha, no. Maybe I should next time.' She grabbed a slice of pizza.

'Why no rematch?'

Miriam shook her head. 'You should've seen the disgust on his face when I told him I was a cleaner.'

'Get out. What a snob. You're better off without that one, babes.'

'No, not a snob. He cares about the environment.' Miriam explained what had happened, and her stomach ached at the thought of never seeing him again. 'He's got a point, too. I looked it up when I got home.'

'What you on, sister? The man trashed your hard-earned business.'

'But he didn't know he was slagging off my business. He was just citing an example.'

'You didn't tell him?'

Miriam shook her head and dumped the pizza back on the table.

'How could I? Oh, Rose, what have I done?'

Rose peered at her. 'Oh girl, you got it bad. There's better out there for you. Forget the opinionated dude.'

'But there isn't, and he wasn't. He's the first man I've connected with since, well, you know...and he ordered dessert first.'

'No way.' Rose's voice softened.

'He did.' Her stomach fizzed at the memory, how their eyes had met in surprise when they both asked for the dessert menu first.

Sleep was not an option. The horrified look on Jerry's face loomed large in her head, and giant bacteria waving flags with murderer written on them, these were followed by red bills, and sleeping rough on the streets. She threw off the bedclothes, grabbed a coffee, switched on her computer, and trawled through everything she could find on cleaning products and bacteria.

After eliminating hype and adverts, she came across a college website which shocked her brain awake. There were more bacteria cells than human cells in the body? What? Most bacteria are good, and over cleaning with strong chemicals can kill the microbes that fight off the harmful ones. Her knee bounced up and down so fast she ended up with cramp in her calf muscle.

Her job was doing more harm than good, but she needed her job. It had taken years to build up her client list. She paced the room.

'You're buzzing, girl. I'll have whatever you had for breakfast,' Rose said with bleary eyes, and a yawn. 'Wait. Did you even go to bed?'

'No,' Miriam flicked on the kettle. 'You'll never believe what I've found out, and it's all because of Jerry.'

'Oh, Mirri babes. He's a bad guy, after all? Men are not worth crying over.'

'No. Not about him.' Although she'd been tempted. 'Those super strong "kills ninety-nine percent of germs" chemicals I use are doing more harm than good. I'm probably making my clients sick, and me too. All those migraines I get could be my fault. And I must tell them. My clients.' She slumped into the chair, resting her forehead on her hands. 'But then I won't have a job, and I'll be on the streets.'

'Too much caffeine and not enough zeds have addled your brain, love,' Rose said, and patted her on the shoulder. 'I'll make you a camomile tea and you reschedule your appointments for today and rest.'

'No, I can't.' Miriam groaned. 'If I tell my clients, they won't want me, and if I don't, I'm harming them. Oh, Ms Winter's asthma? What if it's my fault?' Her chest tightened and she couldn't breathe. Karma?

'And they say I'm the drama queen,' Rose muttered, and handed Miriam a cup of tea. 'Go to work, finish the week, rest on the weekend. I'm sorry I won't be here. But don't you do anything rash, girl. Promise.'

Miriam promised.

She spent the weekend experimenting with lemons, limes, white vinegar, cider vinegar, baking soda, tea tree essential oil, peppermint essential oil, Castile soap, a rosemary plant and olive oil. By Monday her body ached, but the flat was clean despite a slight lingering vinegar smell, and she had several bottles of natural cleaning products ready to fill her car.

She was sticking on the last label when Rose slammed through the front door.

'Damn it, girl, you didn't have a dirty weekend, that's for sure,' Rose said. 'Cleaning on your days off is a sign of something seriously wrong. We need to talk, but I've only time for a shower before work. Later, babes, it's a must.' She glared until Miriam nodded.

Rose vanished into the bathroom and Miriam smiled at her exclamations. The white vinegar and tea tree oil mix had dissolved the ever-growing mould around the shower base and window, with a little elbow grease thrown in. And it smelt fresh rather than chemical.

As Miriam's car spluttered it's morning protest, she was still pondering what to tell her clients. Her business 'The SUPER STRONG CLEANER' - guaranteed to remove ninety-nine percent of all bacteria and one hundred percent of grime–was now a lie. Homemade cleaners would only eliminate the bad bacteria, leaving the good ones to live happily ever after.

Should she use the new cleaning products and see what her clients said? Could she cope with making them rather than ordering online? It was much cheaper, but time consuming. Although, once she'd perfected the recipes, it would be quicker, and they'd last longer if she didn't clean as much. What else did she have to do with her time? Dating was out. Jerry's face filled her head, and she wanted to cry. She was a bacteria killer, destroying the ecosystem one evil cleaning product at a time.

A horn blared, and she flinched. The light was green. She almost stalled the car in her haste to move. Damn the man for getting in her head, and not in her knickers. She blushed. What was wrong with her? She had to stop thinking about him. He'd probably looked her up and was even more disgusted with her.

'But I didn't know,' she said, but then shook her head. Ignorance was not an excuse.

Miriam parked in time to see her first client strapping her third child into the car, the youngest was screaming and scratching her arms, the poor kid had terrible eczema. There was no opportunity to talk to the frantic mum about using a different cleaning product, but when Miriam entered the house, she stared at the work surfaces. Should she use the new stuff without asking? Was it her fault the child had eczema? Or was she blowing this all out of proportion because her libido had awakened like a volcano, as Rose said?

Miriam clung to the kitchen island and made her choice. She couldn't risk harming a child. She'd use the new products in all her client's homes, but say nothing, and see what happened. And after a month, she'd send a letter to explain what she was now doing, and how she was going to change her business name and slogan, and then she would probably be signing on for universal credit.

She was right, her clients were furious she'd not informed them before changing her products. Letters condemned her as a fraud, misleading advertisement, a hippy, jumping on the green bandwagon, using them as an experiment, and betraying their trust. Some refused to pay her for the last month as they didn't want any germs growing in their house, thank you very much.

Only two clients kept her as their cleaner. Two. Her most demanding, who claimed she preferred the smell of the new products and whose asthma had lessened over the month, and the hurried mum, who said her daughter's eczema had calmed down. She'd invited Miriam to come to the mother and toddler group as many of the mums worried about the rise in asthma, eczema, and tummy bugs in their children despite keeping surfaces clean with anti-bacteria products.

Two clients, and both had listened to her advice. They only wanted her once a fortnight.

'Girl, you're screwed,' Rose had said when she'd told her. 'I can cover your share of the rent this month, hon. Give you time to see sense.'

How was she going to pay the bills? At least she had time to design her new business name and slogan, but what should she do with the chemicals stored in boxes in her bedroom? The company didn't do refunds, and she didn't know how to dispose of them.

'Sell 'em on eBay, girl. That's the easiest way,' Rose said, but Miriam's conscience wouldn't let her.

'It's money you need, love,' Rose said with a shake of her head. 'I'll sell them for you.'

'No, it's the same thing. Now I know what it does, I can't.'

Rose patted her shoulder and left for work.

Work. Miriam sighed. At least she wasn't spending much on fuel or cleaning products. She had plenty of ingredients left to make more and had a good idea of which worked best.

She flicked through the local paper looking for people wanting a cleaner. There were several, but after a closer look at their numbers, she blinked away tears. They were her old customers. A wave of despair and regret turned into fierce anger. Miriam threw the paper in the bin.

'Stupid woman. Why did you listen to a man and destroy your perfectly good business?' Although it wasn't a good business, just one that paid the bills. She grabbed the paper back out of the bin and tucked it in to her cleaning basket. It was brilliant for cleaning windows, and better for the environment. Man-made cloths leaked tiny plastic fibres. She froze.

'Oh, no. Rose is right. I've turned into an eco-nerd.' Tears plopped onto the table. Why was it so hard to do the right thing? Or find the right man? Wait. Had she jeopardised her business for a man? She shook her head. No, she was doing this because it was important and felt right, and what was wrong with being an eco-nerd anyway? She could share her knowledge at the toddler group and maybe get more clients, but she wasn't an expert and what if their children got sick?

She stared at her cleaning basket, which was prettier than a plastic box, and the word mental stared back from an advert on the back page of the newspaper.

'That sums me up.' She pulled the paper back out.

'Oh. Environmental Answers. Ha. Let's see if you can answer my list of questions.' She picked up her phone and tapped in the number.

'Environmental Answers. Zara here. How may I help you?'

Fifteen minutes later the woman had convinced Miriam to meet with their environmental projects manager, despite her protest that her problem was about her job, not a community project, and one week later, Miriam was walking into town through the park, with a folder full of research and ideas. It was so pretty, and the fresh air eased her mounting panic.

She stopped. When was the last time she had sat on the grass and read a book, or had a picnic? She listened to the bird song and the buzz of insects. How could she ever use strong chemicals again? This was the right choice, even if she became homeless.

The Environmental Answers offices were above a café in a side street and the scent of coffee was tempting, but she couldn't waste a penny. She swigged cold water from her flask, wiped her sweaty hands on her dress, and entered. She felt like an imposter, but before she could run away, 'please call me Zara' said,

'You must be Miriam. You can go straight in.'

Miriam walked through the open door and froze.

Jerry stood. His face mirrored her surprise.

'Miriam?'

'Oh, I think this is a mistake,' she stepped back and bashed her elbow on the door frame. 'Ouch, ow.' She blinked away tears. What a twit she was. 'I'll leave, and I'm sorry to waste your time. It was such a great night, and I spoilt it and after I looked everything up, and...

sorry.' Shut up, brain. She turned to leave, but Jerry was closing the door and taking her arm, not the one that throbbed, and leading her to a comfy chair.

'Sit down. Elbows hurt like hell. Can I get you something, ice maybe?'

She shook her head.

'I'm fine.'

He sat in the chair opposite but didn't meet her eyes.

'I guess you're here to shout at me,' he said. 'Go ahead. I deserve it. Slagging off your company, although I didn't know it was yours until the next day. I was so embarrassed, and the look on your face. I should have called, but I knew you'd never want to see me again.' He scratched his neck.

Miriam stared. Was he blushing?

'But I did,' she said, and it was her turn to blush. 'I didn't think you'd want to see me. You were horrified when I said I was a cleaner.'

'No, I was horrified I'd insulted you.'

His mouth twitched and within seconds, they were both laughing, although Miriam didn't know why. Her heart thumped louder than a steam train when, somehow, they ended up holding hands.

'Then why are you here, Miriam? Zara said something about mothers and toddler talks, but...?'

He pulled his hand away, raised his eyebrows and looked at her, melting away any coherent thought she had.

'Um, yes, sort of.' She fumbled in her bag for her folder. 'I did some research and changed my products to natural ones. Now I don't have a business, but I do have lots of nasty chemicals I can't dispose of. I can't pay my rent, but I can't sell the stuff. One of my clients wants me to talk to mums about microbes, but what if I say the wrong thing?' Her hands shook and all the pages fluttered out of the folder.

Miriam grabbed the nearest sheets.

'Stop,' Jerry said, picking one up and reading, 'Gentle Green Cleaner–a healthier clean home. Wait, you risked your business because of me?'

'For the environment,' she said. 'But mostly for you.' She groaned. 'Did I say that out loud?'

'You did.' He grinned. 'Shall we discuss your ideas? Zara thinks they have potential for a grant, and after we could try that new desert café, if you'd like?'[1]

---

1. For more information see: https://www.greenstories.org.uk/anthology-for-cop27/solutions/eco-friendly-cleaning/

THE FOREST AWAITS

by Lyndsey Croal

*W*elcome to the Northern Kelp Forest Restoration Project and
Experience. We hope you enjoy your visit to one of Scotland's
*most beautiful protected areas. Please follow our information guides at
all times – we are only visitors here and should leave the forests as we
found them.*

The salty sea air is like the smell of home to Maris. The waves a
sound she'll never forget. It's been fifty years since she first took a boat
to this coastal forest – back then, it had been more of a nursery than a
forest, and she'd been on a motor-run fishing vessel that could only fit
five or six students, including her and Jakob, alongside the crew. Now,
the wind-sail boat moves seamlessly across the waves, and is teeming
with tourists, researchers, and divers.

Maris sits still, content, wrapped up warm with a flask of tea
in hand, as sightseers mill around her. Her granddaughter Sorcha
has gone to find some food for the journey across. She's heard the
hand-cut-kelp soup is quite something, even if she'll never really see

the forest itself as a food source. But, things change, and the Advisory Group made a good case for continuing sustainable harvest alongside species management, which so far, seems to have been a success with little impact on the ecosystems. And nowadays, cheap and sustainable food sources aren't to be scoffed at.

To her left, a guide is explaining the origin of the Kelp Forest to a school group, and Maris listens distantly, enjoying the collective wonder as the guide explains the process of planting and restoration.

'The famous coastal forests began their restoration journey as nurseries of seedlings sequestering around a million tonnes of carbon every year, on their journey to tackle climate change. Now, the forests equal peatlands, forests, and soils on the land as carbon stores, and sequester over six million tonnes of carbon each year, with marine environments and blue carbon around Scotland's coast altogether responsible for sequestering over forty million tonnes. Over the years, the forests have not only helped fight climate change, but have provided lucrative and sustainable opportunities for divers, harvesters, fishers, and tourists alike.'

Maris notices a few of the harvesters and researchers fully kitted out in their gear at the rear of the boat, preparing for their dives into the forest. The guide continues. 'Here we benefit from special marine protected areas, where dredging and bottom-towed fishing and trawling, are no longer allowed. This ensures forests can continue to be a blue carbon haven, with wildlife populations thriving, and still allowing creel and other fishing industries to continue sustainably. Dr Taylor and her husband, founders of the Kelp Forest Restoration Project, wanted the forests to be not only environmental successes, but sites for education and respite too. She wanted future generations to be able to enjoy and experience a legacy of what's possible when people, communities and Government, come together for a better world. That's why we're able to bring you here today.'

The Project was founded in 2026, a flagship initiative to restore and protect the great seaweed forests off the Scottish west coast. In the 2020s and 2030s, warming seas and poor management practices were becoming an ever-growing threat to ecosystems, with kelp disappearing faster than the world's rainforests. However, with new marine protected areas designation following the most ambitious Marine Act of 2030, rewilding and regeneration efforts, alongside global partnerships for seascape restoration, the project was able to help kelp forests thrive as part of a sustainable economy for coastal communities. In return, the forests provide resilient habitats for hundreds of species of marine flora and fauna and every year are one of the most successful nature-based solutions, soaking up and storing millions of tonnes of carbon every year.

Maris remembers her first dive here so clearly that it's imprinted in her mind. It was during university, where she and Jakob met studying marine biology together. They'd come out to the west coast for a field trip, for sampling and research. Signalling to one another, she and Jakob had jumped off the boat, clad in their full dry suits and weighted down with equipment, into the stinging sea. Bubbles and sediment rose like glitter all around, and she remembers feeling the weight of water above and below. The weight of the world.

They dove down to the rocky seabed, the echoey sound of breathing in her ears. The further down they went, the lower the light became, though on a sunny day the sun's rays reached the waiting forest below. There, the sea was calm, kelp swaying slightly in the gentle currents. Row upon row of red, brown and grey-green plants hooked with holdfasts to rocky outcrops along the seabed. Back then, all the kelp had been naturally occurring – not the mix of natural and artificial environments that existed now.

In these forests, their other home, Maris had always marvelled at the wildlife that teemed all around – crabs, urchins, anemones, sea slugs, starfish, limpets, and fish swimming to and fro between fronds. It was a mesmerising sort of magic to watch this underwater world bursting with life – like she was on a different planet altogether.

In those early research trips, Maris often encountered a group of curious seals swimming amidst the forest catching fish. Sometimes, they'd come up to their cameras and nudge the equipment, but it was always with curiosity rather than threat. It was then she knew that if she'd had the choice, she could have stayed down there, watching this world, forever.

Over the years, as her research interests grew, and she began her doctorate with Jakob, Maris began to notice the degradation of her special world. The kelp forests thinning out, receding into patches because of warming temperatures, dredging, bottom trawling, species imbalances, and pollution and waste. Once, she came across an entire area decimated and lifeless from trawling, and afterwards months and months had passed by and she'd barely seen a seal grace the area she had held so dear. So, after graduating with their doctorates, Maris and Jakob knew what they wanted to do – they set up the Kelp Forest Restoration Project, and thus their life together began.

There are two tourist boat trips to the forests per week, with tours benefitting from our cutting-edge drone and award-winning virtual experiences technology, our unique glass-bottomed amphitheatre for easy viewing, and experienced guides on hand to answer questions at all times. All of our boats are fully renewable and run from solar and wind-sail energy for low impact travel. Once a month, these tours double

as research and planting trips – so if you've signed up for a regeneration
experience, you can collect your rock and seedling in the nursery at the
back of the boat.

Maris and Jakob worked for years on the project, putting everything they had into it. At first, there was a lot of trial and error – kelp needed a place to stand, to anchor to, and so to expand the forests they needed to create the perfect habitats. Maris remembers the first regeneration boat, weighted down by rocks so that their approach towards the edge of the receding forests was slow and almost comical. It took them all afternoon to drop the rocks and seedlings with their small team, and they were still working as dusk fell and forced them home. Slowly, after several visits, the kelp seedlings took root and began to grow. But it wasn't enough. The growth couldn't keep up with the changing tides and growing pressures, and they realised everything would need to scale up fast – reintroduction by the thousands, not hundreds, in places all around the coast if they were really going to create a viable carbon sink. For this, the project would need to grow more than Maris and Jakob could tackle alone.

It was Jakob's idea to turn some of their early sites into special environmental experiences – a team building exercise or volunteer day for companies and communities alike. Boatloads started to sail from all around Scotland to new viable forests, teams of volunteers working with the project on reintroduction. Together, they'd gather rocks and seedlings, then drop them carefully into the expanding underwater world below. With funding for kelp planting, the project also supported fishers to join the forest restoration efforts, quickly becoming key players in the fight to protect the marine environment.

As the project grew, so too did their ambition, and they worked hard to find funding from donors and foundations. At the same time, they campaigned for everything from protected areas designation to sustainable fishing practices so that their efforts of regeneration wouldn't be in vain. What was the point of restoring habitats, if they would just be destroyed later by counterproductive activities? There was a time when Maris had felt like giving up – when they seemed to be spending all their time fighting new licences for inshore trawling or dredging in areas where the forests were now growing, rather than making things better, and all seemed lost. But then the communities all came together – the same communities that had become teams of volunteers, had seen the forests for themselves with a renewed connection, or had found a new way of making a living as forests grew. Creel fishers were able to take advantage of growing populations of crabs and lobsters, as well as diversify their income with funding from the restoration project to become keen deployers of the forests themselves.

Divers and tourists benefited from the exciting marine life expansion, and as urchin populations grew in the forests, urchin harvester crews began making regular visits, gathering the prickly kelp-eating nuisances, and selling them on as a delicacy. Everything found a balance, and those who had found this life in the kelp forests came together and campaigned tirelessly against damaging proposals and in the end the support came, along with new designations and legislation. Finally, the tides were changing and the forests were protected, flourishing with a sustainable future. For a while Maris and Jakob could step back and watch the project grow organically.

By that point, Maris was heavily pregnant, with Eilidh on the way. They moved into a small cottage in a quiet coastal village, a house just on the sea, the view only slightly obscured by the seawalls built up to push back the rising water. It was a happy time, despite the challenges that came with living the rural life.

As Eilidh grew up, their daughter took to the land more than the sea. Despite Maris's attempts, Eilidh resisted early morning boat trips, sea swims, and dives, preferring instead to stay at home, explore bogs or woods, or when they would go to the beach, she would sit on the rocks and look out towards the hills and mountains. Later, she met a similar landfaring spirit and they bought a croft together – one that needed a lot of love and care to bring it back. And Maris realised then that she and Eilidh were alike in many ways. That despite the juxtaposition – a child of the earth and a mother of the sea – they both held the same vision for change.

On holidays and summers, Maris and Jakob would retreat inland and spend days on the farm with Eilidh and her partner, and everything felt so opposite to those in Maris's natural habitat. The sounds were clear, not echoey like the mystical ones from under the water. The smells thick, cloying, but in many ways pleasant, while the sea held a fresh sharpness in the air that couldn't be replicated anywhere else. Still, she enjoyed it when Eilidh explained her practices with such enthusiasm that it was clear she'd found her calling. The affinity she had with the land, with her animals, with the earth and the greenery, was just like Maris had with her own second home. When she learned during one visit that the animal feed was mixed with kelp harvested from her own forests, she felt a renewed connection between the two worlds.

Though, after a few weeks of walking the land, helping with harvests, animal care, and tree planting, Maris was always ready to go. She could feel the call of the sea, and when they were back by the coast, she knew she was going home.

While you're on board with us today, why not try one of our sustainably harvested kelp products, hand-cut by our skilled divers and fishers. These provide a direct healthy and sustainable food source, as well as being used around the country as an additive in natural fertilisers and animal feed. All profits from sale go directly into the regeneration project, as well as jobs for local people to continue our important work.

The worst day of Maris and Jakob's journey together came not from the project itself, but when the sea took their home. It felt like an injustice after all their life's work as it rose up amidst the worst storm they'd seen in years. They watched with the rest of the town, holed up in the community centre, as their family cottage was swept away into the waves. They'd gone to live with Eilidh for a time while they tried to get their life back, and the project had to be put on hold for a while.

It helped that during that time, Eilidh shared the news of Sorcha, and that year they welcomed a granddaughter into the world. And as Sorcha grew up, she grew to share the love of both her grandparents' sea and her mother's land. Jakob was besotted, and he took to being a grandparent as if it were his calling. When they moved back to the coast, in a house further from shore, Sorcha would visit every school holiday, and they'd enjoy so many magical trips together – whale watching, beachcombing, rockpool hopping, even seaweed harvesting. It was Sorcha's idea, after one of Jakob's tours that he gave with such enthusiasm, to create the immersive visitor experiences so that everyone could enjoy the forests and take part in the work they'd built. She helped the project with the technology proposals and interactive elements, even designing the guide documents and everything that came with it. It was her and Jakob's special project, and Maris had never been prouder of them both.

As part of your visit today, we welcome you to a fully immersive and interactive experience. Witness the kelp forests in their natural state.

See the thriving habitats, with more than 350 species, invertebrates, mammals, fish, and birds. For hopeful divers, you may wish to apply for a diving tour with our specialist guides, though the majority of our excursions and experiences allow for a visit without the need to go into the water.

The tour boat slows and they arrive near the great kelp forest. Maris feels a tug in her chest, as if a sea current lives within, pulling gently – it's almost time. To her side, schoolchildren gather by the big screen in the on-board open amphitheatre, with its dipped glass bottom so that tourists can look down to the seabed below. The tour operators then drop drones over the side and begin their demonstrations. The children watch in excited silence, staring at the split-screen as they show the drones dive further to the kelp forests below. In the small "experience pod", the kids line up and are given headsets, one by one, so that they can experience the sea almost as it would be diving below, without having to disturb the habitats themselves.

Maris watches on with a quiet satisfaction – the kids battling over who gets to go next, or who gets to move the drone's 360 camera. On one of the drone's screens, a seal swims by and stops, curiously, and tries to bite it playfully as the girl wearing the VR headset screams and giggles, hands reaching all around her as if trying to stroke the creature. On another, a drone is twisting around artificial posts that stick out of the softer seabed areas. From the wear and tear of them and the height of the kelp rooted to the base, they look like they've been standing there, steadfast, for many years. They likely have. Given a place to stand, nature is resilient. It persists.

Sorcha is coming towards Maris holding two tubs of soup, but she stops to watch the demonstrations with a fond smile.

When Sorcha was a wee girl, Jakob had held his arm around her shoulders after a snorkelling visit off this very spot. He'd told her all about the forests and the magic that lay within and that if she spent enough time watching, maybe she'd see it too.

'Mermaids?' Sorcha had asked.

'Maybe,' Jakob said. 'Did you know that some say the seals themselves were almost like mermaids – but they were called Selkies, and they could go between land and sea whenever they wished, their seal forms having an affinity to the water, their human bodies to the land.'

Sorcha had nodded. 'So they're like Mum and Gran put together?'

Jakob had chuckled, looking at Maris with a wink. 'Exactly. Though if your Gran could turn into a seal, I'm not sure she'd ever come out of the water again,' he said, to which Sorcha had giggled. Then, Jakob had whispered something to their granddaughter that he'd later told Maris was their magical secret. To this day when Sorcha is by the sea, she always looks like she's watching out for any magic within the depths, and when the water touches her skin, the smile never leaves her face.

Once the demonstration is over, and the school groups are taken to watch the seals that have just arrived to greet the boats, Sorcha returns to Maris.

With a tear in her eye, Maris looks to her granddaughter, and lets her take her arm as she stands to walk to the side of the boat.

'He always loved to see all of this,' she says to Sorcha. 'All these smiling people.'

'They're here because of you both,' Sorcha says.

Maris nods. 'And you, my wee Selkie,' she says, squeezing her granddaughter's hand. 'What did he tell you, that day on the boat, when you were younger?'

Sorcha looks up at Maris and smiles. 'He said that every second breath we take comes from the sea. So really, we were all made for both land and water, and you and Mum were the balance. He told me I had to help keep that balance.'

Maris smiles. 'Of course he did,' she says. 'Very philosophical, your grandfather.'

'He was right,' Sorcha replies, putting her head on her grandmother's shoulder. 'And I'm glad I get to live in both worlds.'

Maris laughs softly then takes a deep breath, tasting the tanginess of the salt-dry air, familiar in her lungs. It might have taken a whole lifetime to get here, but in the end, they'd made it together. And just look what she and Jakob had made in the process.

Maris takes Sorcha's hand, and they walk to the back of the boat together where things are quiet and still. There, she pulls out the urn from her bag. She closes her eyes and whispers her dreams to the sea, and then opens them to look to the horizon. A single tear falls into the water below, and in the distance a dual rainbow looms bright, a door to the otherworld.

Maris smiles as she opens the urn and tips Jakob's ashes out into the water. They fly upwards for a moment, like a whirl of clouds caught in a breeze, before drifting to settle on the water below, sinking into the kelp forests that had always been, and always will be, their home.[1]

---

1. To find out more about climate solutions included, see: https://www.greenstories.org.uk/anthology-for-cop27/solutions/seagrass-kelp/

PENANG FAIRHAVEN – A VISITOR'S GUIDE

by Steve Willis

N.B. Everything in this short story is fictional (including appendices) but we'd love to make it fact. It follows on from Blue Nation and OasIS.

Fly through this amazing city in 2062. See the amazing climate solutions.

Welcome to Malaysia! Welcome to Penang Fairhaven! This is the METATMHOLOTMGLYUIDETM introductory virtual tour of the city and its history. If you are having trouble with the HOLOglasses TM, please press the help button on the side and a real person will be along straight away to help you. I am your guide, known to most of you as Miss Chan. Fairhaven is my home. I have lived and worked in the city since it was first built, 40 years ago. I will show just a few of the many highlights of the city and also explain a few housekeeping tips which will make your trip much more enjoyable.

We are now hovering above the north dyke, facing the Malacca Strait. The water is two metres higher than it was when the project began in 2025 and I started my first job as a junior engineer on the Bazalgette pumping station. If we turn and face south, we can see the new city of Fairhaven laid out beneath our feet, a beautiful poly-cultural mixture of 18 districts from all around the world, the Arab Quarter, Little India, NewNew Orleans, New Venice, China Town, Russland, NewNew York, Heart of Africa, New Amsterdam and more that you will explore. It is home to ten million people.

Let's swoop down into NewNew Orleans, through the French Quarter. You can see the beautiful wide boulevards filled with trees, pedestrians and bikes. There is a San Francisco style trolley car and numerous stops on the Light Rail Transit which will whisk you anywhere in town. This popular 'Bourbon Street' stop has dozens of cafes, four metres below sea level, links to the river bus which travels the canals to many other parts of town. I love sitting on the top deck of the river buses and watching the world go by. These re-created quarters are a bittersweet reminder of the many beautiful places that have already been lost to sea level rise.

Take a seat with me in this Mamak stall for a moment – there are thousands around the city. I am, of course, biased, but Malaysia makes some of the best food in the world: Nonya, Malay, Indian, Chinese and every blend in between. Be bold, you'll find something you love.

HOUSEKEEPING POINT 1. WATER.

You will see that water is provided in jugs. The tap water tastes great and is totally safe to drink all around the city and the region, so there is no bottled water. There are also no single use plastics. All containers are melamine or Tupperware which are returned to the 'ReUse' slot at the municipal garbage collection points. You can pick up or refill a water bottle at any food outlet for free. It is pretty hot here, so make sure you stay hydrated.

In your hotels, B&Bs, and homestays, you are welcome to take long showers, and even baths – a rare treat for many visitors. Unlike most cities in the world, Penang Fairhaven has no water restrictions because of the large reservoirs and the drain separation. Rainwater joins the canals and runs into the reservoirs. Sewage is collected in a dedicated high solids system. 'Grey' water from showers, washing machines and domestic use is collected separately. This grey water is treated and then pumped inland to provide irrigation for the rice fields. We are constantly diverting fresh reservoir water into this system, so you may as well enjoy the thrill of an unrestricted shower first!

Let's continue. Gaining height, we now head along the great North Dyke which prevents flooding of the low-lying lands of Kedah and northwards, protecting the crucial rice fields – all the more important after the flooding of so much of Vietnam, Bangladesh and parts of China. The new biochar-based farming techniques have boosted yields three-fold.

You can see the fleets of Snow Geese Zeppelins which are recharging from the huge solar arrays floating on the reservoirs. This is their first stop of twelve on their long journey from the famous Equatorial Zeppelin yards around Singapore to Siberia and the Arctic. The Snow Geese spend the summer extinguishing peat fires, and in the darkness of winter help to refreeze the Arctic ice. Thousands of these nearly autonomous craft are working on the top of the world and hundreds of new zeppelins join them every year, expanding the fleet and replacing the losses. They form one of the biggest climate and albedo restoration projects attempted so far.

Further inland you can see the Regional Fast Rail Network that many of you travelled on. Most of it travels on land that is at least 20 metres above sea level and is secure for generations to come. Beyond that, you can see some of the palm oil plantations. These have also become major carbon sinks after switching practices and putting millions of tonnes of biochar into their soil. An impressive transformation.

Let's fly out over the Malacca Straits. Below us are many ships, travelling more slowly that they did in previous decades. You will see that some are also towing a high zeppelin as a water spray platform from which to make reflective clouds – one of our many ongoing climate solution trials. Despite many tankers still running on LNG, the ships are carbon negative as they are used as satellite-guided ocean-nutrification platforms. Once very controversial, this type of ocean nutrification involves fertilising carefully monitored sectors of the ocean to maximise primary productivity, managing algal blooms which are the foundation of the ocean food chain and a great method for blue carbon sequestration.

Heading back to Penang Fairhaven, you will see the fast Wigetworks ferries which connect the coastal towns of Malaysia, Sumatra and ports across the region. They are a lot of fun – the closest most people will ever get to flying in a real plane these days. They are all electrically powered, fast, and remarkably safe.

We are now crossing the first OceanOrchards site in the world. This site was my third real job, installing these remarkably simple seabed structures. They make great low-cost habitats for rebuilding fisheries. I worked alongside the local fishing communities who learned how to care for and harvest them. For tourists, this is a great day out, either in the nearly-a-submarine or actually diving amongst the submerged structures of the OceanOrchards themselves. You will be amazed at the abundance of fish, corals and other sea life. The more practical amongst you will be impressed by the carefully controlled fishing techniques that allow ongoing substantial fish catches while ensuring fish populations which are twenty times that seen in open waters. There are now thousands of these sites around the world and as well as producing a large proportion of the fish consumed, they are truly sustainable and are massive carbon sinks.

Just inland from the OceanOrchards and seagrass meadows, you will see the inundated west coast of Penang. Controversially, it was decided that the land protected by the necessary seawall was too small to justify the construction. Instead, the area has been turned over to mangroves. The northern section is fully natural, and a carefully preserved gene pool of truly wild mangroves. The southern section is the new mono-clonal TurboMangroves which grow five times faster and are coppiced for biochar. The wildlife living there seems indifferent to this, and is thriving. We are running a trial to see if these new mangroves can form the central reinforcement for new dykes that could be literally grown in place and then backfilled – watch this space.

HOUSEKEEPING POINT 2. FREEDOM TO AND FREEDOM FROM

Fairhaven is still very much a Malaysian city, but with 18 distinctly different districts, Fairhaven is also one of the most culturally diverse cities in the world. This diversity is the reason many of you have come here, but does bring some complications. We want everyone to be free to do more or less whatever they want and to be free from criticism or restriction, following the simple principle of: Freedom To and Freedom From. This means that while you can do pretty much whatever you like within the guidance of the law, you can't do it everywhere at all times. This separation in time and space (a classic Triz solution) allows us to all live alongside one another with joy rather than friction.

In the North America district, there are numerous distinct neighbourhoods. The NewNewOrleans area is free and easy and particularly popular amongst visitors. The Amish Community is also fascinating and well worth a visit, just not in the same attire or the same mindset. We residents have come to terms with this, but we realise it is a challenge for visitors. Naturally, there is an app for that, which is downloading on your phones and AI assistants. If you have Bluetooth, it will automatically update so you can get hints and tips in your ear by sound bone-conduction. The system guides you through what you can and can't wear, do, or say in the various districts. While this may seem restrictive, it is also powerfully liberating. The short shorts and spray on attire popular with tourists this season are welcome in some areas, but deeply offensive in others – which may only be one street away. This allows visitors to avoid making embarrassing faux pas and allows people to live in their own areas without too many glaring clashes.

Moving on: We are now at the southern dyke and hovering over the old international airport with its four massive runways. They are still in occasional use, but the area is now the largest aircraft museum in the world. I know the old-tech geeks amongst you will love this place (I know, because I am one too). To the north you'll see two huge freshwater lakes. There are many pleasant lakeside resorts where you'll enjoy a swim without the protective jellyfish suit unfortunately strictly required in the sea.

OCEAN STATE PLAZA.

We now head into the city and to Ocean State Plaza. This will be a highlight for those who consider themselves foremost citizens of The Ocean after respectful relocation as climate refugees. The 19th anniversary of the formation of 'The Ocean as an Independent State' is next week, and you will be able to join the celebrations. All are welcome – we are all citizens, after all.

It still amuses me that 'The Ocean' became an independent state as a result of a short story published in a climate fiction anthology that was written ahead of COP27, as Kim Stanley Robinson's *Ministry for the Future* had been in COP26. It was picked up and cherished by some delegates and then became a memorable episode in the Netflix 'Climate Mirror' series. This was followed by the largest global social media movement ever seen and a popular push to get the land governments of the world to accept the proposal. The revenue that The Ocean receives for present and past services rendered has provided the funds for enormous ocean and coastal restoration projects.

I was one of the first members of The Ocean team, before independence was agreed, and it is the proudest part of my life. Fairhaven is one of five Ocean capitals around the world, and I know that many of you hope to visit them all in time. The Ocean as an Independent State is an astonishing collective achievement, and allowed so many ocean, climate, and refugee-related shared calamities to be addressed from a broader perspective.

The Ocean coordinates the Ocean Orchards and the other Ocean carbon dioxide removal work as well as handling 150 million climate refuges so far. A number which is rising every year. The largest carbon drawdown has been through The Ocean, as reforestation and Carbon Capture and Storage have struggled. The Ocean is also coordinating the refreezing work in the Arctic – we hope to achieve the maximum summer ice extent in 10,000 years very soon. Another team is coordinating the even bolder plan to stabilise the ice sheets in Antarctica – following a plan very similar to the one outlined in Kim Stanley Robinson's classic book, *The Ministry for the Future*.

I will leave you here and let you explore the city virtually and in person at your leisure. All the things we have seen today and many more have links and their own META$_{TM}$HOLO$_{TM}$GLYUIDE$_{TM}$ tours. I am the guide on dozens of them, so will see you again soon!

APPENDIX 1 – THE OCEAN

This was another idea picked off the cutting room floor. It began many years ago with a light-hearted conversation over lunch with the head of sustainability for a major US bank. He pointed out that America only became great after it declared independence from the colonial power. By extension, The Ocean can only resolve its problems and become sustainable by declaring independence from the surrounding countries which currently use/take its resources for free. I love the map, which is the flag you all now know.

THE OCEAN – INDEPENDENT STATE

The Ocean declares independence from the land in order to resolve its own problems. The neighbouring countries will never truly put the interests of The Ocean on a par with their own.

The Ocean declares independence and starts to charge for services that have traditionally been provided/taken for free. Levies of 1% on fishing revenues. 0.1% on shipping. $1 per tonne for CO_2 sequestration. $10 per tonne for effluent. (Perhaps later to avoid advantage being taken of this) $100 per tonne for plastics. The services provided by The Ocean are valued at trillions of dollars and are currently taken for free.

Extensive use of global fishing watch tracker and satellites. The Ocean uses this revenue to fund Marine Protection Areass and other critical restoration activities. The Ocean assumes full authority of the open Ocean. 50/50 of Exclusive Economic Zones. 25% of coastal waters. People of all nations can become citizens of The Ocean.

The bill for each land-country is calculated and posted regardless of whether they are paying or not. Four numbers, from the date of the first UN conference on the Oceans, total from the start of the industrial revolution, annual total and per capita. This highly controversial approach would raise the profile of the issues The Ocean faces and help focus the discussion on how much the actual amounts are, rather than whether or not it is reasonable to charge for the services.

Charging for the services that were previously used/taken for free gave the Ocean the revenue that had never been available before to sort out its own problems and those of the coastal countries. A bright light in a bleak time. There was a lot of resistance initially, but the massive public support through social media for such an out-of-the-box idea quickly won over a small, pivotal group of countries that was just big enough to get the idea off the ground. Switzerland, Uzbekistan, and Kyrgyzstan were keen founder members.

Many people identified with The Ocean as the ultimate underdog, the largest occupied, unrepresented territory in the world. Journalists were particularly supportive – in a time where fake news continued to be a problem, it was thrilling that a fictional story could go on to have such influence.[1]

---

1. Interested to know more about climate solutions included? See https://www.greenstories.org.uk/anthology-for-cop27/stories/penang-fairhaven-a-visitors-guide/

and https://www.greenstories.org.uk/anthology-for-cop27/solutions/ocean-as-a-nation/

SAVING THE TITANICS

by Steve Willis, Martin Hastie, and D.A. Baden

John scanned the circle of chairs. All occupied bar two. The ten people in the room were getting restless. He checked the clock, hoping that they hadn't got lost. The session been moved at the last minute into one of the smaller rooms in the Community Centre to make way for a Zumba class. Finally, two girls stumbled in and sat down, eyes averted.

He stood up and smiled round the group.

'Welcome, everybody. I'm John, I'll be leading you all through the Climate Anxiety Alleviation Program. Over the next six weeks, we'll explore our thoughts and feelings about the climate. Can we have any volunteers to introduce themselves?'

Twelve pairs of eyes studiously avoided his gaze. Eventually, one lad, about twenty raised his hand.

'I'm Ethan, I don't have climate anxiety, I just came along to support my girlfriend.' He squeezed the hand of the girl next to him.

John looked at her, hoping she'd speak, but she dropped her eyes and looked away.

After a moment's awkward silence, Mary, one the late arrivals, stood up and cleared her throat. 'Hello everybody. I'm Mary. And I do have climate anxiety.'

A murmur of support made its way around the circle. Her fellow CAAPers listened intently, relieved that somebody else had taken the initiative.

'Some nights I lie there fretting. Not know what to do. By nature, I'm a reasonably optimistic person. But as I've come to understand more about the climate crisis, I've been prone to bouts of despair. Grief. Despondency. Hopelessness.'

The others watched and nodded, offering warm smiles of encouragement.

'I might be watching a film and suddenly, tears are streaming down my face. I don't know what to do.'

Those same tears came now, dampening her cheeks, misting up her glasses. John leapt from his seat and handed her a box of tissues.

Now that Mary had taken the plunge, other people in the circle introduced themselves and their fears. John was especially interested to hear from Stephen who had worked in the oil and gas industry for over twenty years before taking early retirement. He looked rather out of place amongst the youngsters, but he had a lot to get off his chest, a lifetime of guilt stored up inside and eating away at him.

There were now just two people who hadn't spoken.

John turned to the other latecomer. 'Would you like to go next?'

'Not really. But here goes...' She stood up and took a deep breath. 'My name is Niamh. And I have climate anxiety.'

More supportive nods and a few words of acknowledgment at her bravery for taking the floor. Stephen gave her a sympathetic thumbs up.

'Like Mary, I'm a student. Same course. But I'm angrier than Mary. We watched the Big Oil vs The World documentary last year. I was raging.' She glared at Stephen who shrank back in his chair.

'I'm frightened. We're going to be the generation who has to live through the Mad Max movies. You can see it on the horizon. Hear it. Smell it. Taste it. Feel the vibrations in the ground...' She took a moment to compose herself. John readied the tissue box in case the emotion overwhelmed her, but Niamh was made of sterner stuff.

'I didn't want to come tonight. Mary made me. I don't want moaning, or self-reflection. I want action. I want to see it fixed. And, naïve though it sounds, I want to help fix it.'

'Thank you, Niamh,' said John.

He noticed that the shy girl was clasping Ethan's hand but still looking at the floor. He gave up on her contributing and continued.

'These sessions are, as you know, modelled on the very successful Alcoholics Anonymous programme. They themselves were loosely based on church services, as they are familiar formats that bring people comfort. Today, we're going to have some readings which we will then discuss, as is done in a traditional bible study class.'

John took a book from under his chair and opened it to where a bookmark had been carefully placed.

'These three short stories were written as part of a group exercise with Girl Guides exploring the sinking of the Titanic.'

'Girl Guides!' Ethan snorted, and then shut up when his girlfriend cast him a doleful look.

'A sinking ship. Just what we need,' said Niamh.

John suspected her sarcasm was a defence mechanism against the fear and continued unperturbed.

'The task was to imagine themselves on the ship and consider how they could have averted the crisis. The stories work well as parables and encourage discussion of the problems that people face when presented with seemingly insurmountable problems.'

He stood up and began to read. The group were astonished to hear this straightlaced, serious-looking man affect a plummy young girl's voice, throwing himself into the reading with gusto, bringing the scenes to vivid life.

Good morning, ladies and gentlemen. I'm Jane, roving reporter of the 1st Pinkey's Green Girl Guide Troop, and I'm here to tell you about our thrilling adventure on the Titanic! We are heading to New York as part of a team introducing scouting and guiding to the United States of America.

On Wednesday – the 10th of April – we joined the Titanic in Southampton.

Today is Sunday, the fifth day of our absolutely spiffing trip. All fourteen girls standing together, wrapped up warm as a proper Girl Guide would be. Prepared for anything!

Lady Agnes Baden Powell arranged a packed programme. What fun we've had! The great lady led us on a grand tour of the ship, exploring every nook and cranny – the cathedral-like engine rooms, the bridge, the kitchens. We have become well known in such a short time, smartly presented in our pristine new blue uniforms.

In the spirit of being prepared, on the first day, we explored the lifeboats. Lady Agnes had written to White Star Line, who arranged that the 6th officer, Sub Lieutenant James Moody, would be our liaison. He's a lot of fun and insists we call him James. He let us clamber around the boat as long as everything was put back tidily in place. Dorothy, one of the Girl Guides, knew every detail of the design. She's a walking encyclopaedia! It was such a fun hour. Afterwards, we went back inside for scrumptious hot chocolate.

Dorothy, being a serious sort, asked Lady Agnes why there was only space for 1,178 when there were 2,208 passengers and crew.

'That doesn't sound much like being prepared,' said Dorothy.

Dorothy can be rather direct.

'An excellent point, Dorothy. Think about it and come up with a solution,' said Lady Agnes.

When the iceberg struck, we were on the upper deck, star spotting. It was a beautifully clear night. So cold. So bright. We even saw the iceberg. Then crash!

Instant panic, lots of shouting and finally we're directed towards lifeboats 6 and 7. Lady Agnes is agitated, talking rapidly to James. She looks worried. We all are. We know already there aren't enough lifeboats. Ours nominally had space for just 65.

But Ivy – she's my good friend and a maths whizz – calculated that the lifeboats had displacement equivalent to 206 people. She reminded Dorothy about a trip the Guides had done the previous year on lake Windermere when we'd built a tent on a platform between two canoes and camped over the water at night.

Dorothy had one of her 'ding' moments and rushed to tell Lady Agnes her idea.

We'd lash the lifeboats together and create a similar structure between two lifeboats using the masts and sails.

Lady Agnes had been there and could picture it straightaway. We watched from a slight distance as she convinced Lieutenant James with her booming voice and much gesticulation. She gave us the Girl Guide salute and we got straight to work.

Being lowered down to the water was thrilling! Each boat had ten oars, plenty of rope, a big mast, a gaff and a sail. We laid the masts across the central rowlocks and tied the lashed-together oars between the prows and sterns. The sails were lashed tight over the gap between the boats. The boats' sailors were a tremendous help; together, we all jumped up and down on the sail hammock to show it was safe. Using our sturdy knives and many knots, it took us thirty minutes to join together the first pair of boats.

Once built, we called to boat 3 and transferred everyone onto our pontoon. There was plenty of room – we were able to take passengers from boat 1 as well! The emptied boats returned to the ship to collect more people.

We waved to Lady Agnes who had rounded up the Captain and the officers – she can be extremely forceful. Everyone was pointing at our contraption!

The poor, beautiful Titanic was already low in the water. We Guides returned to the ship to help with the lashings on the next pontoons. After 90 minutes, seven pontoons were carrying over 2,000 people. One of the smaller collapsible boats was used for the dogs. Some had to be muzzled and bound, or even put in sacks, but all were rounded up before the ship foundered.

The Captain and Lady Agnes were on the last lifeboat off the ship and joined our little archipelago of islands as we all watched the ship sink below the waves. The band had brought their small instruments along and we sang hymns to keep us warm and raise our spirits.

It was a mirror calm night. We were lucky; the pontoons would have been harder to build on a rough sea.

Three hours later, the rescue ship appeared and collected us from our pontoons. There was already a buzz amongst the survivors, which was everyone – all the passengers and all the crew and even the dogs! Lady

Agnes proudly presented Ivy and Dorothy as the brains behind the plan
and praised us girls for calmly delivering the prototype under pressure.
New York here we come!

'Wow,' said Mary. 'That was really quite something. They saved all the people.'

'And it sounded plausible, didn't it?' said John.

'That's all very well,' said Niamh. 'But what has it got to do with the climate crisis?'

'Good question, Niamh,' said John. 'Who can tell us?'

Ethan shot his hand up, desperate to be the first to answer, but when John looked at him, his mind was blank.

Mary spoke up instead. 'Well, the way I see it, they were a team. There was Dorothy, the bookish girl, interested in detail, focused, not great with people. She had a need to complete the puzzle. But she wasn't alone. Her friend, Ivy used her mathematical abilities and together they'd produced a solution neither would have found alone.'

'And they used a shortcut to tell Lady Agnes,' chipped in Stephen. 'By saying "it's just like the canoe tent we built on Windermere last year", Lady Agnes could understand what they meant in a flash. And she used her position to speak to Lieutenant James, who then immediately commissioned the building of the first prototype. And after that, she used her own personal forcefulness to twist the captain's arm.'

'Good,' said John. 'You've followed the story very well. So could Dorothy and Ivy have done it without Lady Agnes?'

'Not a chance!' said Ethan. 'They were a couple of geeky girls – no offence – who would listen to them?'

'And could Agnes have done it without them?'

'No way. She'd just not thought about it. Why would she come up with an out of the box solution in a tight corner under time pressure?' Stephen said.

'And the Captain?'

'He'd just made the worst decision of his life and knew he was going to die, go down with the ship. He was falling back on discipline to hold the situation together. Not the best time for generating a creative, radical, untested solution.'

'So all three steps were needed,' said John. 'The idea, the listener/enabler/driver person to get things going and the overall authority to apply the solution across the whole situation.'

He noticed that Niamh had been fidgeting in her chair throughout the discussion, repeatedly checking her watch. He was keen not to lose her from the group. The people who needed persuading that the solutions could work were the most important people in the program.

'So who can answer Niamh's question?' John looked round the group. 'What's the link between this story – Ivy, Dorothy, Lady Agnes, saving the Titanic – and the climate crisis that we are facing in the world today?'

Ethan's brow furrowed. He still didn't see a connection.

'I think I understand the link,' said Mary. 'The authorities don't have all the answers. They might be paralysed into inaction. But they're trying to give the impression that they are still in control.'

'Politicians are voted in by old people,' said Stephen. 'I would say "no offence", but I'm one of the old people I'm talking about. The interests of the old become the priority. The young – school children and future generations – have no vote, no representation at all. So the longer-term policies – things like, oh, you know, trivial little things like the existential threat posed by climate change – these things get pushed to one side. Quite frankly, we're stuffed.'

'So we need participation by the people whose lives are at stake in the political process,' said Niamh.

'Citizen's assemblies maybe?' suggested Stephen.

'Yes,' agreed John. 'These are increasingly used as a way to generate sustainable solutions. They just need to be given greater power.'

'Also an authority needs all of the key players,' said Mary. 'An Agnes needs a Dorothy, a Dorothy needs an Ivy. We need thousands of Dorothys because we need thousands of different solutions.'

'It's not even a good metaphor,' grumbled Ethan. 'Like the iceberg is the problem in the Titanic, but in real life it's a problem that they're melting.'

'Could we refreeze glaciers?' asked Mary.

'Or slow down their melting,' said another.

'Ice stupas?' suggested Stephen.

'Maybe.' John beamed. 'The melting of the Greenland ice cap is incredibly serious. Can we stop it? We need to harness all of man's ingenuity—'

'And women's,' said Niamh.

'Let's face it, it's gonna be men,' said Ethan.

'We need to harness all of humanity's ingenuity to try,' John smiled. He was delighted at the animated discussion. In his day job, he was a teacher. He was skilled at coaxing information from his students, encouraging them to fill in the gaps themselves, pointing them gently in the right direction if they veered off course.

'Got it!' Ethan shouted suddenly. 'The metaphor. Obviously it's nothing like you guys said. It's about leaving the sinking ship. It's the mission to Mars right?'

John's heart sank. He sought for a kind way to address the issues, but Niamh got there first.

'For fuck sake! You do know you won't be on this select crew don't you? You know that when they've siphoned off all the best minds and funds and resources for their escape plan, that you'll be left here with the rest of us to die? We're not going to get funds to refreeze the Arctic or slow down glaciers if they're all funnelled into your Trekkie off world fantasy. Get real.'

John was relentlessly positive, but even he had to admit Niamh was probably right. Funding tended to go towards the sexy projects rather than those that would really make the difference. Eye-candy like CO_2 to vodka, diamonds, fuels or hydrogen, but nothing that would do the necessary millions of tonnes of negative emissions. For years, there had been calls for a dramatic reduction in all kinds of consumption; a complete switch to renewable energy with no more fossil fuels. CO_2 in the atmosphere needed pulling down from its current level of 415ppm back to 350ppm. There was also a pressing necessity to refreeze the Arctic. But consumption had hardly changed, the transition to renewables was too slow, and carbon dioxide removal was the tiniest of the new development areas. And as for the refreezing the Arctic, the process hadn't even begun.

He'd wondered about the second reading, bearing in mind the session was about allaying eco-anxiety. This decided him. They needed to get real.

'Let's have a quick break for a cup of tea and a stretch,' said John. 'And then we'll do the next two stories.'

We all stand together, wrapped up warm as proper Girl Guides would be. Prepared for anything. But not prepared for this. There is quiet sobbing. We are huddled together for warmth as the crew struggles with the lifeboat. It looks big and heavy and frightfully cumbersome.

It is Monday, 1am, the fifth day of our trip on the now-sinking Titanic. I suppose it might have been fun. Now I am just frightened. There was a huge crash when the iceberg struck. The impact sent us tumbling to the floor.

As we were already outside, star spotting, we gathered by the lifeboats, struggling with the bulky life vests. It is horribly cold. Dorothy will be glad she missed all this – she was kicked by a horse the week before we left and wasn't able to join the trip. I miss her. She might have had some thoughts about our predicament.

We silently climb into the lifeboat. An argument breaks out as to whether it can be lowered when full of people. We are already in so we stay put. The boat is only half full. We pull away from the ship. A worried-looking Lady Agnes tries to comfort the sobbing girls. We should have brought more blankets; we'll have hypothermia soon.

Although we are a long way from the ship, we can still hear the band. The stern is high in the air. People are plummeting towards the water. Now the band has stopped. I can hear screams. The stern breaks and crashes into the sea. More bodies fall. There is silence on our boat.

The lights go out on the Titanic.

The great ship disappears beneath the waves. In the near silence, we can hear distant cries for help. We huddle together in the all-encompassing cold.

Helpless.

Hopeless.

John removed his glasses and pinched the bridge of his nose thoughtfully. 'How do you all feel now?'

'Sad,' said one.

'With just one piece missing, without Dorothy there, the whole alternative future just didn't develop,' said Mary.

'In terms of the climate,' said Stephen, 'it feels like this might be where we are. Already too late. Already sinking. Sat in the isolated boats, but with no rescue ship coming to save us. It's pretty scary.'

'This is exactly why I didn't want to come tonight,' said Niamh. 'We already know the world's in dire straits. Who needs to be reminded?'

'We know from the first story that the big solutions really could be out there,' said John. 'But are we making a determined effort to find them?'

John had been tempted to finish with this story. Its stark impact would live long in the memory. But this program was essentially about positivity, and leaving people deflated seemed counterproductive. He wanted to end the session on a high point.

'Are you sitting comfortably?' he said. 'OK, strap yourselves in and hold onto your hats. We're going for one more ride in the time machine!'

Good morning, everyone. I'm Jane, the roving reporter of the...well, you know all that already.

Over dinner on the first evening, Dorothy and her good friend Ivy showed Lady Agnes their solution to the lifeboat problem. Using two gravy boat saucers and a dozen pencils, they showed how two lifeboats could be made into one big pontoon. Two clean handkerchiefs served as sails, demonstrating how the pontoons could be decked over. Ivy had made a lovely isometric sketch and had calculated that one pontoon of two boats might carry as many as 400 people.

On Thursday 11th, Agnes called Dorothy, Ivy and me over and promised us a special treat. That afternoon, after departing from Queenstown, we were to meet Mr Andrews, the designer of the ship. Lady Agnes had spoken with him on the promenade deck and mentioned our pontoon design. Very courteously, he had agreed to speak to us.

We were a bit nervous before we met Mr Andrews. Shoes had been polished and we were well turned out – even Ivy, who often looked a bit tousled. We gathered in the corner of the first-class lounge for tea and scones.

Mr A was polite but serious – I'm sure he had a lot on his mind. Dorothy explained the pontoon design to him, and together we pored over Ivy's skilful illustration of the arrangement. Very good, he muttered, very good. He said it would be an excellent addition to White Star Line's cadet training course. Would we mind awfully if he used our plan? We were, of course, thrilled and said yes!

Mr Andrews then relaxed and called for more tea.

'Do you have any questions for me, girls?' asked Mr A.

'Yes, Sir. A great many!' Dorothy said. 'The first is, have you read 'The Wreck of the Titan' by Morgan Robertson? Where a huge liner hits an iceberg and sinks. We all read it before joining the ship – hugely exciting.'

'Yes, although some parts of the story are rather fantastic,' said Mr A.

'I agree, Sir. Especially the piece about the polar bear. What about the collision with 'Royal Age' and then the iceberg itself?'

'We do all we can to avoid collisions, but when you are moving a ship as big as this they do happen very occasionally,' said Mr Andrews.

'The Titan hit a submerged shelf on the iceberg and quickly capsized – is that likely?' asked Dorothy.

'Icebergs come in all shapes and sizes,' said Mr A.

'Yes, Sir. Ivy and I were thinking about that. A head-on collision would bend the front of the ship and make an awful mess. A strike on the underside would be partly deflected by the double hull, but a glancing blow to the side could make a nasty hole.'

Dorothy grabbed a French loaf from a passing waiter and jabbed the butter knife into the side. There was quite a kerfuffle. Mr Andrews was laughing as he settled the situation with the waiter.

'Oops, sorry, Sir. My enthusiasm got the better of me,' said Dorothy.

'Never mind. I haven't had so much fun in ages.'

'Well, Sir, as Ivy will demonstrate – she's from a farming family so she knows all about this – a slice down the side would be like gutting a pig.'

'And instead of the innards spilling out, the water would gush in,' said Ivy.

'Indeed. The pumps could handle a small leak, but I'm intrigued – now you've solved the lifeboat problem, what would you do with this?' Mr Andrews asked.

'Well, Sir, I'm sure you've heard of fothering – Captain Cook used it in 1770 to save the Endeavour. If there was a glancing blow, it seems likely that it would cause a split down the rivet seams, rather than a punched hole – like a garment will sometimes fail at the stitched seams rather than push through the cloth,' Dorothy said.

'Do go on...'

'So if there's a split, it would be necessary to block it. The Titanic is larger than the Endeavour, so it might be tricky to put a rope all the way around and pull a patch over the split. Though it might be possible to dangle a canvas – the lifeboat cover, perhaps – over the side and see where it gets sucked in.'

'Excellent, girls! I'm impressed.'

We like to think a puzzle through to the end, Sir. Not every idea is a good idea, but there's usually a solution out the somewhere.' Dorothy said.

'And what will you do with these ideas?' asked Mr A.

'We were thinking of rewriting the Titan story to make it more realistic. Even without the bears, the Hashish and the insurance fraud, we're sure there's an interesting tale to tell.'

'Well I'd love to read it. I have had such a pleasant afternoon. I wish my nieces were as engaged as you.'

'But they can be Sir,' I said. 'If they join the Girl Guides, they can be just like us – well, not like Ivy and Dotty, they are rather unusual. But the rest of us are ordinary girls.'

'Well, Jane, that's just the kind of ordinary we need a lot more of. It has been a great pleasure. Good day to you, ladies.'

What a jolly afternoon!

Late on Sunday night we were on the boat deck, enjoying a star-gazing navigation instruction session. At 11.40pm, the ship hit an iceberg.

We were all wrapped up and ready to go, heading straight to our muster station by lifeboat 7. We had just arrived when a midshipman ran up. 'Lady Agnes, your presence is required on the bridge by the Captain and Mr Andrews. Bring Jane, Dorothy and Ivy. Immediately.'

Lady Agnes split the team and delegated construction of the pontoon to the six strongest girls. The rest of us headed to the bridge.

When we arrived, Mr Andrews was just finishing his explanation of the pontoon scheme to the Captain, who said, 'Thank you girls,' and went off to organise the conversion of the lifeboats into pontoons.

Mr Andrews said, 'Follow me,' and we hurried off to the starboard side with several officers.

'Thank goodness you're here, girls,' said Mr. A. 'You have given me the determination to try the impossible. We need to reduce the leak rate by at least 80%. And, by Jove, I believe we can do it! Quickly – what else do we need?'

'All the lifeboat covers, rope, strong men,' said Dorothy.

'You there, fetch 200 strong hands from the 3rd Class deck. You, gather the boat covers and all the canvas you can find. You, bring rope. And I want a continuous reading on the depth of the water in the bilge,' commanded Mr. Andrews.

'And some of those lovely new carpets!' Dorothy added.

'Excellent. You, you and you – sacks, canvas and carpet. Mr Andrews turned to Ivy. 'Ivy – I know you are good with mathematics; I'd like you to keep a running tally on how much time we have. Take my notebook. This is my rough calculation: we are leaking at 1.5 tonnes a second, perhaps more. The pumps will only do a quarter of that. Shout out the time remaining every couple of minutes.'

'And Sir,' Dorothy piped up. 'Close all the portholes! And any hatches that would help slow the water. Every hole stopped up now buys a few minutes of not sinking later.'

'Excellent idea. You – portholes! You – batten down those hatches! You – take three hands and close all the doors you can reach.'

It was a hectic couple of hours. Equipment tumbled into the area, along with groups of worried but eager hands. Lady Agnes and the other Guides helped to organise the rope and canvas teams.

The first attempts, at the bow, were hopeless. We lost several boat canvases, sucked into the holes. When the Axminsters and the Persian carpets arrived, things picked up a bit. Ivy's original plan of sliding things down the back of the canvas didn't work as well as hoped, but multiple patches over the same hole started to do the trick.

Gradually, Ivy's running countdown of the time remaining before the ship sank slowed, stabilised and eventually started to increase. All the pumps were running at full capacity.

By the time the Carpathia arrived, all the passengers, except those working on the fothering teams, were safely on five pontoons. The en-

*gineers and stokers worked gallantly in rising water to keep the power on
and the pumps running flat out.*

*We thought we'd made it, but the sea doesn't give up so easily. One
pump seized. We were losing ground again. People were tired, desperate,
but grimly determined.*

*With the Carpathia and Olympic alongside, hot food and a team
change was organised so a large-sized fothering sheet could be fed under
the ship. Over the next 24 hours, three more sheets were placed over the
holes.*

*Two large warships appeared. The Titanic was lashed between the
two, like a drunken sailor being carried home by his mates. The extra
hands and pumps managed to stop the Titanic sinking and dragging
the other ships down with it.*

*We were transferred to the Olympic and arrived in New York three
days late. The poor old Titanic limped in five days later. We were all on
the dockside to cheer her in.*

*What an exhilarating trip! It feels like we have abundant material
for our new book...*

When John finished his reading, he saw that the mood of the circle had improved. Smiles had replaced apprehension. 'What do you think? Can you see the metaphor now?' he asked.

'Just like they have to bail out the excess water that's sinking the ship, the planet has all these greenhouse gases we need to get rid of,' said Mary.

'That's right. We need to remove carbon dioxide from our atmosphere and store it. Sequester it is the correct term. The whole process is called carbon drawdown,' said John. 'There are already thousands of projects that do this – like restoring seagrass and kelp forests, peat bogs, reforestation, mangroves, biochar. Each location offers different opportunities for carbon drawdown. We just need many thousands more.'

'Or we can just stop chopping down the forests and mangroves and destroying the peat bogs and seabeds in the first place,' said Niamh.

'Good point. Peat will no longer be an allowable ingredient in garden compost for example. But you're right. We need international laws on seafloor trawling and bans on any development that disturbs existing carbon sinks.'

'But why wasn't peat banned years ago? We're still cutting down mangrove forests to build holiday complexes. Why isn't there a law against ecocide? Why isn't the entire ocean a marine protected area?' Niamh cried.

'All good questions. So the other side of the metaphor is just as they need to bailout water that existed, they need to stop more water rushing in,' John explained.

'I get it. It's like a bathtub,' said Ethan. 'Obviously having the plug – carbon drawdown or whatnot – draining carbon dioxide won't be effective if the taps are still full on. So, erm. Like, how do we turn the taps off?'

John looked round pleased at the flurry of comments that followed from the group.

'Stop consuming?'

'Find a way of everyone living well that didn't require making new stuff and then throwing it away.'

'Ration consumption,' said Niamh.

'Fuck off!' Ethan responded.

'Actually, there have been proposals such as personal carbon allowances, or carbon credit cards based on the idea that everyone is responsible for their own carbon footprint,' John said quickly before it developed into a slanging match.

'Yeah. They did it in the war, emergency measures,' said Niamh.

'This is an emergency,' said Mary.

'What about rewarding low-carbon consumption?' suggested Stephen.

'What do you mean?' John asked him, keen to draw out the idea.

'You lot will be too young to remember Green Shield stamps, but my parents used to collect them. You got them when you bought certain goods or services and then you could use them to get other stuff free. It was huge in the seventies. You could change it to Green Planet stamps and get them when you bought low carbon stuff and redeem them against green products.'

'What a wonderful idea, Stephen. It would be a great way to introduce people to new sustainable alternatives too,' said John. 'How about today's homework is you all go and ask any company with a reward scheme, supermarkets for example, to change to a green point system.'

'I don't trust business.' Niamh glowered again at Stephen. 'It's just smoke and mirrors. They call products 'green' for the points but are they really? Like sustainable palm oil. It's bollocks. I did a project on it and there's no such thing. They don't care as long as we buy something. Like if you're worried about fast fashion, they just start talking about organic cotton as if it's a proper solution. It isn't cos it uses twice as much water. We need to just consume less, but that doesn't make them any money. It's all greenwash.'

'It's true,' said Stephen, hoping to redeem himself with Niamh. 'That's why I had to leave. While business's main purpose is maximising profit, they'll never deliver what's needed.'

The room went quiet. Everyone suspected he was right, but where did that leave them?

There was a shuddering breath from Ethan's girlfriend as she started weeping.

'Shut up, everyone.' Ethan shouted at the group and put his arm round the crying girl. 'It's all right sweety, I got you.'

'There's hope,' said John, gently. 'Businesses are changing. France passed a law in 2019 obliging business to consider the social and environmental impacts of business activity. The British Academy is also pushing for changes in corporate purpose. Even the US Business Round Table are moving away from the idea that businesses are just there to serve shareholders to the idea that it should be good for society. In a few years, if the trend continues—'

'Time,' Niamh cut across him brutally. 'That's the key metaphor in your Titanic story. Just like they had to bail fast before too much water got in, we have just eight years left before it's too late and we tip over into runaway warming. Your lot,' Niamh's eyes were daggers as she turned to Stephen, 'lost us decades with their misinformation and climate denial. They fucking screwed us over for fucking profit,' her voice shook with fury.

John attempted to intervene. 'Niamh, I can see you're upset, how about—'

'You don't get it, do you. You're what, fifty?'

John tried not to look offended. He was 39.

'You worry in some abstract way about your kids, but for us it's personal.' Niamh thumped her chest. 'It's me, us, us here, we're all going to die. Of course we're fucking upset. Yes, you cry girl,' Niamh stood up and put her hand on the shy girl's shoulder. 'You cry, we should all cry. And you,' she spat at Ethan. 'How dare you say 'you got her' when you want to piss off to fucking Mars and say 'no fucking way' when we propose that yes, this is enough of an emergency to call in rationing. This is worse than any war. This is all of us and our planet.

And you!' Niamh turned back to Stephen. 'If it was war time, then your lot would be hanged for treason. In the Second World War, anyone who spread lies that favoured the enemy got capital punishment. I watch those interviews with those business CEOs. 'I'm just doing my job' they say. Wasn't that what the Nazi's said? We're just doing our job. Well if your job is killing the fucking planet then just leave.'

Stephen wanted to remind her that he had. But what if she asked why he had left it so late? He had no answer to that.

'Don't you underestimate our anger cos it comes from fear. You'd better do something or your backs will be against the fucking wall.' Niamh stomped back to her chair and sat back down.

John struggled for words. None came.

There was a silence, then a whisper.

'They saved the ship and the people.'

Everyone looked round to see who had spoken. It was Ethan's girlfriend.

Ethan did a double take then shouted out ,'Yes sweet pea, they did. In your Titanic story they saved the ship and the people.'

John knew a lifeline when he saw it.

'Exactly! Once they got stuck into the problem, they were never going to give up. You could feel the determination, hear the grunts, the straining, the strength that was being brought to bear, the camaraderie, the adrenaline, the creak of the ropes. They were heroes.'

'So, climate-wise,' said Stephen, 'I guess it shows that even when you've found a great solution, there may be an even better one out there. This one managed to drag the Titanic back from a certain sinking.'

'Exactly,' said John. 'This group of Girl Guides fixed a hundred and ten-year-old problem with an inspired idea and a focused team. What can we do if we put the right amount of effort into fixing the climate crisis? Of course we can do it!'

This generated the buzz he'd been hoping for, and everyone pitched in, even the shy girl.

'We should act as if our ship is sinking.'

'Go to emergency measures.'

'That's scary.'

'Could we be any more scared?'

The group all shook their heads.

'So just like in war, funds need to go to bringing down the enemy.'

'Greenhouse gas emissions.'

'The people who are in a position to change things need to look at what needs to be done to fix the whole problem.'

'Prevent the sinking of the ship, rather than just a bit of profitable deck chair rearrangement.'

'Harness business to the good of the planet.'

'By law.'

'All business must be benefit corporations or social enterprises.'

'Citizens assemblies.'

'Carbon trading.'

'Green taxation.'

'Renewable energy.'

'Mangrove terraces to store carbon and bolster sea walls.'

'Refreeze the Arctic.'

'Reforestation'

'Restore soil and peat bogs, replant coral and seagrasses and kelp forests.'

'Personal carbon allowances.'

'Green Planet stamps.'

John was delighted with the response. The stories had connected with the listeners, and everyone felt inspired that they could play a part, however large or small, in taking things forward.

'There are some great projects out there. All sorts of stuff. The ideas people just need an easy, supportive framework to connect to. One that doesn't require impossible grant forms, or 200% commitment, or for them to completely mess up their lives. But I'll tell you one thing – we're going do this. We're going to save this sinking ship!'

He received a round of applause and even a few cheers, cut rudely short as they were ushered out of the room to make way for a waiting Pilates class.

Session 1 had been an undoubted success. More chairs and a wider circle would be required for Session 2.

Afterword

This anthology of short stories has been put together with help from the Green Stories Project in association with Herculean Climate Solutions, the Climate Fiction Writers League; Change Agents UK and the University of Southampton.

Each story has an associated webpage accessed via a QR code with more information on how we can achieve the climate solutions proposed e.g . see https://www.greenstories.org.uk/anthology-for-cop27/the-assassin-solutions/ or scan here:

You can find more details about each story, and access audio recordings for some here: https://www.greenstor ies.org.uk/anthology-for-cop27/stories/ or scan

Sign up to the mailing list on www.greenstories.org.uk to keep informed about new writing competitions, green stories publications and research findings related to storytelling for the planet. Also connect on: facebook.com/greenstoriessoton and instagram.com/green storiessoton

If you enjoyed this book, please help to spread the word by leaving a review on sites such as Amazon and Good Reads. These are a huge help to authors.

For more information about the editor go to www.dabaden.com or connect on twitter.com/DABadenauthor.

SCAN ME

We'd love feedback on how you enjoyed the stories if they impacted you in anyway. All feedback is anonymous as personal information is not collected. The questions will help us to polish stories and decide which stories to keep in future editions, although data may be used as part of an article on the impacts of eco-fiction. Scan here for brief survey of 3 questions.

ACKNOWLEDGEMENTS

Thanks are due to the authors in the anthology who worked fast and often in conjunction with climate specialists to create stories that are both engaging and which capture important climate solutions.

We'd also like to thank the climate experts who generously contributed their time and advice. These include: Prof Ken Collins, Ocean and Earth Science, University of Southampton; Jon Copley, Professor of Ocean Exploration and Science Communication, University of Southampton; David Fell, Brook Lyndhurst sustainability consultancy; Dave Goulson Professor of Biology, University of Sussex, and founder of the Bumble Conservation Trust; Jerry Joynson, Herculean Climate Solutions; Dr Kevan Manwaring, Senior Lecturer in Creative Writing, Arts University Bournemouth; Dr Stephen Martin Hon, president of the charity Change Agents UKand WWF Fellow;

Prof William Scott, NAEE chair, University of Bath; Arran Stibbe, Professor of Ecological Linguistics, University of Gloucestershire; Alex Templeton Community Infrastructure Group CIC; Stephen Turnock, Professor of Maritime Fluid Dynamics; Joerg Wiedenmann, Professor of Biological Oceanography, University of Southampton.

Thanks to our beta readers: Alastair JR Ball, SolarPunk Stories; Bridget Blankley; Nancy Houser-Bluhm, author of Whispers for Terra; Jenny Moroney; Liz Ottosson; Anneliese Schultz, MA, MFA, writer; E.A. Smiroldo, author of The Silent Count.

Thanks to Change Agents UK who sponsored our efforts.

Change Agents UK

A final word from the editor

Special mention to Steve Willis from Herculean Climate Solutions whose boundless renewable energy was the fuel behind the anthology. He approached me in April with the proposal to get an anthology of stories together to inspire the delegates at COP27 in November. I like an impossible challenge and I was in. He'd recruited freelance comedy writer Martin Hastie to the cause whose job was to translate his middle of the night rantings into coherent stories. Martin and I retaliated by calling all our bad guys Steve! It's been huge fun working with them and also the authors who went above and beyond to get it all together in time.

Author Bios

E DITOR/AUTHOR: **D.A. Baden** is Professor of Sustain-ability at the University of Southampton and has published numerous book chapters and articles in the academic realm, and a eco-themed rom-com *Habitat Man*, and written several screenplays. Denise set up the series of free Green Stories writing competitions in 2018 to inspire writers to integrate green solutions into their writing. Denise has written three stories for this anthology, and co-written two others. *The Pitch* is adapted from her novel *Habitat Man*. Follow on https://www.dabaden.com/ and @DABadenauthor.

Brian Adams is the author of three romantic comedies (*Love in the Time of Climate Change, KABOOM!, and Offline*), that have won numerous independent book awards. He is a former sex educator and a Professor Emeritus of Environmental Science. His first novel is being adapted into a screenplay, His writings deal with topical issues (climate change, mountain-top removal, cell phone addiction) and straddle the fine line between humor and tragedy. He is the co-owner of Phippenadams Solar which installs solar electric systems on the roofs of non-profits. He lives in Massachusetts in a zero net energy

house with his wife, his cat, and his awesome vegetable garden. www
.brianadamsauthor.wordpress.combrianadamsauthor@gmail.com

Paolo Bacigalupi's writing has been nominated for three Nebula Awards, four Hugo Awards, and won the Theodore Sturgeon
Memorial Award for best science fiction short story of the year. His
debut novel THE WINDUP GIRL was named by TIME Magazine
as one of the ten best novels of 2009, and also won the Hugo, Nebula,
Locus, Compton Crook, and John W. Campbell Memorial Awards,
and many international awards. His debut young adult novel, SHIP
BREAKER, was a Micheal L. Printz Award Winner, and a National
Book Award Finalist, and its sequel, THE DROWNED CITIES, was
a 2012 Kirkus Reviews Best of YA Book, A 2012 VOYA Perfect Ten
Book, and 2012 L.A Times Book Prize Finalist.

Rasha Barrage is a freelance writer, editor and former lawyer with
a particular interest in social justice issues and climate action. Rasha is
the author of non-fiction books for Summersdale Publishers including *The Little Book of Anthropology* and *Say No to Racism*. She was
born in Baghdad, raised in Merseyside and now lives in London. You
can find her on https://twitter.com/rashabarrage

Brian Burt is a science fiction writer whose work focuses on
eco-fiction themes. His eco-fiction short story "The Last Indian War"
won the L. Ron Hubbard Gold Award in the 1991 *Writers of the
Future* contest. His *Aquarius Rising* trilogy of eco-fiction novels, cen-
tered on climate change, won EPIC's eBook Award for Science Fiction and the Readers' Favorite Gold Medal for Science Fiction and
will soon be released as a consolidated volume on Amazon Kindle. A
prequel to *Aquarius Rising*, the short story "Neptune's Children," will

be released in October 2022 in *Tales from the Deep*. You can learn more about Brian's work at https://www.briantburt.com/ or by following him on Twitter.

Jenni Clarke has several books published in a variety of genres. Her short stories have been published in two anthologies and Writing magazine as well as in two flash fiction volumes published as eBooks and paperbacks. Under her fifty- something exterior is an excitable seven-year-old who dances in awe and wonder at nature and dabbles with a thousand creative projects. She enjoys experimenting with ways to use the power of story to inspire thinking about the choices we make. Find out more at www.jenniclarke.com

Lyndsey Croal is a Scottish Book Trust New Writers Awardee. Her work has been published in over fifty anthologies and magazines, including Mslexia's *Best Women's Short Fiction 2021*, Canongate's *Imagine a Country*, and *Shoreline of Infinity Magazine*. Her climate-themed audio drama 'Daughter of Fire and Water' was produced by *Alternative Stories & Fake Realities* and was a 2022 British Fantasy Award finalist. Her professional experience is in climate and nature policy and advocacy, and she currently works at WWF Scotland. She enjoys exploring climate and environmental themes in her writing and is interested in how fictional stories can offer solutions or inspire future action. Find her on Twitter as @writerlynds or via www.lyndseycroal.co.uk

Sara Foster is the bestselling author of seven novels, and her latest, *The Hush*, is a near-future, female-led thriller about a conspiracy that goes right to the heart of the British government. Her fifth novel, *The Hidden Hours*, was shortlisted for a Davitt Award in 2018 and has been optioned by TV production company CJZ. Sara began her publishing career working for a time in the HarperCollins fiction department in London, before freelancing as an editor and then beginning her writing career. She is currently a doctoral candidate at Curtin University, studying the representation of mothers in dystopian fiction with young adult heroines.

Howard Gaukrodger. A full-time author, Howard has been involved in writing all his life. He taught English, studied translation, then operated a language consultancy in Norway, though it was his experience cycling, hiking and flying around the globe that inspired his first novel – a humorous travelogue, recently rewritten under the title *Campervans Gone Wild*. Howard's addresses climate change in his second novel, *Lufianblid: Global Dawning – the countdown begins, which* aims to impassion young adults to engage in this crucial issue. Through climate fiction, Howard is convinced we can increase our awareness of the world's fragility and foster greater efforts to mitigate climate change. LinkedIn; Gaukrodger.com.

Matthew Hanson-Kahn is of Chinese and English parents, and lives in Brighton, U.K. He worked for 25 years on equalities and social care, in both the public and voluntary sectors. He has a partner and two grown up kids. In his early twenties, he undertook voluntary work in a tribal village in India for two years and contracted hepatitis as a result! He has backpacked around the world and loves travelling. He and his partner have travelled with their kids to India, Cambodia and Albania. He has now given up work to concentrate on writing. Matthew's other passion is music and since retiring has formed a band Brighton Strangler, which features in a video game.

Martin Hastie is a freelance writer and editor. Over the last ten years he has written for TV, radio, stage and online. Working in television production, he helped to produce content for shows in Malaysia, the Philippines and Indonesia. He has also taught creative writing and is an award-winning stand-up comedian.

Andrew Dana Hudson is a speculative fiction writer, sustainability researcher, editor and futurist. His stories have appeared in Slate Future Tense, Lightspeed Magazine, Vice Terraform, MIT Technology Review, Grist, and more. His fiction has been nominated for the Pushcart Prize and longlisted for the BSFA. In 2016 his story *Sunshine State* won the first Everything Change Climate Fiction Contest. His 2015 essay *On the Political Dimensions of Solarpunk* has helped define and grow the "solarpunk" subgenre. He has a masters degree in sustainability from Arizona State University, where he is a fellow at the Center for Science and the Imagination. His first book, *Our Shared Storm: A Novel of Five Climate Futures*, was published April 2022 by Fordham University Press.

Elizabeth Kurucz is a Canadian writer who explores the relations between personal and ecological flourishing. Her ecofeminist work *Ground Up* won first prize in the Green Stories Short Story Competition in 2022. She is an Associate Professor of Leadership and Sustainability at the University of Guelph. Her research focuses on challenging individual mindsets to support social-ecological resilience and to build a regenerative future. Her non-fiction book is *Reconstructing Value: Leadership Skills for a Sustainable World* (University of Toronto Press). She lives with her family on the Niagara Escarpment, a UNESCO Biosphere Reserve located in Ontario, Canada. Website: https://www.uoguelph.ca/lang/people/elizabeth-kurucz

Nancy Lord, an Alaska resident and former Alaska Writer Laureate, is the author or editor of ten books related to northern subjects and the environment. She addressed the climate crisis in her narrative nonfiction book *Early Warming: Crisis and Response in the Climate-changed North* (2011) and her novel *pH* (2017.) She is a former commercial salmon fisherman and currently teaches science and medical writing for Johns Hopkins University. Her MFA. degree is from Vermont College of Fine Arts. Her website is www.writerna ncylord.com.

Kim Stanley Robinson is a winner of the Hugo, Nebula, and Locus Awards. He is the author of twelve previous books, including bestseller *Ministry for the Future*, the bestselling *Mars trilogy* and the critically acclaimed *Fifty Degrees Below, Forty Signs of Rain, The Years of Rice and Salt,* and *Antarctica*--for which he was sent to the Antarctic by the U.S. National Science Foundation as part of their Antarctic Artists and Writers' Program. He lives in Davis, California.

Steve Willis is an engineer and innovator who works on industrial and environmental project, and during the lockdowns wrote short, climate fiction stories which explored potential positive outcomes to the climate crisis. Steve's heavy industrial background is combined with sharp observation, a vivid imagination, relentless persistence and a talent for lucid dreaming. He uses these unusual skills to continuously seek massive scale climate solutions, to identify climate start-up opportunities and to write stories which capture some of the essence of working on the climate crisis challenge.

9 781739 980320